STUDY
WAR
NO
MORE

STUDY WAR NO MORE

A SELECTION OF ALTERNATIVES

Edited by
JOE HALDEMAN

ST. MARTIN'S PRESS   NEW YORK

Copyright © 1977 by Joe Haldeman
For information, write:
  St. Martin's Press
  175 Fifth Avenue
  New York, N.Y. 10010
Manufactured in the United States of America
Library of Congress Catalog Card Number: 77-9517

Library of Congress Cataloging in Publication Data

Main entry under title:
Study war no more.

   1. Science fiction, American.   2. War stories.
I. Haldeman, Joe W.
PZ1.S949   [PS648.S3]   813'.0876   77-9517
ISBN 0-312-77315-3

CONTENTS

For Damon Knight and Kate Wilhelm,
who invited me to the party.

Men . . . though under hope
Of heavenly grace; and God proclaiming
peace,
Yet live in hatred, enmitie, and strife
Among themselves, and levie cruel warres,
Wasting the Earth, each other to destroy:
As if (which might induce us to accord)
Man had not hellish foes enow besides,
That day and night for his destruction waite.

John Milton
(from Paradise Lost)

INTRODUCTION

War, von Clausewitz maintained, is only the continuation of a state's policies "by other means." But even the most casual examination of human history shows that he had it backwards: war is the normal instrument of policy and the conference table is only the first or last weapon.

And his viewpoint was far too academic. To most men and women it's immaterial whether war is caused by politics or economics or divine indigestion; their experience and concern is limited to the effect of steel or lead or fire on mortal flesh.

War is waiting terrors—gleam of enemy sail on a placid horizon, beat of massed hooves or engines approaching, drone of unseen bombers laden with random death—and it is sudden trauma, when you meet the easy killer who was always inside you; when you first observe that a man is only a fragile bag of skin filled with obscene mysteries; perhaps when your own body betrays you with a wounding, and you feel the moment of shattering pain and then the seductive, helpless numbness of shock.

And afterwards, with the ominous quiet, it is bottleflies and ants; surprising volumes of blood, crusting; dead men's faces swelling open-mouthed to a caricature of astonishment; a smell that can be neither described nor forgotten. It is searching smoking ruins for a lost past; it is a boy returned rotting on his shield or hidden antiseptically inside a plastic bag.

War is this and worse but, to some degree, we all accept it. We can even grow to depend on it and, finally, to love it.

For one thing, war is useful. It can be a rite of passage, an opportunity for valor, a channel for frustrations and aggressiveness that, turned inward, could be dangerous to the state. It's something to do with your excess population, a tool for expansion, a prop for a sagging economy. And ever and always, a source of excitement. Catharsis on the grand scale.

We might have muddled through all of eternity this way, spending a certain portion of our lives, a certain fraction of our population, marching off to learn again (because the lesson can only be learned first-hand) the various permutations of steel and soul and blood. But a handful of the billions of students of war, not long ago, had to face their final exam not by probing blade or bullet, but by a brilliant spreading flower, and a warm rain of energetic neutrons. Not for the first time, but perhaps with more conviction than ever before, there was a generally-held sentiment that perhaps we ought to cut this stuff out before we get ourselves killed.

Fear of the atom was such an effective deterrent that it was over two weeks before war broke out again. A fellow with a wispy beard seized control of Hanoi. The editor of this anthology was in diapers when that happened; it lasted long enough to give him his first white hairs, and then five years more.

A short time after Uncle Ho made his play, the Greeks started shooting it out; but that was a civil war and didn't really count. Bullet by bullet, the old machine got cranked up again. We had limited, cold and brush-fire wars, and wars of National Liberation. None of them used nuclear "devices" and most of the combatants fought with superannuated bolt-action rifles and their cultures' equivalents of the rusty beer can opener. Nobody would dream of starting the real thing.

But just to be on the safe side, nations who had the wherewithal were busy distilling the earth and sea for plutonium, deuterium, tritium, and the elusive U-235, to store in bombs, rockets, submarines—even suitcases—until they had enough to wipe out all of their enemies and most of their supposed friends. And then they made some more, presumably because you can't have enough of a good thing.

And if there were such a thing as an objective observer of life on this planet, he would shake his head in wonder and confusion, and return to the study of lemmings, who at least get a refreshing swim for their folly.

By way of discussing objectivity, consider the human ear, a remarkable little organ. For primitive man to be an effective hunter, it had to be sensitive enough to detect the faintest snap of a twig and yet not be incapacitated by the billion-times-greater sound of a nearby thunderclap. Like the eye, the ear accommodates this range by delivering a logarithmic response to the amount of sound energy received: a noise one hundred times as loud as the twig snapping seems only twice as loud; a thousand times, three times as loud, and so forth. Therefore, there are very few sounds in nature that cause pain or even temporary damage to the ear.

To find sounds that loud, we have to investigate that corner of nature we call "man-made." A person who leans on a jackhammer all day stuffs his ears with cotton, but the second most common word in his vocabulary is "What?" A rock drummer will be deaf before he's rich enough to run for office. A person who frequently shoots rifles will come down with shooter's ear: an actual physical dent in his eardrum that makes him hear everything as if through the rush of a waterfall.

Getting to the point, there are even louder sounds; things so loud that they don't even register as sound. When twenty or thirty pounds of Chinese high explosive goes off a couple of yards away, you don't hear a thing; you just experience a sensation like being caressed on the ear by a baseball bat and find yourself suddenly horizontal; and, should your experience duplicate the editor's, you find the green jungle suddenly grey with smoke and crimson with sprayed blood; try to stand up and realize you can't feel your legs; look down to see a femoral artery pumping; try to staunch it with both hands; can't spare a hand to wipe the blood out of your eye; try wiping it on your shoulder, which doesn't help, it's like raw hamburger; holler for a medic and see that your medic is lying beside you with both legs blown off, good friend, his dying screams a delicate threnody in a dull, silent universe. They carry you roughly across a field and load you into a helicopter—the only one of the demolition team who lived—and you're thinking a lot of things, but one thing that doesn't cross your mind is that, as a student of war, you've flunked. You will never be objective about it, never again.

The war was kind to me, though—material for two novels and a pension that used to pay the rent. And since there are relatively few science fiction writers who were also footsoldiers in the last war, it set me up to edit an anthology like this one. Which, as any writer will tell you, is such an easy way to make a living, it ought to be illegal. (Professional editors know differently. Editing is hard work; you can write novels sitting on your veranda staring at the sea, dictating an occasional paragraph on the way to the refrigerator.)

But why this anthology? The absurdity and outrage of war may be quite obvious, but trying to find a solution to it has occupied the energies of the race's finest philosophers and poets for thousands of years, to no conspicuous success.

Science fiction writers are generally renowned neither for the depth of their philosophy nor the fineness of their poetry, so isn't it presumptuous of them to take on so formidable, yet subtle, an opponent? The answer is a duet: a soft "no" and a loud "*Hell*, no!"

The soft answer, hopefully turning away the wrath of philosophers and poets, is that no harm can come of it, beyond the felling of a few trees that might otherwise have become books about conversation. The louder answer has to do with a quality always missing in good poets and usually missing in philosophers: anthropological perspective, a dissonant, but accurate, term for being able to step outside of the human condition and write about it as an observer.

Which may be the only way to handle it. A strong argument can be made for the thesis that war is not unnatural; that it is a natural extension of basic biological urges, such as territoriality and sexual aggression. Personally, I think this is wrong; that "perversion" is the operative word, rather than "extension." I feel that humans are basically well disposed toward one enother, that warfare is an atavism, carefully (if unconsciously) nurtured by the people who are in positions of power, to assure that they stay in power; that politics, to turn the Count around in his grave once more, is only warfare by other means—and that we will have war until we find some way to organize human activity without the kind assistance of counts and kings and presidents and central committees and senates. But as stated above, I'm not objective, and maybe I can't think straight.

Herman Kahn says that we have entered a new *belle epoque*—a time of world peace and prosperity. This is probably true in some relative sense. But this morning's paper reports sixteen combat deaths in Beirut and the apparently premeditated axe-murders of two American soldiers on the Korean DMZ, by a truckload of North Korean troops. Religious war smolders in Northern Ireland; race war in Johannesburg. A Hitler-worshipping brain-damage case in central Africa rattles his sword at everybody. In the United States, the budget for what used to be called the War Department is higher than it ever was in time of war. The balance of power requires that the Soviets spend a similar sum: a quarter of a trillion dollars down the rabbit hole. This is enough to buy dinner at Sardi's for every child, woman, and man in the world. Or a year's worth of rice and vegetables.

But that's science fiction, of course. War, to quote von Clausewitz one last time, is part of the intercourse of the human race (the crude pun is an accident of translation)—to end war would be to subvert the animal part of our nature; and the final product of this subversion, even if closer to the angels, would definitely be something other than *homo sapiens.*

Maybe so. But then, it may be time we stopped being so damned human. Concentrate on survival, even though it may mean giving up our precious individual freedom, or illusion of freedom: have our genes manipulated; grow up in Skinner boxes; automatic lobotomy the penalty for any sign of aggression. A race of cloned cowards, of soft passive hedonists. Consider the alternative.

Alternatives are what this book is about. Ten authors have approached from ten different directions the question "If not war, what else?"

When I wrote these people (and a couple of dozen others), asking for contributions to this anthology, I did not expect that many of them would submit really workable alternatives to war. Instead, it seemed likely that most of them would use the theme as a vantage point from which to examine war and aggression in general.

This turned out to be true. A few of these ideas might actually work, if the universe were ruled by logic; but all of the stories—hopeful, chilling, satirical—are entertaining, whether practical or not. And all of them offer food for thought. The ones that offer hope, as well, offer something rare.

—Joe Haldeman
Key West, New York, and Iowa City
September, 1976

Harlan Ellison is the type of person conventionally
described as a dynamo. A more exact electronic metaphor,
though, would be the Van de Graaf generator, that familiar
prop of late-night horror movies: it stands a little over five
feet tall and makes a lot of sparks and noise while whirling
around at an incredible speed. And it makes your hair stand
on end.

Ellison might be the best science fiction writer around.
At least he's gathered a greater tonnage of awards than
anybody else, not only in science fiction writing and editing,
but also for his work in television and films. Those of us who
love science fiction wish he would take a vow of poverty, quit
those other, more remunerative fields and spend all of his
time turning out stories–unique, exciting, muscular-like the
one that follows.

The intent here, and the power, seem similar to Goya's
in his brutal "Disasters of War" etchings. The people who
wage war become anesthetized to its horrors, Ellison says, so
take the ones who merely allow war and make them see its
face.

BASILISK
by HARLAN ELLISON

What though the Moor the basilisk has slain
And pinned him lifeless to the sandy plain,
Up through the spear the subtle venom flies,
The hand imbibes it, and the victor dies.

—Lucan: *Pharsalia*
(Marcus Annaeus Lucanus,

Returning from a night patrol beyond the perimeter of the
firebase, Lance Corporal Vernon Lestig fell into a trail trap set by hostiles. He was bringing up the rear, covering the patrol's withdrawal
from recently overrun sector eight, when he fell too far behind and lost
the bush track. Though he had no way of knowing he was paralleling
the patrol's trail, thirty yards off their left flank, he kept moving forward hoping to intersect them. He did not see the pungi stakes set at
cruel angles, frosted with poison, tilted for top-point efficiency, shar-
pened to infinity.

Two set close together penetrated the barricade of his boot; the first piercing the arch and his weight driving it up and out to emerge just below the ankle bone, still inside the boot; the other ripping through the sole and splintering against the fibula above the heel, without breaking the skin.

Every circuit shorted out, every light bulb blew, every vacuum imploded, snakes shed their skins, wagon wheels creaked, plate-glass windows shattered, dentist drills ratcheted across nerve ends, vomit burned tracks up through throats, hymens were torn, fingernails bent double dragged down blackboards, water came to a boil; lava. Nova pain. Lestig's heart stopped, lubbed, began again, stuttered; his brain went dead refusing to accept the load; all senses came to full stop; he staggered sidewise with his untouched left foot, pulling one of the pungi stakes out of the ground, and was unconscious even during the single movement; and fainted, simply directly fainted with the pain.

This was happening: great black gap-mawed beast padding through outer darkness toward him. On a horizonless journey through myth, coming toward the moment *before* the piercing of flesh. Lizard dragon beast with eyes of oil-slick pools, ultraviolet death colors smoking in their depths. Corded silk-flowing muscles sliding beneath the black hairless hide, trained sprinter from a lost land, smoothest movements of choreographed power. The never-sleeping guardian of the faith, now gentlestepping down through mists of potent barriers erected to separate men from their masters.

In that moment before the boot touched the bamboo spike, the basilisk passed through the final veils of confounding time and space and dimension and thought, to assume palpable shape in the forest world of Vernon Lestig. And in the translation was changed, altered wonderfully. The black, thick and oily hide of the death-breath dragon beast shimmered, heat lightning across flat prairie land, golden flashes seen spattering beyond mountain peaks, and the great creature was a thousand colored. Green diamonds burned up from the skin of the basilisk, the deadly million eyes of a nameless god. Rubies gorged with the water-thin blood of insects sealed in amber from the dawn of time pulsed there. Golden jewels changing from instant to instant, shape and scent and hue . . . they were there in the tapestry mosaic of the skin picture. A delicate, subtle, gaudy flashmaze kaleidoscope of flesh, taut over massive muscled threats.

The basilisk was in the world.

And Lestig had yet to experience his pain.

The creature lifted a satin-padded paw and laid it against the points of the pungi stakes. Slowly, the basilisk relaxed and the stakes pierced the rough sensitive blackmoon shapes of the pads. Dark, steaming serum flowed down over the stakes, mingling with the Oriental poison. The basilisk withdrew its paw and the twin wounds healed in an instant, closed over and were gone.

Were gone. Bunching of muscles, a leap into air, a cauldron roiling of dark air, and the basilisk sprang up into nothing and was gone. Was gone.

As the moment came to an exhalation of end, and Vernon Lestig walked onto the pungi stakes.

It is a well-known fact that one whose blood slakes the thirst of the *vrykolakas*, the vampire, himself becomes one of the drinkers of darkness, becomes a celebrant of the master deity, becomes himself possessed of the powers of the disciples of that deity.

The basilisk had not come from the vampires, nor were his powers those of the blood drinkers. It was not by chance that the basilisk's master had sent him to recruit Lance Corporal Vernon Lestig. There is an order to the darkside universe.

He fought consciousness, as if on some cellular level he knew what pain awaited him with the return of his senses. But the red tide washed higher, swallowed more and more of his deliquescent body, and finally the pain thundered in from the blood-sea, broke in a long, curling comber and coenesthesia was upon him totally. He screamed, and the scream went on and on for a long time, till they came back to him and gave him an injection of something that thinned the pain, and he lost contact with the chaos that had been his right foot.

When he came back again, it was dark and at first he thought it was night; but when he opened his eyes it was still dark. His right foot itched mercilessly. He went back to sleep, no coma, sleep.

When he came back again, it was still night and he opened his eyes and he realized he was blind. He felt straw under his left hand and knew he was on a pallet and knew he had been captured; and then he started to cry because he knew, without even reaching down to find out, that they had amputated his foot. Perhaps his entire leg. He cried about not being able to run down in the car for a pint of half-and-half just before dinner; he cried about not being able to go out to a movie without people trying not to see what had happened to him; he cried about Teresa and what she would have to decide now; he cried about the way clothes would look on him; he cried about the things he would have to say every time; he cried about shoes; and so many other things. He cursed his parents and his patrol and the hostiles and the men who had sent him here and he wanted, wished, prayed desperately that any one of them could change places with him. And when he was long finished crying, and simply wanted to die, they came for him, and took him to a hooch where they began questioning him. In the night. The night he carried with him.

They were an ancient people, with a heritage of enslavement, and so for them anguish had less meaning than the thinnest whisper of crimson cloud high above a desert planet of the farthest star in the sky. But they knew the uses to which anguish could be put, and for them there was no evil in doing so: for a people with a heritage of enslavement, evil is a concept of those who forged the shackles, not those who wore them. In the name of freedom, no monstrousness is too great.

So they tortured Lestig, and he told them what they wanted to know. Every scrap of information he knew. Locations and movements and plans and defenses and the troop strength and the sophistication of armaments and the nature of his mission and rumors he'd picked up and his name and his rank and every serial number he could think of, and the street address of his home in Kansas, and the sequence of his driver's license, and his gas credit card number and the telephone number of Teresa. He told them everything.

As if it were a reward for having held nothing back, a gummed gold star placed beside his chalked name on a blackboard in a kindergarten schoolroom, his eyesight began to come back slightly. Flickering, through a haze of gray; just enough light permitted through to show him shapes, the change from daylight to darkness; and it grew stronger, till he could actually *see* for whole minutes at a time . . . then blindness again. His sight came and went, and when they realized he could see them, they resumed the interrogations on a more strenuous level. But he had nothing left to tell; he had emptied himself.

But they kept at him. They threatened to hammer bamboo slivers into his damaged eyeballs. They hung him up on a shoulder-high wooden wall, his arms behind him, circulation cut off, weight pulling the arms from their shoulder sockets, and they beat him across the belly with lengths of bamboo, with *bojitsu* sticks. He could not even cry any more. They had given him no food and no water, and he could not manufacture tears. But his breath came in deep, husking spasms from his chest, and one of the interrogators made the mistake of stepping forward to grab Lestig's head by the hair, yanking it up, leaning in close to ask another question, and Lestig—falling falling—exhaled deeply, struggling to live; and there was that breath, and a terrible thing happened.

When the reconnaissance patrol from the firebase actualized control of the hostile command position, when the Huey choppers dropped into the clearing, they advised Supermart HQ that every hostile but one in the immediate area was dead, that a Marine Lance Corporal named Lestig, Vernon C. 526-90-5416, had been found lying unconscious on the dirt floor of a hooch containing the bodies of nine enemy officers who had died horribly, most peculiarly, sickeningly, you've gotta see what this place looks like, HQ, jesus you ain't gonna believe what it smells like in here, you gotta see what these slopes look like, it musta been some terrible disease that could of done this kinda thing to 'em, the new lieutenant got really sick an' puked and what do you want us to do with the one guy that crawled off into the bushes before *it* got him, his face is melting, and the troops're scared shitless and. . .

And they pulled the recon group out immediately and sent in the Intelligence section, who sealed the area with Top Security, and they found out from the one with the rotting face—just before he died—that Lestig had talked, and they medivacked Lestig back to a field hospital and then to Saigon and then to Tokyo and then to San Diego, and they decided to court-martial him for treason and conspiring with the enemy, and the case made the papers big, and the court-martial was held behind closed doors, and after a long time Lestig emerged with an honorable, and they paid him off for the loss of his foot and the blindness, and he went back to the hospital for eleven months and in a way regained his sight, though he had to wear smoked glasses.

And then he went home to Kansas.

Between Syracuse and Garden City, sitting close to the coach window, staring out through the film of roadbed filth, Lestig watched the ghost image of the train he rode superimposed over flatland Kansas slipping past outside. The mud-swollen Arkansas River was a thick, syrupy-brown underline to the horizon.

"Hey, you Corporal Lestig?"

Vernon Lestig refocused his eyes and saw the wraith in the window. He turned and the sandwich butcher with his tray of candy bars, soft drinks, ham & cheeses on white or rye, newspapers and *Reader's Digests*, suspended from his chest by a strap around the neck, was his chest by a strap around the neck, was looking at him.

"No thanks," Lestig said, refusing the merchandise.

"No, hey, really, aren't you that Corporal Lestig—" He uncurled a newspaper from the roll in the tray and opened it quickly. "Yeah, sure, here you are. See?"

Lestig had seen most of the newspaper coverage, but this was local, Wichita. He fumbled for change. "How much?"

"Ten cents." There was a surprised look on the butcher's face, but it washed down into a smile as he said, understanding it, "You been out of touch in the service, didn't even remember what a paper cost, huh?"

Lestig gave him two nickels and turned abruptly to the window, folding the paper back. He read the article. It was a stone. There was a note referring to an editorial, and he turned to that page and read it. People were outraged, it said. Enough secret trials, it said. We must face up to our war crimes, it said. The effrontery of the military and the government, it said. Coddling, even ennobling traitors and killers, it said. He let the newspaper slide out of his hands. It clung to his lap for a moment, then fell apart to the floor.

"I didn't say it before, but they should of shot you, you want *my* opinion!" The butcher said it, going fast, fast through the aisle, coming back the other way, gaining the end of the car and gone. Lestig did not turn around. Even wearing the smoked glasses to protect his damaged eyes, he could see too clearly. He thought about the months of blindness and wondered again what had happened in that hooch and considered how much better off he might be if he were *still* blind.

The Rock Island Line was a mighty good road, the Rock Island Line was the way to go. To go home. The land outside dimmed for him, as things frequently dimmed, as though the repair work to his eyes was only temporary, a reserve generator cut in from time to time to sustain the power-feed to his vision, and dimming as the drain drank too deeply. Then light seeped back in and he could see again. But there was a mist over his eyes, over the land.

Somewhere else, through another mist, a great beast sat haunch-back, dripping chromatic fire from jeweled hide, nibbling at something soft in its paw, talons extended from around blackmoon pads. Watching, breathing, waiting for Lestig's vision to clear.

He had rented the car in Wichita and driven back the sixty-five miles to Grafton. The Rock Island Line no longer stopped there. Passenger trains were almost a thing of the past in Kansas.

Lestig drove silently. No radio sounds accompanied him. He did not hum, he did not cough, he drove with his eyes straight ahead, not seeing the hills and valleys through which he passed, features of the land that gave the lie to the myth of a totally flat Kansas. He drove like a man who, had he the power of images, thought of himself as a turtle drawn straight to the salt sea.

He paralleled the belt of sand hills on the south side of the Arkansas, turned off Route 96 at Elmer, below Hutchinson, due south onto 17. He had not driven these roads in three years, but then, neither had he swum or ridden a bicycle in all that time. Once learned, there was no forgetting.

Or Teresa.

Or home. No forgetting.

Or the hooch.

Or the smell of it. No forgetting.

He crossed the North Fork at the western tip of Cheney Reservoir and turned west off 17 above Pretty Prairie. He pulled into Grafton just before dusk, the immense running sore of the sun draining off behind the hills. The deserted buildings of the zinc mine—closed now for twelve years—stood against the sky like black fingers of a giant hand opened and raised behind the nearest hill.

He drove once around the town mall, the Soldiers and Sailors Monument and the crumbling band shell its only ornaments. There was an American flag flying at half-mast from the City Hall. And another from the Post Office.

It was getting dark. He turned on his headlights. The mist over his eyes was strangely reassuring, as if it separated him from a land at once familiar and alien.

The stores on Fitch Street were closed, but the Utopia Theater's marquee was flashing, and a small crowd was gathered waiting for the ticket booth to open. He slowed to see if he recognized anyone, and people stared back at him. A teen-aged boy he didn't know pointed and then turned to his friends. In the rearview mirror Lestig saw two of them leave the queue and head for the candy shop beside the movie house. He drove through the business section and headed for his home.

He stepped on the headlight brightener but it did little to dissipate the dimness through which he marked his progress. Had he been a man of images, he might have fantasized that he now saw the world through the eyes of some special beast. But he was not a man of images.

The house in which his family had lived for sixteen years was empty.

There was a realtor's FOR SALE sign on the unmowed front lawn.

Gramas and buffalo grass were taking over. Someone had taken a chain saw to the oak tree that had grown in the front yard. When it had fallen, the top branches had torn away part of the side porch of the house.

He forced an entrance through the coal chute at the rear of the house, and through the sooty remains of his vision he searched every room, both upstairs and down. It was slow work: he walked with an aluminum crutch.

They had left hurriedly, mother and father and Neola. Coat hangers clumped together in the closets like frightened creatures huddling for comfort. Empty cartons from a market littered the kitchen floor, and in one of them a teacup without a handle lay upside-down. The fireplace flue had been left open, and rain had reduced the ashes in the grate to a black paste. Mold grew in an open jar of blackberry preserves left on a kitchen cabinet shelf. There was dust.

He was touching the ripped shade hanging in a living room window when he saw the headlights of the cars turning into the driveway. Three of them pulled in, bumper-to-bumper. Two more slewed in at the curb, their headlights flooding the living room with a dim glow. Doors slammed.

Lestig crutched back and to the side.

Hard-lined shapes moved in front of the headlights, seemed to be grouping, talking. One of them moved away from the pack, and an arm came up, and something shone for a moment in the light; then a Stillson wrench came crashing through the front window in an explosion of glass.

"Lestig, you motherfuckin' bastard, come on out of there!"

He moved awkwardly but silently through the living room, into the kitchen and down the basement stairs. He was careful opening the coal chute window from the bin, and through the narrow slit he saw someone moving out there. They were all around the house. Coal shifted under his foot.

He let the window fall back smoothly and turned to go back upstairs. He didn't want to be trapped in the basement. From upstairs he heard the sounds of windows being smashed.

He took the stairs clumsily, clinging to the banister, his crutch useless, but moved quickly through the house and climbed the stairs to the upper floor. The top porch doorway was in what had been his parents' room; he unlocked and opened it. The screen door was hanging off at an angle, leaning against the outer wall by one hinge. He stepped out onto the porch, careful to avoid any places where the falling tree had weakened the structure. He looked down, back flat to the wall, but could see no one. He crutched to the railing, dropped the aluminum prop into the darkness, climbed over and began shinnying down one of the porch posts, clinging tightly with his thighs, as he had when he'd been a small boy, sneaking out to play after he'd been sent to bed.

It happened so quickly, he had no idea, even later, what had actually transpired. Before his foot touched the ground, someone grabbed him from behind. He fought to stay on the post, like a monkey on a stick, and even tried to kick out with his good foot; but he was pulled loose from the post and thrown down violently. He tried to roll, but he came up against a mulberry bush. Then he tried to dummy-up, fold into a bundle, but a foot caught him in the side, and he fell over onto his back. His smoked glasses fell off, and through the sooty fog he could just make out someone dropping down to sit on his chest, something thick and long being raised above the head of the shape . . . he strained to see . . . strained. . .

And then the shape screamed, and the weapon fell out of the hand and both hands clawed at the head, and the someone staggered to its feet and stumbled away, crashing through the mulberry bushes, still screaming.

Lestig fumbled around and found his glasses, pushed them onto his face. He was lying on the aluminum crutch. He got to his foot with the aid of the prop, like a skier righting himself after a spill.

He limped away behind the house next door, circled and came up on the empty cars still headed-in at the curb, their headlights splashing the house with dirty light. He slid in behind the wheel, saw it was a stick shift and knew that with one foot he could not manage it. He slid out, moved to the second car, saw it was an automatic, and quietly opened the door. He slid behind the wheel and turned the key hard. The car thrummed to life and a mass of shapes erupted from the side of the house.

But he was gone before they reached the street.

He sat in the darkness, he sat in the sooty fog that obscured his sight, he sat in the stolen car. Outside Teresa's home. Not the house in which she'd lived when he'd left three years ago, but in the house of the man she'd married six months before, when Lestig's name had been first splashed across newspaper front pages.

He had driven to her parents' home, but it had been dark. He could not—or would not—break in to wait, but there had been a note taped to the mailbox advising the mailman to forward all letters to Teresa McCausland to this house.

He drummed the steering wheel with his fingers. His right leg ached from the fall. His shirt sleeve had been ripped, and his left forearm bore a long, shallow gash from the mulberry bush. But it had stopped bleeding.

Finally, he crawled out of the car, dropped his shoulder into the crutch's padded curve, and rolled like a man with sea legs, up to the front door.

The white plastic button in the baroque backing was lit by a tiny nameplate bearing the word HOWARD. He pressed the button, and a chime sounded somewhere on the other side of the door.

She answered the door wearing blue denim shorts and a man's white shirt, button-down and frayed; a husband's castoff.

"Vern. . ." her voice cut off the sentence before she could say *oh* or *what are you* or *they said* or *no*!

"Can I come in?"

"Go away, Vern. My husband's—"

A voice from inside called, "Who is it, Terry?"

"Please go away," she whispered.

"I want to know where Mom and Dad and Neola went."

"Terry?"

"I can't talk to you . . . go away!"

"What the hell's going on around here, I *have* to know."

"Terry? Someone there?"

"Good-by, Vern. I'm. . ." She slammed the door and did not say the word *sorry*.

He turned to go. Somewhere great corded muscles flexed, a serpentine throat lifted, talons flashed against the stars. His vision fogged, cleared for a moment, and in that moment rage sluiced through him. He turned back to the door and leaned against the wall and banged on the frame with the crutch.

There was the sound of movement from inside; he heard Teresa arguing, pleading, trying to stop someone from going to answer the noise, but a second later the door flew open and Gary Howard stood in the doorway, older and thicker across the shoulders and angrier than Lestig had remembered him from senior year in high school, the last time they'd seen each other. The annoyed look of expecting Bible salesman, heart fund solicitor, girl scout cookie dealer, evening door-bell prankster changed into a smirk.

Howard leaned against the jamb, folded his arms across his chest so that the off-tackle pectorals bunched against his Sherwood-green tank top.

"Evening, Vern. When'd you get back?"

Lestig straightened, crutch jammed back into armpit. "I want to talk to Terry."

"Didn't know just when you'd come rolling in, Vern, but we knew you'd show. How was the war, old buddy?"

"You going to let me talk to her?"

"Nothing's stopping her, old buddy. My wife is a free agent when it comes to talking to ex-boy friends. My *wife*, that is. You get the word . . . old buddy?"

"*Terry?*" He leaned forward and yelled past Howard.

Gary Howard smiled a ladies'-choice-dance smile and put one hand flat against Lestig's chest. "Don't make a nuisance of yourself, Vern."

"I'm talking to her, Howard. Right now, even if I have to go through you."

Howard straightened, hand still flat against Lestig's chest. "You miserable cowardly sonofabitch," he said, very gently, and shoved. Lestig flailed backward, the crutch going out from under him, and he tumbled off the front step.

Howard looked down at him, and the president-of-the-senior-class smile vanished. "Don't come back, Vern. The next time I'll punch out your fucking heart."

The door slammed and there were voices inside. High voices, and then the sound of Howard slapping her.

Lestig crawled to the crutch, and using the wall stood up. He thought of breaking in through the door, but he was Lestig, track . . . once . . . and Howard had been football. Still was. Would be, on Sunday afternoons with the children he'd made on cool Saturday nights in a bed with Teresa.

He went back to the car and sat in the darkness. He didn't know he'd been sitting there for some time, till the shadow moved up to the window and his head came around sharply.

"Vern . . . ?"

"You'd better go back in. I don't want to cause you any more trouble."

"He's upstairs doing some sales reports. He got a very nice job as a salesman for Shoop Motors when he got out of the Air Force. We live nice, Vern. He's really very good to me . . . oh, Vern . . . why? Why'd you *do* it?"

"You'd better go back in."

"I waited, God, you *know* I waited, Vern. But then all that terrible thing happened . . . Vern, why did you *do* it?"

"Come on, Terry. I'm tired, leave me alone."

"The whole town, Vern. They were so ashamed. There were reporters and TV people, they came in and talked to *every*one. Your mother and father, Neola, they couldn't stay here any more . . . ."

"Where are they, Terry?"

"They moved away, Vern. Kansas City, I think."

"Oh, Jesus."

"Neola's living closer."

"Where?"

"She doesn't want you to know, Vern. I think she got married. I know she changed her name . . . Lestig isn't such a good name around here any more."

"I've got to talk to her, Terry. Please. You've got to tell me where she is."

"I can't Vern. I promised."

"Then call her. Do you have her number? Can you get in touch with her?"

"Yes, I think so. Oh, Vern. . ."

"Call her. Tell her I'll stay here in town till I can talk to her. Tonight. Please, Terry!"

She stood silently. Then said, "All right, Vern. Do you want her to meet you at your house?"

He thought of the hard-lined shapes in the glare of headlamps, and of the thing that had run screaming as he lay beside the mulberry bush. "No. Tell her I'll meet her in the church."

"St. Matthew's?"

"No. The Harvest Baptist."

"But it's closed, it has been for years."

"I know. It closed down before I left. I know a way in. She'll remember. Tell her I'll be waiting."

Light erupted through the front door, and Teresa Howard's face came up as she stared across the roof of the stolen car. She didn't even say goodbye; but her hand touched his face, cool and quick; and she ran back.

Knowing it was time once again to travel, the dragonbreath death-beast eased sinuously to its feet and began treading down carefully through the fogs of limitless forevers. A soft, expectant purring came from its throat, and its terrible eyes burned with joy.

He was lying full out in one of the pews when the loose boards in the vestry wall creaked, and Lestig knew she had come. He sat up, wiping sleep from his fogged eyes, and replaced the smoked glasses. Somehow, they helped.

She came through the darkness in the aisle in front of the altar, and stopped. "Vernon?"

"I'm here, Sis."

She came toward the pew, but stopped three rows away. "Why did you come back?"

His mouth was dry. He would have liked a beer. "Where else should I have gone?"

"Haven't you made enough trouble for Mom and Dad and me?"

He wanted to say things about his right foot and his eyesight, left somewhere in Southeast Asia. But even the light smear of skin he could see in the darkness told him her face was older, wearier, changed, and he could not do that to her.

"It was terrible, Vernon. Terrible. They came and talked to us and they wouldn't let us alone. And they set up television cameras and made movies of the house and we couldn't even go out. And when they went away the people from town came, and they were even worse; oh God, Vern, you can't believe what they did. One night they came to break things, and they cut down the tree and Dad tried to stop them and they beat him up so bad, Vern. You should have seen him. It would have made you cry, Vern."

And he thought of his foot.

"We went away, Vern. We had to. We hoped—" She stopped.

"You hoped I'd be convicted and shot or sent away."

She said nothing.

He thought of the hooch and the smell.

"Okay, Sis. I understand."

"I'm sorry, Vernon. I'm really sorry, dear. But why did you do this to us? Why?"

He didn't answer for a long time, and finally she came to him, and put her arms around him and kissed his neck, and then she slipped away in the darkness; and the wall boards creaked; and he was alone.

He sat there in the pew, thinking nothing. He stared at the shadows till his eyes played him tricks and he thought he saw little speckles of light dancing. Then the light glimmers changed and coalesced and turned red and he seemed to be staring first into a mirror and then into the eyes of some monstrous creature, and his head hurt and his eyes burned. . .

And the church changed, melted, swam before his eyes, and he fought for breath and pulled at his throat, and the church re-formed, and he was in the hooch again; they were questioning him.

He was crawling.

Crawling across a dirt floor, pulling himself forward with his fingers leaving flesh-furrows in the earth, trying to crawl away from them.

"Crawl! Crawl and perhaps we will let you live!"

He crawled and their legs were at his eye level, and he tried to reach up to touch one of them, and they hit him. Again and again. But the pain was not the worst of it. The monkey cage where they kept him boxed for endless days and nights. Too small to stand, too narrow to lie down, open to the rain, open to the insects that came and nested in the raw stump of his leg and laid their eggs, and the itching that sent Lilliputian arrows up into his side, and the light that hung from jury-rigged wires through the trees, the light that never went out, day or night, and no sleep, and the questions, the endless questions . . . and he crawled . . . God how he crawled . . . if he could have crawled around the world on both bloody hands and one foot, scouring away the knees of his pants, he would have crawled, just to sleep, just to stop the arrows of pain . . . he would have crawled to the center of the earth and drunk the menstrual blood of the planet . . . for only a time of quiet, a straightening of his legs, a little sleep. . .

Why did you do this to us, why?

Because I'm a human being and I'm weak and no one should be expected to be able to take it. Because I'm a man and not a book of rules that says I have to take it. Because I was in a place without sleep and I didn't want to be there and there was no one to save me. Because I wanted to live.

He heard boards creaking.

He blinked his eyes and sat silently and listened, and there was movement in the church. He reached for his smoked glasses, but they were out of reach, and he reached farther and the crutch slid away from the pew seat and dropped with a crash. Then they were on him.

Whether it was the same bunch, he never knew.

They came for him and vaulted the pews and smashed into him before he could use whatever it was he'd used on the kid at the house, the kid who lay on a table in the City Hall, covered with a sheet through which green stains and odd rotting smells oozed.

They jumped him and beat him, and he flailed up through the mass of bodies and was staring directly into a wild-eyed mandrill face, and he *looked* at him.

Looked at him. As the deathbeast struck.

The man screamed, clawed at his face, and his face came away in handfuls, the rotting flesh dripping off his fingers. He fell back, carrying two others with him, and Lestig suddenly remembered what had happened in the hooch, remembered breathing and looking, and here in this house of a God gone away he spun on them, one by one, and he breathed deeply and exhaled in their faces and stared at them across the evil night wasteland of another universe, and they shrieked and died, and he was all alone once more. The others, coming through the vestry wall, having followed Neola, having been telephoned by Gary Howard, who had beaten the information from his wife, the others stopped and turned and ran. . .

So that only Lestig, brother to the basilisk, who was itself the servant of a nameless dark one far away, only Lestig was left standing amid the twisted body shapes of things that had been men.

Stood alone, felt the power and the fury pulsing in him, felt his eyes glowing, felt the death that lay on his tongue, deep in his throat, the wind death in his lungs. And knew night had finally fallen.

They had roadblocked the only two exits out of town. Then they took eight-cell battery flashlights and Coleman lanterns and cave-crawling lamps, and some of them who had worked the zinc mine years before, they donned their miner's helmets with the lights on them, and they even wound rags around clubs and dipped them in kerosene and lit them, and they went out searching for the filthy traitor who had killed their sons and husbands and brothers, and not one of them laughed at the scene of crowd lights moving through the town, like something from an old film. A film of hunting the monster. They did not draw the parallel, for had they drawn the parallel, they would still never have laughed.

And they searched through the night, but did not find him. And when the dawn came up and they doused their lamps, and the parking lights replaced headlights on the caravans of cars that ringed the town, they still had not found him. And finally they gathered in the mall, to decide what to do.

And he was there.

He stood on the Soldiers and Sailors Monument high above them, where he had huddled all through the night, at the feet of a World War I doughboy with his arm upraised and a Springfield in his fist. He was there, and the symbolism did not escape them.

"Pull him down!" someone shouted. And they surged toward the marble and bronze monument.

Vernon Lestig stood watching them come out of the pale, chill, aluminum-dawn mist and he seemed unconcerned at the rifles and clubs and war-souvenir Lugers coming toward him.

The first man to scale the plinth was Gary Howard, with the bro-ken-field-cheers-of-the-crowd smile on his face. Lestig's eyes widened behind the smoked glasses, and very casually he removed them, and he *looked* at the big, many-toothed car salesman.

The crowd screamed in one voice, and the forward rush was halted as the still-smoking body of Teresa's husband fell back on them, arms flung out wide, torso twisted.

In the rear, they tried to run. He cut them down. The crowd stopped. One man tried to raise a revolver to kill him, but he dropped, his face burned away, smoking pustules of ruined flesh where his eyes had been.

They stopped. Frozen in a world of muscles that trembled, of run-ning energy with no place to go.

"I'll show you!" he yelled. "I'll show you what it's like! You want to know, so I'll show you!"

Then he breathed, and men died. Then he looked and others fell. Then he said, very quietly, so that they would hear him: "It's easy, till it happens. You never know, Patriots! You live all the time and you say one thing or another, all your rules about what it takes to be brave, but you never *know*, till that one time when you find out. *I* found out, it's not so easy. Now *you'll* find out."

He pointed to the ground.

"Get down on your knees and crawl, Patriots! Crawl to me and maybe I'll let you live. Get down like animals and crawl on your bellies to me."

There was a shout from the crowd; and the man died.

"*Crawl, I said!* Crawl to me!"

Here and there in the crowd people dropped from sight. At the rear a woman tried to run away and he burned her out and the husk fell, and all around her, within sight of the wisps of smoke from her face, people fell to their knees. Then entire groups dropped; then one whole side of the mob went down. Then they were all on their knees.

"Crawl! Crawl, brave ones, crawl nice my people! Crawl and learn it's better to *live*, any way at all, to stay alive, because you're human! Crawl and you'll understand your slogans are shit, your rules are for others! Crawl for your goddamned lives and you'll understand! *Crawl!*"

And they crawled. They crept forward on hands and knees, across the grass, across cement and mud and the branches of small bushes, across the dirt. They crawled toward him.

And far away, through mists of darkness, the Helmeted-Headed One sat on his throne, high above all, with the basilisk at his feet, and he smiled.

"Crawl, God damn you!"

But he did not know the name of the God he served.

"Crawl!"

And in the middle of the mob, a woman who had hung a gold star in her front window, crawled across a .32 Police Positive, and her hand touched it, and she folded her fingers around it, and suddenly she raised up and screamed, "For Kennyyyyy. . . !" and she fired.

The bullet smashed Lestig's collarbone and he spun sidewise, up against the Yank's puttees, and he tried to regain his stance, but the crutch had fallen, and now the crowd was on its feet and firing . . . and firing. . .

They buried the body in an unmarked grave, and no one talked of it. And far away, on a high throne, tickling the sleek hide of the basilisk that reclined at his feet like a faithful mastiff, even the Armed One did not speak of it. There was no need to speak of it. Lestig was gone, but that was to have been expected.

The weapon had been de-activated; but Mars, the Eternal One, the God Who Never Dies, the Lord of Futures, Warden of the Dark Places, Ever-Potent Scion of Conflict, Master of Men, Mars sat content.

The recruiting had gone well. Power to the people.

Ben Bova seems to have structured his life toward being an emissary between those "two cultures," science and the arts. Educated in journalism and foreign service, but with an abiding love for science, he used to divide his time between writing (both popular science and science fiction) and being Manager of Marketing for a large space-oriented R&D laboratory.

Since 1970, he has edited the enduring science fiction magazine Analog *and has been given four Hugo Awards for excellence in editing.*

Analog *being a journal dedicated to the celebration and preservation of the "hard science" science fiction story, Ben was the logical person to ask for a piece offering a possible alternative to war, via technology. He responded with this story of a marvelous machine that allows warriors to act out their battles in perfect realism, without anybody getting hurt.*

But anything can be made a weapon, they teach you in commando training; you can send a person to Valhalla by striking him hard enough, in the right place, with the corner of a Holy Bible's binding. . . .

THE DUELING MACHINE
by BEN BOVA

Dulaq rode the slide to the upper pedestrian level, stepped off and walked over to the railing. The city stretched out all around him—broad avenues thronged with busy people, pedestrian walks, vehicle thoroughfares, aircars gliding between the gleaming, towering buildings.

And somewhere in this vast city was the man he must kill. The man who would kill him, perhaps.

It all seemed so real! The noise of the streets, the odors of the perfumed trees lining the walks, even the warmth of the reddish sun on his back as he scanned the scene before him.

It is an illusion, Dulaq reminded himself, *a clever man-made hallucination. A figment of my own imagination amplified by a machine.*

But it seemed so very real.

Real or not, he had to find Odal before the sun set. Find him and kill him. Those were the terms of the duel. He fingered the stubby cylindrical stat-wand in his tunic pocket. That was the weapon he had chosen, his weapon, his own invention. And this was the environment he had picked: his city, busy, noisy, crowded, the metropolis Dulaq had known and loved since childhood.

Dulaq turned and glanced at the sun. It was halfway down toward the horizon, he judged. He had about three hours to find Odal. When he did—kill or be killed.

Of course no one is actually hurt. That is the beauty of the machine. It allows one to settle a score, to work out aggressive feelings, without either mental or physical harm.

Dulaq shrugged. He was a roundish figure, moonfaced, slightly stooped shoulders. He had work to do. Unpleasant work for a civilized man, but the future of the Acquataine Cluster and the entire alliance of neighboring star systems could well depend on the outcome of this electronically synthesized dream.

He turned and walked down the elevated avenue, marveling at the sharp sensation of hardness that met each footstep on the paving. Children dashed by and rushed up to a toyshop window. Men of commerce strode along purposefully, but without missing a chance to eye the girls sauntering by.

I must have a marvelous imagination, Dulaq thought smiling to himself.

Then he thought of Odal, the blond, icy professional he was pitted against. Odal was an expert at all the weapons, a man of strength and cool precision, an emotionless tool in the hands of a ruthless politician. But how expert could he be with a stat-wand, when the first time he saw one was the moment before the duel began? And how well acquainted could he be with the metropolis, when he had spent most of his life in the military camps on the dreary planets of Kerak, sixty light-years from Acquatainia?

No, Odal would be lost and helpless in this situation. He would attempt to hide among the throngs of people. All Dulaq had to do was to find him.

The terms of the duel restricted both men to the pedestrian walks of the commercial quarter of the city. Dulaq knew the area intimately, and he began a methodical hunt through the crowds for the tall, fair-haired, blue-eyed Odal.

And he saw him! After only a few minutes of walking down the major thoroughfare, he spotted his opponent, strolling calmly along a crosswalk, at the level below.

Dulaq hurried down the next ramp, worked his way through the crowd, and saw the man again. Tall and blond, unmistakable. Dulaq edged along behind him quietly, easily. No disturbance. No pushing.

Plenty of time. They walked along the street for a quarter hour while the distance between them slowly shrank from fifty feet to five.

Finally Dulaq was directly behind him, within arm's reach. He grasped the stat-wand and pulled it from his tunic. With one quick motion he touched it to the base of the man's skull and started to thumb the button that would release the killing of energy. . .

The man turned suddenly. It wasn't Odal!

Dulaq jerked back in surprise. It couldn't be. He had seen his face. It was Odal—and yet this man was definitely a stranger.

He stared at Dulaq as the duelist backed away a few steps, then turned and walked quickly from the place.

A mistake, Dulaq told himself. *You were overanxious. A good thing this is an hallucination, or else the autopolice would be taking you in by now.*

And yet . . . he had been so certain that it was Odal. A chill shuddered through him. He looked up, and there was his antagonist, on the thoroughfare above, at the precise spot where he himself had been a few minutes earlier. Their eyes met, and Odal's lips parted in a cold smile.

Dulaq hurried up the ramp. Odal was gone by the time he reached the upper level, *He could not have gotten far,* Dulaq reasoned. Slowly, but very surely, Dulaq's hallucination turned into a nightmare. He spotted Odal in the crowd, only to have him melt away. He saw him again, lolling in a small park, but when he got closer, the man turned out to be another stranger. He felt a chill of the duelist's ice-blue eyes on him again and again, but when he turned to find his antagonist, no one was there but the impersonal crowd.

Odal's face appeared again and again. Dulaq struggled through the throngs to find his opponent, only to have him vanish. The crowd seemed to be filled with tall, blond men crisscrossing before Dulaq's dismayed eyes.

The shadows lengthened. The sun was setting, Dulaq could feel his heart pounding within him and perspiration pouring from every square inch of his skin.

There he is! Definitely, positively him! Dulaq pushed through the homeward-bound crowds toward the figure of a tall, blond man leaning against the safety railing of the city's main thoroughfare. It was Odal, the damned smiling confident Odal.

Dulaq pulled the wand from his tunic and battled across the surging crowd to the spot where Odal stood motionless, hands in pockets, watching him.

Dulaq came within arm's reach. . .
"TIME, GENTLEMEN. TIME IS UP, THE DUEL IS ENDED."

High above the floor of the antiseptic-white chamber that housed the dueling machine was a narrow gallery. Before the machine had been installed, the chamber had been a lecture hall in Acquatainia's largest university. Now the rows of students' seats, the lecturer's dais and rostrum were gone. The chamber held only the machine, the grotesque collection of consoles, control desks, power units, association circuits, and booths where the two antagonists sat.

In the gallery—empty during ordinary duels—sat a privileged handful of newsmen.

"Time limit is up," one of them said. "Dulaq didn't get him."

"Yes, but he didn't get Dulaq, either."

The first one shrugged. "The important thing is that now Dulaq has to fight Odal on *his* terms. Dulaq couldn't win with his own choice of weapons and situation, so—"

"Wait, they're coming out."

Down on the floor below, Dulaq and his opponent emerged from their enclosed booths.

One of the newsmen whistled softly. "Look at Dulaq's face . . . it's positively gray."

"I've never seen the Prime Minister so shaken."

"And take a look at Kanus' hired assassin." The newsmen turned toward Odal, who stood before his booth, quietly chatting with his seconds.

"Hm-m-m. There's a bucket of frozen ammonia for you."

"He's enjoying this."

One of the newsmen stood up. "I've got a deadline to meet. Save my seat."

He made his way past the guarded door, down the rampway circling the outer walls of the building, to the portable tri-di transmitting unit that the Acquatainian government had permitted for the newsmen on the campus grounds outside the former lecture hall.

The newsman huddled with his technicians for a few minutes, then stepped before the transmitter.

"Emile Dulaq, Prime Minister of the Acquataine Cluster and acknowledged leader of the coalition against Chancellor Kanus of the Kerak Worlds, has failed in the first part of his psychonic duel against Major Par Odal of Kerak. The two antagonists are now undergoing the routine medical and psychological checks before renewing their duel."

By the time the newsman returned to his gallery seat, the duel was almost ready to begin again.

Dulaq stood in the midst of the group of advisors before the looming impersonality of the machine.

"You need not go through with the next phase of the duel immediately," his Minister of Defense was saying. "Wait until tomorrow. Rest and calm yourself."

Dulaq's round face puckered into a frown. He cocked an eye at the chief meditech, hovering at the edge of the little group.

Meditch, one of the staff that ran the dueling machine, pointed out, "The Prime Minister has passed the examinations. He is capable, within the agree-upon rules of the contest, of resuming."

"But he has the option of retiring for the day, does he not?"

"If Major Odal agrees."

Dulaq shook his head impatiently. "No. I shall go through with it. Now."

"But—"

The prime minister's face suddenly hardened; his advisors lapsed into a respectful silence. The chief meditech ushered Dulaq back into his booth. On the other side of the room, Odal glanced at the Acquatainians, grinned humorlessly, and strode to his own booth.

Dulaq sat and tried to blank out his mind while the meditechs adjusted the neurocontacts to his head and torso. They finished at last and withdrew. He was alone in the booth now, looking at the dead-white walls, completely bare except for the viewscreen before his eyes. The screen finally began to glow slightly, then brightened into a series of shifting colors. The colors merged and changed, swirled across his field of view. Dulaq felt himself being drawn into them gradually, compellingly, completely immersed in them.

The mists slowly vanished, and Dulaq found himself standing on an immense and totally barren plain. Not a tree, not a blade of grass; nothing but bare, rocky ground stretching in all directions to the horizon and disturbingly harsh yellow sky. He looked down and at his feet saw the weapon that Odal had chosen.

A primitive club.

With a sense of dread, Dulaq picked up the club and hefted it in his hand. He scanned the plain. Nothing. No hills or trees or bushes to hide in. No place to run to.

And off on the horizon he could see a tall, lithe figure holding a similar club walking slowly and deliberately toward him.

The press gallery was practically empty. The duel had more than an hour to run, and most of the newsmen were outside, broadcasting their hastily-drawn guesses about Dulaq's failure to win with his own choice of weapon and environment.

Then a curious thing happened.

On the master control panel of the dueling machine, a single light flashed red. The meditech blinked at it in surprise, then pressed a series of buttons on his board. More red lights appeared. The chief meditech rushed to the board and flipped a single switch.

One of the newsmen turned to his partner. "What's going on down there?"

"I think it's all over. . . Yes, look, they're opening up the booths. Somebody must've scored a victory."

They watched intently while the other newsmen quickly filed back into the gallery.

"There's Odal. He looks happy."

"Guess that means—"

"Good Lord! Look at Dulaq!"

II

Dr. Leoh was lecturing at the Carinae Regional University when the news of Dulaq's duel reached him. An assistant professor perpetrated the unthinkable breach of interrupting the lecture to whisper the news in his ear.

Leoh nodded grimly, hurriedly finished his lecture, and then accompanied the assistant professor to the University president's office. They stood in silence as the slideway whisked them through the strolling students and blossoming greenery of the quietly-busy campus.

Leoh remained wrapped in his thoughts as they entered the administration building and rode the lift tube. Finally, as they stepped through the president's doorway, Leoh asked the assistant professor:

"You say he was in a state of catatonic shock when they removed him from the machine?"

"He still is," the president answered from his desk. "Completely withdrawn from the real world. Cannot speak, hear, or even see—a living vegetable."

Leoh plopped down in the nearest chair and ran a hand across his fleshy face. He was balding and jowly, but his face was creased from a smile that was almost habitual, and his eyes were active and alert.

"I don't understand it," he admitted. "Nothing like this has ever happened in a dueling machine before."

The university president shrugged. "I don't understand it either. But, this is your business." He put a slight emphasis on the last word, unconsciously perhaps.

"Well, at least this will not reflect on the university. That is why I formed Psychonics as a separate business enterprise." Then he added, with a grin, "The money was, of course, only a secondary consideration."

The president managed a smile. "Of course."

"I suppose the Acquatainians want to see me?" Leoh asked academically.

"They're on the tri-di now, waiting for you."

"They're holding a transmission frequency open over eight hundred parsecs?" Leoh looked impressed. "I must be an important man."

"You're the inventor of the dueling machine and the head of Psychonics, Inc. You're the only man who can tell them what went wrong."

"Well, I suppose I shouldn't keep them waiting."

"You can take the call here," the president said, starting to get up from his chair.

"No, no, stay there at your desk," Leoh insisted. "There's no reason for you to leave. Or you either," he said to the assistant professor.

The president touched a button on his desk communicator. The far wall of the office glowed momentarily, then seemed to dissolve. They were looking into another office, this one on Acquatainia. It was crowded with nervous-looking men in business clothes and military uniforms.

"Gentlemen," Dr. Leoh said.

Several of the Acquatainians tried to answer him at once. After a few seconds of talking together, they all looked toward one of their members—a tall, purposeful, shrewd-faced civilian who bore a neatly-trimmed black beard.

"I am Fernd Massan, the Acting Prime Minister of Acquatainia. You realize, of course, the crisis that has been precipitated in my Government because of this duel?"

Leoh blinked. "I realize that apparently there has been some difficulty with the dueling machine installed on the governing planet of your star cluster. Political crises are not in my field."

"But your dueling machine has incapacitated the Prime Minister," one of the generals bellowed.

"And at this particular moment," the defense minister added, "in the midst of our difficulties with the Kerak Worlds."

"If the Prime Minister is not—"

"Gentlemen!" Leoh objected. "I cannot make sense of your story if you all speak at once."

Massan gestured them to silence.

"The dueling machine," Leoh said, adopting a slightly professorial tone, "is nothing more than a psychonic device for alleviating human aggressions and hostilities. It allows two men to share a dream world created by one of them. There is nearly-complete feedback between the two. Within certain limits, the two men can do anything they wish within their dream world. This allows men to settle grievances with violence—in the safety of their own imaginations. If the machine is operated properly, no physical or mental harm can be done to the participants. They can alleviate their tensions safely—without damage of any sort to anyone, and without hurting society.

"Your own Government tested one of the machines and approved its use on Acquatainia more than three years ago. I see several of you who were among those to whom I personally demonstrated the device. Dueling machines are in use through wide portions of the galaxy, and I am certain that many of you have used the machine. You have, general, I'm sure."

The general blustered. "That has nothing to do with the matter at hand!"

"Admittedly," Leoh conceded. "But I do not understand how a therapeutic machine can possibly become entangled in a political crisis."

Massan said; "Allow me to explain. Our Government has been conducting extremely delicate negotiations with the stellar governments of our neighboring territories. These negotiations concern the rearmaments of the Kerak Worlds. You have heard of Kanus of Kerak?"

"I recall the name vaguely," Leoh said. "He's a political leader of some sort."

"Of the worst sort. He has acquired complete dictatorship of the Kerak Worlds, and is now attempting to rearm them for war. This is in direct countervention of the Treaty of Acquatainia, signed only thirty Terran years ago."

"I see. The treaty was signed at the end of the Acquataine-Kerak war, wasn't it?"

"A war that we won," the general pointed out.

"And now the Kerak Worlds want to rearm and try again," Leoh said.

"Precisely."

Leoh shrugged. "Why not call in the Star Watch? This is their type of police activity. And what has all this to do with the dueling machine?"

Massan explained patiently, "The Acquataine Cluster has never become a full-fledged member of the Terran Commonwealth. Our neighboring territories are likewise unaffiliated. Therefore the Star Watch can intervene only if all parties concerned agree to intervention. Unless, of course, there is an actual military emergency. The Kerak Worlds, of course, are completely isolationist—unbound by any laws except those of force."

Leoh shook his head.

"As for the dueling machine," Massan went on, "Kanus of Kerak has turned it into a political weapon—"

"But that's impossible. Your government passed strict laws concerning the use of the machine; I recommended them and I was in your Council chambers when the laws were passed. The machine may be used only for personal grievances. It is strictly outside the realm of politics."

Massan shook his head sadly. "Sir, laws are one thing—people are another. And politics consists of people, not words on paper."

"I don't understand," Leoh said.

Massan explained, "A little more than one Terran year ago, Kanus picked a quarrel with a neighboring star-group—the Safad Federation. He wanted an especially favorable trade agreement with them. Their minister of trade objected most strenuously. One of the Kerak negotiators—a certain Major Odal—got into a personal argument with the minister. Before anyone knew what had happened, they had challenged each other to a duel. Odal won the duel, and the minister resigned his post. He said that he could no longer effectively fight against the will of Odal and his group . . . he was psychologically incapable of it. Two weeks later he was dead—apparently a suicide, although I have doubts."

"That's . . . extremely interesting," Leoh said.

"Three days ago," Massan continued, "the same Major Odal engaged Prime Minister Dulaq in a bitter personal argument. Odal is now a military attaché of the Kerak Embassy here. He accused the Prime Minister of cowardice, before a large group of an Embassy party.

The Prime Minister had no alternative but to challenge him. And now—"

"And now Dulaq is in a state of shock, and your government is tottering."

Massan's back stiffened. "Our Government shall not fall, nor shall the Acquataine Cluster acquiesce to the rearmament of the Kerak Worlds. But"—and his voice lowered—"without Dulaq, I fear that our neighboring governments will give in to Kanus' demands and allow him to rearm. Alone, we are powerless to stop him."

"Rearmament itself might not be so bad," Leoh mused, "if you can keep the Kerak Worlds from using their weapons. Perhaps the Star Watch might—"

"Kanus could strike a blow and conquer a star system before the Star Watch could be summoned and arrive to stop him. Once Kerak is armed, this entire area of the galaxy is in peril. In fact, the entire galaxy is endangered."

"And he's using the dueling machine to further his ambitions," Leoh said. "Well, gentlemen, it seems I have no alternative but to travel to the Acquataine Cluster. The dueling machine is my responsibility, and if there is something wrong with it, or with the use of it, I will do my best to correct the situation."

"That is all we ask," Massan said. "Thank you."

The Acquatainian scene faded away, and the three men in the university president's office found themselves looking at a solid wall once again.

"Well," Dr. Leoh said, turning to the president, "it seems that I must request an indefinite leave of absence."

The president frowned. "And it seems that I must grant your request—even though the year is only half-finished."

"I regret the necessity," Leoh said; then, with a broad grin, he added, "My assistant professor, here, can handle my courses for the remainder of the year very easily. Perhaps he will even be able to deliver his lectures without being interrupted."

The assistant professor turned red.

"Now then," Leoh muttered, mostly to himself, "who is this Kanus, and why is he trying to turn the Kerak Worlds into an arsenal?"

III

Chancellor Kanus, the supreme leader of the Kerak Worlds, stood at the edge of the balcony and looked across the wild, tumbling gorge to the rugged mountains beyond.

"These are the forces that mold men's actions," he said to his small audience of officials and advisors, "the howling winds, the mighty mountains, the open sky and the dark powers of the clouds."

The men nodded and made murmurs of agreement.

"Just as the mountains thrust up from the pettiness of the lands below, so shall we rise above the common walk of men," Kanus said. "Just as a thunderstorm terrifies them, we will make them bend to our will!"

"We will destroy the past," said one of the ministers.

"And avenge the memory of defeat," Kanus added. He turned and looked at the little group of men. Kanus was the smallest man on the balcony: short, spare, sallow-faced; but he possessed piercing dark eyes and a strong voice that commanded attention.

He walked through the knot of men and stopped before a tall, lean, blond youth in light-blue military uniform. "And you, Major Odal, will be a primary instrument in the first steps of conquest."

Odal bowed stiffly. "I only hope to serve my leader and my worlds."

"You shall. And you already have," Kanus said, beaming. "Already the Acquatainians are thrashing about like a snake whose head has been cut off. Without Dulaq, they have no head, no brain to direct them. For your part in this triumph"—Kanus snapped his fingers, and one of his advisors quickly stepped to his side and handed him a small ebony box—"I present you with this token of the esteem of the Kerak Worlds, and of my personal high regard."

He handed the box to Odal, who opened it and took out a small jeweled pin.

"The Star of Kerak," Kanus announced. "This is the first time it has been awarded to anyone except a warrior on the battlefield. But then, we have turned their so-called civilized machine into our own battlefield, eh?"

Odal grinned. "Yes, sir, we have. Thank you very much sir. This is the supreme moment of my life."

"To date, major. Only to date. There will be other moments, even higher ones. Come, let's go inside. We have many plans to discuss . . . more duels . . . more triumphs."

They all filed in to Kanus' huge, elaborate office. The leader walked across the plushly ornate room and sat at the elevated desk, while his followers arranged themselves in the chairs and couches placed about the floor. Odal remained standing, near the doorway.

Kanus let his fingers flick across a small control board set into his desktop, and a tri-dimensional star map glowed into existence on the far wall. As its center were the eleven stars that harbored the Kerak Worlds. Around them stood neighboring stars, color-coded to show their political groupings. Off to one side of the map was the Acquataine Cluster, a rich mass of stars—wealthy, powerful, the most important political and economic power in the section of the galaxy. Until yesterday's duel.

Kanus began one of his inevitable harangues. Objectives, political and military. Already the Kerak Worlds were unified under his dominant will. The people would follow wherever he led. Already the political alliances built up by Acquatainian diplomacy since the last war were tottering, now that Dulaq was out of the picture. Now was the time to strike. A political blow *here*, at the Szarno Confederacy, to bring them and their armaments industries into line with Kerak. Then more political strikes to isolate the Acquataine Cluster from its allies, and to build up subservient states for Kerak. Then, finally, the military blow—against the Acquatainians.

"A sudden strike, a quick, decisive series of blows, and the Acquatainians will collapse like a house of paper. Before the Star Watch can interfere, we will be masters of the Cluster. Then, with the resources of Acquatainia to draw on, we can challenge any force in the galaxy—even the Terran Commonwealth itself!"

The men in the room nodded their assent.

They've heard this story many, many times, Odal thought to himself. This was the first time he had been privileged to listen to it. If you closed your eyes, or looked only at the star map, the plan sounded bizarre, extreme, even impossible. But, if you watched Kanus, and let those piercing, almost hypnotic eyes fasten on yours, then the leader's wildest dreams sounded not only exciting, but inevitable.

Odal leaned a shoulder against the paneled wall and scanned the other men in the room.

There was fat Greber, the vice chancellor, fighting desperately to stay awake after drinking too much wine during the luncheon and afterward. And Modal, sitting on the couch next to him, was bright-eyed and alert, thinking only of how much money and power would come to him as Chief of Industries once the rearmament program began in earnest.

Sitting alone on another couch was Kor, the quiet one, the head of Intelligence, and—technically—Odal's superior. Silent Kor, whose few words were usually charged with terror for those whom he spoke against.

Marshal Lugal looked bored when Kanus spoke of politics, but his face changed when military matters came up. The marshal lived for only one purpose; to avenge his army's humiliating defeat in the war against the Acquatainians, thirty Terran years ago. What he didn't realize, Odal thought, smiling to himself, was that as soon as he had reorganized the army and re-equipped it, Kanus planned to retire him and place younger men in charge. Men whose only loyalty was not to the army, nor even to the Kerak Worlds and their people, but to the chancellor himself.

Eagerly following every syllable, every gesture of the leader was little Tinth. Born to the nobility, trained in the arts, a student of philosophy, Tinth had deserted his heritage and joined the forces of Kanus. His reward had been the Ministry of Education; many teachers had suffered under him.

And finally there was Romis, the Minister of Intergovernmental Affairs. A professional diplomat, and one of the few men in government before Kanus' sweep to power to survive this long. It was clear that Romis hated the chancellor. But he served the Kerak Worlds well. The diplomatic corps was flawless in their handling of intergovernmental affairs. It was only a matter of time, Odal knew, before one of them— Romis or Kanus—killed the other.

The rest of Kanus' audience consisted of political hacks, roughnecks-turned-bodyguards, and a few other hangers-on who had been with Kanus since the days when he held his political monologues in cellars, and haunted the alleys to avoid the police. Kanus had come a long way: from the blackness of oblivion to the dazzling heights of the chancellor's rural estate.

Money, power, glory, revenge, patriotism: each man in the room, listening to Kanus, had his reasons for following the chancellor.

And my reasons? Odal asked himself. *Why do I follow him? Can I see into my own mind as easily as I see into theirs?*

There was duty, of course. Odal was a soldier, and Kanus was the duly-elected leader of the government. Once elected, though, he had dissolved the government and solidified his powers as absolute dictator of the Kerak Worlds.

There was gain to be had by performing well under Kanus. Regardless of his political ambitions and personal tyrannies, Kanus rewarded well when he was pleased. The medal—the Star of Kerak—carried with it an annual pension that would nicely accommodate a family. *If I had one,* Odal thought, sardonically.

There was power, of sorts, also. Working the dueling machine in his special way, hammering a man into nothingness, finding the weaknesses in his personality and exploiting them, pitting his mind against others, turning sneering towers of pride like Dulaq into helpless whipped dogs—that was power. And it was a power that did not go unnoticed in the cities of the Kerak Worlds. Already Odal was easily recognized on the streets; women especially seemed to be attracted to him now.

"The most important factor," Kanus was saying, "and I cannot stress it overmuch, is to build up an aura of invincibility. This is why your work is so important, Major Odal. You must be invincible! Because today you represent the collective will of the Kerak Worlds. Today you are the instrument of my own will—and you must triumph at every turn. The fate of your people, of your government, of your chancellor rests squarely on your shoulders each time you step into a dueling machine. You have borne that responsibility well, major. Can you carry it even further?"

"I can, sir," Odal answered crisply," and I will."

Kanus beamed at him. "Good! Because your next duel—and those that follow it—will be to the death."

IV

It took the starship two weeks to make the journey from Carinae to the Acquataine Cluster. Dr. Leoh spent the time checking over the Acquatainian dueling machine, by direct tri-di beam; the Acquatainian government gave him all the technicians, time and money he needed for the task.

Leoh spent as much of his spare time as possible with the other passengers of the ship. He was gregarious, a fine conversationalist, and had a nicely-balanced sense of humor. Particularly, he was a favorite of the younger women, since he had reached the age where he could flatter them with his attention without making them feel endangered.

But still, there were long hours when he was alone in his stateroom with nothing but his memories. At times like these, it was impossible not to think back over the road he had been following.

Albert Robertus Leoh, Ph.D., Professor of Physics, Professor of

Electronics, master of computer technology, inventor of the interstellar tri-di communications system; and more recently, student of psychology, Professor of Psychophysiology, founder of Psychonics, Inc., inventor of the dueling machine.

During his earlier years, when the supreme confidence of youth was still with him, Leoh had envisioned himself as helping mankind to spread his colonies and civilizations throughout the galaxy. The bitter years of galactic war had ended in his childhood, and now human societies throughout the Milky Way were linked together—in greater or lesser degree of union—into a more-or-less peaceful coalition of star groups.

There were two great motivating forces at work on those human societies spread across the stars, and these forces worked toward opposite goals. On the one hand was the urge to explore, to reach new stars, new planets, to expand the frontiers of man's civilizations and found new colonies, new nations. Pitted against this drive to expand was an equally-powerful force: the realization that technology had finally put an end to physical labor and almost to poverty itself on all the civilized worlds of man. The urge to move off to the frontier was penned in and buried alive under the enervating comforts of civilization.

The result was inescapable. The civilized worlds became constantly more crowded as time wore on. They became jampacked islands of humanity sprinkled thinly across the sea of space that was still full of unpopulated islands.

The expense and difficulty of interstellar travel was often cited as an excuse. The starships *were* expensive: their power demands were frightful. Only the most determined—and the best financed—groups of colonists could afford them. The rest of mankind accepted the ease and safety of civilization, lived in the bulging cities of the teeming planets. Their lives were circumscribed by their neighbors, and by their governments. Constantly more people crowding into a fixed living space meant constantly less freedom. The freedom to dream, to run free, to procreate, all became state-owned, state-controlled monopolies.

And Leoh had contributed to this situation.

He had contributed his thoughts and his work. He had contributed often and regularly—the interstellar communications systems was only the one outstanding achievement in a long career of achievements.

Leoh had been nearly at the voluntary retirement age for scientists when he realized what he, and his fellow scientists, had done. Their efforts to make life richer and more rewarding for mankind had made life only less strenuous and more rigid.

And with every increase in comfort, Leoh discovered, came a corresponding increase in neuroses, in crimes of violence, in mental abberations. Senseless wars of pride broke out between star-groups for the first time in generations. Outwardly, the peace of the galaxy was assured; but beneath the glossy surface of the Terran Commonwealth there smoldered the beginnings of a volcano. Police actions fought by the Star Watch were increasing ominously. Petty wars between once-stable peoples were flaring up steadily.

Once Leoh realized the part he had played in this increasingly-tragic drama, he was confronted with two emotions—a deep sense of guilt, both personal and professional; and, countering this, a determination to do something, anything, to restore at least some balance to man's collective mentality.

Leoh stepped out of physics and electronics, and entered the field of psychology. Instead of retiring, he applied for a beginner's status in his new profession. It had taken considerable bending and straining of the Commonwealth's rules—but for a man of Leoh's stature, the rules could be flexed somewhat. Leoh became a student once again, then a researcher, and finally a Professor of Psychophysiology.

Out of this came the dueling machine. A combination of electroencephalograph and autocomputer. A dream machine, that amplified a man's imagination until he could engulf himself into a world of his own making.

Leoh envisioned it as a device to enable men to rid themselves of hostility and tension safety. Through his efforts, and those of his colleagues, dueling machines were quickly becoming accepted as devices for settling disputes.

When two men had a severe difference of opinion—deep enough to warrant legal action—they could go to the dueling machine instead of the courts. Instead of sitting helplessly and watching the machinations of the law grind impersonally through their differences, the two antagonists could allow their imaginations free rein in the dueling machine. They could settle their differences personally, as violently as they wished, without hurting themselves or anyone else. On most civilized worlds, the results of properly-monitored duels were accepted as legally binding.

The tensions of civilized life could be escaped—albeit temporarily—in the dueling machine. This was a powerful tool, much too powerful to allow it to be used indiscriminately. Therefore Leoh safeguarded his invention by forming a private company—Psychonics,

Inc.—and securing an exclusive license from the Terran Common-wealth to manufacture, sell, install and maintain the machines. His customers were government health and legal agencies; his responsibilities were: legally, to the Commonwealth; morally, to all mankind; and, finally, to his own restless conscience.

The dueling machines succeeded. They worked as well, and often better, than Leoh had anticipated. But he knew that they were only a stopgap, only a temporary shoring of a constantly-eroding dam. What was needed, really needed, was some method of exploding the status quo, some means of convincing people to reach out for those unoccupied, unexplored stars that filled the galaxy, some way of convincing men that they should leave the comforts of civilization for the excitement of colonization.

Leoh had been searching for that method when the news of Dulaq's duel against Odal reached him.

Now he was speeding across parsecs of space, praying to himself that the dueling machine had not failed.

The two-week flight ended. The starship took up a parking orbit around the capital planet of the Acquataine Cluster. The passengers transhipped to the surface.

Dr. Leoh was met at the landing disk by an official delegation, headed by Massan, the acting prime minister. They exchanged formal greetings there at the base of the ship, while the other passengers hurried by.

As Leoh and Massan, surrounded by the other members of the delegation, rode the slideway to the port's administration building, Leoh commented:

"As you probably know, I have checked through your dueling machine quite thoroughly via tri-di for the past two weeks. I can find nothing wrong with it."

Massan shrugged. "Perhaps you should have checked then, the machine on Szarno."

"The Szarno Confederation? Their dueling machine?"

"Yes. This morning Kanus' hired assassin killed a man in it."

"He won another duel," Leoh said.

"You do not understand," Massan said grimly. "Major Odal's opponent—an industrialist who had spoken out against Kanus—was actually killed in the dueling machine. The man is dead!"

V

One of the advantages of being Commander-in-Chief of the Star Watch, the old man thought to himself, is that you can visit any planet in the Commonwealth.

He stood at the top of the hill and looked out over the green tableland of Kenya. This was the land of his birth, Earth was his homeworld. The Star Watch's official headquarters may be in the heart of a globular cluster of stars near the center of the galaxy, but Earth was the place the commander wanted most to see as he grew older and wearier.

An aide, who had been following the commander at a respectful distance, suddenly intruded himself in the old man's reverie.

"Sir, a message for you."

The commander scowled at the young officer. "I gave orders that I was not to be disturbed."

The officer, slim and stiff in his black-and-silver uniform, replied, "Your chief of staff has passed the message on to you, sir. It's from Dr. Leoh, of Carinae University. Personal and urgent, sir."

The old man grumbled to himself, but nodded. The aide placed a small crystalline sphere on the grass before him. The air above the sphere started to vibrate and glow.

"Sir Harold Spencer here," the commander said.

The bubbling air seemed to draw in on itself and take solid form. Dr. Leoh sat at a desk chair and looked up at the standing commander.

"Harold, it's a pleasure to see you once again."

Spencer's stern eyes softened, and his beefy face broke into a well-creased smile. "Albert, you ancient scoundrel. What do you mean by interrupting my first visit home in fifteen years?"

"It won't be a long interruption," Leoh said.

"You told my chief of staff that it was urgent," Sir Harold groused.

"It is. But it's not the sort of problem that requires much action on your part. Yet. You are familiar with recent political developments on the Kerak Worlds?"

Spencer snorted. "I know that a barbarian named Kanus has established himself as a dictator. He's a trouble-maker. I've been talking to the Commonwealth Council about the advisability of quashing him before he causes grief, but you know the Council . . . first wait until the flames have sprung up, then thrash about and demand that the Star Watch do something!"

Leoh grinned. "You're as irascible as ever."

"My personality is not the subject of this rather expensive discussion. What about Kanus? And what are you doing, getting yourself involved in politics? About to change your profession again?"

"No, not at all," Leoh answered, laughing. Then, more seriously, "It seems as though Kanus has discovered some method of using the dueling machines to achieve political advantages over his neighbors."

"What?"

Leoh explained the circumstances of Odal's duels with the Acquatainian prime minister and Szarno industrialist.

"Dulaq is completely incapacitated and the other poor fellow is dead?" Spencer's face darkened into a thundercloud. "You were right to call me. This is a situation that could easily become intolerable."

"I agree," Leoh said. "But evidently Kanus has not broken any laws or interstellar agreements. All that meets the eye is a disturbing pair of accidents, both of them accruing to Kanus' benefit."

"Do *you* believe that they were accidents?"

"Certainly not. The dueling machine cannot cause physical or mental harm . . . unless someone has tampered with it in some way."

"That is my thought, too." Spencer was silent for a moment, weighing the matter in his mind. "Very well. The Star Watch cannot act officially, but there is nothing to prevent me from dispatching an officer to the Acquataine Cluster, on detached duty, to serve as liaison between us."

"Good. I think that will be the most effective method of handling the situation, at present."

"It will be done," Sir Harold pronounced. His aide made a mental note of it.

"Thank you very much," Leoh said. "Now, go back to enjoying your vacation."

"Vacation? This is no vacation," Spencer rumbled. "I happen to be celebrating my birthday."

"So? Well, congratulations. I try not to remember mine," Leoh said.

"Then you must be older than I," Spencer replied, allowing only the faintest hint of a smile to appear.

"I suppose it's possible."

"But not very likely, eh?"

They laughed together and said good-by. The Star Watch commander tramped through the hills until sunset, enjoying the sight of the grasslands and distant purple mountains he had known in his childhood. As dusk closed in, he told his aide he was ready to leave.

The aide pressed a stud on his belt and a two-place aircar skimmed silently from the far side of the hills and hovered beside them. Spencer climbed in laboriously while the aide remained discreetly at his side. While the commander settled his bulk into his seat the aide hurried around the car and hopped into his place. The car glided off toward Spencer's personal planetship, waiting for him at a nearby field.

"Don't forget to assign an officer to Dr. Leoh," the commander muttered to his aide. Then he turned and watched the unmatchable beauty of an Earthly sunset.

The aide did not forget the assignment. That night, as Sir Harold's ship spiraled out to a rendezvous with a starship, the aide dictated the necessary order into an autodispatcher that immediately beamed it to the Star Watch's nearest communications center, on Mars.

The order was scanned and routed automatically and finally beamed to the Star Watch unit commandant in charge of the area closest to the Acquataine Cluster, on the sixth planet circling the star Perseus Alpha. Here again, the order was processed automatically and routed through the local headquarters to the personnel files. The automated files selected three microcard dossiers that matched the requirements of the order.

The three microcards and the order itself appeared simultaneously on the desktop viewer of the Star Watch personnel officer. He looked at the order, then read the dossiers. He flicked a button that gave him an updated status report on each of the three men in question. One was due for leave after an extensive period of duty. The second was the son of a personal friend of the local commandant. The third had just arrived a few weeks ago, fresh from the Star Watch Academy on Mars.

The personnel officer selected the third man, routed his dossier and Sir Harold's order back into the automatic processing system, and returned to the film of primitive dancing girls he had been watching before this matter of decision had arrived at his desk.

VI

The space station orbiting around Acquatainia—the capital planet of the Acquataine Cluster—served simultaneously as a transfer point from starships to planet-ships, a tourist resort, meteorological station, communications center, scientific laboratory, astronomical observatory, medical haven for allergy and cardiac patients, and military base. It was, in reality, a good-sized city with its own markets, its own local government, and its own way of life.

Dr. Leoh had just stepped off the debarking ramp of the starship from Szarno. The trip there had been pointless and fruitless. But he had gone anyway, in the slim hope that he might find something wrong with the dueling machine that had been used to murder a man.

A shudder went through him as he edged along the automated customs scanners and paper-checkers. What kind of people could these men of Kerak be? To actually kill a human being in cold blood; to plot and plan the death of a fellow man. Worse than barbaric. Savage.

He felt tired as he left customs and took the slideway to the planetary shuttle ships. Halfway there, he decided to check at the communications desk for messages. That Star Watch officer that Sir Harold had promised him a week ago should have arrived by now.

The communications desk consisted of a small booth that contained the output printer of a communications computer and an attractive young dark-haired girl. Automation or not, Leoh thought smilingly, there were certain human values that transcended mere efficiency.

A lanky, thin-faced youth was half-leaning on the booth's counter, trying to talk to the girl. He had curly blond hair and crystal blue eyes; his clothes consisted of an ill-fitting pair of slacks and tunic. A small traveler's kit rested on the floor at his feet.

"So, I was sort of, well, thinking . . . maybe somebody might, uh, show me around . . . a little," he was stammering to the girl. "I've never been, uh, here. . ."

"It's the most beautiful planet in the galaxy," the girl was saying. "Its cities are the finest."

"Yes . . . well, I was sort of thinking . . . that is, I know we just, uh, met a few minutes ago . . . but, well, maybe . . . if you have a free day or so coming up . . . maybe we could, uh, sort of—"

She smiled coolly. "I have two days off at the end of the week, but I'll be staying here at the station. There's so much to see and do here, I very seldom leave."

"Oh—"

"You're making a mistake," Leoh interjected dogmatically. "If you have such a beautiful planet for your homeworld, why in the name of the gods of intellect don't you go down there and enjoy it? I'll wager you haven't been out in the natural beauty and fine cities you spoke of since you started working here on the station."

"Why, you're right," she said, surprised.

"You see? You youngsters are all alike. You never think further than the ends of your noses. You should return to the planet, young lady, and see the sunshine again. Why don't you visit the University at the capital city? Plenty of open space and greenery, lots of sunshine and available young men!"

Leoh was grinning broadly, and the girl smiled back at him. "Perhaps I will," she said.

"Ask for me when you get to the University. I'm Dr. Leoh. I'll see to it that you're introduced to some of the girls and gentlemen of your own age."

"Why . . . thank you, doctor. I'll do it this week end."

"Good. Now then, any messages for me? Anyone aboard the station looking for me?"

The girl turned and tapped a few keys on the computer's control console. A row of lights flicked briefly across the consol's face. She turned back to Leoh:

"No, sir, I'm sorry. No messages and no one has asked for you."

"Hm-m-m. That's strange. Well, thank you . . . and I'll expect to see you at the end of this week."

The girl smiled a farewell. Leoh started to walk away from the booth, back toward the slideway. The young man took a step toward him, stumbled on his own traveling kit, and staggered across the floor for a half-dozen steps before regaining his balance. Leoh turned and saw that the youth's face bore a somewhat ridiculous expression of mixed indecision and curiosity.

"Can I help you?" Leoh asked, stopping at the edge of the moving slideway.

"How . . . how did you do that, sir?"

"Do what?"

"Get that girl to agree to visit the university. I've been talking to her for half an hour, and, well, she wouldn't even look straight at me."

Leoh broke into a chuckle. "Well, young man, to begin with, you were much too flustered. It made you appear overanxious. On the other hand, I am at an age where I can be strictly platonic. She was on guard against you, but she knows she has very little to fear from me."

"I see . . . I think."

"Well," Leoh said, gesturing toward the slideway, "I suppose this is where we go our separate ways."

"Oh, no, sir. I'm going with you. That is, I mean, you *are* Dr. Leoh, aren't you?"

"Yes, I am. And you must be—" Leoh hesitated. *Can this be a Star Watch officer?* he wondered.

The youth stiffened to attention and for an absurd flash of a second, Leoh thought he was going to salute. "I am Junior Lieutenant Hector, sir; on special detached duty from the cruiser SW4-J188, home base Perseus Alpha VI."

"I see," Leoh replied. "Um-m-m . . . is Hector your first name or your last?"

"Both, sir."

I should have guessed, Leoh told himself. Aloud, he said, "Well, lieutenant, we'd better get to the shuttle before it leaves without us."

They took to the slideway. Half a second later, Hector jumped off and dashed back to the communications desk for his traveling kit. He hurried back to Leoh, bumping into seven bewildered citizens of various descriptions and nearly breaking both his legs when he tripped as he ran back onto the moving slideway. He went down on his face, sprawled across two lanes moving at different speeds, and needed the assistance of several persons before he was again on his feet and standing beside Leoh.

"I . . . I'm sorry to cause all that, uh, commotion, sir."

"That's all right. You weren't hurt, were you?"

"Uh, no . . . I don't think so. Just embarrassed."

Leoh said nothing. They rode the slideway in silence through the busy station and out to the enclosed berths where the planetary shuttles were docked. They boarded one of the ships and found a pair of seats.

"Just how long have you been with the Star Watch, lieutenant?"

"Six weeks, sir. Three weeks aboard a starship bringing me out to Perseus Alpha VI, a week at the planetary base there, and two weeks aboard the cruiser SW4-J188. That is, it's been six weeks since I received my commission. I've been at the Academy . . . the Star Watch Academy on Mars . . . for four years."

"You got through the Academy in four years?"

"That's the regulation time, sir."

"Yes, I know."

The ship eased out of its berth. There was a moment of free-fall, then the drive engine came on and the gray-field equilibrated.

"Tell me, lieutenant, how did you get picked for this assignment?"

"I wish I knew, sir," Hector said, his lean face twisting into a puzzled frown. "I was working out a program for the navigation officer . . . aboard the cruiser. I'm pretty good at that . . . I can work out computer programs in my head, mostly. Mathematics was my best subject at the Academy—"

"Interesting."

"Yes, well, anyway, I was working out this program when the captain himself came on deck and started shaking my hand and telling me that I was being sent on special duty on Acquatainia by direct orders of the Commander-in-Chief. He seemed very happy . . . the captain, that is."

"He was no doubt pleased to see you get such an unusual assignment," Leoh said tactfully.

"I'm not so sure," Hector said truthfully. "I think he regarded me as some sort of a problem, sir. He had me on a different duty-berth practically every day I was on board the ship."

"Well now," Leoh changed the subject, "what do you know about psychonics?"

"About what, sir?"

"Eh . . . electroencephalography?"

Hector looked blank.

"Psychology, perhaps?" Leoh suggested, hopefully. "Physiology? Computer molectronics?"

"I'm pretty good at mathematics!"

"Yes, I know. Did you, by any chance, receive any training in diplomatic affairs?"

"At the Star Watch Academy? No, sir."

Leoh ran a hand through his thinning hair. "Then why did the Star Watch select you for this job? I must confess, lieutenant, that I can't understand the workings of a military organization."

Hector shook his head ruefully, "Neither do I, sir."

VII

The next week was an enervatingly slow one for Leoh, evenly divided between tedious checking of each component of the dueling machine, and shameless rouses to keep Hector as far away from the machine as possible.

The Star Watchman certainly wanted to help, and he actually *was* little short of brilliant in doing intricate mathematics completely in his head. But he was, Leoh found, a clumsy, chattering, whistling, scatterbrained, inexperienced bundle of noise and nerves. It was impossible to do constructive work with him nearby.

Perhaps you're judging him too harshly, Leoh warned himself. *You just might be letting your frustrations with the dueling machine get the better of your sense of balance.*

The professor was sitting in the office that the Acquatainians had given him in one end of the former lecture hall that held the dueling machine. Leoh could see its impassive metal hulk through the open office door.

The room he was sitting in had been one of a suite of offices used by the permanent staff of the machine. But they had moved out of the building completely, in deference to Leoh, and the Acquatainian government had turned the other cubbyhole offices into sleeping rooms for the professor and the Star Watchman, and an autokitchen. A combination cook-valet-handyman appeared twice each day—morning and evening—to handle any special chores that the cleaning machines and autokitchen might miss.

Leoh slouched back in his desk chair and cast a weary eye on the stack of papers that recorded the latest performances of the machine. Earlier that day he had taken the electroencephalographic records of clinical cases of catatonia and run them through the machine's input unit. The machine immediately rejected them, refused to process them through the amplification units and association circuits.

In other words, the machine had recognized the EEG traces as something harmful to a human being.

Then how did it happen to Dulaq? Leoh asked himself for the thousandth time. It couldn't have been the machine's fault; it must have been something in Odal's mind that simply overpowered Dulaq's.

"Overpowered?" That's a terribly unscientific term, Leoh argued against himself.

Before he could carry the debate any further, he heard the main door of the big chamber slide open and then bang shut, and Hector's off-key whistle shrilled and echoed through the high-vaulted room.

Leoh sighed and put his self-contained argument off to the back of his mind. Trying to think logically near Hector was a hopeless prospect.

"Are you in, doctor?" Hector's voice rang out.

"In here."

Hector ducked in through the doorway and plopped his rangy frame on the office's couch.

"Everything going well, sir?"

Leoh shrugged. "Not very well, I'm afraid. I can't find anything wrong with the dueling machine. I can't even *force* it to malfunction."

"Well, that's good, isn't it?" Hector chirped happily.

"In a sense," Leoh admitted, feeling slightly nettled at the youth's boundless, pointless optimism. "But, you see, it means that Kanus' people can do things with the machine that I can't."

Hector frowned, considering the problem. "Hm-m-m . . . yes, I guess that's right, too, isn't it?"

"Did you see the girl back to her ship safely?" Leoh asked.

"Yes, sir," Hector replied, bobbing his head vigorously. "She's on her way back to the communications booth at the space station. She said to tell you she enjoyed her visit very much."

"Good. It was, eh, very good of you to escort her about the campus. It kept her out of my hair . . . what's left of it, that is."

Hector grinned. "Oh, I liked showing her around, and all that— And, well, it sort of kept *me* out of your hair, too, didn't it?"

Leoh's eyebrows shot up in surprise.

Hector laughed. "Doctor, I may be clumsy, and I'm certainly no scientist . . . but I'm not completely brainless."

"I'm sorry if I gave you that impression—"

"Oh no . . . don't be sorry. I didn't mean that to sound so . . . well, the way it sounded . . . that is, I know I'm just in your way—" He started to get up.

Leoh waved him back to the couch. "Relax, my boy, relax. You know, I've been sitting here all afternoon wondering what to do next. Somehow, just now, I came to a conclusion."

"Yes?"

"I'm going to leave the Acquaurine Cluster and return to Carinae."

"What? But you can't! I mean—"

"Why not? I'm not accomplishing anything here. Whatever it is that this Odal and Kanus have been doing, it's basically a political problem, and not a scientific one. The professional staff of the machine here will catch up to their tricks sooner or later."

"But sir, if you can't find the answer, how can they?"

Frankly, I don't know. But, as I said, this is a political problem more than a scientific one. I'm tired and frustrated and I'm feeling my years. I want to return to Carinae and spend the next few months considering beautifully abstract problems about instantaneous transportation devices. Let Massan and the Star Watch worry about Kanus."

"Oh! That's what I came to tell you. Massan has been challenged to a duel by Odal!"

"What?"

"This afternoon, Odal went to the Council building. Picked an argument with Massan right in the main corridor and challenged him."

"Massan accepted?" Leoh asked.

Hector nodded.

Leoh leaned across his desk and reached for the phone unit. It took a few minutes and a few levels of secretaries and assistants, but finally Massan's dark, bearded face appeared on the screen above the desk.

"You have accepted Odal's challenge?" Leoh asked, without preliminaries.

"We meet next week," Massan replied gravely.

"You should have refused."

"On what pretext?"

"No pretext. A flat refusal, based on the certainty that Odal or someone else from Kerak is tampering with the dueling machine."

Massan shook his head sadly. "My dear learned sir, you still do not comprehend the political situation. The Government of the Acquataine Cluster is much closer to dissolution than I dare to admit openly. The coalition of star groups that Dulaq had constructed to keep the Kerak Worlds neutralized has broken apart completely. This morning, Kanus announced that he would annex Szarno. This afternoon, Odal challenges me."

"I think I see—"

"Of course. The Acquatainian Government is paralyzed now, until the outcome of the duel is known. We cannot effectively intervene in the Szarno crisis until we know who will be heading the Government next week. And, frankly, more than a few members of our Council are now openly favoring Kanus and urging that we establish friendly relations with him before it is too late."

"But, that's all the more reason for refusing the duel," Leoh insisted.

"And be accused of cowardice in my own Council meetings?" Massan smiled grimly. "In politics, my dear sir, the *appearance* of a man means much more than his substance. As a coward, I would soon be out of office. But, perhaps, as the winner of a duel against the invincible Odal . . . or even as a martyr . . . I may accomplish something useful."

Leoh said nothing.

Massan continued, "I put off the duel for a week, hoping that in that time you might discover Odal's secret. I dare not postpone the duel any longer; as it is, the political situation may collapse about our heads at any moment."

"I'll take this machine apart and rebuild it again, molecule by molecule," Leoh promised.

As Massan's image faded from the screen, Leoh turned to Hector. "We have one week to save his life."

"And avert a war, maybe," Hector added.

"Yes." Leoh leaned back in his chair and stared off into infinity.

Hector shuffled his feet, rubbed his nose, whistled a few bars of off-key tunes, and finally blurted, "How can you take apart the dueling machine?"

"Hm-m-m?" Leoh snapped out of his reverie.

"How can you take apart the dueling machine?" Hector repeated. "Looks like a big job to do in a week."

"Yes, it is. But, my boy, perhaps we . . . the two of us . . . can do it."

Hector scratched his head. "Well, uh, sir . . . I'm not very . . . that is, my mechanical aptitude scores at the Academy—"

Leoh smiled at him. "No need for mechanical aptitude, my boy. You were trained to fight, weren't you? We can do the job mentally."

VIII

It was the strangest week of their lives.

Leoh's plan was straightforward: to test the dueling machine, push it to the limits of its performance, by actually operating it—by fighting duels.

They started off easily enough, tentatively probing and flexing their mental muscles. Leoh had used the dueling machines himself many times in the past, but only in tests of the machines' routine performance. Never in actual combat against another human being. To Hector, of course, the machine was a totally new and different experience.

The Acquatainian staff plunged into the project without question, providing Leoh with invaluable help in monitoring and analyzing the duels.

At first, Leoh and Hector did nothing more than play hide-and-seek, with one of them picking an environment and the other trying to find his opponent in it. They wandered through jungles and cities, over glaciers and interplanetary voids, seeking each other—without ever leaving the booths of the dueling machine.

Then, when Leoh was satisfied that the machine could reproduce and amplify thought patterns with strict fidelity, they began to fight light duels. They fenced with blunted foils—Hector won, of course, because of his much faster reflexes. Then they tried other weapons—

pistols, sonic beams, grenades—but always with the precaution of imagining themselves to be wearing protective equipment. Strangely, even though Hector was trained in the use of these weapons, Leoh won almost all the bouts. He was neither faster nor more accurate, when they were target-shooting. But when the two of them faced each other, somehow Leoh almost always won.

The machine projects more than thoughts, Leoh told himself. *It projects personality.*

They worked in the dueling machine day and night now, enclosed in the booths for twelve or more hours a day, driving themselves and the machine's regular staff to near-exhaustion. When they gulped their meals, between duels, they were physically ragged and sharp-tempered. They usually fell asleep in Leoh's office, while discussing the results of the day's work.

The duels grew slowly more serious. Leoh was pushing the machine to its limits now, carefully extending the rigors of each bout. And yet, even though he knew exactly what and how much he intended to do in each fight, it often took a conscious effort of will to remind himself that the battles he was fighting were actually imaginary.

As the duels became more dangerous, and the artificially-amplified hallucinations began to end in blood and death, Leoh found himself winning more and more frequently. With one part of his mind he was driving to analyze the cause of his consistent success. But another part of him was beginning to really enjoy his prowess.

The strain was telling on Hector. The physical exertion of constant work and practically no relief was considerable in itself. But the emotional effects of being "hurt" and "killed" repeatedly were infinitely worse.

"Perhaps we should stop for a while," Leoh suggested after the fourth day of tests.

"No. I'm all right."

Leoh looked at him. Hector's face was haggard, his eyes bleary.

"You've had enough," Leoh said quietly.

"Please don't make me stop," Hector begged. "I . . . I can't stop now. Please give me a chance to do better. I'm improving . . . I lasted twice as long in this afternoon's two duels as I did in the ones this morning. Please, don't end it now . . . not while I'm completely lost—"

Leoh stared at him. "You want to go on?"

"Yes, sir."

"And if I say no?"

Hector hesitated. Leoh sensed he was struggling with himself. "If you say no," he answered dully, "then it will be no. I can't argue against you any more."

Leoh was silent for a long moment. Finally he opened a desk drawer and took a small bottle from it. "Here, take a sleep capsule. When you wake up we'll try again."

It was dawn when they began again. Leoh entered the dueling machine determined to allow Hector to win. He gave the youthful Star Watchman his choice of weapon and environment. Hector picked one-man scoutships, in planetary orbits. Their weapons were conventional force beams.

But despite his own conscious desire, Leoh found himself winning! The ships spiraled about an unnamed planet, their paths intersecting at least once in every orbit. The problem was to estimate your opponent's orbital position, and then program your own ship so that you arrived at that position either behind or to one side of him. Then you could train your guns on him before he could turn on you.

The problem should have been an easy one for Hector, with his knack for intuitive mental calculation. But Leoh scored the first hit— Hector had piloted his ship into an excellent firing position, but his shot went wide; Leoh maneuvered around clumsily, but managed to register an inconsequential hit on the side of Hector's ship.

In the next three passes, Leoh scored two more hits. Hector's ship was badly damaged now. In return, the Star Watchman had landed one glancing shot on Leoh's ship.

They came around again, and once more Leoh had outguessed his younger opponent. He trained his guns on Hector's ship, then hesitated with his hand poised above the firing button.

Don't kill him again, he warned himself. *His mind can't accept another defeat.*

But Leoh's hand, almost of its own will, reached the button and touched it lightly. Another gram of pressure and the guns would fire.

In that instant's hesitation. Hector pulled his crippled ship around and aimed at Leoh. The Watchman fired a searing blast that jarred Leoh's ship from end to end. Leoh's hand slammed down on the firing button, whether he intended to do it or not, he did not know.

Leoh's shot raked Hector's ship but did not stop it. The two vehicles were hurling directly at each other. Leoh tried desperately to avert a collision, but Hector bored in grimly, matching Leoh's maneuvers with his own.

The two ships smashed together and exploded.

Abruptly, Leoh found himself in the cramped booth of the dueling machine, his body cold and damp with perspiration, his hands trembling.

He squeezed out of the booth and took a deep breath. Warm sunlight was streaming into the high-vaulted room. The white walls glared brilliantly. Through the tall windows he could see trees and people and clouds in the sky.

Hector walked up to him. For the first time in several days, the Watchman was smiling. Not much, but smiling. "Well, we broke even on that one."

Leoh smiled back, somewhat shakily. "Yes. It was . . . quite an experience. I've never died before."

Hector fidgeted. "It's, uh, not so bad, I guess—It does sort of, well, shatter you, you know."

"Yes. I can see that now."

"Another duel?" Hector asked, nodding his head toward the machine.

"Let's get out of this place for a few hours. Are you hungry?"

"Starved."

They fought seven more duels over the next day and a half. Hector won three of them. It was late afternoon when Leoh called a halt to the tests.

"We can still get in another one or two," the Watchman pointed out.

"No need," Leoh said. "I have all the data I require. Tomorrow Massan meets Odal, unless we can put a stop to it. We have much to do before tomorrow morning."

Hector sagged into the couch. "Just as well. I think I've aged seven years in the past seven days."

"No, my boy," Leoh said gently. "You haven't aged. You've matured."

IX

It was deep twilight when the groundcar slid to a halt on its cushion of compressed air before the Kerak Embassy.

"I still think it's a mistake to go in there," Hector said. "I mean, you could've called him on the tri-di just as well, couldn't you?"

Leoh shook his head. "Never give an agency of any government the opportunity to say 'hold the line a moment' and then huddle together to consider what to do with you. Nineteen times out of twenty, they'll end by passing your request up to the next higher echelon, and you'll be left waiting for weeks."

"Still," Hector insisted, "you're simply stepping into enemy territory. It's a chance you shouldn't take."

"They wouldn't dare touch us."

Hector did not reply, but he looked unconvinced.

"Look," Leoh said, "there are only two men alive who can shed light on this matter. One of them is Dulaq, and his mind is closed to us for an indefinite time. Odal is the only other one who knows what happened."

Hector shook his head skeptically. Leoh shrugged, and opened the door of the groundcar. Hector had no choice but to get out and follow him as he walked up the pathway to the main entrance of the Embassy. The building stood gaunt and gray in the dusk, surrounded by a precisely-clipped hedge. The entrance was flanked by a pair of tall evergreen trees.

Leoh and Hector were met just inside the entrance by a female receptionist. She looked just a trifle disheveled—as though she had been rushed to the desk at a moment's notice. They asked for Odal, were ushered into a sitting room, and within a few minutes—to Hector's surprise—were informed by the girl that Major Odal would be with them shortly.

"You see," Leoh pointed out jovially, "when you come in person they haven't as much of a chance to consider how to get rid of you."

Hector glanced around the windowless room and contemplated the thick, solidly closed door. "There's a lot of scurrying going on on the other side of that door, I'll bet. I mean . . . they may be considering how to, uh, get rid of us . . . permanently."

Leoh shook his head, smiling wryly. "Undoubtedly the approach closest to their hearts—but highly improbable in the present situation. They have been making most efficient and effective use of the dueling machine to gain their ends."

Odal picked this moment to open the door.

"Dr. Leoh . . . Lt. Hector . . . you asked to see me?"

"Thank you, Major Odal; I hope you will be able to help me," said Leoh. "You are the only man living who may be able to give us some clues to the failure of the Dueling Machine."

Odal's answering smile reminded Leoh of the best efforts of the robot-puppet designers to make a machine that smiled like a man. "I am afraid I can be of no assistance, Dr. Leoh. My experiences in the machine are . . . private."

"Perhaps you don't fully understand the situation," Leoh said. "In the past week, we have tested the dueling machine here on Acquatainia exhaustively. We have learned that its performance can be greatly influenced by a man's personality, and by training. You have fought may duels in the machines. Your background of experience, both as a professional soldier and in the machines, gives you a decided advantage over your opponents.

"However, even with all this considered, I am convinced that you cannot kill a man in the machine—under normal circumstances. We have demonstrated that fact in our tests. An unsabotaged machine cannot cause actual physical harm.

"Yet you have already killed one man and incapacitated another. Where will it stop?"

Odal's face remained calm, except for the faintest glitter of fire deep in his eyes. His voice was quiet, but had the edge of a well-honed blade to it: "I cannot be blamed for my background and experience. And I have not tampered with your machines."

The door to the room opened, and a short, thick-set, bullet-headed man entered. He was dressed in a dark street suit, so that it was impossible to guess his station at the Embassy.

"Would the gentlemen care for refreshments?" he asked in a low-pitched voice.

"No, thank you," Leoh said.

"Some Kerak wine, perhaps?"

"Well—"

"I don't, uh, think we'd better, sir," Hector said. "Thanks all the same."

The man shrugged and sat at a chair next to the door.

Odal turned back to Leah. "Sir, I have my duty. Massan and I duel tomorrow. There is no possibility of postponing it."

"Very well," Leoh said. "Will you at least allow us to place some special instrumentation into the booth with you, so that we can monitor the duel more fully? We can do the same with Massan. I know that duels are normally private and you would be within your legal rights to refuse the request. But, morally—"

The smile returned to Odal's face. "You wish to monitor my thoughts. To record them and see how I perform during the duel. Interesting. Very interesting—"

The man at the door rose and said, "If you have no desire for refreshments, gentlemen—"

Odal turned to him. "Thank you for your attention."

Their eyes met and locked for an instant. The man gave a barely perceptible shake of his head, then left.

Odal returned his attention to Leoh. "I am sorry, professor, but I cannot allow you to monitor my thoughts during the duel."

"But—"

"I regret having to refuse you. But, as you yourself pointed out, there is no legal requirement for such a course of action. I must refuse. I hope you understand."

Leoh rose from the couch, and Hector popped up beside him. "I'm afraid I do understand. And I, too, regret your decision."

Odal escorted them out to their car. They drove away, and the Kerak major walked slowly back into the Embassy building. He was met in the hallway by the darksuited man who had sat in on the conversation.

"I could have let them monitor my thoughts and still crush Massan," Odal said. "It would have been a good joke on them."

The man grunted. "I have just spoken to the Chancellor on the tri-di, and obtained permission to make a slight adjustment in our plans."

"An adjustment, Minister Kor?"

"After your duel tomorrow, your next opponent will be the eminent Dr. Leoh," Kor said.

X

The mists swirled deep and impenetrable about Fernd Massan. He stared blindly through the useless viewplate in his helmet, then reached up slowly and carefully to place the infrared detector before his eyes.

I never realized an hallucination could seem so real, Massan thought.

Since the challenge by Odal, he realized, the actual world had seemed quite unreal. For a week, he had gone through the motions of life, but felt as though he were standing aside, a spectator mind watching its own body from a distance. The gathering of his friends and associates last night, the night before the duel—that silent, funereal group of people—it had all seemed completely unreal to him.

But now, in this manufactured dream, he seemed vibrantly alive. Every sensation was solid, stimulating. He could feel his pulse throbbing through him. Somewhere out in those mists, he knew, was Odal.

And the thought of coming to grips with the assassin filled him with a strange satisfaction.

Massan had spent a good many years serving his government on the rich but inhospitable high-gravity planets of the Acquataine Cluster. This was the environment he had chosen: crushing gravity; killing pressures; atmosphere of ammonia and hydrogen, laced with free radicals of sulphur and other valuable but deadly chemicals; oceans of liquid methane and ammonia; "solid ground" consisting of quickly crumbling, eroding ice; howling superpowerful winds that could pick up a mountain of ice and hurl it halfway around the planet; darkness; danger; death.

He was encased in a one-man protective outfit that was half armored suit, half vehicle. There was an internal grav-field to keep him comfortable in 3.7 gees, but still the suit was cumbersome, and a man could move only very slowly in it, even with the aid of servomotors.

The weapon he had chosen was simplicity itself—a hand-sized capsule of oxygen. But in a hydrogen/ammonia atmosphere, oxygen could be a deadly explosive. Massan carried several of these "bombs"; so did Odal. *But the trick,* Massan thought to himself, *is to know how to throw them under these conditions; the proper range, the proper trajectory. Not an easy thing to learn, without years of experience.*

The terms of the duel were simple: Massan and Odal were situated on a rough-topped iceberg that was being swirled along one of the methane/ammonia ocean's vicious currents. The ice was rapidly crumbling; the duel would end when the iceberg was completely broken up.

Massan edged along the ragged terrain. His suit's grippers and rollers automatically adjusted to the roughness of the topography. He concentrated his attention on the infrared detector that hung before his viewplate.

A chunk of ice the size of a man's head sailed through the murky atmosphere in a steep glide peculair to heavy gravity and banged into the shoulder of Massan's suit. The force was enough to rock him slightly off-balance before the servos readjusted. Massan withdrew his arm from the sleeve and felt the inside of the shoulder seam. *Dented, but not penetrated.* A leak would have been disastrous, possibly fatal. Then he remembered: *Of course–I cannot be killed except by direct action of my antagonist. That is one of the rules of the game.*

Still, he carefully fingered the dented shoulder to make certain it was not leaking. The dueling machine and its rules seemed so very remote and unsubstantial, compared to this freezing, howling inferno.

He diligently set about combing the iceberg, determined to find Odal and kill him before their floating island disintegrated. He thoroughly explored every projection, every crevice, every slope, working his way slowly from one end of the 'berg toward the other. Back and forth, cross and re-cross, with the infrared sensors scanning three hundred sixty-degrees around him.

It was time-consuming. Even with the suit's servomotors and propulsion units, motion across the ice, against the buffeting wind, was a cumbersone business. But Massan continued to work his way across the iceberg, fighting down a gnawing, growing fear that Odal was not there at all.

And then he caught just the barest flicker of a shadow on his detector. Something, or someone, had darted behind a jutting rise of the ice, off by the edge of the iceberg.

Slowly and carefully, Massan made his way toward the base of the rise. He picked one of the oxy-bombs from his belt and held it in his right-hand claw.

Massan edged around the base of the ice cliff, and stood on a narrow ledge between the cliff and the churning sea. He saw no one. He extended the detector's range to maximum, and worked the scanners up the sheer face of the cliff toward the top.

There he was! The shadowy outline of a man etched itself on the detector screen. And at the same time, Massan heard a muffled roar, then a rumbling toward him. *That devil set off a bomb at the top of the cliff!*

Massan tried to back out of the way, but it was too late. The first chunk of ice bounced harmlessly off his helmet, but the others knocked him off-balance so repeatedly that the servos had no chance to recover. He staggered blindly for a few moments, as more and more ice cascaded down on him, and then toppled off the ledge into the boiling sea.

Relax! he ordered himself. *Do not panic! The suit will float you. The servos will keep you right-side-up. You cannot be killed accidentally; Odal must perform the* coup-de-grace *himself.*

Then he remembered the emergency rocket units in the back of the suit. If he could orient himself properly, a touch of a control stud on his belt would set them off, and he would be boosted back onto the iceberg. He turned slightly inside the suit and tried to judge the iceberg's distance through the infrared detector. It was difficult, especially since he was bobbing madly in the churning currents.

Finally he decided to fire the rocket and make final adjustments of distance and landing site after he was safely out of the sea.

But he could not move his hand.

He tried, but his entire right arm was locked fast. He could not budge it an inch. And the same for the left. Something, or someone, was clamping his arms tight. He could not even pull them out of their sleeves.

Massan thrashed about, trying to shake off whatever it was. No use.

Then his detector screen was lifted slowly from the viewplate. He felt something birating on his helmet. The oxygen tubes! They were being disconnected.

He screamed and tried to fight free. No use. With a hiss, the oxygen tubes pulled free of his helmet. Massan could feel the blood pounding through his veins as he fought desperately to free himself.

Now he was being pushed down into the sea. He screamed again and tried to wrench his body away. The frothing sea filled his viewplate. He was under. He was being held under. And now . . . now the viewplate itself was being loosened.

No! Don't! The scalding cold methane ammonia sea seeped in through the opening viewplate.

"It's only a dream!" Massan shouted to himself. "Only a dream. A dream. A—"

XI

Dr. Leoh stared at the dinner table without really seeing it. Coming to this restaurant had been Hector's idea. Three hours earlier, Massan had been removed from the dueling machine—dead.

Leoh sat stolidly, hands in lap, his mind racing in many different directions at once. Hector was off at the phone, getting the latest information from the meditechs. Odal had expressed his regret perfunctorily, and then left for the Kerak Embassy, under a heavy escort of his own plainclothes guards. The government of the Acquataine Cluster was quite literally falling apart, with no man willing to assume responsibility . . . and thereby expose himself. One hour after the duel, Kanus' troops had landed on all the major planets of the Szarno Confederacy; the annexation was a *fait accompli*.

And what have I done since I arrived on Acquatainia? Leoh demanded of himself. *Nothing. Absolutely nothing. I have sat back like a doddering old professor and played academic games with the machine, while younger, more vigorous men have USED the machine to suit their purposes.*

Used the machine. There was a fragment of an idea in that phrase. Something nebulous, that must be approached carefully or it will fade away. Used the machine . . . used it . . . Leoh toyed with the phrase for a few moments, then gave it up with a sigh of resignation. *Lord, I'm too tired even to think.*

Leoh focused his attention on his surroundings and scanned the busy dining room. It was a beautiful place, really; decorated with crystal and genuine woods and fabric draperies. Not a synthetic in sight. The waiters and cooks and busboys were humans, not the autocookers and servers that most restaurants employed. Leoh suddenly felt touched at Hector's attempt to restore his spirits—even if it *was* being done at Star Watch expense.

He saw the young Watchman approaching the table, coming back from the phone. Hector bumped two waiters and stumbled over a chair before reaching the relative safety of his own seat.

"What's the verdict?" Leoh asked.

Hector's lean face was bleak. "Couldn't revive him. Cerebral hemorrhage, the meditechs said—induced by shock."

"Shock?"

"That's what they said. Something must've, uh, overloaded his nervous system . . . I guess."

Leoh shook his head. "I just don't understand any of this. I might as well admit it. I'm no closer to an answer now than I was when I arrived here. Perhaps I should have retired years ago, before the dueling machine was invented."

"Nonsense."

"No, I mean it." Leoh said. "This is the first real intellectual puzzle I've had to contend with in years. Tinkering with machinery . . . that's easy. You know what you want, all you need is to make the machinery perform properly. But this . . . I'm afraid I'm too old to handle a real problem like this."

Hector scratched his nose thoughtfully, then answered. "If you can't handle the problem, sir, then we're going to have a war on our hands in a matter of weeks. I mean, Kanus won't be satisfied with swallowing the Szarno group . . . the Acquataine Cluster is next . . . and he'll have to fight to get it."

"Then the Star Watch can step in," Leoh said, resignedly.

"Maybe . . . but it'll take time to mobilize the Star

Watch . . . Kanus can move a lot faster than we can. Sure, we could throw in a task force . . . a token group, that is. But Kanus' gang will chew them up pretty quick. I . . . I'm no politician, sir, but I think I can see what will happen. Kerak will gobble up the Acquataine Cluster . . . a Star Watch task force will be wiped out in the battle . . . and we'll end up with Kerak at war with the Terran Commonwealth. And it'll be a real war . . . a big one."

Leoh began to answer, then stopped. His eyes were fixed on the far entrance of the dining room. Suddenly every murmur in the busy room stopped dead. Waiters stood still between tables. Eating, drinking, conversation hung suspended.

Hector turned in his chair and saw at the far entrance the slim, stiff, blue-uniformed figure of Odal.

The moment of silence passed. Everyone turned to his own business and avoided looking at the Kerak major. Odal, with a faint smile on his thin face, made his way slowly to the table where Hector and Leoh were sitting.

They rose to greet him and exchanged perfunctory salutations. Odal pulled up a chair and sat with them.

"I assume that you've been looking for me," Leoh said. "What do you wish to say?"

Before Odal could answer the waiter assigned to the table walked up, took a position where his back would be to the Kerak major, and asked firmly, "Your dinner is ready gentlemen. Shall I serve it now?"

Leoh hesitated a moment, then asked Odal, "Will you join us?"

"I'm afraid not."

"Serve it now," Hector said. "The major will be leaving shortly."

Again the tight grin broke across Odal's face. The waiter bowed and left.

"I have been thinking about our conversation of last night," Odal said to Leoh.

"Yes?"

"You accused me of cheating in my duels."

Leoh's eyebrows arched. "I said someone was cheating, yes—"

"An accusation is an accusation."

Leoh said nothing.

"Do you withdraw your words, or do you still accuse me of deliberate murder? I am willing to allow you to apologize and leave Acquatainia in peace."

Hector cleared his throat noisily. "This is no place to have an argument . . . besides, here comes our dinner."

Odal ignored the Watchman. "You heard me, professor. Will you leave? Or do you accuse me of murdering Massan this afternoon?"

"I—"

Hector banged his fist on the table and jerked up out of his chair—just as the waiter arrived with a large tray of food. There was a loud crash. A tureen of soup, two bowls of salad, glasses, assorted rolls, vegetables, cheeses and other delicacies cascaded over Odal.

The Kerak major leaped to his feet, swearing violently in his native tongue. He sputtered back into basic Terran: "You clumsy, stupid oaf! You maggot-brained misbegotten peasant-faced—"

Hector calmly picked a salad leaf from the sleeve of his tunic. Odal abruptly stopped his tirade.

"I am clumsy," Hector said, grinning. "As for being stupid, and the rest of it, I resent that. I am highly insulted."

A flash of recognition lighted Odal's eyes. "I see. Of course. My quarrel here is not with you. I apologize." He turned back to Leoh, who was also standing now.

"Not good enough," Hector said. "I don't, uh, like the . . . tone of your apology."

Leoh raised a hand, as if to silence the younger man.

"I apologized; that is sufficient," Odal warned.

Hector took a step toward Odal. "I guess I could insult your glorious leader, or something like that . . . but this seems more direct." He took the water pitcher from the table and poured it calmly and carefully over Odal's head.

A wave of laughter swept the room. Odal went white. "You are determined to die." He wiped the dripping water from his eyes. "I will meet you before the week is out. And you have saved no one." He turned on his heel and stalked out.

"Do you realize what you've done?" Leoh asked, aghast.

Hector shrugged. "He was going to challenge you—"

"He will still challenge me, after you're dead."

"Uu-m-m, yes, well, maybe so. I guess you're right—Well, anyway, we've gained a little more time."

"Four days." Leoh shook his head. "Four days to the end of the week. All right, come on, we have work to do."

Hector was grinning broadly as they left the restaurant. He began to whistle.

"What are you so happy about?" Leoh grumbled.

"About you, sir. When we came in here, you were, uh, well . . . almost beaten. Now you're right back in the game again."

Leoh glanced at the Star Watchman. "In your own odd way, Hector, you're quite a boy . . . I think."

XII

Their groundcar glided from the parking building to the restaurant's entrance ramp, at the radio call of the doorman. Within minutes, Hector and Leoh were cruising through the city, in the deepening shadows of night.

"There's only one man," Leoh said, "who has faced Odal and lived through it."

"Dulaq," Hector agreed. "But . . . for all the information the medical people have been able to get from him, he might as well be, uh, dead."

"He's still completely withdrawn?"

Hector nodded. "The medicos think that . . . well, maybe in a few months, with drugs and psychotherapy and all that . . . they might be able to bring him back."

"It won't be soon enough. We've only got four days."

"I know."

Leoh was silent for several minutes. Then: "Who is Dulaq's closest living relative? Does he have a wife?"

"I think his wife is, uh, dead. Has a daughter though. Pretty girl. Bumped into her in the hospital once or twice—"

Leoh smiled in the darkness. Hector's term, "bumped into," was probably completely literal.

"Why are you asking about Dulaq's next-of-kin?"

"Because," Leoh replied, "I think there might be a way to make Dulaq tell us what happened during his duel. But it is a very dangerous way. Perhaps a fatal way."

"Oh."

They lapsed into silence again. Finally he blurted, "Come on, my boy, let's find the daughter and talk to her."

"Tonight?"

"Now."

She certainly is a pretty girl, Leoh thought as he explained very carefully to Geri Dulaq what he proposed to do. She sat quietly and politely in the spacious living room of the Dulaq residence. The glittering chandelier cast touches of fire on her chestnut hair. Her slim body was slightly rigid with tension, her hands were clasped in her lap.

Her face—which looked as though it could be very expressive—was completely serious now.

"And that is the sum of it." Leoh concluded. "I believe that it will be possible to use the dueling machine itself to examine your father's thoughts and determine exactly what took place during his duel against Major Odal!"

She asked softly, "But you are afraid that the shock might be repeated, and this could be fatal to my father?"

Leoh nodded wordless'y.

"Then I am very sorry, sir, but I must say no." Firmly.

"I understand your feelings," Leoh replied. "but I hope you realize that unless we can stop Odal and Kanus immediately, we may very well be faced with war."

She nodded. "I know. But you must remember that we are speaking of my father, of his very life. Kanus will have his war in any event, no matter what I do."

"Perhaps," Leoh admitted, "Perhaps."

Hector and Leoh drove back to the University campus and their quarters in the dueling machine chamber. Neither of them slept well that night.

The next morning, after an unenthusiastic breakfast, they found themselves standing in the antiseptic-white chamber, before the looming, impersonal intricacy of the machine.

"Would you like to practice with it?" Leoh asked.

Hector shook his head. "Maybe later."

The phone chimed in Leoh's office. They both went in. Geri Dulaq's faced showed on the tri-di screen.

"I have just heard the news. I did not know that Lieutenant Hector has challenged Odal." Her face was a mixture of concern and reluctance.

"He challenged Odal," Leoh answered, "to prevent the assassin from challenging me."

"Oh—You are a very brave man, Lieutenant."

Hector's face went through various contortions and slowly turned a definite red, but no words issued from his mouth.

"Have you reconsidered your decision?" Leoh asked.

The girl closed her eyes briefly, then said flatly "I am afraid I cannot change my decision. My father's safety is my first responsibility. I am sorry."

They exchanged a few meaningless trivialities—with Hector still thoroughly tongue-tied—and ended the conversation on a polite but strained note.

Leoh rubbed his thumb across the phone switch for a moment, then turned to Hector. "My boy, I think it would be a good idea for you to go straight to the hospital and check on Dulaq's condition."

"But . . . why—"

"Don't argue, son. This could be vitally important."

Hector shrugged and left the office. Leoh sat down at his desk and drummed his fingers on the top of it. Then he burst out of the office and began pacing the big chamber. Finally, even that was too confining. He left the building and started stalking through the campus. He walked past a dozen buildings, turned and strode as far as the decorative fence that marked the end of the main campus, ignoring students and faculty alike.

Campuses are all alike, he muttered to himself, *on every human planet, for all the centuries there have been universities. There must be some fundamental reason for it.*

Leoh was halfway back to the dueling machine facility when he spotted Hector walking dazedly toward the same building. For once, the Watchman was not whistling. Leoh cut across some lawn and pulled up beside the youth.

"Well?" he asked.

Hector shook his head, as if to clear away an inner fog. "How did you know she'd be at the hospital?"

"The wisdom of age. What happened?"

"She kissed me. Right there in the hallway of the—"

"Spare me the geography," Leoh cut in. "What did she say?"

"I bumped into her in the hallway. We, uh, started talking . . . sort of. She seemed, well . . . worried about me. She got upset. Emotional. You know? I guess I looked pretty forlorn and frightened. I am . . . I guess. When you get right down to it, I mean."

"You aroused her maternal instinct."

"I . . . I don't think it was that . . . exactly. Well, anyway, she said that if I was willing to risk my life to save yours, she couldn't protect her father any more. Said she was doing it out of selfishness, really, since he's her only living relative. I don't believe she meant that, but she said it anyway."

They had reached the building by now. Leoh grabbed Hector's arm and steered him clear of a collision with the half-open door.

"She's agreed to let us put Dulaq in the dueling machine?"

"Sort of."

"Eh?"

"The medical staff doesn't want him to be moved from the hospital . . . especially not back to here. She agrees with them."

Leoh snorted. "All right. In fact, so much the better. I'd rather not have the Kerak people see us bring Dulaq to the dueling machine. So instead, we shall smuggle the dueling machine to Dulaq!"

XIII

They plunged to work immediately. Leoh preferred not to inform the regular staff of the dueling machine about their plan, so he and Hector had to work through the night and most of the next morning. Hector barely understood what he was doing, but with Leoh's supervision, he managed to dismantle part of the dueling machine's central network, insert a few additional black boxes that the professor had conjured up from the spare parts bins in the basement, and then reconstruct the machine so that it looked exactly the same as before they had started.

In between his frequent trips to oversee Hector's work, Leoh had jury-rigged a rather bulky headset and a handsized override control circuit.

The late morning sun was streaming through the tall windows when Leoh finally explained it all to Hector.

"A simple matter of technological inprovisation," he told the bewildered Watchman. "You have installed a short-range transceiver into the machine, and this headset is a portable transceiver for Dulaq. Now he can sit in his hospital bed and still be 'in' the dueling machine."

Only the three most trusted members of the hospital staff were taken into Leoh's confidence, and they were hardly enthusiastic about Leoh's plan.

"It is a waste of time," said the chief psychophysician, shaking his white-maned head vigorously. "You cannot expect a patient who has shown no positive response to drugs and therapy to respond to your machine."

Leoh argued, Geri Dulaq coaxed. Finally the doctors agreed. With only two days remaining before Hector's duel with Odal, they began to probe Dulaq's mind. Geri remained by her father's bedside while the three doctors fitted the cumbersome transceiver to Dulaq's head and attached the electrodes for the automatic hospital equipment that monitored his physical condition. Hector and Leoh remained at the dueling machine, communicating with the hospital by phone.

Leoh made a final check of the controls and circuitry, then put in the last call to the tense little group in Dulaq's room. All was ready.

He walked out to the machine, with Hector beside him. Their footsteps echoed hollowly in the sepulchral chamber. Leoh stopped at the nearer booth.

"Now remember," he said, carefully, "I will be holding the emergency control unit in my hand. It will stop the duel the instant I set it off. However, if something should go wrong, you must be prepared to act quickly. Keep a close watch on my physical condition; I've shown you which instruments to check on the control board—"

"Yes, sir."

Leoh nodded and took a deep breath. "Very well then."

He stepped into the booth and sat down. The emergency control unit rested on a shelf at his side; he took it in his hands. He leaned back and waited for the semihypnotic effect to take hold. Dulaq's choice of this very city and the stat-wand were known. But beyond that, everything was locked and sealed in Dulaq's subconscious mind. Could the machine reach into that subconscious, probe past the lock and seal of catatonia, and stimulate Dulaq's mind into repeating the duel?

Slowly, lullingly, the dueling machine's imaginary yet very real mists enveloped Leoh. When the mists cleared, he was standing on the upper pedestrian level of the main commercial street of the city. For a long moment, everything was still.

Have I made contact? Whose eyes am I seeing with, my own or Dulaq's?

And then he sensed it—an amused, somewhat astonished marveling at the reality of the illusion. Dulaq's thoughts!

Make your mind a blank, Leoh told himself. *Watch. Listen. Be passive.*

He became a spectator, seeing and hearing the world through Dulaq's eyes and ears as the Acquatainian Prime Minister advanced through his nightmarish ordeal. He felt the confusion, frustration, apprehension and growing terror as, time and again, Odal appeared in the crowd—only to melt into someone else and escape.

The first part of the duel ended, and Leoh was suddenly buffeted by a jumble of thoughts and impressions. Then the thoughts slowly cleared and steadied.

Leoh saw an immense and totally barren plain. Not a tree, not a blade of grass; nothing but bare, rocky ground stretching in all directions to the horizon and a disturbingly harsh yellow sky. At his feet was the weapon Odal had chosen. A primitive club.

He shared Dulaq's sense of dread as he picked up the club and hefted it. Off on the horizon he could see a tall, lithe figure holding a similar club walking toward him.

Despite himself, Leoh could feel his own excitement. He had broken through the shock-created armor that Dulaq's mind had erected! Dulaq was reliving the part of the duel that had caused the shock.

Reluctantly, he advanced to meet Odal. But as they drew closer together, the one figure of his opponent seemed to split apart. Now there were two, four, six of them. Six Odals, six mirror images, all armed with massive, evil clubs, advancing steadily on him.

Six tall, lean, blond assassins, with six cold smiles on their intent faces.

Horrified, completely panicked, he scrambled away, trying to evade the six opponents with the half-dozen clubs raised and poised to strike.

Their young legs and lungs easily outdistanced him. A smash on his back sent him sprawling. One of them kicked his weapon away.

They stood over him for a malevolent, gloating second. Then six strong arms flashed down, again and again, mercilessly. Pain and blood, screaming agony, punctuated by the awful thudding of solid clubs hitting fragile flesh and bone, over and over again, endlessly,

Everything went blank.

Leoh opened his eyes and saw Hector bending over him.

"Are you all right, sir?"

"I . . . I think so."

"The controls all hit the danger mark at once. You were . . . well, sir, you were screaming."

"I don't doubt it," Leoh said.

They walked, with Leoh leaning on Hector's arm, from the dueling machine booth to the office.

"That was . . . an experience," Leoh said, easing himself onto the couch.

"What happened? What did Odal do? What made Dulaq go into shock? How does—"

The old man silenced Hector with a wave of his hand. "One question at a time, please."

Leoh leaned back on the deep couch and told Hector every detail of both parts of the duel.

"Six Odals," Hector muttered soberly, leaning back against the doorframe, "Six against one."

"That's what he did. It's easy to see how a man expecting a polite, formal duel can be completely shattered by the visciousness of such an attack. And the machine amplifies every impulse, every sensation."

"But how does he do it?" Hector asked, his voice suddenly loud and demanding.

"I've been asking myself the same question. We've checked over the dueling machine time and again. There is no possible way for Odal to plug in five helpers . . . unless—"

"Unless?"

Leoh hesitated, seemingly debating with himself. Finally he nodded his head sharply, and answered, "Unless Odal is telepath."

"Telepath? But—"

"I know it sounds farfetched. But there have been well-documented cases of telepathy for centuries throughout the Commonwealth."

Hector frowned. "Sure, everybody's heard about it . . . natural telepaths . . . but they're so unpredictable . . . I don't see how—"

Leoh leaned forward on the couch and clasped his hands in front of his chin. "The Terran races have never developed telepathy, or any of the extrasensory talents. They never had to, not with tri-di communications and superlight starships. But perhaps the Kerak people are different—"

Hector shook his head. "If they had uh, telepathic abilities, they would be using them everywhere. Don't you think?"

"Probably so. But only Odal has shown such an ability, and only . . . *of course!*"

"What?"

"Odal has shown telepathic ability only in the dueling machine."

"As far as we know."

"Certainly. But look, suppose he's a natural telepath . . . the same as a Terran. He has an erratic, difficult-to-control talent. Then he gets into a dueling machine. The machine amplifies his thoughts. And it also amplifies his talent!"

"Ohhh."

"You see . . . outside the machine, he's no better than any wandering fortuneteller. But the dueling machine gives his natural abilities the amplification and reproducibility that they could never have unaided."

Hector nodded.

"So it's a fairly straightforward matter for him to have five associates in the Kerak Embassy sit in on the duel, so to speak. Possibly they are natural telepaths also, but they needn't be."

"They just, uh, pool their minds with his, hm-m-m? Six men show up in the duel . . . pretty nasty." Hector dropped into the desk chair.

"So what do we do now?"

"Now?" Leoh blinked at his young friend. "Why . . . I suppose the first thing we should do is call the hospital and see how Dulaq came through."

Leoh put the call through. Geri Dulaq's face appeared on the screen.

"How's your father?" Hector blurted.

"The duel was too much for him," she said blankly. "He is dead."

"No," Leoh groaned.

"I . . . I'm sorry," Hector said. "I'll be right down there. Stay where you are."

The young Star Watchman dashed out of the office as Geri broke the phone connection. Leoh stared at the blank screen for a few moments, then leaned far back in the couch and closed his eyes. He was suddenly exhausted, physically and emotionally. He fell asleep, and dreamed of men dead and dying.

Hector's nerve-shattering whistling woke him up. It was full night outside.

"What are you so happy about?" Leoh groused as Hector popped into the office.

"Happy? Me?"

"You were whistling."

Hector shrugged. "I always whistle, sir. Doesn't mean I'm happy."

"All right," Leoh said, rubbing his eyes. "How did the girl take her father's death?"

"Pretty hard. Cried a lot."

Leoh looked at the younger man. "Does she blame . . . me?"

"You? Why, no, sir. Why should she? Odal . . . Kanus . . . the Kerak Worlds. But not you."

The old professor sighed, relieved. "Very well. Now then, we have much work to do, and little more than a day in which to finish it."

"What do you want me to do?" Hector asked.

"Phone the Star Watch Commander—"

"My commanding officer, all the way back at Alpha Perseus VI? That's a hundred light-years from here."

"No, no, no." Leoh shook his head. "The Commander-in-Chief, Sir Harold Spencer. At Star Watch Central Headquarters. That's several hundred parsecs from here. But get through to him as quickly as possible."

With a low whistle of astonishment, Hector began punching buttons on the phone switch.

XIV

The morning of the duel arrived, and precisely at the agreed-upon hour, Odal and a small retinue of Kerak representatives stepped through the double doors of the dueling machine changer.

Hector and Leoh were already there, waiting. With them stood another man, dressed in the black-and-silver of the Star Watch. He was a blocky, broad-faced veteran with iron-gray hair and hard, unsmiling eyes.

The two little groups of men knotted together in the center of the room, before the machine's control board. The white-uniformed staff meditechs emerged from a far doorway and stood off to one side.

Odal went through the formality of shaking hands with Hector. The Kerak major nodded toward the other Watchman. "Your replacement?" he asked mischievously.

The chief meditech stepped between them. "Since you are the challenged party, Major Odal, you have the first choice of weapon and environment. Are their any instructions or comments necessary before the duel begins?"

"I think not," Odal replied. "The situation will be self-explanatory. I assume, of course, that Star Watchmen are trained to be warriors and not merely technicians. The situation I have chosen is one in which many warriors have won glory."

Hector said nothing.

"I intend," Leoh said firmly, "to assist the staff in monitoring this duel. Your aides may, of course, sit at the control board with me."

Odal nodded.

"If you are ready to begin, gentlemen," the chief meditech said.

Hector and Odal went to their booths. Leoh sat at the control console, and one of the Kerak men sat down next to him.

Hector felt every nerve and muscle tense as he sat in the booth, despite his efforts to relax. Slowly the tension eased, and he began to feel slightly drowsy. The booth seemed to melt away . . .

He was standing on a grassy meadow. Off in the distance were wooded hills. A cool breeze was hustling puffy white clouds across a calm blue sky.

Hector heard a snuffling noise behind him, and wheeled around. He blinked, then stared.

It had four legs, and was evidently a beast of burden. At least, it carried a saddle on its back. Piled atop the saddle was a conglomeration of what looked to Hector—at first glance—like a pile of junk. He went over to the animal and examined it carefully. The "junk" turned out to be a long spear, various pieces of armor, a helmet, sword, shield, battle-ax and dagger.

The situation I have chosen in one in which many warriors have won glory. Hector puzzled over the assortment of weapons. They came straight out of Kerak's Dark Ages. No doubt Odal had been practicing with them for months, even years. He may not need five helpers.

Warily, Hector put on the armor. The breastplate seemed too big, and he was somehow unable to tighten the greaves on his shins properly. The helmet fit over his head like an ancient oil can, flattening his ears and nose and forcing him to squint to see through the narrow eye-slit.

Finally, he buckled on the sword and found attachments on the saddle for the other weapons. The shield was almost too heavy to lift, and he barely struggled into the saddle with all the weight he was carrying.

And then he just sat. He began to feel a little ridiculous. *Suppose it rains?* He wondered. But of course it wouldn't.

After an interminable wait, Odal appeared, on a powerful trotting charger. His armor was black as space, and so was his animal. *Naturally,* Hector thought.

Odal saluted gravely with his great spear from across the meadow. Hector returned the salute, nearly dropping his spear in the process.

Then, Odal lowered his spear and aimed it—so it seemed to Hector—directly at the Watchman's ribs. He pricked his mount into a canter. Hector did the same, and his steed jogged into a bumping, jolting gallop. The two warriors hurtled toward each other from opposite ends of the meadow.

And suddenly there were six black figures roaring down on Hector!

The Watchmen's stomach wrenched within him. Automatically he tried to turn his mount aside. But the beast had no intention of going anywhere except straight ahead. The Kerak warriors bore in, six abreast, with six spears aimed menacingly.

Abuptly, Hector heard the pounding of other hoofbeats right beside him. Through a corner of his helmet-slit he glimpsed at least two other warriors charging with him into Odal's crew.

Leoh's gamble had worked. The transceive that had allowed Dulaq to make contact with the dueling machine from his hospital bed was now allowing five Star Watch officers to join Hector, even though they were physically sitting in a starship orbiting high above the planet.

The odds were even now. The five additional Watchmen were the roughest, hardiest, most aggressive man-to-man fighters that the Star Watch could provide on a one-day notice.

Twelve powerful chargers met head on, and twelve strong men smashed together with an ear-splitting CLANG! Shattered spears showered splinters everywhere. Men and animals went down.

Hector was rocked back in his saddle, but somehow managed to avoid falling off.

On the other hand, he could not really regain his balance, either. Dust and weapons filled the air. A sword hissed near his head and rattled off his shield.

With a supreme effort, Hector pulled out his own sword and thrashed at the nearest rider. It turned out to be a fellow Watchman, but the stroke bounced harmlessly off his helmet.

It was so confusing. The wheeling, snorting animals. Clouds of dust. Screaming, raging men. A black-armored rider charged into Hector, waving a battle-ax over his head. He chopped savagely, and the Watchman's shield split apart. Another frightening swing—Hector tried to duck and slid completely out of the saddle, thumping painfully on the ground, while the ax cleaved the air where his head had been a split-second earlier.

Somehow his helmet had been turned around. Hector tried to decide whether to thrash around blindly or lay down his sword and straighten out the helmet. The problem was solved for him by the *crang!* of a sword against the back of his helmet. The blow flipped him into a somersault, but also knocked the helmet completely off his head.

Hector climbed painfully to his feet, his head spinning. It took him several moments to realize that the battle had stopped. The dust drifted away, and he saw that all the Kerak fighters were down—except one. The black-armored warrior took off his helmet and tossed it aside. It was Odal. Or was it? They all looked alike. *What difference does it make?* Hector wondered. *Odal's mind is the dominant one.*

Odal stood, legs braced apart, sword in hand, and looked uncertainly at the other Star Watchmen. Three of them were afoot and two still mounted. The Kerak assassin seemed as confused as Hector felt. The shock of facing equal numbers had sapped much of his confidence.

Cautiously, he advanced toward Hector, holding his sword out before him. The other Watchmen stood aside while Hector slowly backpedaled, stumbling slightly on the uneven ground.

Odal feinted and cut at Hector's arm. The Watchman barely parried in time. Another feint, at the head, and a slash in the chest; Hector missed the parry but his armor saved him. Grimly, Odal kept advancing. Feint, feint, crack! and Hector's sword went flying from his hand.

For the barest instant everyone froze. Then Hector leaped desperately straight at Odal, caught him completely by surprise, and wrestled him to the ground. The Watchman pulled the sword from his opponent's hand and tossed it away. But with his free hand, Odal clouted Hector on the side of the head and knocked him on his back. Both men scrambled up and ran for the nearest weapons.

Odal picked up a wicked-looking double-bladed ax. One of the mounted Star Watchmen handed Hector a huge broadsword. He gripped it with both hands, but still staggered off-balance as he swung it up over his shoulder.

Holding the broadsword aloft, Hector charged toward Odal, who stood dogged, short-breathed, sweat-streaked, waiting for him. The broadsword was quite heavy, even for a two-handed grip. And Hector did not notice his own battered helmet laying on the ground between them.

Odal, for his part, had Hector's charge and swing timed perfectly in his own mind. He would duck under the swing and bury his ax in the Watchman's chest. Then he would face the others. Probably with their leader gone, the duel would automatically end. But, of course, Hector would not really be dead; the best Odal could hope for now was to win the duel.

Hector charged directly into Odal's plan, but the Watchman's timing was much poorer than anticipated. Just as he began the downswing of a mighty broadsword stroke, he stumbled on the helmet. Odal started to duck, then saw that the Watchman was diving facefirst into the ground, legs flailing, and that heavy broadsword was cleaving through the air with a will of its own.

Odal pulled back in confusion, only to have the wildswinging broadsword strike him just above the wrist. The ax dropped out of his hand, and Odal involuntarily grasped the wounded forearm with his left hand. Blood seeped through his fingers.

He shook his head in bitter resignation, turned his back on the prostrate Hector, and began walking away.

Slowly, the scene faded, and Hector found himself sitting in the booth of the dueling machine.

XV

The door opened and Leoh squeezed into the booth. "You're all right?"

Hector blinked and refocused his eyes on reality. "Think so—"

"Everything went well? The Watchmen got through to you?"

"Good thing they did. I was nearly killed anyway."

"But you survived."

"So far."

Across the room, Odal stood massaging his forehead while Kor demanded: "How could they possibly have discovered the secret? Where was the leak?"

"That is not important now," Odal said quietly. "The primary fact is that they have not only discovered our secret, but they have found a way of duplicating it."

"The sanctimonious hypocrites," Kor snarled, "accusing us of cheating, and then they do the same thing."

"Regardless of the moral values of our mutual behavior," Odal said dryly, "it is evident that there is no longer any use in calling on telepathically-guided assistants. I shall face the Watchman alone during the second half of the duel."

"Can you trust them to do the same?"

"Yes. They easily defeated my aides a few minutes ago, then stood aside and allowed the two of us to fight by ourselves."

"And you failed to defeat him?"

Odal frowned. "I was wounded by a fluke. He is a very . . . unusual opponent. I cannot decide whether he is actually as clumsy as he appears to be, or whether he is shamming and trying to make me overconfident. Either way, it is impossible to predict his behavior. Perhaps he is also telepathic."

Kor's gray eyes became flat and emotionless. "You know, of

course, how the Chancellor will react if you fail to kill this Watchman. Not merely defeat him. He must be killed. The aura of invincibility must be maintained."

"I will do my best," Odal said.

"He must be killed."

The chime that marked the end of the rest period sounded. Odal and Hector returned to their booths. Now it was Hector's choice of environment and weapons.

Odal found himself enveloped in darkness. Only gradually did his eyes adjust. He saw that he was in a spacesuit. For several minutes he stood motionless, peering into the darkness, every sense alert, every muscle coiled for immediate action.

Dimly he could see the outlines of jagged rock against a background of innumerable stars. Experimentally, he lifted one foot. It stuck, tackily, to the surface. *Magnetized boots,* Odal thought. *This must be a planetoid.*

As his eyes grew accustomed to the dimness, he saw that he was right. It was a small planetoid, perhaps a mile or so in diameter. Almost zero gravity. Airless.

Odal swiveled his head inside the fishbowl helmet of his spacesuit and saw, over his right shoulder, the figure of Hector—lank and ungainly even with the bulky suit. For a moment, Odal puzzled over the weapon to be used. Then Hector bent down, picked up a loose stone, straightened, and tossed it softly past Odal's head. The Kerak major watched it sail by and off into the darkness of space, never to return to the tiny planetoid.

A *warning shot,* Odal thought to himself. He wondered how much damage one could do with a nearly weightless stone, then remembered that inertial mass was unaffected by gravitational fields, or lack of them. A fifty-pound rock might be easier to lift, but it would be just as hard to throw—and it would do just as much damage when it hit, regardless of its gravitational "weight."

Odal crouched down and selected a stone the size of his fist. He rose carefully, sighted Hector standing a hundred yards or so away, and threw as hard as he could.

The effort of his throw sent him tumbling off-balance, and the stone was far off-target. He fell to his hands and knees, bounced lightly and skidded to a stop. Immediately he drew his feet up under his body and planted the magnetized soles of his boots firmly on the iron-rich surface.

But before he could stand again, a small stone *pinged* slightly off his oxygen tank. The Star Watchman had his range already!

Odal scrambled to the nearest upjutting rocks and crouched behind them. *Lucky I didn't rip open the spacesuit*, he told himself. Three stones, evidently hurled in salvo, ticked off the top of the rocks he was hunched behind. One of the stones bounced into his fishbowl helmet.

Odal scooped up a handful of pebbles and tossed them in Hector's general direction. *That should make him duck. Perhaps he'll stumble and crack his helmet open.*

Then he grinned to himself. *That's it. Kor wants him dead, and that is the way to do it. Pin him under a big rock, then bury him alive under more rocks. A few at a time, stretched out nicely. While his oxygen supply gives out. That should put enough stress on his nervous system to hospitalize him, at least. Then he can be assassinated by more conventional means. Perhaps he will even be as obliging as Massan, and have a fatal stroke.*

A large rock. One that is light enough to lift and throw, yet also big enough to pin him for a few moments. Once he is down, it will be easy enough to bury him under more rocks.

The Kerak major spotted a boulder of the proper size, a few yards away. He backed toward it, throwing small stones in Hector's direction to keep the Watchman busy. In return, a barrage of stones began striking all around him. Several hit him, one hard enough to knock him slightly off-balance.

Slowly, patiently, Odal reached his chosen weapon—an oblong boulder, about the size of a small chair. He crouched behind it and tugged at it experimentally. It moved slightly. Another stone *zinged* off his arm, hard enough to hurt. Odal could see Hector clearly now, standing atop a small rise, calmly firing pellets at him. He smiled as he coiled, catlike, and tensed himself. He gripped the boulder with his arms and hands.

Then in one vicious uncoiling motion he snatched it up, whirled around, and hurled it at Hector. The violence of his action sent him tottering awkwardly as he released the boulder. He fell to the ground, but kept his eyes fixed on the boulder as it tumbled end over end, directly at the Watchman.

For an eternally-long instant Hector stood motionless, seemingly entranced. Then he leaped sideways, floating dreamlike in the low gravity, as the stone hurtled inexorably past him.

Odal pounded his fist on the ground in fury. He started up, only to have a good-sized stone slam against his shoulder, and knock him flat again. He looked up in time to see Hector fire another. The stone puffed into the ground inches from Odal's helmet. The Kerak major flattened himself, Several more stones clattered on his helmet and oxygen tank. Then silence.

Odal looked up and saw Hector squatting down, reaching for more ammunition. The Kerak warrior stood up quickly, his own fists filled with throwing stones. He cocked his arm to throw—

But something made him turn to look behind him. The boulder looked before his eyes, still tumbling slowly, as it had when he had thrown it. It was too close and too big to avoid. It smashed into Odal, picked him off his feet and slammed against the upjutting rocks a few yards away.

Even before he started to feel the pain in his midsection, Odal began trying to push the boulder off. But he could not get enough leverage. Then he saw the Star Watchman's form standing over him.

"I didn't really think you'd fall for it," Odal heard Hector's voice in his earphones. "I mean . . . didn't you realize that the boulder was too massive to escape completely after it had missed me? You could've calculated its orbit . . . you just threw it into a, uh, six-minute orbit around the planetoid. It *had* to come back to perigee . . . right where you were standing when you threw it, you know."

Odal said nothing, but strained every cell in his painwracked body to get free of the boulder. Hector reached over his shoulder and began fumbling with the valves that were pressed against the rocks.

"Sorry to do this . . . but I'm not, uh, killing you, at least . . . just defeating you. Let's see . . . one of these is the oxygen valve, and the other, I think, is the emergency rocket pack . . . now, which is which?" Odal felt the Watchman's hands searching for the proper valve. "I shouldn've dreamed up suits without the rocket pack . . . confuses things . . . there, that's it."

Hector's hand tightened on a valve and turned it sharply. The rocket roared to life and Odal was hurtled free of the boulder, shot uncontrolled completely off the planetoid. Hector was bowled over by the blast and rolled halfway around the tiny chink of rock and metal.

Odal tried to reach around to throttle down the rocket, but the pain in his body was too great. He was slipping into unconsciousness. He fought against it. He knew he must return to the planetoid and somehow kill the opponent. But gradually the pain overpowered him. His eyes were closing, closing—

And quite abruptly, he found himself sitting in the booth of the dueling machine. It took a moment for him to realize that he was back in the real world. Then his thoughts cleared. He had failed to kill Hector.

And at the door of the booth stood Kor, his face a grim mask of anger.

XVI

The office was that of the new prime minister of the Acquataine Cluster. It had been loaned to Leoh for his conversation with Sir Harold Spencer. For the moment, it seemed like a great double room: half of it was dark, warm woods, rich draperies, floor-to-ceiling bookcases. The other half, from the tri-di screen onward, was the austere, metallic utility of a starship compartment.

Spencer was saying, "So this hired assassin, after killing four men and nearly wrecking a government, has returned to his native worlds."

Leoh nodded. "He returned under guard. I suppose he is in disgrace, or perhaps even under arrest."

"Servants of a dictator never know when they will be the ones who are served—on a platter." Spencer chuckled. "And the Watchman who assisted you, this Junior Lieutenant Hector, what of him?"

"He's not here just now. The Dulaq girl has him in tow, somewhere. Evidently it's the first time he's been a hero—"

Spencer shifted his weight in his chair. "I have long prided myself on the conviction that any Star Watch officer can handle almost any kind of emergency anywhere in the galaxy. From your description of the past few weeks, I was beginning to have my doubts. However, Junior Lieutenant Hector seems to have won the day . . . almost in spite of himself."

"Don't underestimate him," Leoh said, smiling. "He turned out to be an extremely valuable man. I think he will make a fine officer."

Spencer grunted an affirmative.

"Well," Leoh said, "that's the complete story, to date. I believe that Odal is finished. But the Kerak Worlds have made good their annexation of the Szarno Confederacy, and the Acquataine Cluster is still very wobbly, politically. We haven't heard the last of Kanus—not by a long shot."

Spencer lifted a shaggy eyebrow. "Neither," he rumbled, "has *he* heard the last from *us*."

*Besides having written over fifty books and having
served a busy term as President of the Science Fiction Writers
of America, Poul Anderson has long been active in a strange
outfit called The Society for Creative Anachronism—a group
organized to preserve such useful and nearly forgotten skills
as jousting and dueling with broadsword, morning star,
poleax and so on. Members gather in grassy glades and have
at each other with bogus weapons of wood and plastic.
Wounds are never more serious than an occasional turned
ankle, bruise or cracked rib; but still, you would expect a
man who does this sort of thing for fun to turn in a story
awash with blood and gore, with more groans per square line
than ideas.*

*Not so. The story that follows, like the man himself, is
rather quiet and introspective. And it fulfils a soldier's
fantasy that was probably an old tradition before the Punic
Wars and was certainly still current when I was in Viet Nam:
if Johnson and Uncle Ho want whatever they want so badly,
why don't they just get together someplace and shoot it out?*

*In Poul Anderson's world of the near future, there are
only two classes, with few members, who can fall victim to
war. One class is made up of Presidents and Commissars and
Secretaries of War.*

A MAN TO MY WOUNDING
By Poul Anderson

> *I have slain a man to my wounding, and a young man to my hurt.*
> —Genesis, iv. 23

His names were legion and his face was anybody's. Because a
Senator was being hunted, I stood on a corner and waited for him.

The arm gun was a slight, annoying drag under my tunic. Lord
knew the thing should be almost a part of me after so many years, but
today I had the jaggers. It's always harder on the nerves to defend than
to stalk. A vending machine was close by, and I might have bought a
reefer, or even a cigaret, to calm me down; but I can't smoke. I got a
whiff of chlorine several years ago, during an assassination in Morocco,
and the regenerated lung tissue I now use is a bit cranky. Nor did my
philosophical tricks work: meditation on the koans of Zen, recital of
elementary derivatives and integrals.

I was alone at my post. In some towns, where private autos

haven't yet been banned from congested areas, my assignment would have given me trouble. Here, though, only pedestrians and an occasional electroshuttle got between me and my view, kittycorner across the intersection of Grant and Jefferson to The Sword Called Precious Pearl. I stood as if waiting for a particular ride. A public minivid was on the wall behind me, and after a while I decided it wouldn't hurt to see if anything had happened. Not that I expected it yet. The Senator's escorted plane was still airborne. I hardly thought the enemy would have gotten a bomb aboard. However—

I dropped a coin in the box and turned the dials in search of a newscast.

"—development was inevitable, toward greater and greater ferocity. For example, we think of the era between the Peace of Westphalia and the French Revolution as one of limited conflicts. But Heidelberg and Poltava suffice to remind us how easily they got out of hand. Likewise, the relative chivalry of the post-Napoleonic nineteenth century evolved into the trench combat of the First World War, the indiscriminate aerial bombings of the Second, and the atomic horrors of the Third."

Interested, I leaned closer to the little screen. I only needed one eye to watch that bar. The other could study this speaker. He was a fortyish man with sharp, intelligent features. I liked his delivery, vivid without being sentimental. I couldn't quite place him, though, so I thumbed the info switch. He disappeared for a moment while a sign in the screen told me this was a filmed broadcast of an address by Juan Morales, the new president of the University of California, on the topic: *Clausewitz's Analysis Reconsidered.*

It was refreshing to hear a college president voice something besides noises about Education in the Cybernetic Age. I recalled, now, that Morales was a historian of note, and moderately active in the Libertarian Party. Doubtless the latter experience had taught him to speak with vigor. The fact that the Enterprise Party had won the last election seemed only to have honed him more fine-edged.

"The Third World War, short and inconclusive as it was, made painfully clear that mass destruction had become ridiculous," he went on. "War was traditionally an instrument of national policy, a means of getting acquiescence to something from another state when less drastic measures had failed. But a threat to instigate mutual suicide has no such meaning. At the same time, force remains the *ultima ratio*. It is no use to preach that killing is wrong, that human life is infinitely valuable, and so on. I'm afraid that in point of blunt, regrettable fact, human life has always been a rather cheap commodity. From a man defending his wife against a homicidal maniac, on to the most complex international problems, issues are bound to arise occasionally which cannot be resolved. If these issues are too important to ignore, men will then fight.

"The need of the world today is, therefore, not to plan grandiose renunciations of violence. I know that many distinguished thinkers regard our present system of killing—not whole populations, but the leaders of those populations—as a step forward. Certainly it is more efficient, even more humane, than war. But it does not lead logically to a next step of killing no one at all. Rather, it has merely shifted the means of enforcing the national will.

"Our task is to understand this process. That will not be easy. Assassination evolved slowly, almost unconsciously, like every other viable institution. Like old-fashioned war, it has its own reaction upon the political purposes for which it is used. Also like war, it has its own evolutionary tendencies. Once we thought we had contained war, made it a safely limited duel between gentlemen. We learned better. Let us not make the same complacent mistake about our new system of assassination. Let us not—"

"Shine, mister?"

I looked down into a round face and black almond eyes. The boy was perhaps ten years old, small, quick, brilliant in the Mandarin tunic affected by most Chinatown youngsters these days. (A kind of defiance, an appeal: Look, we're Americans too, with a special and proud heritage; our ancestors left the old country before the Kung She rose up to make humans into machinery.) He carried a box under his arm.

"What time machine did you get off of?" I asked him.

"A shoe blaster's no good," he grinned. "I give you a hand shine, just like the Nineties. The Gay Nineties, I mean, not the Nasty Nineties." As I hesitated: "You could ride in my cable car too, only I'm still saving money to get one built. Have a shoe shine and help make San Francisco picturesque again!"

I laughed. "Sure thing, bucko. I may have to take off in a hurry, though, so let me pay you in advance."

He made a sparrow's estimate of me. "Five dollars."

The cost of a slug of bourbon didn't seem excessive for a good excuse to loiter here. Besides, I like kids. Once I hoped to have a few of my own. Most people in the Bureau of National Protection (good old Anglo-Saxon hypocrisy!) do; they keep regular hours, like any other office worker. However, the field agent—or trigger man, if you don't want euphemisms—has no business getting married. I tried, but shouldn't have. A few years later, when the memory wasn't hurting quite so much, I saw how justified she had been.

I flipped the boy a coin. He speared it in midair and broke out his apparatus. Morales was still talking in the screen. The boy cocked an eye that way. "What's he so thermal about, mister? The assassination that's on?"

"The whole system." I switched the program off hastily, not wanting to draw even this much attention to my real purpose.

But the kid was too bright. Smearing wax on a shoe, he said, "Gee, I don't get it. How long we been fighting those old Chinese, anyhow? Seven months? And nothing's happened. I bet pretty soon they'll call the whole show off and talk some more. It don't make sense. Why not *do* something first?"

"The two countries might agree on an armistice," I said with care. "But that won't be for lack of trying to do each other dirt. A lot of wars in early days got called off too, when neither side found it could make any headway. Do you think it's easy to pot the President, or Chairman Kao-Tsung?"

"I guess not. But Secretive Operative Dan Steelman on the vid—"

"Yeah," I grunted. "Him."

If I'd been one of those granite-jawed microcephalics with beautiful female assistants, whom you see represented as agents of the BNP, everything would have looked clear-cut. The United States of America and the Grand Society of China were in a formally declared state of assassination, weren't they? Our men were gunning for their leaders, and vice versa, right?

Specifically, Senator Greenstein was to address an open meeting in San Francisco tonight, rallying a somewhat reluctant public opinion behind the Administration's firm stand on the Cambodian question. He could do it, too. He was not only floor leader of the Senate Enterprisers, but a brilliant speaker and much admired personally, a major engine of our foreign policy. At any time the Chinese would be happy to bag him. The Washington branch of my corps had already parried several attempts. Here on the West Coast he'd be more vulnerable.

So Secretive Operative Dan Steelman would have arrested the man for whom I stood waiting, the minute he walked into the bar where I'd first spotted him. After a fist fight which tore apart the whole saloon, we'd get the secret papers that showed the Chinese consulate was the local HQ of their organization, we'd raid the joint, fadeout to happy ending and long spiel about Jolt, the New Way to Take LSD.

Haw. To settle a single one of those clichés, how stupid is an assassination corps supposed to be? A consulate or embassy is the last place to work out of. Quite apart from its being watched as a matter of routine, diplomatic relations are too valuable to risk by such a breach of international law.

Furthermore, I didn't want to give the Chinese the slightest tip-off that we knew The Sword Called Precious Pearl was a rendezvous of theirs. Johnny Wang had taken months to get himself contacted by their agents, months more to get sucked into their outfit, a couple of years to work up high enough that he could pass on an occasional bit of useful information to us, like the truth about that bar. If they learned that we'd learned this, they'd simply find another spot.

They might also trace back the leak and find Johnny, whom we could ill afford to lose. He was one of our best. In fact, he'd bagged Semyanov by himself, during the Russo-American assassination a decade ago. (He passed as a Buryat Mongol, got a bellhop job in the swank new hotel at Kosygingrad, and smuggled in his equipment piece by piece; when the Soviet Minister of Production finally visited that Siberian town on one of his inspection trips, Johnny Wang was all set to inject the air conditioning of the official suite with hydrogen cyanide.)

My sarcasm surprised the boy. "Well, gee," he said, "I hadn't thought much about it. But I guess it is tough to get a big government man. Real tough. Why do they even try?"

"Oh, they have ways," I said, not elaborating. The ways can be too unpleasant. Synergic poison, for example. Slip your victim the first component, harmless in itself, weeks ahead of time; then, at your leisure, give him the other dose, mixed in his food or sprayed as an aerosol in his office.

Though nowadays, with the art of guarding a man twenty-four hours a day so highly developed, the trend is back again toward more colorful brute force. If he is not to become a mere figurehead, an important man has to move around, appear publicly, attend conferences; and that sometimes lays him open to his hunters.

"Like what?" the boy persisted.

"Well," I said, "if the quarry makes a speech behind a shield of safety plastic, your assassin might wear an artificial arm with a gun inside. He might shoot a thermite slug through the plastic and the speaker, then use a minijato pack to get over the police cordon and across the rooftops."

Actually, such a method is hopelessly outdated now. And it isn't as horrid as some of the things the laboratories are working on—like remote-control devices to burn out a brain or stop a heart. I went on quickly:

"A state of assassination is similar to a football game, son. A contest, not between individual oafs such as you see on the vid, but between whole organizations. The guy who makes the touchdown depends on line backs, blocking, a long pass. The organizations might probe for months before finding a chink in the enemy armor. But if we knock off enough of their leaders, one after the next, eventually men will come to power who're so scared, or otherwise ready to compromise, that negotiations can recommence to our advantage."

I didn't add that two can play at that game.

As a matter of fact, we and the Chinese had been quietly nibbling at each other. Their biggest prize so far was the Undersecretary of State; not being anxious to admit failure, our corps let the coroner's verdict of accidental death stand, though we had ample evidence to the contrary. Our best trophy was the Commissar of Internal Waterways for Hopeh Province. That doesn't sound like much till you realize what a lot of traffic still goes by water in China and that his replacement, correspondingly influential, favored conciliating the Americans.

To date there hadn't been any really big, really decisive coups on either side. But Johnny Wang had learned that four top agents of the Chinese corps were due in town—at the same time as Senator Greenstein.

More than that he had not discovered. The cell type of organization limits the scope of even the most gifted spy. We did not know exactly where, when, or how those agents were to arrive: submarine, false bottom of a truck, stratochute, or what. We did not know their assignments, though the general idea seemed obvious.

Naturally, our outfit was alerted to protect Greenstein and the other bigwigs who were to greet him. Every inch of his route, before and after the speech, had been pre-planned in secret and was guarded one way or another. Since the Chinese presumably expected us to be so careful, we were all the more worried that they should slip in their crack hunters at this exact nexus. Why waste personnel on a hopeless task? Or was it hopeless?

Very few men could be spared from guard duty. I was one. They had staked me out in front of The Sword Called Precious Pearl and told me to play by ear.

The shoeshine rag snapped around my feet. The boy's mind had jumped to my example, football, which was a relief. I told him I didn't think we'd make the Rose Bowl this year, but he insisted otherwise. It was a lot of fun arguing with him. I wished I could keep on.

"Well." He picked up his kit. "How's that, mister? Pretty good, huh? I gotta go now. If I was you, I wouldn't wait any longer for some old girl."

His small form vanished in the crowd as I looked at my watch and realized I'd been here almost an hour. What was going on in that building I was supposed to have under surveillance?

What did I already know?

For the thousandth time I ran through the list. We knew the joint was a meeting place of the enemy, that only the owner and a single bartender were Chinese agents, that the rest of the help were innocent and unaware. Bit by bit, we'd studied them and the layout. We'd gotten a girl of our own in, as a waitress. We knew about a storeroom upstairs, always kept locked and burglar-alarmed; we hadn't risked making a sneak entry, but doubtless it was a combination office, file room, and cache for tools and weapons.

Posting myself today at the dragon-shaped bar, I had seen a little man enter. He was altogether ordinary, not be distinguished from the rest of the Saturday afternoon crowd. His Caucasian face might be real or surgical; the Kung She does have a lot of whites in its pay, just as we have friends of Oriental race. Nothing had differentiated this man except that he spoke softly for a while with that bartender who was a traitor, and then went upstairs. I'd faded back outside. The building had no secret passages or any such nonsense. My man could emerge from the front door onto Grant Street, or out a rear door and a blind alley to Jefferson. My eyes covered both possibilities.

But I'd been waiting an hour now.

He might simply be waiting too. However, the whole thing smelled wrong.

I reached my decision and slipped into the grocery store behind me. A phone booth stood between the bok choy counter and the candied ginger shelf. I dialed local HQ, slipped a scrambler on the mouthpiece, and said to the recorder at the other end what I'd observed and what I planned. There wasn't much the corps could do to help or even to stop me, nailed down as they were by the necessity of protecting the Senator and his colleagues. But if I never reported back, it might be useful for them to know what I'd been about.

I pushed through the crowd, hardly conscious of them. Not that I needed to be. I knew them by heart. The Chinatown citizens, selling their Asian wares, keeping alive their Cantonese language after a cen-

tury or more over here. Other San Franciscans, looking for amusement. The tourists from Alaska, Massachusetts, Iowa, cratered Los
Angeles. The foreigners—Canadians, self-conscious about belonging to
the world's wealthiest nation, leaning backward to be good fellows;
Europeans, gushing over our old buildings and quaint little shops; Russians, bustling earnestly about with cameras and guidebooks; an Israeli
milord, immaculate, reserved, veddy veddy Imperial; a South African
or Indonesian in search of a white clerk to order around; and a few
Chinese proper—consular officials or commercial representatives, stiff
in their drab uniforms but retaining a hint of old Confucian politeness.

Possibly, face remodeled, speech and gait and tastes recon-
ditioned, a Chinese assassin, stalking me. But I couldn't linger to worry
about that. I had one of my own to hunt.

Crossing the street, I bent my attention to a koan I'd found helpful
before—"What face did you wear before your mother and father conceived you?"—and re-entered The Sword Called Precious Pearl in a
more relaxed and efficient state. I stood by the entrance a moment, letting my pupils adjust to cool smoky dimness.

A waitress passed near. Not ours, unfortunately; Joan didn't come
on duty till twenty hundred. But I'd read the dossiers on everyone
working here. The girl I saw was a petite blonde. Surgery had slanted
her blue eyes, which made for a startling effect; the slit-skirt rig she
wore on the job added to that. Our inquiries, Joan's reports, everything
tagged her as being impulsive, credulous, and rather greedy.

My scheme was chancy, but an instinctive sense of desperation
was growing on me. I tapped her arm and donned a sort of smile.
"Excuse me, miss."

"Yes?" She stopped. "Can I bring you something, sir?"

"Just a little information. I'm trying to locate a friend." I slipped
her a two hundred dollar bill. She nodded very brightly, tucked the
bill in her belt pouch, and led me into a cavernous rear booth. I seated
myself opposite her and closed curtains which I recognized as being of
sound-absorbent material.

"Yes, sir?" she invited.

I studied her through the twilight. Muffled, the talk and laughter
and footsteps in the bar room seemed far away, not quite real. "Don't
get excited, sis," I said. "I'm only looking for a guy. You probably saw
him. He came in an hour or so ago, talked to Slim at the bar, then
went upstairs. A short baldish fellow. Do you remember?"

Her sudden start took me by surprise. I hadn't expected her to attach any significance to this. "No," she whispered. "I can't—you'd better—"

My pulse flipflopped, but I achieved a chuckle. "He's a bit shy, but I am too. I just want a chance to talk with him privately, without Slim knowing. It's a business deal, see, and I want him to hear my offer. All I'm asking you to do is tell me if he's still in that storeroom." As her eyes grew round: "Yes, I know that's the only possible place for him to have gone. Nothing else up there but an office and such, and those're much too public."

"I don't know," she said jaggedly.

"Well, can you find out?" I took my wallet forth, extracted ten kilobuck notes, and shuffled them before her. "This is yours for the information, and nobody has to be told. In fact, nobody had better be told. Ever."

Fine beads of sweat glittered on her forehead, catching the wan light. She was scared. Not of me. I don't look tough, and anyhow she was used to petty gangsters. But she had seen something lately which disconcerted her, and when I showed up and touched on the same nerve, it was a shock.

"You under contract here?" I asked, keeping my voice mild.

Her golden head shook.

"Then I'd quit if I were you," I said. "Today. Go work somewhere else—the other end of town or a different city altogether."

I decided to take a further risk, and pulled my right sleeve back far enough for her to glimpse the gun barrel strapped to my forearm.

"This is not a healthy spot," I went on. "Slim's got himself mixed up with something."

I observed her closely. My next line could go flat on its face, it was so straight from the tall corn country. Or it could be a look at hell. She was so rattled by now that I decided she might fall for it.

"Zombie racket," I said.

"Oh, no!" She had shrunk away from me when I showed the gun. At my last words, she sagged against the booth wall, and her oblique blue eyes went blank.

I had her hooked. Finding someone who'd believe that story on so little evidence was my first break today. And I needed one for damn sure.

Not that the racket doesn't still exist, here and there. And where it does, it's the ghastliest form of enslavement man has yet invented. But mostly it's been wiped out. Not even legitimate doctors do much psychosurgery any more, and certainly not for zombie merchants. (I refer to the civilized world; totalitarian governments continue to find the procedures useful.)

"You needn't tell Slim, or anyone, why you're quitting," I said, placing the bills on the table. "That's jet fare to any other spot in the world, and a stake till you get another job. I understand there are lots of openings around Von Braunsville these days, what with the spaceport being expanded."

She nodded, stiff in the neck muscles.

"Okay, sis," I finished. "Believe me, you needn't get involved in this at all. I just want to know whatever you noticed about that little guy."

"I saw him talk to Slim and then go upstairs by himself." She spoke so low I could barely hear. "That was kind of funny—unusual, I mean. A couple of us girls talked about it. Then I saw him come down again maybe fifteen minutes ago. You know, in this business you got to keep watching everywhere, see if the customers are happy and so on."

"Uh-huh," I said. That was the main reason I'd returned here.

"Well, he came down again," she said. "He must have been the same man, because nobody else goes upstairs this time of day. And like you said, he must have gone in the storeroom. They don't ever allow anybody else in there, I guess you know. Well, when he came back, he didn't look like himself. He wore different clothes—red tunic, green pants, and he had thick black hair and walked different, and he carried a little bag or satchel—"

Her voice trailed off. I tried to imagine how a man might strangle himself. Of course that private room would have disguise materials! Not that a skilled agent needs much; it's fantastic what a simple change of posture will do.

My man had altered his looks, collected whatever tools he needed, and sauntered out the front door under my eye like any departing patron.

For a moment I debated coldly whether the enemy knew this place was known to us. Probably not. They had merely been taking a sensible extra precaution. The fault was ours—no, mine—for underestimating their thoroughness.

I looked hard at the girl. To be sure, I consoled myself, they in their turn had underestimated her and her companions. That's a characteristic failing of the present-day Chinese: to forget that the unregimented common man is able to see and think about things he hasn't been conditioned to see and think about. Nonetheless, they were now ahead on points: because I had no idea where my mouse-turned-cat was bound.

"What's the matter?" The girl's tones became shrill. "I told you everything I know. It scared me some—wasn't the first funny goings-on I'd noticed here—but I figured it was Slim's business. Then you came along and—Go on! Get out of here!"

"I don't suppose you observed which way he turned as he went out the door?" I asked.

She shook her head. The rest of her was shaking too.

I sighed. "Makes no difference. Well, thanks, sis. If you don't want to attract attention to yourself, you better take a happypill before going back to work."

She agreed by fumbling in her pouch. So as not to be noticed either, I remained slumped for another few minutes. By then the girl was in orbit. She looked at me rosily, giggled, and said, "Care to offer me a job yourself? You bought quite a few hours of my time already, you know."

"I bought your plane fare," I told her sharply, and left. Sometimes I think a temporary zombie is as gruesome as a permanent one, and more dangerous to civilization.

I had been racing around in my own skull while I waited, like any trapped rat, getting nowhere. A full-dress attempt on Senator Greenstein—even with the hope of also bagging the Governor, the state chairman of the Enterprise Party, and various other jupiters—didn't seem plausible. The only way I could see to get them at once would be by, say, a light super-fast rocket bomber, descending from the stratosphere with ground guidance. But such weapons were banned by the World Disarmament Convention. If the Chinese were about to break *that*. . . . Impossible! What use is it to be the chief corpse in a radioactive desert?

Had the enemy research labs come up with a new technique: The virus gun, the invisibility screen, or any of those dream gadgets? Conceivable, but doubtful. One of our own major triumphs had been a raid on their central R & D plant in Shanghai. We hadn't gotten Grandfather Scientist Feng as hoped, but our agents had machine-gunned a number of valuable lesser men and blown up the main building. There was every reason to believe we were ahead of them in armaments development. The Chinese had nothing we didn't have more of, except perhaps imagination.

And yet they wouldn't slip four of their best killers into this country merely for a lark. The trigger man of real life bears no resemblance to the one on your living-room screen. He has to have the potentialities to start with, and such genes are rare. Then a lot of expensive talent goes into training him, peeling off ordinary humanness and installing the needful reflexes. I say this quite without modesty, sometimes wishing to hell I'd flunked out. But at any rate, a top-grade field agent is not expended lightly.

So where was my boy?

I slouched down Grant Street, under the dragon lamps and the peaked tile roofs, thinking that I might already know the answer. The prominent men in this area didn't total so very many. If the agent murdered cleverly enough, as he was trained to do, the result would pass for an accident—though naturally, whenever a big name dies during a state of assassination, the presumption is that it was engineered. The corps can't investigate every case of home electrocution, iodine swallowed by mistake for cough cyrup, drowning, suicide. . . . However, no operative kills obscure folk. He has no rational motive for it, and we aren't sadists; we are the kings who die for the people, that little boys with shoeshine kits may not again be fried on molten streets. . . .

I don't know what put the answer in my head. Hunch, subconscious ratiocination, esp, lucky guess—I just don't know. But I have said that a trigger man is a special and lonely creature.

I stood unmoving for an instant. The crowd milled around me, frantic in search of something to fill the rest of the thirty-hour week; I was a million light-years elsewhere and it was cold.

Then I started running.

I slowed down after a while, which was more efficient under these conditions. I told myself that $d\sin y$ equals $\cos y \, dy$ and $d\cos y$ equals minus $\sin y \, dy$, I asked myself how high is green, and presently I arrived in front of New Old St. Mary's Church, where the taxis patrol. Somebody's mother was hailing one. As it drew up I pushed her aside, hopped into the bubble, closed it on her gray hairs, and said, "Berkeley!"

No use urging speed on the pilot. I had to sit and fume. The knowledge that it followed the guide cables faster and more safely than any human chauffeur was scant consolation. I could have browbeaten a man.

The Bay looked silver, down a swooping length of street. The far side was a gleam of towers and delicate colors; they rebuilt well over there, though of course it so happened the bomb left them a clearer field than in San Francisco. The air was bright and swift, and I could see the giant whale-shape of a transpolar merchant submarine standing in past Alcatraz Peace Memorial. Looking at that white spire, I wondered if the old German idea about a human race mind might not be correct; and if so, how grisly a sense of humor does it have?

But I had business on hand. As the taxi swooped into the Bay tunnel I took the city index off its shelf by the phone and leafed through. The address I wanted . . . yes, here . . . "2878 Buena Vista," I told the pilot.

I had no idea if the resident was at home; but neither did my opponent, I supposed. I should call ahead, warn. . . . No. If my man was actually there, he mustn't be tipped off that I knew.

We came out onto the freeway and hummed along at an even 150 KPH, another drop in the river of machines. The land climbed rapidly on this side too. We skirted the city within a city which is the UC campus, dropped off the freeway at Euclid, and followed that avenue between canyonlike apartment house walls to Buena Vista. This street was old and narrow and dignified. We had to slow, while I groaned.

"2878 Buena Vista," my voice played back to me. The change from my money jingled down. I scooped it up and threw back a coin.

"Drive on past," I said. "Let me off around the next bend."

I heard a clicking. The pilot didn't quite understand, bucked my taped words on to a human dispatcher across the Bay, got its coded orders, and obeyed.

I walked back, the street on my right and a high hedge on my left. Roofs and walls swept away below me, falling to the glitter of great waters. San Francisco and Marin County lifted their somehow unreal hills on the farther side. A fresh wind touched my skin. My footfalls came loudly and the arm gun weighed a million kilograms.

At the private driveway I turned and walked in. Landscaped grounds enclosed a pleasant modernistic mansion; the University does well by its president. An old gardener was puttering with some roses. I began to realize just how thin my hunch was.

He straightened and peered at me. His face was wizened, his clothes fifty years out of date, his language quaint. "What's the drag, man?"

"Looking for a chap," I said. "Important message. Any strangers been around?"

"Well, I dunno. Like, we get a lot of assorted cats."

I flipped a ten-dollar coin up and down in a cold hand. "Medium height, thin," I said, "black hair, smallish nose, red tunic, green slacks, carrying a bag."

"Dunno," repeated the gardener. "I mean, like hard to remember."

"Have a beer on me," I said, my heartbeat accelerating. I slipped him the coin.

"Cat went in· about fifteen minutes ago. Said he was doing the Sonaclean repair bit, like."

That was a good gimmick. Having your things cleaned with super-sonics is expensive, but once you've bought the apparatus it's so damned automatic it diagnoses its own troubles and calls for its own service men. I took the porch steps fast and leaned on the chimes. A voice from the scanner cooed, "How do you do, sir. Your business, please."

"I'm from Sonaclean," I snapped. "Something appears to be wrong with your set."

"We have a repairman here now, sir."

"The continuator doesn't mesh with the hypostat. We got an alarm. You'd better let me talk to him."

"Very good, sir. One moment, please."

I waited for about sixty geological epochs till the door was opened manually, by the same house maintenance technician who'd quizzed me. I'd know that pigeon voice in hell, where as a matter of fact I was.

"This way, please, sir." She led me down a hall, past a library loaded with books and microspools, and opened a panel on a downward stair. "Straight that way."

I looked into fluorescent brightness. Perhaps, I thought in a remote volume of myself, death is not black; perhaps death is just this featureless luminosity, forever. I went down the stairs.

The brains as well as the guts and sinews of the house were down here. A monitor board blinked many red eyes at me; a dust precipitator buzzed within an air shaft. I looked across the glazed plastic floor and saw my man beside an open Sonaclean. His tools were spread out in front of him, and he stood in a posture that looked easy but wasn't. If need be, he could lift his arm and shoot in the same motion that drop-ped him on the floor and bounced him sideways. And yet his face was kindly, the eyes tired, the skin sagging a bit with surgical middle age.

"Hello," he said. "What brings you here?"

He wasn't expecting anyone from the company, of course. He'd disconnected the Sonaclean the moment he arrived. I didn't believe he meant to plant a bomb, or any such elaborate deal. He'd fiddle around a while, put the machine back together, go upstairs. Maybe this was simply a reconnoitering expedition, or maybe he knew where Morales was and would slay him this same day. Yes, probably the latter.

He'd slip to Juan Morales' study, kill him with a single karate chop, arrange a rug or stool to make the death look accidental, come back to the head of this stairway, and take his leave. Quite likely no one would ever check with the Sonaclean people. Even if somebody did, my man would have vanished long ago; and he was unmemorable. Here, now, a few meters from him, realizing he must have a gun beneath his tunic sleeve, I found it hard to fix him in my mind. That mediocrity was the work of a great artist.

Was he, even, the one I sought? His costume combination was being worn this instant by a million harmless citizens; his face was anyone's; the sole deadliness might be housed in my own sick brain.

I grunted. "Air filter inspection."

He turned back to his dojiggling with the machine. And I knew that he was my man.

He took seconds to comprehend what I had said. An American would have protested at once, "Hey, this is Saturday—" As he whipped about on his heel, my right arm lifted.

Our guns hissed together, but mine was aimed. He lurched back from sheer impact. The needle stood full in his neck. For an instant he sagged against the wall, then blindness seized his eyes. I crouched, waiting for him to lose consciousness.

Instead, the lips peeled from his teeth, his spine arched, and he left the wall in a stiff rigadoon. While he screamed, I cursed and ran up the stairs, three at a time.

The housie came into the library from the opposite side. "What's the matter?" she cried. "Wait! Wait, you can't—"

I was already at the phone. I fended her off with an elbow while I dialed local HQ, emergency extension. That's one line which is always open, with human monitors, during a state of assassination. I rattled off my identification number said: "I'm at 2878 Buena Vista, Berkeley. Get a revival squad here. Regular police, if our own medics aren't handy. I plugged one of the opposition with a sleepydart, but they seem to have found some means of sensitizing. He went straight into tetany. . . . 2878 Buena Vista, yes. Snap to it, and we may still get some use out of him!"

The woman wailed behind me as I pounded back down the stairs. My man was dead, hideously rigid on the floor. I picked him up. A corpse isn't really heavier than an organic, but it feels that way.

"The deep freeze!" I roared. "Where the obscenity is your freezer? If we can keep the process from—Don't stand there and gawp! Every second at room temperature, more of his brain cells are disintegrating! Do you want them to revive an idiot?"

If he could be resurrected at all. I wasn't sure what had been done to his biochemistry, to make him react so to plain old neurocaine. For his sake I could almost hope he wouldn't be viable. I could have done worse in life than be a trigger man, I guess: might have ended on an interrogation team. Not that prisoners undergo torture, nothing that crude, but—oh, well.

The housie squealed, nearly fainted, but finally led me to a chest behind the kitchen. After which she ran off again. I dumped out several hundred dollars' worth of food to make room for my burden.

As I closed the lid, Dr. Juan Morales arrived. He was quite pale, but he asked me steadily, "What happened to that man?"

"I think he had a heart attack." I mopped my face and sat down on the coldbox; my knees were like rubber.

Morales stood a while, regarding me. Some of his color returned, but a bleakness was also gathering in him. "Miss Thomas said something about your using a needle gun," he told me, very low.

"Miss Thomas babbles," I replied.

I saw his fists clench till the knuckles stood white. "I have a family to think of," he said. "Doesn't that give me a right to know the truth?"

I sighed. "Could be. Come on, let's talk privately. Afterward you can persuade Miss Thomas she misheard me on the phone. Best to keep this off the newscasts, you realize."

He led me to this study, seated me, and poured some welcome brandy. Having refilled the glasses and offered cigars, he sat down too. The room was comfortable and masculine, lined with books, a window opening on the bayview grandeur. We smoked in a brief and somehow friendly silence.

At last he said, "I take it you're from the Bureau of National Protection."

I nodded. "Been chasing that fellow. He gave me the slip. I didn't know where he was headed, but I got a hunch that turned out to be correct."

"But why me?" he breathed—the question which every man must ask, at least once in this life.

I chose to interpret it literally. "They weren't after Senator

Greenstein or the other big politicos, not really," I said. "They simply picked this time to strike because they knew most of our manpower would be occupied, giving them a clear field everywhere else. I was wrestling with the problem of what they actually planned to do, and a bit from your lecture came back to me."

"My lecture?" His laugh was nervous, but it meant much that he could laugh in any fashion. "Which one?"

"On the vid earlier today. About the evolution of war. You were remarking on how it started as a way to break the enemy's will, and finished trying to destroy the enemy himself—not only armies, but factories, fields, cities, women, children. You were speculating if assassination might not develop along similar lines. Evidently it has."

"But me . . . I am no one! A university president, a minor local figure in a party that lost the last election—"

"It's still a major party," I said. "Its turn will come again one of these years. You're among its best thinkers, and young as politicians go. Wilson and Eisenhower were once university presidents too."

I saw a horror in his eyes, and it was less for himself, who must now live under guard and fear, than for all of us. But that, I suppose, is one of the reasons he was a target.

"Sure," I said, "they're gunning for the current President, for Senator Greenstein, for the other Americans who stand in their way in this crisis. Maybe they'll succeed, maybe they won't. In either case, it won't be the last such conflict. They're looking ahead—twenty years, thirty years. As long as we have a state of assassination anyway, they figure they might as well weaken us for the future by killing off our most promising leaders of the next generation."

I heard a siren. That must be the revival squad. I rose. "You might try to guess who else they'll hunt," I told him. "Three other operatives are loose that I know of, and we may not extract enough information from the one I got."

He shook his head in a blind, dazed way. "I'm thinking of more than that," he said. "It's like being one of the old atomic scientists on Hiroshima Day. Suddenly an academic proposition has become real."

I paused at the door. He went on, not looking at me, talking only to his nightmare:

"It's more than the coming necessity of guarding every man who could possibly interest them—though God knows that will be a heavy burden, and when we have to start guarding every gifted child. . . . It's more, even, than our own retaliation in kind; more than the targets spreading, from potential leaders to potential scientists to potential teachers and artists and I dare not guess what else. It's that the bounds have been broken.

"I see the rules laid aside once more, in the future. Sneak-attack assassinations. Undeclared assassinations. Assassination with massive weapons that take a thousand bystanders. Permanent states of assassination, dragging on for decade after decade, and no reason for them except the gnawing down of the others because they are the others.

"Whole populations mobilized against the hidden enemy, with each man watching his neighbor like a shark, with privacy, decency, freedom gone. Where is it going to end?" he asked the sky and the broad waters. "Where is it going to end?"

Harry Harrison made clear his contempt for war and warriors in his satirical novel Bill, the Galactic Hero. *Strangely enough, he looks and talks like a casting director's dream for the part of a crusty field-grade officer, come up from the ranks. A quick stocky man with close-cropped white hair, he is usually angry about something and prepared to defend his point of view with a staccato thousand words a minute—in any of five languages—and erudition equal to any opponent.*

Being science fiction's foremost Esperanto freak, the compleat internationalist, Harry would naturally write a story showing a way the passions and energies of war might be used to bring the various peoples of the world closer together.

This method has been tried, you're going to say, and wasn't exactly a smashing success. But maybe they just didn't try hard enough.

COMMANDO RAID

By Harry Harrison

Private Truscoe and the captain had left the truck, parked out of sight in the jungle, and had walked a good hundred yards further down the road. They were crouched now in the dense shadows of the trees, with the silver light of the full moon picking out every rut and hollow of the dirt track before them.

"Be quiet!" the captain whispered, putting a restraining hand on the soldier's arm, listening. Truscoe held his breath and struggled to keep absolutely still. Captain Carter was a legendary jungle fighter, with the scars and medals to prove it. If he thought there was something dangerous, creeping closer in the darkness . . . Truscoe suppressed an involuntary shudder.

"It's all right," the captain said, this time in a normal speaking tone. "Something big out there, buffalo or deer. But it's downwind and it took off as soon as it caught our smell. You can smoke if you want to."

The soldier hesitated, not sure how to answer. Finally, he said, "Sir, aren't we supposed . . . I mean someone could see the flame?"

"We're not hiding, Private Truscoe. William—do they call you Billy?"

"Why, yes sir."

"We picked this spot, Billy, because none of the locals normally come this way at night. Light up. The smoke will let all the wildlife know that we're here and they'll keep their distance. They are a lot more afraid of us than you are of them. And our informant can find us by the smell too. One whiff and he'll know that it's not the local leaf. That trail over there leads to the village and he'll probably come that way."

Billy looked but could see neither trail nor opening in the jungle wall where the officer pointed. But if the captain said so it had to be true. He clutched his M-16 rifle tightly and looked around at the buzzing, clattering darkness.

"It's not so much the critters out there, sir. I've done plenty of hunting in Alabama and I know this gun can stop anything around. Except maybe another gun. I mean, this geek, sir, the one that's coming. Isn't he kind of a traitor? You know, if he finks on his own people how do we know he won't do the same to us?"

Carter's voice was patient and gave no indication of how much he loathed the work *geek*.

"The man's an informant, not a traitor, and he is more eager than we are for this deal to go through. He was originally a refugee from a village in the south, one that was wiped out by that earthquake some years back. You have to understand that these people are very provincial, and he'll be a 'foreigner' in this village as long as he lives. His wife is dead, he has nothing to stay here for. When we approached him for information he jumped at the chance. We'll pay him enough so that he won't ever have to work again. He'll retire to a village close to the one where he was raised. It's a good deal."

Billy was emboldened by the darkness and the presence of the solitary officer. "Still, seems sort of raw for the people he lived with. Selling them out."

"No one is being sold out." The captain was much more positive now. "What we are doing for them is for their own good. They may not see it that way now, but it is. It is the long-term results that count."

The captain sounded a little peeved. Billy shifted uneasily and did not answer. He should have remembered you don't talk to officers like they were real people or something.

"Stand up, here he comes," Carter said.

Billy had the feeling that maybe the captain could have outhunted him even in his own stand of woods back in Alabama. He neither saw nor heard a thing. Only when the short, turbaned figure appeared at their sides did he know that the informant had arrived.

"*Tuan?*" the man whispered, and Carter spoke to him quietly in his own tongue. It was so much geek talk to Billy: they had had lectures on the language, but he had never bothered to listen. When they stepped out into the flood of moonlight he saw that the man was a typical geek, too. Scrawny and little and old. There was more cloth in the turban than in his loincloth. All of his possessions, the accumulation of a lifetime, were rolled in a straw mat that he carried in one hand. And he sounded frightened.

"Let's get back to the truck," Captain Carter ordered. "He won't talk here. Too afraid the villagers will find him."

He'd got cause to worry, Billy thought, following the disproportionate pair back down the road. The captain was half bent over as he talked to the little man.

. Once the truck had coughed to life and the driver was tooling her back to camp the informant relaxed. He talked steadily in a high, birdlike voice, and the captain put a sheet of paper on his map case and sketched in the details of the village and the surrounding area. Billy nodded, bored, with his rifle between his legs, looking forward to some chow and hitting the sack. There was an all-night cook in the MP mess who would fry up steak and eggs for you if you were on night duty. The voice twittered on and the map grew.

"Don't want to drop government property, do you, Billy?" Carter asked, and Billy realized that he had dozed off and the M-16 had fallen from his fingers. But the captain had caught it and held it safe for him. The sharp blue illumination of the mercury vapor lights of the camp poured into the open back of the truck. Billy opened his mouth, but did not know what to say. Then the officer was gone, with the tiny native scrambling after him, and Billy was alone. He jumped down, boots squelching in the mud, and stretched. Even though the captain had saved his neck rather than report him, he still wasn't sure whether he liked him or not.

Less than three hours after he had fallen asleep the light came on above him in the tent, and the recorded notes of reveille sawed out of the speaker mounted next to it. Billy blinked at his watch and saw that it was just after two.

"What the hell is all this about?" someone shouted. "Another damn night maneuver?"

Billy knew, but before he could open his mouth the CO came on the speaker and told them first.

"We're going in, men. This is it. The first units jump off in two hours' time. H Hour will be at first light, at exactly 0515. Your unit commanders will give you complete and detailed instructions before we roll. Full field packs. This is what you have been training for—and this is the moment that you have been waiting for. Don't get rattled, do your job, and don't believe all the latrine rumors that you hear. I'm talking particularly to you new men. I know you have been chewed out a lot, and you have been called 'combat virgins' and a lot worse. Forget it. You're a team now—and after tomorrow you won't even be virgins."

The men laughed at that, but not Billy. He recognized the old bushwa when it was being fed to him. At home, at school, it was the same old crap. Do or die for our dear old High. Crap.

"Let's go, let's go," the sergeant shouted, throwing open the flap of the tent. "We don't have all night and you guys are creeping around like grandmas in a sack race."

That was more like it. The sergeant didn't horse around. With him you knew just where you stood, all the time.

"Roll the packs tighter, they look like they're stuffed full of turds." The sergeant had never really taken the orders on use of language to heart.

It was still hot, dark and hot and muggy, and Billy could feel the sweat already soaking into his clean dungarees. They double-timed to chow, stuffed it down, and double-timed back. Then, packs on backs, they lined up at the QM stores for field issue. A tired and yellowish corporal signed in Billy's M-16, checked the serial number, then handed him a Mark-13 and a sack of reloads. The cool metal slipped through Billy's hands and he almost dropped it.

"Keep that flitgun out of the mud or you'll be signing a statement of charges for life." The corporal growled, by reflex, and was already turning to the next man.

Billy gave him the finger—as soon as his back was turned—and went out into the company street. Under a light he looked at the riot gun, turning it over and over. It was new, right out of the cosmoline, smooth and shining, with a wide stock, a thick barrel, and a thicker receiver. Heavy, too, eighteen pounds, but he didn't mind.

"Fall in, fall in," the sergeant was still in good voice.

They fell into ranks and waited at ease for a long time. Hurry up and wait, it was always like this, and Billy slipped a piece of gum into his mouth when all the noncoms had their backs turned, then chewed it slowly. His squad was finally called out and dogtrotted off to the copters, where Captain Carter was waiting.

"Just one thing before we board," the captain said. "You men here are in the shock squad and you have the dirty work to do. I want you to stay behind me at all times, in loose order, and watch on all sides and still watch me at the same time. We can expect trouble. But no matter what happens, do not—and I repeat that—do *not* act upon your own initiative. Look to me for orders. We want this to be a model operation and we don't want any losses."

He unrolled a big, diagrammatic map, then pointed to the front rank. "You two men, hold this up so the others can see. This is the target we are going to hit. The village is on the river, with the rice fields between it and the houses. The hovercraft will come in right over the fields, so no one will get out that way. There is a single dirt road in through the jungle, and that will be plugged, and there will be squads on every trail out of there. The villagers can dive into the jungle if they want, but they won't get far. They'll have to cut their way through and we can follow them easily and bring them back. There are men assigned to all these duties and they will all be in position at H Hour. Then we hit. We come in low and fast so we can sit down in the center of the houses, in this open spot, before anyone even knows that we are on the way. If we do it right the only resistance will be the dogs and chickens."

"Shoot the dogs and eat the chickens," someone shouted from the back, and everyone laughed. The captain smiled slightly to know that he appreciated the joke, but disapproved of chatter while they were fallen in. He tapped the map.

"As we touch down the other units will move in. The headman in the village, this is his house here, is an old rogue with military service and a bad temper. Everyone will be too shocked to provide much resistance—unless he orders it. I'll take care of him. Now—are there any questions?" He looked around at the silent men. "All right then, let's load up."

The big, double-rotored copters squatted low, their wide doors close to the ground. As soon as the men were aboard, the starters whined and the long blades began to turn slowly. The operation had begun.

When they rose above the trees they could see the lightening of the eastern horizon. They stayed low, their wheels almost brushing the leaves, like a flock of ungainly birds of prey. It wasn't a long flight, but the sudden tropical dawn was on them almost before they realized it.

The ready light flashed on and the captain came down from the cockpit and gave them the thumbs-up signal. They went in.

It was a hard landing, almost a drop, and the doors banged open as they touched. The shock squad hit the ground and Captain Carter went first.

The pounded dirt compound was empty. The squad formed on the captain and watched the doorways of the rattan-walled buildings, where people were beginning to appear. The surprise had been absolute. There was the grumble of truck engines from the direction of the road and a roar of sound from the river. Billy glanced that way and saw the hovercraft moving over the paddies in a cloud of spray. Then he jumped, raising the riot gun, as a shrill warbling ripped at his ears.

It was the captain. He had a voice gun with a built-in siren. The sound wailed, shriller and shriller, then died away as he flipped the switch. He raised it and spoke into the microphone, and his voice filled the village.

Billy couldn't understand the geek talk, but it sounded impressive. For the first time he realized that the captain was unarmed—and even wore a garrison cap instead of his helmet. That was taking a big chance. Billy raised the flitgun to the ready and glanced around at the people who were slowly emerging from the houses.

Then the captain pointed toward the road and his echoing voice stopped. All of the watching heads, as though worked by a single string, turned to look where he indicated. A half-track appeared, engine bellowing, trailing a thick column of dust. It braked, skidding to a stop, and a corporal jumped from the back and ran the few paces to the town well. He had a bulky object in his arms, which he dropped into the well—then dived aside.

With a sharp explosion the well blew up. Dirt flew and mud and water spattered down. The walls collapsed. Where the well had once been there remained only a shallow, smoking pit. The captain's voice cut through the shocked silence that followed.

Yet, even as his first amplified words swept the compound, a hoarse shout interrupted them. A gray-haired man had emerged from the headman's house. He was shouting, pointing at the captain, who waited, then answered back. He was interrupted before he was finished. The captain tried to argue, but the headman ran back inside the building.

He was fast. A moment later he came out—with an archaic steel helmet on his head, waving a long-bladed sword over his head. There hadn't been a helmet made like that in forty years. And a *sword*. Billy almost laughed out loud until he realized that the headman was playing it for real. He ran at the captain, sword raised, ignoring the captain's voice completely. It was like watching a play, being in a play, with no one moving and only the captain and the old man playing their roles.

The headman wasn't listening. He attacked, screeching, and brought the sword down and around in a wicked, decapitating cut. The captain blocked the blow with the voice gun, which coughed and died. He was still trying to reason with the old man, but his voice sounded smaller and different now—and the headman wasn't listening.

Twice he struck, and a third time, and each time the captain backed away a bit and parried with the voice gun, which was rapidly being reduced to battered junk. As the sword came up again, the captain called back over his shoulder.

"Private Truscoe, take this man out. This has gone far enough."

Billy was well trained and knew what to do without even thinking about it. A step forward, the flitgun raised to his shoulder and aimed, the safety off, and when the old man's head filled the sight he squeezed off the shot.

With a throat-clearing cough the cloud of compressed gas blasted out and struck the headman full in the face.

"Masks on," Captain Carter ordered, and once more the movement was automatic.

Small of the stock in his left hand, right hand free, grasp the handle (gas mask, actuating) under the brim of his helmet, and pull. The transparent plastic reeled down and he hooked it under his chin. All by the numbers.

But then something went wrong. The Mace-IV that the flitgun expelled was supposed to take anyone out. Down and out. But the headman was not going down. He was retching, his belly working in and out uncontrollably, while the vomit ran down his chin and onto his bare chest. He still clutched the long sword and, with his free hand, he threw his helmet to the ground and pried open one streaming eye. He must have made out Billy's form through his tears, because he turned from the captain and came on, sword raised, staggering.

Billy brought the flitgun up, but it was in his left hand and he couldn't fire. He changed the grip, fumbling with it, but the man was still coming on. The sword glistened as the rising sun struck it.

Billy swung the gun around like a club and caught the headman across the temple with a thick barrel. The man pitched face forward to the ground and was still.

Billy pointed the gun down at him and pulled the trigger, again and again, the gas streaming out and covering the sprawled figure. . .

Until the captain knocked the gun from his hand and pulled him about, almost throwing him to the ground.

"Medic!" The captain shouted then, almost whispering through his clenched teeth, "You fool, you fool."

Billy just stood, dazed, trying to understand what had happened, as the ambulance pulled up. There were injections, cream on the man's face, oxygen from a tank, then he was loaded onto a stretcher and the doctor came over.

"It's touch and go, captain. Possible skull fracture, and he breathed in a lot of your junk. How did it happen?"

"It will be in my report," Captain Carter answered in a toneless voice.

The doctor started to speak, thought better of it, and turned and climbed into the ambulance. It pulled away, dodging around the big trucks that were coming into the village. The people were out of the houses now, huddled in knots, talking under their breaths. There would be no more resistance.

Billy was aware that the captain was looking at him, looking as if he wanted to kill. The gas mask was suddenly hot on Billy's face and he pulled it free.

"It wasn't my fault, sir," Billy explained. "He just came at me. . ."

"He came at me too. I didn't fracture his skull. It *was* your fault."

"No, it's not. Not when some old geek swings a rusty damn pig-sticker at me."

"He is not a geek, Private, but a citizen of this country and a man of stature in this village. He was defending his home and was within his rights—"

Billy was angry now. He knew it was all up with him and the Corps and his plans, and he didn't give a damn. He turned to the officer, fists clenched.

"He's a crummy geek from geeksville, and if he got rights what are we doing here, just tell me that?"

The captain was coldly quiet now. "We were invited here by the country's President and the Parliament, you know that as well as I do." His voice was drowned out as a truck passed close by and the exhaust blatted out at them. It stopped and men jumped down and began to unload lengths of plastic piping. Billy looked the captain square in the eye and told him off, what he had always wanted to say.

"In a pig's ass we were invited here. Some bigshot these local geeks never heard of says okay and we drop down their throats and spend a couple billion dollars of the US taxpayers' money to give some geeks the good life they don't know nothing about and don't need—so what the hell!" He shouted the last words. The captain was much quieter.

"I suppose it would be better if we helped them the way we helped in Vietnam? Came in and burned them and shot them and blasted them right back to the Stone Age?"

Another truck stopped and began unloading sinks, toilets, electric stoves.

"Well, why not? Why not! If they trouble Uncle Sam—then knock them out. We don't need anything from these kind of broken-down raggedy people. Now Uncle Sam is Uncle Sap and taking care of the world and the taxpayers are footing the bill. . ."

"Shut up and listen, Private." There was an edge to the captain's voice that Billy had never heard before and he shut up. "I don't know how you got into the Aid Corps, but I do know that you don't belong in it. This is one world and it gets smaller every year. The Eskimos in the Arctic have DDT poisoning from the farms in the Midwest. The strontium ninety from a French atom test in the Pacific gives bone cancer to a child in New York. This is spaceship Earth and we're all aboard it together, trying to stay alive on it. The richest countries better help the poorest ones because it's all the same spaceship. And it's already almost too late. In Vietnam we spent five million dollars a head to kill the citizens of that country, and our profit was the undying hatred of everyone there, both north and south, and the loathing of the civilized world. We've made our mistakes, now let's profit from them.

"For far less than one thousandth of the cost of killing a man, and making his friends our enemies, we can save a life and make the man our friend. Two hundred bucks a head, that's what this operation costs. We've blown up the well here because it was a cesspit of infection, and we are drilling a new well to bring up pure water from the strata below. We are putting toilets into the houses, and sinks. We are killing the disease-breeding insects. We are running in power lines and bringing in a medical mission to save their lives. We are opening a birth-control clinic so they can have families like people, not breed like rats and pull the world down with them. They are going to have scientific agriculture so they can eat better, and education so they can be more than working animals. We are going to bring them about five percent of the 'benefits' you enjoy in the sovereign state of Alabama and we are doing it from selfish motives. We want to stay alive. But at least we are doing it."

The captain looked at his clenched fist, then slowly opened it. "Sergeant," he called out as he turned away. "Put this man under arrest and see that he is sent back to the camp at once."

A crate of flush toilets thudded to the ground almost at Billy's feet and a thread of hot anger snapped inside of him. Who were these people to get waited on like this? He had grown up in a sharecropper's shack and had never seen a toilet like these until he was more than eight years old. Now he had to help give them away too. . .

"Niggers, that's what these people are! And we give them everything on a silver platter. It's bleeding hearts like you, Captain, crying your eyes out for these poor helpless people, that are causing the trouble!"

Captain Carter stopped, and slowly turned about. He looked at the young man who stood before him and felt only a terrible feeling of depression.

"No, Private William Truscoe, I don't cry for these people. I don't cry. But if I ever could—I would cry for you."

After that he went away.

*George Alec Effinger once confided in me that he had
never written a killing or an overtly sexual scene into a
story—not that he couldn't, or that he thought such writing
reprehensible. His stories just didn't evolve along those lines.*

*So the following story, written especially for this volume,
might be something of a landmark. Effinger kills off people
here, by ones and twos and dozens and cities.*

*It's interesting to compare "Curtains" with the story that
follows it, by Mack Reynolds (who has been gleefully
dispatching people with his typewriter for twenty years);
since both of them consider a future where soldiers are
performers, and wars are choreographed shows. The
difference is in what motivates the performers. And who
watches them.*

CURTAINS
by George Alec Effinger

It seemed to Sgt. Weinraub that they only had two kinds of
weather on the battlefield. Sometimes it was unbelievably cold, so that
the ragged little troupe huddled beneath torn blankets and tried to
thaw its bandaged fingers with warm cups of thin coffee. Just as often it
was blisteringly hot, and the weight of the rifle alone was enough to
drive a soldier crazy. On the endless marches beneath the fiery sun the
soldiers dropped pieces of equipment to lighten their burden; their
trail could easily be followed, as one essential item after another was
discarded in the dust. Then later, when the weather grew suddenly
icy, the men cursed themselves for losing the very things that might
keep them alive. There was never any moderate climate; it was either
cold or very, very hot.

Today it was sweltering beneath the blazing sun. The seventy-five
men were resting in the scant shade of a few stumpy trees. Weinraub
looked at them for a moment. They leaned against the gnarled trunks
wearily, eyes shut, faces shiny with sweat, beards black, mouths open.
No one talked. No one smoked or laughed. They all sat there, panting
in the heat, waiting for Weinraub to order them to fall in. He was in
no hurry, himself. But they had a mission to accomplish.

Master sergeant Steve Weinraub was trying to put up a good
front for the men. The command had fallen to him suddenly, and he
hadn't adjusted to the responsibility yet. But that made no practical
difference at all. He was expected to perform as though he had been

trained for the job. He walked over to one of the men. "I want to talk with you, Corporal Staefler," he said.

The man looked up. He said nothing. Weinraub sighed and sat down in the dirt next to Staefler. "I'm going to hand you some of my old duties," said the sergeant. "Now that I have to look after all seventy-five of you, I don't have the time anymore."

"Sure," said Staefler flatly. "Like what?"

Weinraub slipped out of his pack's harness and rummaged among his personal effects. He brought out a small black book. "This is the company record book. I want you to carry it from now on. You can see how I've been working it. Just keep track of the reviews, paste them in, make the appropriate notes. It doesn't take that much time, but I just don't want to be bothered." Staefler took the book, looking past Weinraub, still too exhausted to waste energy talking. "I got the new *Stars and Stripes* here," said Weinraub. "Why don't you cut out the review on our next rest stop?"

"What did they say?"

Sgt. Weinraub turned the pages until he found the right place. " 'On The Home Front'," read the sergeant. " 'By Brig. Gen. Robert W. Hanson'."

"Hanson!" said Staefler. "How did we rate him? I didn't think he bothered to notice us poor slobs."

"He was right out there, last time," said Weinraub. "*I* saw him. I figure Lt. Marquand must have heard ahead of time."

Staefler spit into the dust. "Yeah," he said softly. "I wish I'd known."

" 'And then there's Delta Company,' " said Weinraub, continuing to read from the magazine, " 'a rather shabby troupe seemingly dedicated to defending our borders in the tritest ways imaginable. This week, in preparation for the first great offensive of the war, rumored to be a massive invasion of the European enemy's homeland, Delta Company attempted to consolidate its gains of the previous months. There was no secret about the importance of this performance. But, for some reason, the company dragged out the oldest, silliest ploy known to modern warfare. Dressed in civilian clothes, the company divided itself into two equal 'gangs' and staged a sort of teenage street fight. I don't know about my colleagues, but I myself have grown excessively weary of such tired examples of low-level creativity.' "

"Uh oh," said Staefler. "Sounds like he didn't like us."

"Yeah," said Weinraub. " 'The farce continued in predictable fashion until the company's senior officer, Lt. Rod Marquand, cried out against the injustice of the soldier's fate and threw himself on an opponent's switchblade knife. Although the stunned look on the face of the poor soldier holding the blade was worth a few minutes of the tedious exhibition, Marquand's cheap tactic destroyed whatever tiny shred of interest the performance may have generated. When will we have enough of sordid emotionalism and such sensational novelties as Marquand's? I suspect not until the officers responsible have learned to their dismay the results they may earn; we can hope these officers will take heed from Marquand's poor example, but I fear that's asking too much. We shall see.' "

"I want to know something," said Staefler. "You're telling me that Lt. Marquand got himself killed to save us, and this idiot Hanson is saying it was all for nothing?"

Weinraub closed the magazine and handed it to the other man. "Seems like it."

"And now you're in charge?"

Weinraub nodded. That was the same question he kept asking himself.

"I know what you better not do," said Staefler bitterly. "You better not throw yourself on any bayonets."

"Right," said Sgt. Weinraub. "Okay, men," he called. "Fall in."

Over a year before, when the war first began, Weinraub and others like him had been very excited. He could remember the declaration itself with strange clarity. The Representative of North America had appeared on television one evening after dinner. There had been no advance notice. The situation comedy re-run had ended, the station had played a couple of commercials, and then the handsome face of the Representative filled the screen. Weinraub had glanced across the room at his wife, who was sewing. "Hey," he said. "It's the Representative." She had looked up and smiled, but otherwise had shown no interest in what the Representative had to say.

"Good evening, my fellow citizens of North America," he said. "I come before you tonight to make an announcement that will affect you all, and to explain the situation so that you may understand the reasons behind my decision. As of midnight tonight, New York time, the North American people will be officially at war with the people of Europe. It has been many years since our two great continents have engaged in such a conflict, but nevertheless I feel that you will all support me now, and come to the defense of our noble land."

The next morning the newspapers reported plans for the first draft call for the North American Havoc Forces since the end of the African war, six years before. Seized by the powerful patriotic spirit, Weinraub had not waited to be called. He was proud to be the first citizen of his tiny Pennsylvania hometown to enlist. In the months since then he had distinguished himself in a modest way, enough to warrant promotion to master sergeant. And now, with the fruitless death of Lt. Marquand, Weinraub found himself in command of an increasingly discontent force. He understood that the North American invasion of Europe could be adversely affected, even ruined, by the performance of his Delta Company. But he didn't like to think about that.

The Delta Company was only one small theater of operations, of course. But one couldn't hide from the critical gaze of the Representatives. Even though the little band of soldiers thought themselves isolated and ineffectual, so mythic a figure as General Hanson had been assigned to observe one of their actions. Weinraub had no idea if Hanson would be there again in four days, when Delta Company was scheduled for another. He thought about the review, and prayed that someone out of the NAHF would be sent.

The column marched slowly, shuffling through the dry dust of the road. The sun was going down at last, but the heat did not abate. When it got too dark, Weinraub called a halt and the men moved off the trail to make camp for the night. He threw his own things down next to Staefler.

"You got any ideas yet?" asked the corporal.

"Yeah, I'm working on something. Nothing definite. Nothing I want to talk about yet."

"You'd think the NAHF guys would give us a break," said Staefler, still burning over the bad notice Lt. Marquand's sacrifice had received. "I mean, we're on the same side."

"I don't think so," said Weinraub. In the light of the campfire, he could see that Staefler was giving him a quizzical look. The sergeant hurried to explain. "Well, look," he said. "Sometimes we get an African attaché assigned to review us, sometimes an Asian, sometimes even a European. And they're the enemy. But they're all answerable to their particular Representative, and those guys are a lot rougher on their juniors than you think. The military liaison fellows have an awful short lifespan unless they play clean. As a matter of fact, we can usually count on worse treatment from one of our own than from some neutral power. That way the Representatives won't think the NAHF man is favoring us."

"And the whole system works fine," said Staefler. "But only as long as the Representatives are honest. What do they get out of it? I could never understand that. They must have some kind of deal worked out. And if the Representatives aren't on the level, what we're doing is really kind of pointless."

"Shut up, corporal," said Weinraub sharply.

"Sorry, sir." Staefler spit into the dust again and moved away from the fire. A couple of the privates waited until Staefler had gone, then moved into the circle of firelight.

"We heard about Lt. Marquand's review," said one of the men. "We were wondering if it was true."

"Yeah, Nicholl," said Sgt. Weinraub. "*Stars and Stripes* didn't seem too thrilled."

Another man tossed a few branches into the fire. "Was it really Gen. Hanson that wrote the review?"

"Yeah. He's one of the *new* critics. I don't really know what they want."

"We better find out some way," said the second man. "Any idea what's going to happen with the Evaluation?"

"Not yet," said Weinraub. "Lt. Marquand had a fine record going until that idiot Hanson spoiled it. The Evaluations have been pretty good to us. We haven't lost that many men, and the NAHF has gained a lot of ground on our account. This one flop shouldn't hurt us too bad."

"Maybe if we look at what's happening on the other fronts, we can get a better notion of what they want," said Nicholl.

"I don't know," said Sgt Weinraub. "Some South American company did the Battle of Maldon thing. You know, a losing cause but loyal warriors, fighting to the last man to avenge the death of their stupid leader. I would have figured that would really tickle the audience, the whole company of them going out in a huge blaze of glory. But the review just said something about 'pyrotechnic nonsense'. They want simple, basic stuff these days. The tear-jerkers aren't getting points anymore."

"I heard where South America is really losing," said a third soldier. "Asia managed to wipe out most of the Brazilian coast a couple of months ago, and the SAHF is going all out. They wasted that whole company for a major retaliation, but I guess it didn't work out."

"Asia killed off the Brazilian coast?" asked Nicholl. "I didn't know about that. I was just down there about four years ago."

"From what I hear, you won't be able to go back there for a while," said Weinraub. "It's going to be a long time before it cools down."

"What about Africa?" asked the second man.

"Nothing for sure," said Weinraub. "Rumors are that Africa's going to declare against Asia. That would be good news for South America."

"I don't know that they'd be much good," said Nicholl. "We took care of most of Africa's bigger production companies seven years ago."

Sgt. Weinraub stood up, his cramped legs aching. "You got to remember that the Representatives try to keep their own domains in the running," he said. "The Representative of Africa is as shrewd as any of them."

"Yeah," said the second soldier, "and I bet they all got some kind of helping-hand fund to dip into."

"That's pretty rotten talk," said Weinraub. "I'm tired of hearing you idiots going on like that. It shows a lack of discipline. Lt. Marquand was a good officer. He didn't allow that kind of thinking, and I won't, either."

There were a few mumbled "Yes, sarges", but Weinraub paid little attention. He was looking for Staefler. The new action had to be planned, and the necessary materiel requisitioned. He found Staefler sitting among a group of men, all of them arguing loudly about the death of Lt. Marquand.

"Corporal," said Weinraub, "would you come here for a minute? We have less than four days now, and I want you to help me go over the outline."

"All right," said Staefler. He stood and followed the sergeant to where a couple of privates were setting up the senior officer's tent.

"Sit down," said Weinraub. "I wish these guys would finish putting up the HQ already. Never mind, we can talk here. Frankly, I want your advice. I've never planned an entire action by myself; it's also no secret that you're the most talented man in the company, now that Lt. Marquand's dead."

"Thank you, sarge," said Staefler. "I'm pleased you feel that way."

"Not at all. But it does load certain responsibilities on you. The rest of these soldiers don't really have much to worry about. A couple of them win parts in each action, but every time there's less to choose from. Do you follow me? Every one of us *wants* to be used. I mean, that's why we're here. We all want to give the best performance we're capable of; otherwise the EHF will crush North America, and then there'll be no stopping them. But the commanding officer has it a whole lot harder. He has to compromise between spending all his talent on one big action, and reserving material for the next one. And most of all, he has to exercise judgment in choosing his own role."

"You making a dig at Lt. Marquand?" asked Staefler angrily.

"No, no. I was just trying to say that I have to play an active and important part, but still keep myself able to continue in command. It's a very critical job of planning."

"I think the best thing now is to play it conservative," said Staefler. "It's pretty clear that the brass isn't looking for the kind of stuff we were giving them at the beginning of the war."

"Yeah, right," said Weinraub. "Straight out of Clausewitz. He always hated the kind of complicated stratagems our newer officers are so crazy about. Clausewitz said the best thing was just to hit the enemy in the face, hard."

"Hanson's bunch of critics is going back to old-fashioned themes," said Staefler thoughtfully. "We have to come up with something traditional. Make it short and simple. When I was in school, my coaches never stopped telling me that the professional athlete needs concentration, total commitment, and good form. The guys that don't make it are looking for easy ways around the hard work."

"All right," said Weinraub. "Instead of trying to burn out the observers' mind with a flash of brilliant footwork, let's come up with something nice and substantial." The two men chatted while the privates completed putting up the company headquarters. Then they went into the tent and began drawing up the first outline of the action.

The next morning, as Weinraub was eating his spare field rations, a soldier called into the tent that a command jeep was approaching along the road.

"Thanks, private," said Sgt. Weinraub, hurriedly putting on his trousers and buttoning his tunic. "That has to be the brass with the Evaluation of our last action. Have the men police the area. I don't want a prejudiced audience for the next one." He felt a tightening in his stomach, a fearful anticipation of what the Evaluation would say. He knew that at the same moment a copy of the Evaluation was being presented to the staff of the Representative of North America. All of the NAHF, in effect, was waiting anxiously with him.

He stepped out of the tent, into the torrid sun. The men were frantically trying to give the place an organized appearance, but the jeep was already rattling to a halt on the dusty track beside the camp. Weinraub took a deep breath and walked toward the waiting officers.

Before he had gone halfway, the sergeant realized that Gen. Hanson himself was waiting in the jeep. Weinraub suddenly felt light-headed; he wasn't sure that he could put on a cool show now, knowing what kind of an Evaluation he could expect. He took another breath, saluted, and presented himself to the officers.

Master Sergeant Weinraub, acting commanding officer of Delta Company," he said, his mouth dry and his head still buzzing.

General Hanson returned his salute. "I've admired your work, Sgt. Weinraub," he said. "I've had the pleasure of following Delta Company for several months now, though I've only actually reviewed one of your actions."

"Will you be reviewing us again, sir?"

Hanson gave him a quick smile. "It's against our policy to advise the troupes along those lines, but, yes, I'll be writing the notices for your next action. That's three days from now, isn't it?"

"Yes, sir. We hope you like it, sir."

"I do, too," said the general, giving Weinraub a piercing look. Even though Hanson was compelled to be impartial, it was clear that he was still a superior officer in the NAHF, and his private desires were in no way affected by his public duties. He reached into his tunic and took out a sealed red envelope. "Here is the Evaluation of Lt. Marquand's last action. I want you to study it. I want you to realize the importance of what you're doing, and take the appropriate precautions. Use your judgment, and use your good taste. I'm confident we won't have any more mistakes from this company. All of North America is counting on you." The general's driver started the jeep's engine at a signal from Hanson, and Weinraub took the envelope and saluted. He stood in place while the jeep's wheels spat gravel and dust, then clattered away down the road. He tore a strip from the side of the red envelope and slipped out the Evaluation sheet, meanwhile walking slowly back to the tent. When he got there he lay on the folding bunk and read the paper.

"Sgt. Weinraub?" It was Cpl. Staefler.

"Come in, corporal. Hear the bad news."

Staefler entered the tent and sat in the single camp chair by the bunk. "How bad is it?"

"You remember how Fox Company made some terrific coup and won a staging area in the south of England?"

"That was two or three months ago, right?"

"Yeah," said Weinraub. "We really needed it; without it we wouldn't be able to launch any kind of attack. We had to get on the offensive. Well, not only did the Europeans recapture that staging outpost, but three flights of long-range bombers got through the aerial defenses and wiped out Baltimore, Washington, and Charleston, South Carolina."

Staefler stared for several seconds, stunned by the harshness of the Evaluation. "They got *Washington*?" he said at last.

"That's not so bad," said Weinraub wearily. "The NAHF had twenty-four hour notice, and everything important was evacuated. What really hurts is the loss of the English base. We're right back where we were a year ago. The Europeans are taking their time, knocking out our cities one by one, and we haven't had the first shot at hitting them on their own ground."

"It's really up to us to get that base back, then," said Staefler.

"Yeah, we got to make it good. An advisory note in the Evaluation reported that some European troupe did an awful fine job in an action a few days ago, and when they get evaluated we may be in for a real tough time."

"There's at least three guys in the company from Baltimore and Washington. It'll be hard telling them the news. Especially since they still haven't gotten over the rotten review Lt. Marquand got. They all respected him. He was the best damn officer I ever knew."

"Look, do me a favor. Find out which of our men had families in those cities, and send them in to me. With the lieutenant gone, that's another ugly thing I have to do." Staefler gave him a sympathetic grin, turned, and left the tent. Weinraub was lost in thought until another corporal called in to ask if the men should be formed up for the day's march.

"No, thank you, corporal," said Weinraub. "We'll be staying here for a while longer. Let the men relax. I think I want to begin shaping up the new action." He was interrupted again a short time later by the men affected by the European raid. He handled the difficult task and dismissed the shocked soldiers with a few words of condolence. Then he went back to the job of devising a simple and effective action.

About noon, Weinraub left the tent to find Cpl. Staefler. The men were engaged in various improvised recreations: baseball, boxing, or just plain loafing. Staefler was standing in a circle about two huge soldiers, both of them naked to the waist and trading punches to the cheers of their fellows. Weinraub touched the corporal on the shoulder. Staefler immediately began to break up the fight, thinking that Weinraub disapproved. "No, don't interrupt them," said the sergeant. "Come on, I want you to hear what I've planned."

"Is it done?"

"Just about," said Weinraub. "If you help me put the finishing touches on it, we'll have almost three days to prepare. That's about thirty-six hours more than usual. There won't be any excuse for a foul-up."

"Great, but what can I do?"

Weinraub pulled a dead branch from one of the twisted trees as he passed. He was silent for several seconds, dragging the stick in the dirt and trying to frame what he wanted to say. "You know as well as I do that you're the best of the lot, Bo," he said finally. "There isn't time for modesty. If we don't do a first-class job this time out, the invasion may never get going, and who knows what the Representatives will award to the Europeans. This is going to be your show. I have to lead from strength, and you're it."

Staefler was stunned. "Look, Sarge, don't get me wrong. I've been nearly bursting for months now, waiting for Lt. Marquand to let me carry the ball. I knew I could do one hell of a good job. But now I'm not so sure. It's not that I'm afraid of what it means personally. I don't suppose any of us are, really. But this is such a *big* thing. . . ." His words faded away; the two men stopped along the side of the road, and Weinraub studied the corporal intently.

"It's not just for me," he said. "It's not even for all the other guys in the company. And it goes further than just this one crummy theater of operations. We got to do it for Lt. Marquand. So he didn't die for nothing."

"When you start the locker-room pep talk, I know you're desperate," said Staefler, grinning. "I can't say how much I'm glad for the chance. It's just that I'm not sure I can stand this kind of pressure."

Weinraub clapped the other man on the shoulder. "I've thought it all out, Bo," he said. "there isn't another soldier in the troupe that I can trust on this one."

Staefler shook his head. "Yeah, well, we'll see," he said. "What's it going to be?"

"I figure World War II. It's clean, direct, and there's a lot going for it as far as audience identification. It will be a simple demolitions job, an ambush, and a single act of heroism. You'll have a sort of long solo at the climax. I stole the idea from a movie."

"Great. I didn't want to say anything to you before, but I thought World War II was the best choice. Have you made up a list of supplies?"

"Yeah," said Weinraub. "Come on back to the HQ tent and I'll give it to you. Get on the phone and have the stuff sent out as soon as possible. We need a good river with at least one bank wide enough for the action and the audience. NAHF Dispatch has two full days to find us one around here, so we may even get a rehearsal in."

"That would be nice for a change," said Staefler, more confidently.

Later that day the list of equipment, uniforms, and weapons was radioed to the NAHF depot. Weinraub was informed that the nearest suitable river was some three hundred miles away; the trucks would arrive about noon of the following day, and the company would arrive at the site in the late afternoon or evening. They would have only a couple hours of daylight to sketch out the positions for the action, and a little time the next morning before the audience began to arrive. It was unfortunate that the river was so far away, but Sgt. Weinraub had wisely written a simple scenario that had no complicated movements. Only Staefler had to understand his part perfectly. If he performed well, the whole action would be an impressive success. And Staefler was the best soldier in the company.

When the trucks and the materiel arrived the following day, Weinraub called his men together to explain the action. "I'm going to split you up now," he said. "Fall in in a straight line and count off by threes." After the soldiers had done so, he detailed the men numbered one or three to be Americans, and all the number twos to be German soldiers. This put the American forces about twice that of the mock-Nazis, fifty to twenty-five. The troupe changed into the appropriate uniforms supplied by the NAHF quartermaster corps, loaded the American equipment into the American trucks, the German equipment into the German trucks, and climbed into the remaining space for the long drive to the river.

Weinraub and Staefler were both German soldiers, dressed in the field green trousers and jacket, high black boots, and peaked cap of officers in the Nazi *Waffen-SS.* They rode in a light open Volkswagen personnel carrier, with one of the other members of the company as driver.

It was after eight o'clock when the company got to the chosen site. Weinraub got out of the Volkswagen jeep and walked slowly down to the bank of the river with Staefler. "This is fine, Bo," said the sergeant. "We'll camp on this side tonight. The American troops will go on ahead; there's supposed to be a bridge a little over ninety miles further downstream. I'll run through the plan with them now and synchronize our watches. Then they'll leave to take their positions. After that, it'll all be up to you and me."

The American forces consisted of three regular transport vehicles and two jeep command cars. They were well on their way before darkness fell, and Weinraub gathered the remainder of his men, all dressed in the field uniforms of the *Waffen-SS* or regular Army, some wearing the insignia of the Combat and Construction Engineers. "All right, listen up," he said. "The first thing, the important thing we have to do is throw a light bridge across the river here. The water is just under eighty-two feet wide. We've got plenty of authentic bridging equipment, so the only problem is going to be time. We may have to work right through the night, and give the performance tomorrow on little or no sleep. I'm sorry. If NAHF Dispatch could have found us a suitable site a little closer, we could have had more time to plot out the action. Never mind.

"In the back of one of the trucks are a couple of dozen eight-foot sections of the *Leichte Z Brücke*. These are portable steel sections which are joined in two parallel rows across the river, and then connected by a wooden platform roadbed which is also cut into sections in one of the trucks. We're going to need to improvise supporting stanchions where the *Brücke* units meet. That's twenty-two junctions. Siekewicz, I want you to pick ten men and take care of that. Meanwhile, I want to meet with Cpl. Staefler, Pvt. Wilson, Pvt. Segura, and Cpl. Leskey. The rest of you start working. Cpl. Naegle's had experience with this type of operation, so while I'm busy in my meeting he'll be in charge."

The troupe worked strenuously, far into the night. By the time Weinraub had finished his conference, the bridge extended almost halfway across the river. Men waded chest-deep in the black, moonsparkled water, securing the Z sections to short pillars constructed of rock and sturdy tree limbs. After the sections had been laid across the water, there would remain only the simple task of putting down the roadway and fastening it with light girders. The whole job ought to be completed before four a.m.; Weinraub was satisfied.

"Is there going to be any problem?" asked Staefler nervously. "I mean, you said you got the idea from a movie."

"That's never been any trouble at all," said Sgt. Weinraub. "The critical staff doesn't care where we get our source material, as long as the action is carried out with skill and integrity."

"I'll bet your mother would kill you, if she could see you now."

Weinraub looked startled. "What the hell do you mean?" he asked.

"Nothing," said Staefler quickly. "I mean, just that you're all dressed up like some Nazi butcher. And with a name like Weinraub, too."

"I see what you're getting at. No, my parents were Lutherans."

"I didn't mean anything by it," said Staefler. "I don't know. I guess I'm just trying to work off some of this stage fright."

"Sure. Come on, let's see if anybody's got the coffee going."

The bridge inched its way across the river and, at last, it reached the other side and was secured to the opposite bank. While the men, stripped to the waist, exhausted now by their labors, fastened down the sections of roadbed, Weinraub ordered the company's three demolitions experts to place explosive charges along the length of the bridge.

"Are we going to blow the thing up tomorrow?" asked Pvt. Wilson.

"If everything goes well, we will," said Weinraub. "I want all the charges wired in series, so that one push on the plunger will set off the entire length of bridge. After you men finish that, we can turn in."

"Thank God," said Cpl. Leskey. The soldiers set to work, and the tasks of laying the roadway and secreting the explosives were finished within the hour. Sgt. Weinraub congratulated his men and let them get some sleep, knowing that the inspection group would arrive right on time the next morning.

It was only nine o'clock when Weinraub was awakened by the sound of the jeeps. They pulled to a stop fifty yards from Delta Company's camp; the reviewing committee walked slowly toward the men, chatting and laughing easily among themselves. Once more Weinraub felt an irrational anger, wondering how those critics would feel if they had to go out and be judged, week after week. Belonging to a combat troupe was hard work. The hours were long and the rewards were few, beyond the knowledge that one was helping the war effort against the Europeans. But the worst thing was the emotional strain of performing. Weinraub could never completely conquer it.

The reviewing committee was setting up folding chairs. Cpl. Staefler, as usual, had assumed the responsibility of directing the committee to the best vantage point and assisted in whatever trivial favors the critics required. Weinraub guessed that it was keeping Staefler's mind off his solo.

Soon it was time for Weinraub to order his men to their places. He gathered the fragment of his company and ran through the general instructions once more. "Above all else," he said, "don't get in the way. I don't want any of you spear-carriers ruining the action. If something seems to go wrong, *ignore it*. You may be wrong yourself. Let Cpl. Staefler or myself handle any emergency." He gave Staefler and Segura their special directions, and then waved the soldiers to their places. Staefler and Weinraub took a position in a sandbag bunker near the committee's seats. The two *Waffen-SS* officers were armed with M.P. 40 submachine guns and Walther Pistole 38s. With them in the bunker were five sharpshooters, and two soldiers manning an M.G. 42 machine gun. The other men were scattered about the clearing, some protected by bunkers or foxholes, others sheltered behind stumps and boulders.

Weinraub nodded to one of the privates, who gave the signal by radio to the American forces waiting across the river. In the stillness the sergeant could hear the roar of the transport trucks as they were started up. Looking through his field glasses, he soon saw the first of the convoy approaching the river and the bridge. Weinraub took a quick glance behind him; there had been a rumor that the Representative of North America himself might observe this crucial action. A seat had been prepared for him, but it was empty. Gen Hanson caught Weinraub's eye and nodded grimly. The sergeant returned his gaze to the far side of the river, where the first of the American trucks was rolling onto the bridge.

In a sudden instant of panic, Weinraub swung the glasses to the ignition device, sitting isolated in the middle of the clearing for dramatic effect. The box was small and green, standing up in the mud, its familiar T-shaped firing mechanism making the situation obvious to the observers. He scanned the device through his glasses, but everything seemed to be in order; the wires from the explosive charges were connected properly, he thought. In the matters of armaments and equipment, he had to trust the skill of his engineers. He hoped for his own and Lt. Marquand's sake they hadn't fouled up.

The plan was simple. The Germans would wait until the entire American convoy was on the bridge, then blast it all to pieces. There was a murmur of approval from the reviewing committee. Weinraub had planned well. The simple, classic idea had gained him a positive edge already. The sergeant smiled to Staefler, who grinned back nervously.

Suddenly, a shot cracked from one of the German bunkers. A groan went up from the audience, but Weinraub only smiled again. That was Pvt. Segura, firing on schedule. It seemed as though he had revealed the plan prematurely; the American trucks came to a sudden halt in the middle of the bridge. Infantrymen poured from the backs of the vehicles, running out along the bridge and lying flat, searching for the hidden ambushers. Weinraub gave the signal, and the three German machine guns opened fire. Four Americans died immediately, trying to rush the German position. Seeing that, the rest of the Americans sought shelter. The Germans were all safely hidden, and it was the Americans who were caught in a predicament. Sgt. Weinraub shouted to Cpt. Leskey to run out and blow up the bridge. Of course, Leskey knew that he'd never make it. He was proud that Weinraub had chosen him. Before he had gone ten yards, an American marksman had cut him down. The reviewing committee applauded, suddenly realizing the interesting situation Weinraub had developed. It seemed to be a stalemate. If the Germans could somehow destroy the bridge and its occupants, or if the Americans could somehow manage to over-run the Nazi position, the action would be a great debut for Sgt. Weinraub.

Muffled shouts were heard from the bridge. Most of the American soldiers ran back toward the trucks; it seemed that they were going to try and drive across, ignoring the dense storm of shells coming from the German emplacements. Before they achieved their goal, half of the Americans were slain, sprawling horribly on the white wood planking of the bridge. The others tried hastily to pull the bodies of their mates out of the path of the trucks. More Americans were slaughtered. At last they gave up and sprinted for the safety of the trucks. Four American sharpshooters remained at their posts near the end of the bridge to cover their fellows' attack.

Weinraub signalled again. Pvt. Wilson ran out to the ignition box, making perhaps twenty yards before an American bullet ripped through his neck. The trucks had almost reached the end of the bridge. "Now," cried Weinraub, slapping Staefler's back loudly. In the midst of the action, the corporal would have no time to feel anxious. He had a job to do. The idea was for Staefler to race to the box, nearly succeed, and then be shot by the American snipers. Dying, he would fall over the T-plunger and blast the bridge and the enemy in a last dramatic, heroic gesture.

It worked perfectly. Just before he reached the igniter, several rounds of fire caught Staefler, jerking him about like a kite on a string. He clutched his abdomen and looked straight at Weinraub. "The plunger," muttered Weinraub, clenching his fists. Behind him the committee was perfectly still. The trucks were moving, the first one just inching off the bridge onto the bank. "The plunger!" screamed Weinraub. "Fall on the plunger!" Staefler was obviously in great pain. His knees buckled; he knelt in the mud of the clearing, his jaw slack, and stared at the ignition box. At last, just when Weinraub was about to go mad with frustration, he fell over the plunger.

Nothing happened.

Weinraub felt tears on his cheek. Not caring about the bullets whacking into the sandbags, he ran out to Staefler. "You idiot!" he shouted, grabbing the suffering man. "The plunger! Why didn't you push the plunger?"

Staefler stared at him, his eyes half-closed. He still held his lower abdomen, where the tunic was fouled with a rapidly spreading bloody stain. "*Zünden,*" he whispered hoarsely.

"What the hell do you mean, '*Zünden*'?"

A bubble of red froth burst on Staefler's lips and trickled down his chin. Weinraub looked up helplessly. Confused, the American soldiers had stopped their unscheduled progress. The committee was on its feet. The sergeant could see Gen. Hanson already stalking back toward his jeep. "We closed after one performance," said Weinraub bitterly. He dropped Staefler to the ground and knelt by the igniter. One of the soldiers called out to him.

"It's not a plunger," said the soldier. "I don't know, maybe the NAHF made a mistake, or Staefler gave them the wrong order number. It's got a key where it says '*Zünden*'. You got to turn the key."

"They'll probably wipe us out in an aerial bombardment for this," said Weinraub, sobbing. He picked up the ignition box and turned the T-shaped key in the *Zünden* socket. The bridge exploded in a boiling orange and black cloud, harmlessly as all the American vehicles and personnel were by now safely on the German bank. Weinraub stood and looked around him. His men, dressed in Nazi uniforms and American, their expressions showing only despair, all holding their weapons slackly, turned toward him to hear his orders. "We got to keep going, though," said the helpless sergeant. "That's the way it's done. The show's got to go on." Then he savagely kicked the twisted body of Cpl. Staefler.

Mack Reynolds seems to have lived the kind of life that most people, Hemingway's memory still fresh, feel is the optimum model for a writer. Twenty years an expatriate, adventurer, world traveler–Mack has lived in or travelled through more than 75 countries; endured seven or eight wars and revolutions (usually, he admits, from behind the most solid thing available); has been kidnapped by the ferocious Tuareg and bitten by a rabid vampire bat.

Always fascinated by politics–his father once ran for President–Mack has made his mark on science fiction with carefully reasoned, consistent, sometimes outrageous extrapolations of current socio-economic trends. In Mercenary, *he postulates a chilling static society where war between nations is unknown. But the alternative is rather ugly.*

MERCENARY
by Mack Reynolds

Joseph Mauser spotted the recruiting line-up from two or three blocks down the street, shortly after driving into Kingston. The local offices of Vacuum Tube Transport, undoubtedly. Baron Haer would be doing his recruiting for the fracas with Continental Hovercraft there, if for no other reason than to save on rents. The Baron was watching pennies on this one and that was bad.

In fact, it was bad that even as Joe Mauser let his sport hovercar sink to a parking level and vaulted over its side he was still questioning his decision to sign up with the Vacuum Tube outfit rather than with their opponents. Joe was an old pro and old pros do not get to be old pros in the Category Military without developing an instinct to stay away from losing sides.

Fine enough for Low-Lowers and Mid-Lowers to sign up with this outfit, as opposed to that, motivated by no other reasoning than the snappiness of the uniform and the stock shares offered, but an old pro considered carefully such matters as budget. Baron Haer was watching every expense, was, it was rumored, figuring on commanding himself and calling upon relatives and friends for his staff. Continental Hovercraft, on the other hand, was heavy with variable capital and was in a position to hire Stonewall Cogswell himself for their tactician.

However, the die was cast. You didn't run up a caste level, not to speak of two at once, by playing it careful. Joe had planned this out; for once, old pro or not, he was taking risks.

Recruiting line-ups were not for such as he. Not for many a year, many a fracas. He strode rapidly along this one, heading for the offices ahead, noting only in passing the quality of the men who were taking service with Vacuum Tube Transport. These were the soldiers he'd be commanding in the immediate future and the prospects looked grim. There were few veterans among them. Their stance, their demeanor, their . . . well, you could tell a veteran even though he be Rank Private. You could tell a veteran of even one fracas. It showed.

He knew the situation. The word had gone out. Baron Malcolm Haer was due for a defeat. You weren't going to pick up any lush bonuses signing up with him, and you definitely weren't going to jump a caste. In short, no matter what Haer's past record, choose what was going to be the winning side—Continental Hovercraft. Continental Hovercraft and old Stonewall Cogswell who had lost so few fracases that many a Telly buff couldn't remember a single one.

Individuals among these men showed promise, Joe Mauser estimated even as he walked, but promise means little if you don't live long enough to cash in on it.

Take that small man up ahead. He'd obviously got himself into a hassel maintaining his place in line against two or three heftier wouldbe soldiers. The little fellow wasn't backing down a step in spite of the attempts of the other Lowers to usurp his place. Joe Mauser liked to see such spirit. You could use it when you were in the dill.

As he drew abreast of the altercation, he snapped from the side of his mouth, "Easy, lads. You'll get all the scrapping you want with Hovercraft. Wait until then."

He'd expected his tone of authority to be enough, even though he was in mufti. He wasn't particularly interested in the situation, beyond giving the little man a hand. A veteran would have recognized him as an old timer and probable officer, and heeded, automatically.

These evidently weren't veterans.

"Says who?" one of the Lowers growled back at him. "You one of Baron Haer's kids, or something?"

Joe Mauser came to a halt and faced the other. He was irritated, largely with himself. He didn't want to be bothered. Nevertheless, there was no alternative now.

The line of men, all Lowers so far as Joe could see, had fallen silent in an expectant hush. They were bored with their long wait. Now something would break the monotony.

By tomorrow, Joe Mauser would be in command of some of these men. In as little as a week he would go into a full fledged fracas with them. He couldn't afford to lose face. Not even at this point when all, including himself, were still civilian garbed. When matters pickled, in a fracas, you wanted men with complete confidence in you.

The man who had grumbled the surly response was a near physical twin of Joe Mauser which put him in his early thirties, gave him five foot eleven of altitude and about one hundred and eighty pounds. His clothes casted him Low-Lower—nothing to lose. As with many who have nothing to lose, he was willing to risk all for principle. His face now registered that ideal. Joe Mauser had no authority over him, nor his friends.

Joe's eyes flicked to the other two who had been pestering the little fellow. They weren't quite so aggressive and as yet had come to no conclusion about their stand. Probably the three had been unacquainted before their bullying alliance to deprive the smaller man of his place. However, a moment of hesitation and Joe would have a trio on his hands.

He went through no further verbal preliminaries. Joe Mauser stepped closer. His right hand lanced forward, not doubled in a fist but fingers close together and pointed, spearlike. He sank it into the other's abdomen, immediately below the rib cage—the solar plexus.

He had misestimated the other two. Even as his opponent crumpled, they were upon him, coming in from each side. And at least one of them, he could see now, had been in hand-to-hand combat before. In short, another pro, like Joe himself.

He took one blow, rolling with it, and his feet automatically went into the shuffle of the trained fighter. He retreated slightly to erect defenses, plan attack. They pressed him strongly, sensing victory in his retreat.

The one mattered little to him. Joe Mauser could have polished off the oaf in a matter of seconds, had he been allotted seconds to devote. But the second, the experienced one, was the problem. He and Joe were well matched and with the oaf as an ally really he had all the best of it.

Support came from a forgotten source, the little chap who had been the reason for the whole hassel. He waded in now as big as the next man so far as spirit was concerned, but a sorry fate gave him to attack the wrong man, the veteran rather than the tyro. He took a crashing blow to the side of his head which sent him sailing back into

the recruiting line, now composed of excited, shouting verbal participants of the fray.

However, the extinction of Joe Mauser's small ally had taken a
moment or two and time was what Joe needed most. For a double second he had the oaf alone on his hands and that was sufficient. He
caught a flailing arm, turned his back and automatically went into the
movements which result in that spectacular hold of the wrestler, the
Flying Mare. Just in time he recalled that his opponent was a future
comrade-in-arms and twisted the arm so that it bent at the elbow,
rather than breaking. He hurled the other over his shoulder and as far
as possible, to take the scrap out of him, and twirled quickly to meet
the further attack of his sole remaining foe.

That phase of the combat failed to materialize.

A voice of command bit out, "Hold it, you lads!"

The original situation which had precipitated the fight was being
duplicated. But while the three Lowers had failed to respond to Joe
Mauser's tone of authority, there was no similar failure now.

The owner of the voice, beautifully done up in the uniform of Vac-
cum Tube Transport, complete to kilts and the swagger stick of the
officer of Rank Colonel or above, stood glaring at them. Age, Joe estimated, even as he came to attention, somewhere in the late twen-
ties—an Upper in caste. Born to command. His face holding that
arrogant, contemptuous expression once common to the patricians of
Rome, the Prussian Junkers, the British ruling class of the Nineteenth
Century. Joe knew the expression well. How well he knew it. On more
than one occasion, he had dreamt of it.

Joe said, "Yes, sir."

"What in Zen goes on here? Are you lads overtranked?"

"No, sir," Joe's veteran opponent grumbled, his eyes on the
ground, a schoolboy before the principal.

Joe said, evenly, "A private disagreement, sir."

"Disagreement!" the Upper snorted. His eyes went to the three
fallen combatants, who were in various stages of reviving. "I'd hate to
see you lads in a real scrap."

That brought a response from the non-combatants in the recruiting
line. The *bon mot* wasn't that good but caste has its privileges and the
laughter was just short of uproarious.

Which seemed to placate the kilted officer. He tapped his swagger
stick against the side of his leg while he ran his eyes up and down Joe
Mauser and the others, as though memorizing them for future refer-
ence.

"All right," he said. "Get back into the line, and you trouble makers quiet down. We're processing as quickly as we can." And at that point he added insult to injury with an almost word for word repetition of what Joe had said a few moments earlier. "You'll get all the fighting you want from Hovercraft, if you can wait until then."

The four original participants of the rumpus resumed their places in various stages of sheepishness. The little fellow, nursing an obviously aching jaw, made a point of taking up his original position even while darting a look of thanks to Joe Mauser who still stood where he had when the fight was interrupted.

The Upper looked at Joe. "Well, lad, are you interested in signing up with Vacuum Tube Transport or not?"

"Yes, sir," Joe said evenly. Then, "Joseph Mauser, sir. Category Military, Rank Captain."

"Indeed." The officer looked him up and down all over again, his nostrils high. "A Middle, I assume. And brawling with recruits." He held a long silence. "Very well, come with me." He turned and marched off.

Joe inwardly shrugged. This was a fine start for his pitch—a fine start. He had half a mind to give it all up, here and now, and head on up to Catskill to enlist with Continental Hovercraft. His big scheme would wait for another day. Nevertheless, he fell in behind the aristocrat and followed him to the offices which had been his original destination.

Two Rank Privates with 45-70 Springfields and wearing the Haer kilts in such wise as to indicate permanent status in Vacuum Tube Transport came to the salute as they approached. The Upper preceding Joe Mauser flicked his swagger stick in an easy nonchalance. Joe felt envious amusement. How long did it take to learn how to answer a salute with that degree of arrogant ease?

There were desks in here, and typers humming, as Vacuum Tube Transport office workers, mobilized for this special service, processed volunteers for the company forces. Harried noncoms and junior-grade officers buzzed everywhere, failing miserably to bring order to the chaos. To the right was a door with a medical cross newly painted on it. When it occasionally popped open to admit or emit a recruit, white-robed doctors, male nurses and half nude men could be glimpsed beyond.

Joe followed the other through the press and to an inner office at which door he didn't bother to knock. He pushed his way through, waved in greeting with his swagger stick to the single occupant who looked up from the paper- and tape-strewn desk at which he sat.

Joe Mauser had seen the face before on Telly though never so tired as this and never with the element of defeat to be read in the expression. Bullet-headed, barrel-figured Baron Malcolm Haer of Vacuum Tube Transport. Category Transportation, Mid-Upper, and strong candidate for Upper-Upper upon retirement. However, there would be few who expected retirement in the immediate future. Hardly. Malcolm Haer found too obvious a lusty enjoyment in the competition between Vacuum Tube Transport and its stronger rivals.

Joe came to attention, bore the sharp scrutiny of his chosen commander-to-be. The older man's eyes went to the kilted Upper officer who had brought Joe along. "What is it, Balt?"

The other gestured with his stick at Joe. "Claims to be Rank Captain. Looking for a commission with us, Dad. I wouldn't know why." The last sentence was added lazily.

The older Haer shot an irritated glance at his son. "Possibly for the same reason mercenaries usually enlist for a fracas, Balt." His eyes came back to Joe.

Joe Mauser, still at attention even though in mufti, opened his mouth to give his name, category and rank, but the older man waved a hand negatively. "Captain Mauser, isn't it? I caught the fracas between Carbonaceous Fuel and United Miners, down on the Panhandle Reservation. Seems to me I've spotted you once or twice before, too."

"Yes, sir," Joe said. This was some improvement in the way things were going.

The older Haer was scowling at him. "Confound it, what are you doing with no more rank than captain? On the face of it, you're an old hand, a highly experienced veteran."

An old pro, we call ourselves, Joe said to himself. *Old pros, we call ourselves, among ourselves.*

Aloud, he said, "I was born a Mid-Lower, sir."

There was understanding in the old man's face, but Balt Haer said loftily, "What's that got to do with it? Promotion is quick and based on merit in Category Military."

At a certain point, if you are good combat officer material, you speak your mind no matter the rank of the man you are addressing. On this occasion, Joe Mauser needed few words. He let his eyes go up and down Balt Haer's immaculate uniform, taking in the swagger stick of the Rank Colonel or above. Joe said evenly, "Yes, sir."

Balt Haer flushed quick temper. "What do you mean by—"

But his father was chuckling. "You have spirit, captain. I need spirit now. You are quite correct. My son, though a capable officer, I assure you, has probably not participated in a fraction of the fracases you have to your credit. However, there is something to be said for the training available to we Uppers in the academies. For instance, captain, have you ever commanded a body of lads larger than, well, a *company*?"

Joe said flatly, "In the Douglas-Boeing versus Lockheed-Cessna fracas we took a high loss of officers when the Douglas-Boeing outfit rang in some fast-firing French *mitrailleuse* we didn't know they had. As my superiors took casualties I was field promoted to acting battalion commander, to acting regimental commander, to acting brigadier. For three days I held the rank of acting commander of brigade. We won."

Balt Haer snapped his fingers. "I remember that. Read quite a paper on it." He eyes Joe Mauser, almost respectfully. "Stonewall Cogswell got the credit for the victory and received his marshal's baton as a result."

"He was one of the few other officers that survived," Joe said dryly.

"But, Zen! You mean you got no promotion at all?"

Joe said, "I was upped to Low-Middle from High-Lower, sir. At my age, at the time, quite a promotion."

Baron Haer was remembering, too. "That was the fracas that brought on the howl from the Sovs. They claimed those *mitrailleuse* were post-1900 and violated the Universal Disarmament Pact. Yes, I recall that. Douglas-Boeing was able to prove that the weapon was used by the French as far back as the Franco-Prussian War." He eyed Joe with new interest now. "Sit down, captain. You too, Balt. Do you realize that Captain Mauser is the only recruit of officer rank we've had today?"

"Yes," the younger Haer said dryly. "However, it's too late to call the fracas off now. Hovercraft wouldn't stand for it, and the Category Military Department would back them. Our only alternative is unconditional surrender, and you know what that means."

"It means our family would probably be forced from control of the firm," the older man growled. "But nobody has suggested surrender on any terms. Nobody, thus far." He glared at his officer son who took it with an easy shrug and swung a leg over the edge of his father's desk in the way of a seat.

Joe Mauser found a chair and lowered himself into it. Evidently, the foppish Balt Haer had no illusions about the spot his father had got the family corporation into. And the younger man was right, of course.

But the Baron wasn't blind to reality any more than he was a coward. He dismissed Balt Haer's defeatism from his mind and came back to Joe Mauser. "As I say, you're the only officer recruit today. Why?"

Joe said evenly, "I wouldn't know, sir. Perhaps free lance Category Military men are occupied elsewhere. There's always a shortage of trained officers."

Baron Haer was waggling a finger negatively. "That's not what I mean, captain. You are an old hand. This is your category and you must know it well. Then why are *you* signing up with Vacuum Tube Transport rather than Hovercraft?"

Joe Mauser looked at him for a moment without speaking.

"Come, come, captain. I am an old hand too, in my category, and not a fool. I realize there is scarcely a soul in the West-world that expects anything but disaster for my colors. Pay rates have been widely posted. I can offer only five common shares of Vacuum Tube for a Rank Captain, win or lose. Hovercraft is doubling that, and can pick and choose among the best officers in the hemisphere."

Joe said softly, "I have all the shares I need."

Balt Haer had been looking back and forth between his father and the newcomer and becoming obviously more puzzled. He put in, "Well, what in Zen motivates you if it isn't the stock we offer?"

Joe glanced at the younger Haer to acknowledge the question but he spoke to the Baron. "Sir, like you said, you're no fool. However, you've been sucked in, this time. When you took on Hovercraft, you were thinking in terms of a regional dispute. You wanted to run one of your vacuum tube deals up to Fairbanks from Edmonton. You were expecting a minor fracas, involving possibly five thousand men. You never expected Hovercraft to parlay it up, through their connections in the Category Military Department, to a divisional magnitude fracas which you simply aren't large enough to afford. But Hovercraft was getting sick of your corporation. You've been nicking away at them too long. So they decided to do you in. They've hired Marshal Cogswell and the best combat officers in North America, and they're hiring the most competent veterans they can find. Every fracas buff who watches Telly, figures you've had it. They've been watching you come up the aggressive way, the hard way, for a long time, but now they're all going to be sitting on the edges of their sofas waiting for you to get it."

Baron Haer's heavy face had hardened as Joe Mauser went on

relentlessly. He growled, "Is this what everyone thinks?"

"Yes. Everyone intelligent enough to have an opinion." Joe made a motion of his head to the outer offices where the recruiting was proceeding. "Those men out there are rejects from Catskill, where old Baron Zwerdling is recruiting. Either that or they're inexperienced Low-Lowers, too stupid to realize they're sticking their necks out. Not one man in ten is a veteran. And when things begin to pickle, you want veterans."

Baron Malcolm Haer sat back in his chair and stared coldly at Captain Joe Mauser. He said, "At first I was moderately surprised that an old time mercenary like yourself should chose my uniform, rather than Zwerdling's. Now I am increasingly mystified about motivation. So all over again I ask you, captain: Why are you requesting a commission in my forces which you seem convinced will meet disaster?"

Joe wet his lips carefully. "I think I know a way you can win."

II

His permanent military rank the Haers had no way to alter, but they were short enough of competent officers that they gave him an acting rating and pay scale of major and command of a squadron of cavalry. Joe Mauser wasn't interested in a cavalry command this fracas, but he said nothing. Immediately, he had to size up the situation; it wasn't time as yet to reveal the big scheme. And, meanwhile, they could use him to whip the Rank Privates into shape.

He had left the offices of Baron Haer to go through the red tape involved in being signed up on a temporary basis in the Vacuum Tube Transport forces and reentered the confusion of the outer offices where the Lowers were being processed and given medicals. He reentered in time to run into a Telly team which was doing a live broadcast.

Joe Mauser remembered the news reporter who headed the team. He'd run into him two or three times in fracases. As a matter of fact, although Joe held the standard Military Category prejudices against Telly, he had a basic respect for this particular newsman. On the occasions he'd seen him before, the fellow was hot in the midst of the action even when things were in the dill. He took as many chances as did the average combatant, and you can't ask for more than that.

The other knew him, too, of course. It was part of his job to be able to spot the celebrities and near celebrities. He zeroed in on Joe now, making flicks of his hand to direct the cameras. Joe, of course, was fully aware of the value of Telly and was glad to co-operate.

"Captain! Captain Mauser, isn't it? Joe Mauser who held out for four days in the swamps of Louisiana with a single company while his ranking officers reformed behind him."

That was one way of putting it, but both Joe and the newscaster who had covered the debacle knew the reality of the situation. When the front had collapsed, his commanders—of Upper caste, of course—had hauled out, leaving him to fight a delaying action while they mended their fences with the enemy, coming to the best terms possible. Yes, that had been the United Oil versus Allied Petroleum fracas, and Joe had emerged with little either in glory or pelf.

The average fracas fan wasn't on an intellectual level to appreciate anything other than victory. The good guys win, the bad guys lose—that's obvious, isn't it? Not one out of ten Telly followers of the fracases was interested in a well conducted retreat or holding action. They wanted blood, lots of it, and they identified with the winning side.

Joe Mauser wasn't particularly bitter about this aspect. It was part of his way of life. In fact, his pet peeve was the *real* buff. The type, man or woman, who could remember every fracas you'd ever been in, every time you'd copped one, and how long you'd been in the hospital. Fans who could remember, even better than you could, every time the situation had pickled on you and you'd had to fight your way out as best you could. They'd tell you about it, their eyes gleaming, sometimes a slightest trickle of spittle at the sides of their mouths. They usually wanted an autograph, or a souvenir such as a uniform button.

Now Joe said to the Telly reporter, "That's right, Captain Mauser. Acting major, in this fracas, ah—"

"Freddy. Freddy Soligen. You remember me, captain—"

"Of course I do, Freddy. We've been in the dill, side by side, more than once, and even when I was too scared to use my side arm, you'd be scanning away with your camera."

"Ha, ha, listen to the captain, folks. I hope my boss is tuned in. But seriously, Captain Mauser, what do you think the chances of Vacuum Tube Transport are in this fracas?"

Joe looked into the camera lens, earnestly. "The best, of course, or I wouldn't have signed up with Baron Haer, Freddy. Justice triumphs, and anybody who is familiar with the issues in this fracas, knows that Baron Haer is on the side of true right."

Freddy said, holding any sarcasm he must have felt, "What would you say the issues were, captain?"

"The basic North American free enterprise right to compete. Hovercraft has held a near monopoly in transport to Fairbanks. Vacuum Tube Transport wishes to lower costs and bring the consumers of Fairbanks better service through running a vacuum tube to that area. What could be more in the traditions of the Westworld? Continental Hovercraft stands in the way and it is they who have demanded of the Category Military Department a trial by arms. On the face of it, justice is on the side of Baron Haer."

Freddy Soligen said into the camera, "Well, all you good people of the Telly world, that's an able summation the captain has made, but it certainly doesn't jibe with the words of Baron Zwerdling we heard this morning, does it? However, justice triumphs and we'll see what the field of combat will have to offer. Thank you, thank you very much, Captain Mauser. All of us, all of us tuned in today, hope that you personally will run into no dill in this fracas."

"Thanks, Freddy. Thanks all," Joe said into the camera, before turning away. He wasn't particularly keen about this part of the job, but you couldn't underrate the importance of pleasing the buffs. In the long run it was your career, your chances for promotion both in military rank and ultimately in caste. It was the way the fans took you up, boosted you, idolized you, worshipped you if you really made it. He, Joe Mauser, was only a minor celebrity, he appreciated every chance he had to be interviewed by such a popular reporter as Freddy Soligen.

Even as he turned, he spotted the four men with whom he'd had his spat earlier. The little fellow was still to the fore. Evidently, the others had decided the one place extra that he represented wasn't worth the trouble he'd put in their way defending it.

On an impulse he stepped up to the small man who began a grin of recognition, a grin that transformed his fiesty face. A revelation of an inner warmth beyond average in a world which had lost much of its human warmth.

Joe said, "Like a job, soldier?"

"Name's Max. Max Mainz. Sure I want a job. That's why I'm in this everlasting line."

Joe said, "First fracas for you, isn't it?"

"Yeah, but I had basic training in school."

"What do you weigh, Max?"

Max's face soured. "About one twenty."

"Did you check out on semaphore in school?"

"Well, sure. I'm Category Food, Sub-division Cooking, Branch Chef, but, like I say, I took basic military training, like most everybody else."

"I'm Captain Joe Mauser. How'd you like to be my batman?"

Max screwed up his already not overly handsome face. "Gee, I don't know. I kinda joined up to see some action. Get into the dill. You know what I mean."

Joe said dryly, "See here, Mainz, you'll probably find more pickled situations next to me than you'll want—and you'll come out alive."

The recruiting sergeant looked up from the desk. It was Max Mainz's turn to be processed. The sergeant said, "Lad, take a good opportunity when it drops in your lap. The captain is one of the best in the field. You'll learn more, get better chances for promotion, if you stick with him."

Joe couldn't remember ever having run into the sergeant before, but he said, "Thanks, sergeant."

The other said, evidently realizing Joe didn't recognize him. "We were together on the Chihuahua Reservation, on the jurisdictional fracas between the United Miners and the Teamsters, sir."

It had been almost fifteen years ago. About all that Joe Mauser remembered of that fracas was the abnormal number of casualties they'd taken. His side had lost, but from this distance in time Joe couldn't even remember what force he'd been with. But now he said, "That's right. I thought I recognized you, sergeant."

"It was my first fracas, sir." The sergeant went businesslike. "If you want I should hustle this lad through, captain—"

"Please do, sergeant." Joe added to Max, "I'm not sure where my billet will be. When you're through all this, locate the officer's mess and wait there for me."

"Well, O.K.," Max said doubtfully, still scowling but evidently a servant of an officer, if he wanted to be or not.

"Sir," the sergeant added ominously. "If you've had basic, you know enough how to address an officer."

"Well, yes sir," Max said hurriedly.

Joe began to turn away, but then spotted the man immediately behind Max Mainz. He was one of the three with whom Joe had tangled earlier, the one who'd obviously had previous combat experience. He pointed the man out to the sergeant. "You'd better give this lad at least temporary rank of corporal. He's a veteran and we're short of veterans."

The sergeant said, "Yes, sir. We sure are." Joe's former foe looked properly thankful.

Joe Mauser finished off his own red tape and headed for the street to locate a military tailor who could do him up a set of the Haer kilts and fill his other dress requirements. As he went, he wondered vaguely just how many different uniforms he had worn in his time.

In a career as long as his own from time to time you took semi-permanent positions in bodyguards, company police, or possibly the permanent combat troops of this corporation or that. But largely, if you were ambitious, you signed up for the fracases and that meant into a uniform and out of it again in as short a period as a couple of weeks.

At the door he tried to move aside but was too slow for the quick moving young woman who caromed off him. He caught her arm to prevent her from stumbling. She looked at him with less than thanks.

Joe took the blame for the collision. "Sorry," he said. "I'm afraid I didn't see you, Miss."

"Obviously," she said coldly. Her eyes went up and down him, and for a moment he wondered where he had seen her before. Somewhere, he was sure.

She was dressed as they dress who have never considered cost and she had an elusive beauty which would have been even the more hadn't her face projected quite such a serious outlook. Her features were more delicate than those to which he was usually attracted. Her lips were less full, but still— He was reminded of the classic ideal of the British Romantic Period, the women sung of by Byron and Keats, Shelly and Moore.

She said, "Is there any particular reason why you should be staring at me, Mr.—"

"Captain Mauser," Joe said hurriedly. "I'm afraid I've been rude, Miss—Well, I thought I recognized you."

She took in his civilian dress, typed it automatically, and came to an erroneous conclusion. She said, "Captain? You mean that with everyone else I know drawing down ranks from Lieutenant Colonel to Brigadier General, you can't make anything better than Captain?"

Joe winced. He said carefully, "I came up from the ranks, Miss. Captain is quite an achievement, believe me."

"Up from the ranks!" She took in his clothes again. "You mean you're a Middle? You neither talk nor look like a Middle, captain." She used the caste rating as though it was not *quite* a derogatory term.

Not that she meant to be deliberately insulting, Joe knew, wearily. How well he knew. It was simply born in her. As once a well-educated aristocracy had, not necessarily unkindly, named their status inferiors *niggers*; or other aristocrats, in another area of the country, had named theirs *greasers*. Yes, how well he knew.

He said very evenly, "Mid-Middle now, Miss. However, I was born in the Lower castes."

An eyebrow went up. "Zen! You must have put in many an hour studying. You talk like an Upper, captain." She dropped all interest in him and turned to resume her journey.

"Just a moment," Joe said. "You can't go in there, Miss—"

Her eyebrows went up again. "The name is Haer," she said. "Why can't I go in here, captain?"

Now it came to him why he had thought he recognized her. She had basic features similar to those of that overbred poppycock, Balt Haer.

"Sorry," Joe said. "I suppose under the circumstances, you can. I was about to tell you that they're recruiting with lads running around half clothed. Medical inspections, that sort of thing."

She made a noise through her nose and said over her shoulder, even as she sailed on. "Besides being a Haer, I'm an M.D., captain. At the ludicrous sight of a man shuffling about in his shorts, I seldom blush."

She was gone.

Joe Mauser looked after her. "I'll bet you don't," he muttered.

Had she waited a few minutes he could have explained his Upper accent and his unlikely education. When you'd copped one you had plenty of opportunity in hospital beds to read, to study, to contemplate—and to fester away in your own schemes of rebellion against fate. And Joe had copped many in his time.

III

By the time Joe Mauser called it a day and retired to his quarters he was exhausted to the point where his basic dissatisfaction with the trade he followed was heavily upon him.

He had met his immediate senior officers, largely dilettante Uppers with precious little field experience, and was unimpressed. And he'd met his own junior officers and was shocked. By the looks of things at this stage, Captain Mauser's squadron would be going into this fracas both undermanned with Rank Privates and with junior officers composed largely of temporarily promoted noncoms. If this was typical of Baron Haer's total force, then Balt Haer had been correct; unconditional surrender was to be considered, no matter how disastrous to Haer family fortunes.

Joe had been able to take immediate delivery of one kilted

uniform. Now, inside his quarters, he began stripping out of his jacket. Somewhat to his surprise, the small man he had selected earlier in the day to be his barman entered from an inner room, also resplendent in the Haer uniform and obviously happily so.

He helped his superior out of the jacket with an ease that held no subservience but at the same time was correctly respectful. You'd have thought him a batman specially trained.

Joe grunted, "Max, isn't it? I'd forgotten about you. Glad you found our billet all right."

Max said, "Yes, sir. Would the captain like a drink? I picked up a bottle of applejack. Applejack's the drink around here, sir. Makes a topnotch highball with gingerale and a twist of lemon."

Joe Mauser looked at him. Evidently his tapping this man for orderly had been sheer fortune. Well, Joe Mauser could use some good luck on this job. He hoped it didn't end with selecting a batman.

Joe said, "An applejack highball sounds wonderful, Max. Got ice?"

"Of course, sir." Max left the small room.

Joe Mauser and his officers were billeted in what had once been a motel on the old road between Kingston and Woodstock. There was a shower and a tiny kitchenette in each cottage. That was one advantage in a fracas held in an area where there were plenty of facilities. Such military reservations as that of the Little Big Horn in Montana and particularly some of those in the South West and Mexico, were another thing.

Joe lowered himself into the room's easy-chair and bent down to untie his laces. He kicked his shoes off. He could use that drink. He began wondering all over again if his scheme for winning this Vacuum Tube Transport versus Continental Hovercraft fracas would come off. The more he saw of Baron Haer's inadequate forces, the more he wondered. He hadn't expected Vacuum Tube to be in *this* bad a shape. Baron Haer had been riding high for so long that one would have thought his reputation for victory would have lured many a veteran to his colors. Evidently they hadn't bitten. The word was out all right.

Max Mainz returned with the drink.

Joe said, "You had one yourself?"

"No, sir."

Joe said, "Well, Zen, go get yourself one and come on back and sit down. Let's get acquainted."

"Well, yessir." Max disappeared back into the kitchenette to return almost immediately. The little man slid into a chair, drink awkwardly in hand.

His superior sized him up, all over again. Not much more than a kid, really. Surprisingly aggressive for a Lower who must have been raised from childhood in a trank bemused, Telly entertained household. The fact that he'd broken away from that environment at all was to his credit, it was considerably easier to conform. But then it is always easier to conform, to run with the herd, as Joe well knew. His own break hadn't been an easy one. "Relax," he said now.

Max said, "Well, this is my first day."

"I know. And you've been seeing Telly shows all your life showing how an orderly conducts himself in the presence of his superior." Joe took another pull and yawned. "Well, forget about it. With any man who goes into a fracas with me. I like to be on close terms. When things pickle, I want him to be on my side, not nursing some peeve brought on by his officer trying to give him an inferiority complex."

The little man was eyeing him in surprise.

Joe finished his highball and came to his feet to get another one. He said, "On two occasions I've had an orderly save my life. I'm not taking any chances but that there might be a third opportunity."

"Well, yessir. Does the captain want me to get him—"

"I'll get it," Joe said.

When he'd returned to his chair, he said, "Why did you join up with Baron Haer, Max?"

The other shrugged it off. "The usual. The excitement. The idea of all those fans watching me on Telly. The share of common stock I'll get. And, you never know, maybe a promotion in caste. I wouldn't mind making Upper-Lower."

Joe said sourly, "One fracas and you'll be over that desire to have the buffs watching you on Telly while they sit around in their front rooms sucking on tranks. And you'll probably be over the desire for the excitement, too. Of course, the share of stock is another thing."

"You aren't just countin' down, captain," Max said, an almost surly overtone in his voice. "You don't know what it's like being born with no more common stock shares than a Mid-Lower."

Joe held his peace, sipping at his drink, taking this one more slowly. He let his eyebrows rise to encourage the other to go on.

Max said doggedly, "Sure, they call it People's Capitalism and everybody gets issued enough shares to insure him a basic living all the way from the cradle to the grave, like they say. But let me tell you, you're a Middle and you don't realize how basic the basic living of a Lower can be."

Joe yawned. If he hadn't been so tired, there would have been more amusement in the situation.

Max was still dogged. "Unless you can add to those shares of stock, it's pretty drab, captain. You wouldn't know."

Joe said, "Why don't you work? A Lower can always add to his stock by working."

Max stirred in indignity. "Work? Listen, sir, that's just one more field that's been automated right out of existence. Category Food Preparation, Sub-division Cooking, Branch Chef. Cooking isn't left in the hands of slobs who might drop a cake of soap into the soup. It's done automatic. The only new changes made in cooking are by real top experts, almost scientists like. And most of them are Uppers, mind you."

Joe Mauser sighed inwardly. So his find in batmen wasn't going to be as wonderful as all that, after all. The man might have been born into the food preparation category from a long line of chefs, but evidently he knew precious little about his field. Joe might have suspected. He himself had been born into Clothing Category, Sub-division Shoes, Branch Repair—Cobbler—a meaningless trade since shoes were no longer repaired but discarded upon showing signs of wear. In an economy of complete abundance, there is little reason for repair of basic commodities. It was high time the government investigated category assignment and reshuffled and reassigned half the nation's population. But then, of course, was the question of what to do with the technologically unemployed.

Max was saying, "The only way I could figure on a promotion to a higher caste, or the only way to earn stock shares, was by crossing categories. And you know what that means. Either Category Military, or Category Religion and I sure as Zen don't know nothing about religion."

Joe said mildly, "Theoretically, you can cross categories into any field you want, Max."

Max snorted. "Theoretically is right . . . sir. You ever heard about anybody born a Lower, or even a Middle like yourself, cross categories to, say, some Upper category like banking?"

Joe chuckled. He liked this peppery little fellow. If Max worked out as well as Joe thought he might, there was a possibility of taking him along to the next fracas.

Max was saying, "I'm not saying anything against the old time way of doing things or talking against the government, but I'll tell you, captain, every year goes by it gets harder and harder for a man to raise his caste or to earn some additional stock shares."

The applejack had worked enough on Joe for him to rise against one of his pet peeves. He said, "That term, the old time way, is strictly Telly talk, Max. We don't do things *the old time way*. No nation in history ever has—with the possible exception of Egypt. Socio-economics are in a continual flux and here in this country we no more do things in the way they did fifty years ago, than fifty years ago they did them the way the American Revolutionists outlined back in the Eighteenth Century."

Max was staring at him. "I don't get that, sir."

Joe said impatiently, "Max, the politico-economic system we have today is an outgrowth of what went earlier. The welfare state, the freezing of the status quo, the Frigid Fracas between the West-world and the Sov-world, industrial automation until useful employment is all but needless—all these things were to be found in embryo more than fifty years ago."

"Well, maybe the captain's right, but you gotta admit, sir, that mostly we do things the old way. We still got the Constitution and the two-party system and—"

Joe was wearying of the conversation now. You seldom ran into anyone, even in Middle caste, the traditionally professional class, interested enough in such subjects to be worth arguing with. He said, "The Constitution, Max, has got to the point of the Bible. Interpret it the way you wish, and you can find anything. If not, you can always make a new amendment. So far as the two-party system is concerned, what effect does it have when there are no differences between the two parties? That phase of pseudo-democracy was beginning as far back as the 1930s when they began passing State laws hindering the emerging of new political parties. By the time they were insured against a third party working its way through the maze of election laws, the two parties had become so similar that elections became almost as big a farce as over in the Sov-world."

"A farce?" Max ejaculated indignantly, forgetting his servant status. "That means not so good, doesn't it? Far as I'm concerned, election day is tops. The one day a Lower is just as good as an Upper. The one day how many shares you got makes no difference. Everybody has everything."

"Sure, sure, sure," Joe sighed. "The modern equivalent of the Roman Baccanalia. Election day in the West-world when no one, for just that one day, is freer than anyone else."

"Well, what's wrong with that?" The other was all but belligerent. "That's the trouble with you Middles and Uppers, you don't know how it is to be a Lower and—"

Joe snapped suddenly, "I was born a Mid-Lower myself, Max. Don't give me that nonsense."

Max gaped at him, utterly unbelieving.

Joe's irritation fell away. He held out his glass. "Get us a couple of more drinks, Max, and I'll tell you a story."

By the time the fresh drink came, Joe Mauser was sorry he'd made the offer. He thought back. He hadn't told anyone the Joe Mauser story in many a year. And, as he recalled, the last time had been when he was well into his cups, on an election day at that, and his listener had been a Low-Upper, a hereditary aristocrat, one of the one per cent of the upper strate of the nation. Zen! How the man had laughed. He'd roared his amusement till the tears ran.

However, Joe said, "Max, I was born in the same caste you were—average father, mother, sisters and brothers. They subsisted on the basic income guaranteed from birth, sat and watched Telly for an unbelievable number of hours each day, took trank to keep themselves happy. And thought I was crazy because I didn't. Dad was the sort of man who'd take his belt off to a child of his who questioned such school taught slogans as *What was good enough for Daddy is good enough for me.*

"They were all fracas fans, of course. As far back as I can remember the picture is there of them gathered around the Telly, screaming excitement." Joe Mauser sneered, uncharacteristically.

"You don't sound much like you're in favor of your trade, captain," Max said.

Joe came to his feet, putting down his still half-full glass. "I'll make this epic story short, Max. As you said, the two actually valid methods of rising above the level in which you were born are in the Military and Religious Categories. Like you, even I couldn't stomach the latter."

Joe Mauser hesitated, then finished it off. "Max, there have been few societies that man has evolved that didn't allow in some manner for the competent or sly, the intelligent or the opportunist, the brave or the strong, to work his way to the top. I don't know which of these I personally fit into, but I rebel against remaining in the lower categories of a stratified society. Do I make myself clear?"

"Well, no sir, not exactly."

Joe said flatly, "I'm going to fight my way to the top, and nothing is going to stand in the way. Is that clearer?"

"Yessir," Max said, taken aback.

IV

After routine morning duties, Joe Mauser returned to his billet and mystified Max Mainz by not only changing into mufti himself but having Max do the same.

In fact, the new batman protested faintly. He hadn't nearly, as yet, got over the glory of wearing his kilts and was looking forward to parading around town in them. He had a point, of course. The appointed time for the fracas was getting closer and buffs were beginning to stream into town to bask in the atmosphere of threatened death. Everybody knew what a military center, on the outskirts of a fracas reservation such as the Catskills, was like immediately preceding a clash between rival corporations. The high strung gaiety, the drinking, the overtranking, the relaxation of mores. Even a Rank Private had it made. Admiring civilians to buy drinks and hang on your every word, and more important still, sensuous-eyed women, their faces slack in thinly suppressed passion. It was a recognized phenomenon, even Max Mainz knew—this desire on the part of women Telly fans to date a man, and then watch him later, killing or being killed.

"Time enough to wear your fancy uniform," Joe Mauser growled at him. "In fact, tomorrow's a local election day. Parlay that up on top of all the fracas fans gravitating into town and you'll have a wingding the likes of nothing you've seen before."

"Well yessir," Max begrudged. "Where're we going now, captain?"

"To the airport. Come along."

Joe Mauser led the way to his sports hovercar and as soon as the two were settled into the bucket seats, hit the lift lever with the butt of his left hand. Aircushion borne, he tread down on the accelerator.

Max Mainz was impressed. "You know," he said. "I never been in one of these swanky sports jobs before. The kinda car you can afford on the income of a Mid-Lower's stock aren't—"

"Knock it off," Joe said wearily. "Carping we'll always have with us evidently, but in spite of all the beefing in every strata from Low-Lower to Upper-Middle, I've yet to see any signs of organized protest against our present politico-economic system."

"Hey," Max said. "Don't get me wrong. What was good enough for

Dad, is good enough for me. You won't catch me talking against the government."

"Hm-m-m," Joe murmured. "And all the other cliches taught to us to preserve the status quo, our People's Capitalism." They were reaching the outskirts of town, crossing the Esopus. The airport lay only a mile or so beyond.

It was obviously too deep for Max, and since he didn't understand, he assumed his superior didn't know what he was talking about. He said, tolerantly. "Well, what's wrong with People's Capitalism? Everybody owns the corporations. Damnsight better than the Sovs have."

Joe said sourly. "We've got one optical illusion, they've got another, Max. Over there they claim the proletariat owns the means of production. Great. But the Party members are the ones who control it, and, as a result they manage to do all right for themselves. The Party hierarchy over there are like our Uppers over here."

"Yeah." Max was being particularly dense. "I've seen a lot about it on Telly. You know, when there isn't a good fracas on, you tune to one of them educational shows, like—"

Joe winced at the term *educational*, but held his peace.

"It's pretty rugged over there. But in the West-world, the people own a corporation's stock and they run it and get the benefit."

"At least it makes a beautiful story," Joe said dryly. "Look, Max. Suppose you have a corporation that has two hundred thousand shares out and they're distributed among one hundred thousand and one persons. One hundred thousand of these own one share apiece, but the remaining stockholder owns the other hundred thousand."

"I don't know what you're getting at," Max said.

Joe Mauser was tired of the discussion. "Briefly," he said, "we have the illusion that this is a People's Capitalism, with all stock in the hands of the People. Actually, as ever before, the stock is in the hands of the Uppers, all except a mere dribble. They own the country and they run it for their own benefit."

Max shot a less than military glance at him. "Hey, you're not one of these Sovs yourself, are you?"

They were coming into the parking area near the Administration Building of the airport. "No," Joe said so softly that Max could hardly hear his words. "Only a Mid-Middle on the make."

Followed by Max, he strode quickly to the Administration Building, presented his credit identification at the desk and requested a light aircraft for a period of three hours. The clerk, hardly looking up, began going through motions, speaking into telescreens.

The clerk said finally, "You might have a small wait, sir. Quite a few of the officers involved in this fracas have been renting out taxi-planes almost as fast as they're available."

That didn't surprise Joe Mauser. Any competent officer made a point of an aerial survey of the battle reservation before going into a fracas. Aircraft, of course, couldn't be used *during* the fray, since they post-dated the turn of the century, and hence were relegated to the cemetery of military devices along with such items as nuclear weapons, tanks, and even gasoline propelled vehicles of size to be useful.

Use an aircraft in a fracas, or even *build* an aircraft for military usage and you'd have a howl go up from the military attaches from the Sov-world that would be heard all the way to Budapest. Not a fracas went by but there were scores, if not hundreds, of military observers, keeneyed to check whether or not any really modern tools of war were being illegally utilized. Joe Mauser sometimes wondered if the West-world observers, over in the Sov-world, were as hair fine in their living up to the rules of the Universal Disarmament Pact. Probably. But, for that matter, they didn't have the same system of fighting fracases over there, as in the West.

Max took a chair while he waited and thumbed through a fan magazine. From time to time he found his own face in such publications. He was a third-rate celebrity, really. Luck hadn't been with him so far as the buffs were concerned. They wanted spectacular victories, murderous situations in which they could lose themselves in vicarious sadistic thrills. Joe had reached most of his peaks while in retreat, or commanding a holding action. His officers appreciated him and so did the ultra-knowledgable fracas buffs—but he was all but an unknown to the average dim wit who spent most of his life glued to the Telly set, watching men butcher each other.

On the various occasions when matters had pickled and Joe had to fight his way out against difficult odds, using spectacular tactics in desperation, he was almost always off camera. Purely luck. On top of skill, determination, experience and courage, you have to have luck in the Military Category to get anywhere.

This time Joe was going to manufacture his own.

A voice said, "Ah, Captain Mauser."

Joe looked up, then came to his feet quickly. In automatic reflex, he began to come to the salute but then caught himself. He said stiffly, "My compliments, Marshall Cogswell."

The other was a smallish man, but strikingly strong of face and strongly built. His voice was clipped, clear and had the air of command as though born with it. He, like Joe, wore mufti and now extended his hand to be shaken.

"I hear you've signed up with Baron Haer, captain. I was rather expecting you to come in with me. Had a place for a good aide de camp. Liked your work in that last fracas we went through together."

"Thank you, sir," Joe said. Stonewall Cogswell was as good a tactician as freelanced and he was more than that. He was a judge of men and a stickler for detail. And right now, if Joe Mauser knew Marshal Stonewall Cogswell as well as he thought, Cogswell was smelling a rat. There was no reason why old pro Joe Mauser should sign up with a sure loser like Vacuum Tube when he could have earned more shares taking a commission with Hovercraft.

He was looking at Joe brightly, the question in his eyes. Three or four of his staff were behind a few paces, looking polite, but Cogswell didn't bring them into the conversation. Joe knew most by sight. Good men all. Old pros all. He felt another twinge of doubt.

Joe had to cover. He said. "I was offered a particularly good contract, sir. Too good to resist."

The other nodded, as though inwardly coming to a satisfactory conclusion. "Baron Haer's connections, eh? He's probably offered to back you for a bounce in caste. Is that it, Joe?"

Joe Mauser flushed. Stonewall Cogswell knew what he was talking about. He'd been born into Middle status himself and had become an Upper the hard way. His path wasn't as long as Joe's was going to be, but long enough and he knew how rocky the climb was. How very rocky.

Joe said, stiffly, "I'm afraid I'm in no position to discuss my commander's military contracts, marshal. We're in mufti, but after all—"

Cogswell's lean face registered one of his infrequent grimaces of humor. "I understand, Joe. Well, good luck and I hope things don't pickle for you in the coming fracas. Possibly we'll find ourselves aligned together again at some future time."

"Thank you, sir," Joe said, once more having to catch himself to prevent an automatic salute.

Cogswell and his staff went off, leaving Joe looking after them. Even the marshal's staff members were top men any of whom could have conducted a divisional magnitude fracas. Joe felt the coldness in his stomach again. Although it must have looked like a cinch, the enemy wasn't taking any chances whatsoever. Cogswell and his officers were undoubtedly here at the airport for the same reason as Joe. They wanted a thorough aerial reconnaissance of the battlefield to be, before the issue was joined.

Max was standing at his elbow. "Who was that, sir? Looks like a real tough one."

"He is a real tough one," Joe said sourly. "That's Stonewall Cogswell, the best field commander in North America."

Max pursed his lips. "I never seen him out of uniform before. Lots of times on Telly, but never out of uniform. I thought he was taller than that."

"He fights with his brains," Joe said, still looking after the craggy field marshal. "He doesn't have to be any taller."

Max scowled. "Where'd he ever get that nickname, sir?"

"Stonewall?" Joe was turning to resume his chair and magazine. "He's supposed to be a student of a top general back in the American Civil War. Uses some of the original Stonewall's tactics."

Max was out of his depth. "American Civil War? Was that much of a fracas, captain? It musta been before my time."

"It was quite a fracas," Joe said dryly. "Lot of good lads died. A hundred years after it was fought, the *reasons* it was fought seemed about as valid as those we fight fracases for today. Personally I—"

He had to cut it short. They were calling him on the address system. His aircraft was ready. Joe made his way to the hangars, followed by Max Mainz. He was going to pilot the airplane himself and old Stonewall Cogswell would have been surprised at what Joe Mauser was looking for.

V

By the time they had returned to quarters, there was a message waiting for Captain Mauser. He was to report to the officer commanding reconnaissance.

Joe redressed in the Haer kilts and proceeded to headquarters.

The officer commanding reconnaissance turned out to be none other than Balt Haer, natty as ever, and, as ever, arrogantly tapping his swagger stick against his leg.

"Zen! Captain," he complained. "Where have you been? Off on a trank kick? We've got to get organized."

Joe Mauser snapped him a salute. "No, sir. I rented an aircraft to scout out the terrain over which we'll be fighting."

"Indeed. And what were your impressions, captain?" There was an overtone which suggested that it made little difference what impressions a captain of cavalry might have gained.

Joe shrugged. "Largely mountains, hills, woods. Good reconnaissance is going to make the difference in this one. And in the fracas itself cavalry is going to be more important than either artillery or infantry. A Nathan Forrest fracas, sir. A matter of getting there fustest with the mostest."

Balt Haer said amusedly. "Thanks for your opinion, captain. Fortunately, our staff has already come largely to the same conclusions. Undoubtedly, they'll be glad to hear your wide experience bears them out."

Joe said evenly, "It's a rather obvious conclusion, of course." He took this as it came, having been through it before. The dilettante amateur's dislike of the old pro. The amateur in command who knew full well he was less capable than many of those below him in rank.

"Of course, captain," Balt Haer flicked his swagger stick against his leg. "But to the point. Your squadron is to be deployed as scouts under my overall command. You've had cavalry experience, I assume."

"Yes, sir. In various fracases over the past fifteen years."

"Very well. Now then, to get to the reason I have summoned you. Yesterday in my father's office you intimated that you had some grandiose scheme which would bring victory to the Haer colors. But then, on some thin excuse, refused to divulge just what the scheme might be."

Joe Mauser looked at him unblinkingly.

Balt Haer said: "Now I'd like to have your opinion on just how Vacuum Tube Transport can extract itself from what would seem a poor position at best."

In all there were four others in the office, two women clerks fluttering away at typers, and two of Balt Haer's junior officers. They seemed only mildly interested in the conversation, between Balt and Joe.

Joe wet his lips carefully. The Haer scion was his commanding officer. He said, "Sir, what I had in mind is a new gimmick. At this stage, if I told anybody and it leaked, it'd never be effective, not even this first time."

Haer observed him coldly. "And you think me incapable of keeping your secret, ah, *gimmick*, I believe is the idiomatic term you used."

Joe Mauser's eyes shifted around the room, taking in the other four, who were now looking at him.

Balt Haer rapped, "These members of my staff are all trusted Haer employees, Captain Mauser. They are not fly-by-night freelancers hired for a week or two."

Joe said, "Yes, sir. But it's been my experience that one person can hold a secret. It's twice as hard for two, and from there on it's a decreasing probability in a geometric ratio."

The younger Haer's stick rapped the side of his leg, impatiently. "Suppose I inform you that this is a command, captain? I have little confidence in a supposed gimmick that will rescue our forces from disaster and I rather dislike the idea of a captain of one of my squadrons dashing about with such a bee in his bonnet when he should be obeying my commands."

Joe kept his voice respectful. "Then, sir, I'd request that we take the matter to the Commander in Chief, your father."

"Indeed!"

Joe said, "Sir, I've been working on this a long time. I can't afford to risk throwing the idea away."

Balt Haer glared at him. "Very well, captain. I'll call your bluff, come along." He turned on his heel and headed from the room.

Joe Mauser shrugged in resignation and followed him.

The old Baron wasn't much happier about Joe Mauser's secrets than was his son. It had only been the day before that he had taken Joe on, but already he had seemed to have aged in appearance. Evidently, each hour that went by made it increasingly clear just how perilous a position he had assumed. Vacuum Tube Transport had elbowed, buffaloed, bluffed and edged itself up to the outskirts of the really big time. The Baron's ability, his aggressiveness, his flair, his political pull, had all helped, but now the chips were down. He was up against one of the biggies, and this particular biggy was tired of ambitious little Vacuum Tube Transport.

He listened to his son's words, listened to Joe's defense.

He said, looking at Joe, "If I understand this, you have some scheme which you think will bring victory in spite of what seems a disasterous situation."

"Yes, sir."

The two Haers looked at him, one impatiently, the other in weariness.

Joe said, "I'm gambling everything on this, sir. I'm no Rank Private in his first fracas. I deserve to be given some leeway."

Balt Haer snorted. "Gambling everything! What in Zen would *you* have to gamble, captain? The whole Haer family fortunes are tied up. Hovercraft is out for blood. They won't be satisfied with a token victory and a negotiated compromise. They'll devastate us. Thousands of mercenaries killed, with all that means in indemnities; millions upon millions in expensive military equipment, most of which we've had to hire and will have to recompensate for. Can you imagine the value of our stock after Stonewall Cogswell has finished with us? Why, every two by four trucking outfit in North America will be challenging us, and we won't have the forces to meet a minor skirmish."

Joe reached into an inner pocket and laid a sheaf of documents on the desk of Baron Malcolm Haer. The Baron scowled down at them.

Joe said simply, "I've been accumulating stock since before I was eighteen and I've taken good care of my portfolio in spite of taxes and the various other pitfalls which make the accumulation of capital practically impossible. Yesterday, I sold all of my portfolio I was legally allowed to sell and converted to Vacuum Tube Transport." He added, dryly, "Getting it at an excellent rate, by the way."

Balt Haer mulled through the papers, unbelievingly. "Zen!" he ejaculated. "The fool really did it. He's sunk a small fortune into our stock."

Baron Haer growled at his son, "You seem considerably more convinced of our defeat than the captain, here. Perhaps I should reverse your positions of command."

His son grunted, but said nothing.

Old Malcolm Haer's eyes came back to Joe. "Admittedly, I thought you on the romantic side yesterday, with your hints of some scheme which would lead us out of the wilderness, so to speak. Now I wonder if you might not really have something. Very well, I respect your claimed need for secrecy. Espionage is not exactly an antiquated military field."

"Thank you, sir."

But the Baron was still staring at him. "However, there's more to it than that. Why not take this great scheme to Marshal Cogswell? And yesterday you mentioned that the Telly sets of the nation would be tuned in on this fracas, and obviously you are correct. The question becomes, what of it?"

The fat was in the fire now. Joe Mauser avoided the haughty stare of young Balt Haer and addressed himself to the older man. "You have political pull, sir. Oh, I know you don't make and break presidents.

You couldn't even pull enough wires to keep Hovercraft from making this a divisional magnitude fracas—but you have pull enough for my needs."

Baron Haer leaned back in his chair, his barrellike body causing that article of furniture to creak. He crossed his hands over his stomach. "And what are your needs, Captain Mauser?"

Joe said evenly, "If I can bring this off, I'll be a fracas buff celebrity. I don't have any illusions about the fickleness of the Telly fans, but for a day or two I'll be on top. If at the same time I had your all out support, pulling what string you could reach—"

"Why then, you'd be promoted to Upper, wouldn't you captain?" Balt Haer finished for him, amusement in his voice.

"That's what I'm gambling on," Joe said evenly.

The younger Haer grinned at his father superciliously. "So our captain says he will defeat Stonewall Cogswell in return for you sponsoring his becoming a member of the nation's elite."

"Good Heavens, is the supposed cream of the nation now selected on no higher a level than this?" There was sarcasm in the words.

The three men turned. It was the girl Joe had bumped into the day before. The Haers didn't seem surprised at her entrance.

"Nadine," the older man growled. "Captain Joseph Mauser who has been given a commission in our forces."

Joe went through the routine of a Middle of officer's rank being introduced to a lady of Upper caste. She smiled at him, somewhat mockingly, and failed to make standard response.

Nadine Haer said, "I repeat, what is this service the captain can render the house of Haer so important that pressure should be brought to raise him to Upper Caste? It would seem unlikely that he is a noted scientist, an outstanding artist, a great teacher—"

Joe said, uncomfortably, "They say the military is a science, too."

Her expression was almost as haughty as that of her brother. "Do they? I have never thought so."

"Really, Nadine," her father grumbled. "This is hardly your affair."

"No? In a few days I shall be repairing the damage you have allowed, indeed sponsored, to be committed upon the bodies of possibly thousands of now healthy human beings."

Balt said nastily, "Nobody asked you to join the medical staff, Nadine. You could have stayed in your laboratory, figuring out new methods of preventing the human race from replenishing itself."

The girl was obviously not the type to redden, but her anger was manifest. She spun on her brother. "If the race continues its present maniac course, possibly more effective methods of birth control *are* the most important development we could make. Even to the ultimate discovery of preventing all future conception."

Joe caught himself in mid-chuckle.

But not in time. She spun on him in his turn. "Look at yourself in that silly skirt. A professional soldier! A killer! In my opinion the most useless occupation ever devised by man. Parasite on the best and useful members of society. Destroyer by trade!"

Joe began to open his mouth, but she overrode him. "Yes, yes. I know. I've read all the nonsense that has accumulated down through the ages about the need for, the glory of, the sacrfice of the professional soldier. How they defend their country. How they give all for the common good. Zen! What nonsense."

Balt Haer was smirking sourly at her. "The theory today is, Nadine, old thing, that professionals such as the captain are gathering experience in case a serious fracas with the Sovs ever develops. Meanwhile his training is kept at a fine edge fighting in our inter-corporation, inter-union, or union-corporation fracases that develop in our private enterprise society."

She laughed her scorn. "And what a theory! Limited to the weapons which prevailed before 1900. If there was ever real conflict between the Sov-world and our own, does anyone really believe either would stick to such arms? Why, aircraft, armored vehicles, yes, and nuclear weapons and rockets, would be in overnight use."

Joe was fascinated by her furious attack. He said, "Then, what would you say was the purpose of the fracases, Miss—"

"Circuses," she snorted. "The old Roman games, all over again, and a hundred times worse. Blood and guts sadism. The quest of a frustrated person for satisfaction in another's pain. Our Lowers of today are as useless and frustrated as the Roman proletariat and potentially they're just as dangerous as the mob that once dominated Rome. Automation, the second industrial revolution, has eliminated for all practical purposes the need for their labor. So we give them bread and circuses. And every year that goes by the circuses must be increasingly sadistic, death on an increasing scale, or they aren't satisfied. Once it was enough to have fictional mayhem, cowboys and Indians, gangsters, or G.I.s versus the Nazis, Japs or Commies, but that's passed. Now we need *real* blood and guts."

Baron Haer snapped finally, "All right, Nadine. We've heard this lecture before. I doubt if the captain is interested, particularly since you don't seem to be able to get beyond the protesting stage and have yet to come up with an answer."

"I have an answer!"

"Ah?" Balt Haer raised his eyebrows, mockingly.

"Yes! Overthrow this silly status society. Resume the road to progress. Put our people to useful endeavor, instead of sitting in front of their Telly sets, taking trank pills to put them in a happy daze and watching sadistic fracases to keep them in thrills, and their minds from their condition."

Joe had figured on keeping out of the controversy with this firebrand, but now, really interested, he said, "Progress to where?"

She must have caught in his tone that he wasn't needling. She frowned at him. "I don't know man's goal, if there is one. I'm not even sure it's important. It's the road that counts. The endeavor. The dream. The effort expended to make a world a better place than it was at the time of your birth."

Balt Haer said mockingly, "That's the trouble with you, Sis. Here we've reached Utopia and you don't admit it."

"Utopia!"

"Certainly. Take a poll. You'll find nineteen people out of twenty happy with things just the way they are. They have full tummies and security, lots of leisure and trank pills to make matters seem even rosier than they are—and they're rather rosy already."

"Then what's the necessity of this endless succession of bloody fracases, covered to the most minute bloody detail on the Telly?"

Baron Haer cut things short. "We've hashed and rehashed this before, Nadine and now we're too busy to debate further." He turned to Joe Mauser. "Very well, captain, you have my pledge. I wish I felt as optimistic as you seem to be about your prospect. That will be all for now, captain."

Joe saluted and executed an about face.

In the outer offices, when he had closed the door behind him, he rolled his eyes upward in mute thanks to whatever powers might be. He had somehow gained the enmity of Balt, his immediate superior, but he'd also gained the support of Baron Haer himself, which counted considerably more.

He considered for a moment Nadine Haer's words. She was obviously a malcontent, but, on the other hand, her opinions of his chosen profession weren't too different than his own. However, given this victory, this upgrading in caste, and Joe Mauser would be in a position to retire.

The door opened and shut behind him and he half turned.

Nadine Haer, evidently still caught up in the hot words between herself and her relatives, glared at him. All of which stressed the beauty he had noticed the day before. She was an almost unbelievably pretty girl, particularly when flushed with anger.

It occurred to him with a blowlike suddenness that, if his caste was raised to Upper, he would be in a position to woo such as Nadine Haer.

He looked into her furious face and said, "I was intrigued, Miss Haer with what you had to say, and I'd like to discuss some of your points. I wonder if I could have the pleasure of your company at some nearby refreshment—"

"My, how formal an invitation, captain. I suppose you had in mind sitting and flipping back a few trank pills."

Joe looked at her. "I don't believe I've had a trank in the past twenty years, Miss Haer. Even as a boy, I didn't particularly take to having my senses dulled with drug induced pleasure."

Some of her fury was abating, but she was still critical of the professional mercenary. Her eyes went up and down his uniform in scorn. "You seem to make pretenses of being cultivated, captain. Then why your chosen profession?"

He'd had the answer to that for long years. He said now, simply, "I told you I was born a Lower. Given that, little counts until I fight my way out of it. Had I been born in a feudalist society, I would have attempted to better myself into the nobility. Under classical capitalism, I would have done my utmost to accumulate a fortune, enough to reach an effective position in society. Now, under People's Capitalism. . ."

She snorted, "Industrial Feudalism would be the better term."

". . . I realize I can't even start to fulfill myself until I am a member of the Upper Caste."

Her eyes had narrowed, and the anger was largely gone. "But you chose the military field in which to better yourself?"

"Government propaganda to the contrary, it is practically impossible to raise yourself in other fields. I didn't build this world, possibly I don't even approve of it, but since I'm in it I have no recourse but to follow its rules."

Her eyebrows arched. "Why not try to change the rules?"

Joe blinked at her.

Nadine Haer said, "Let's look up that refreshment you were talking about. In fact, there's a small coffee bar around the corner where it'd be possible for one of Baron Haer's brood to have a cup with one of her father's officers of Middle caste."

VI

The following morning, hands on the pillow beneath his head, Joe Mauser stared up at the ceiling of his room and rehashed his session with Nadine Haer. It hadn't taken him five minutes to come to the conclusion that he was in love with the girl, but it had taken him the rest of the evening to keep himself under rein and not let the fact get through to her.

He wanted to talk about the way her mouth tucked in at the corners, but she was hot on the evolution of society. He would have liked to have kissed that impossibly perfectly shaped ear of hers, but she was all for exploring the reasons why man had reached his present impasse. Joe was for holding hands, and staring into each other's eyes, she was for delving into the differences between the West-world and the Sov-world and the possibility of resolving them.

Of course, to keep her company at all it had been necessary to suppress his own desires and to go along. It obviously had never occurred to her that a Middle might have romantic ideas involving Nadine Haer. It had simply not occurred to her, no matter the radical teachings she advocated.

Most of their world was predictable from what had gone before. In spite of popular fable to the contrary, the division between classes had become increasingly clear. Among other things, tax systems were such that it became all but impossible for a citizen born poor to accumulate a fortune. Through ability he might rise to the point of earning fabulous sums—and wind up in debt to the tax collector. A great inventor, a great artist, had little chance of breaking into the domain of what finally became the small percentage of the population now known as Uppers. Then, too, the rising cost of a really good education became such that few other than those born into the Middle or Upper castes could afford the best of schools. Castes tended to perpetuate themselves.

Politically, the nation had fallen increasingly deeper into the two-party system, both parties of which were tightly controlled by the same group of Uppers. Elections had become a farce, a great national holiday in which stereotyped patriotic speeches, pretenses of unity between all castes, picnics, beer busts and trank binges predominated for one day.

Economically, too, the augurs had been there. Production of the basics had become so profuse that poverty in the old sense of the word had become nonsensical. There was an abundance of the necessities of life for all. Social security, socialized medicine, unending unemployment insurance, old age pensions, pensions for veterans, for widows and children, for the unfit, pensions and doles for this, that and the other, had doubled, and doubled again, until everyone had security for life. The Uppers, true enough, had opulence far beyond that known by the Middles and lived like Gods compared to the Lowers. But all had security.

They had agreed, thus far, Joe and Nadine. But then had come debate.

Then why," Joe had asked her, "haven't we achieved what your brother called it? Why isn't this Utopia? Isn't it what man has been yearning for, down through the ages? Where did the wheel come off? What happened to the dream?"

Nadine had frowned at him—beautifully, he thought. "It's not the first time man has found abundance in a society, though never to this degree. The Incas had it, for instance."

"I don't know much about them," Joe admitted. "An early form of communism with a sort of military-priesthood at the top."

She had nodded, her face serious, as always. "And for themselves, the Romans more or less had it—at the expense of the nations they conquered, of course."

"And—" Joe prodded.

"And in these examples the same thing developed. Society ossified. Joe," she said, using his first name for the first time, and in a manner that set off a new count down in his blood, "a ruling caste and a socio-economic system perpetuates itself, just so long as it ever can. No matter what damage it may do to society as a whole, it perpetuates itself even to the point of complete destruction of everything.

"Remember Hitler? Adolf the Aryan and his Thousand Year Reich? When it became obvious he had failed, and the only thing that could result from continued resistance would be destruction of Germany's cities and millions of her people, did he and his clique resign or surrender? Certainly not. They attempted to bring down the whole German structure in a Götterdammerung."

Nadine Haer was deep into her theme, her eyes flashing her conviction. "A socio-economic system reacts like a living organism. It attempts to live on, indefinitely, agonizingly, no matter how antiquated it might have become. The Roman politico-economic system continued for centuries after it should have been replaced. Such reformers as the Gracchus brothers were assassinated or thrust aside so that the entrenched elements could perpetuate themselves, and when Rome finally fell, darkness descended for a thousand years on Western progress."

Joe had never gone this far in his thoughts. He said now, somewhat uncomfortably. "Well, what would replace what we have now? If you took power from you Uppers, who could direct the country? The Lowers? That's not even funny. Take away their fracases and their trank pills and they'd go berserk. They don't *want* anything else."

Her mouth worked. "Admittedly, we've already allowed things to deteriorate much too far. We should have done something long ago. I'm not sure I know the answer. All I know is that in order to maintain the status quo, we're not utilizing the efforts of more than a fraction of our people. Nine out of ten of us spend our lives sitting before the Telly, sucking tranks. Meanwhile, the motivation for continued progress seems to have withered away. Our Upper political circles are afraid some seemingly minor change might avalanche, so more and more we lean upon the old way of doing things."

Joe had put up mild argument. "I've heard the case made that the Lowers are fools and the reason our present socio-economic system makes it so difficult to rise from Lower to Upper is that you cannot make a fool understand he is one. You can only make him angry. If some, who are not fools, are allowed to advance from Lower to Upper, the vast mass who are fools will be angry because they are not allowed to. That's why the Military Category is made a channel of advance. To take that road, a man gives up his security and he'll die if he's a fool."

Nadine had been scornful. "That reminds me of the old contention by racial segregationalists that the Negroes *smelled* bad. First they put them in a position where they had insufficient bathing facilities, their diet inadequate, and their teeth uncared for, and then protested that they couldn't be associated with because of their odor. Today, we are born within our castes. If an Upper is inadequate, he nevertheless remains an Upper. An accident of birth makes him an aristocrat; environment, family, training, education, friends, traditions and laws maintain him in that position. But a Lower who potentially has the greatest of value to society, is born handicapped and he's hard put not to wind up before a Telly, in a mental daze from trank. Sure he's a fool, he's never been *allowed* to develop himself."

Yes, Joe reflected now, it had been quite an evening. In a life of more than thirty years devoted to rebellion, he had never met anyone so outspoken as Nadine Haer, nor one who had thought it through as far as she had.

He grunted. His own revolt was against the level at which he had found himself in society, not the structure of society itself. His whole *raison d'etre* was to lift himself to Upper status. It came as a shock to him to find a person he admired who had been born into Upper caste, desirous of tearing the whole system down.

His thoughts were interrupted by the door opening and the face of Max Mainz grinning in at him. Joe was mildly surprised at his orderly not knocking before opening the door. Max evidently had a lot to learn.

The little man blurted, "Come on, Joe. Let's go out on the town!"

"*Joe?*" Joe Mauser raised himself to one elbow and stared at the other. "Leaving aside the merits of your suggestion for the moment, do you think you should address an officer by his first name?"

Max Mainz came fully into the bedroom, his grin still wider. "You forgot! It's election day!"

"Oh," Joe Mauser relaxed into his pillow. "So it is. No duty for today eh?"

"No duty for anybody," Max crowed. "Whatd' you say we go into town and have a few drinks in one of the Upper bars?"

Joe grunted, but began to arise. "What'll that accomplish? On election day, most of the Uppers get done up in their oldest clothes and go slumming down in the Lower quarters."

Max wasn't to be put off so easily. "Well, wherever we go, let's get going. Zen! I'll bet this town is full of fracas buffs from as far as Philly. And on election day, to boot. Wouldn't it be something if I found me a real fracas fan, some Upper-Upper dame?"

Joe laughed at him, even as he headed for the bathroom. As a matter of fact, he rather liked the idea of going into town for the show. "Max," he said over his shoulder, "you're in for a big disappointment. They're all the same. Upper, Lower, or Middle."

"Yeah?" Max grinned back at him. "Well, I'd like the pleasure of finding out if that's true by personal experience."

VII

In a far away past, Kingston had once been the capital of the United States. For a short time, when Washington's men were in flight after the debacle of their defeat in New York City, the government of the United Colonies had held session in this Hudson River town. It had been its one moment of historic glory, and afterward Kingston had slipped back into being a minor city on the edge of the Catskills, approximately halfway between New York and Albany.

Of most recent years, it had become one of the two recruiting centers which bordered the Catskill Military Reservation, which in turn was one of the score or so population cleared areas throughout the continent where rival corporations or unions could meet and settle their differences in combat—given permission of the Military Category Department of the government. And permission was becoming ever easier to acquire.

It had slowly evolved, the resorting to trial by combat to settle disputes between competing corporations, disputes between corporations and unions, disputes between unions over jurisdiction. Slowly, but predictably. Since the earliest days of the first industrial revolution, conflict between these elements had often broken into violence, sometimes on a scale comparable to minor warfare. An early example was the union organizing in Colorado when armed elements of the Western Federation of Miners shot it out with similarly armed "detectives" hired by the mine owners, and later with the troops of an unsympathetic State government.

By the middle of the Twentieth-Century, unions had become one of the biggest businesses in the country, and by this time a considerable amount of the industrial conflict had shifted to fights between them for jurisdiction over dues-paying members. Battles on the waterfront, assassination and counter-assassination by gun-toting goon squads dominated by gangsters, industrial sabotage, frays between pickets and scabs—all were common occurrences.

But it was the coming of Telly which increasingly brought such conflicts literally before the public eye. Zealous reporters made ever greater effort to bring the actual mayhem before the eyes of their viewers, and never were their efforts more highly rewarded.

A society based upon private endeavor is as jealous of a vacuum as is mother nature. Give a desire that can be filled profitably, and the means can somehow be found to realize it.

At one point in the nation's history, the railroad lords had dominated the economy, later it became the petroleum princes of Texas and elsewhere, but toward the end of the Twentieth Century the communications industries slowly gained prominence. Nothing was more greatly in demand than feeding the insatiable maw of the Telly fan, nothing, ultimately, became more profitable.

And increasingly, the Telly buff endorsed the more sadistic of the fictional and nonfictional programs presented him. Even in the earliest years of the industry, producers had found that murder and mayhem, war and frontier gunfights, took precedence over less gruesome subjects. Music was drowned out by gunfire, the dance replaced by the shuffle of cowboy and rustler advancing down a dustry street toward each other, their fingertips brushing the grips of their six-shooters, the comedian's banter fell away before the chatter of the gangster's tommy gun.

And increasing realism was demanded. The Telly reporter on the scene of a police arrest, preferably a murder, a rumble between rival gangs of juvenile delinquents, a longshoreman's fray in which scores of workers were hospitalized. When attempts were made to suppress such broadcasts, the howl of freedom of speech and the press went up, financed by tycoons clever enough to realize the value of the subjects they covered so adequately.

The vacuum was there, the desire, the *need*. Bread the populace had. Trank was available to all. But the need was for the circus, the vicious, sadistic circus, and bit by bit, over the years and decades, the way was found to circumvent the country's laws and traditions to supply the need.

Aye, a way is always found. The final Universal Disarmament Pact which had totally banned all weapons invented since the year 1900 and provided for complete inspection, had not ended the fear of war. And thus there was excuse to give the would-be soldier, the potential defender of the country in some future international conflict, practical experience.

Slowly tolerance grew to allow union and corporation to fight it out, hiring the services of mercenaries. Slowly rules grew up to govern such fracases. Slowly a department of government evolved. The Military Category became as acceptable as the next, and the mercenary a valued, even idolized, member of society. And the field became practically the only one in which a status quo oriented socio-economic system allowed for advancement in caste.

Joe Mauser and Max Mainz strolled the streets of Kingston in an extreme of atmosphere seldom to be enjoyed. Not only was the advent of a divisional magnitude fracas only a short period away, but the freedom of an election day as well. The carnival, the Mardi Gras, the fete, the fiesta, of an election. Election Day, when each aristocrat became only a man, and each man an aristocrat, free of all society's artifically conceived, caste perpetuating rituals and taboos.

Carnival! The day was young, but already the streets were thick with revelers, with dancers, with drunks. A score of bands played, youngsters in particular ran about attired in costume, there were barbeques and flowing beer kegs. On the outskirts of town were roller coasters and ferris wheels, fun houses and drive-it-yourself miniature cars. Carnival!

Max said happily, "You drink, Joe? Or maybe you like trank, better." Obviously, he loved to roll the other's first name over his tongue.

Joe wondered in amusement how often the little man had found occasion to call a Mid-Middle by his first name. "No trank," he said. "Alcohol for me. Mankind's old faithful."

"Well," Max debated, "get high on alcohol and bingo, a hangover in the morning. But trank? You wake up with a smile."

"And a desire for more trank to keep the mood going," Joe said wryly. "Get smashed on alcohol and you suffer for it eventually."

"Well, that's one way of looking at it," Max argued happily. "So let's start off with a couple of quick ones in this here Upper joint."

Joe looked the place over. He didn't know Kingston overly well, but by the appearance of the building and by the entry, it was probably the swankiest hotel in town. He shrugged. So far as he was concerned, he appreciated the greater comfort and the better service of his Middle caste bars, restaurants and hotels over the ones he had patronized was a Lower. However, his wasn't an immediate desire to push into the preserves of the Uppers; not until he had won rightfully to their status.

But on this occasion the little fellow wanted to drink at an Upper bar. Very well, it was election day. "Let's go," he said to Max.

In the uniform of a Rank Captain of the Military Category, there was little to indicate caste level, and ordinarily given the correct air of nonchalance, Joe Mauser, in uniform, would have been able to go anywhere, without so much as a raised eyebrow—until he had presented his credit card, which indicated his caste. But Max was another thing. He was obviously a Lower, and probably a Low-Lower at that.

But space was made for them at a bar packed with election day celebrants, politicians involved in the day's speeches and voting, higher ranking officers of the Haer forces, having a day off, and various Uppers of both sexes in town for the excitement of the fracas to come.

"Beer," Joe said to the bartender.

"Not me," Max crowed. "Champagne. Only the best for Max Mainz. Give me some of that champagne liquor I always been hearing about."

Joe had the bill credited to his card, and they took their bottles and glasses to a newly abandoned table. The place was too packed to have awaited the services of a waiter, although poor Max probably would have loved such attention. Lower, and even Middle bars and restaurants were universally automated, and the waiter or waitress a thing of yesteryear.

Max looked about the room in awe. "This is living," he announced. "I wonder what they'd say if I went to the desk and ordered a room."

Joe Muster wasn't as highly impressed as his batman. In fact, he'd often stayed in the larger cities, in hostelries as sumptuous as this, though only of Middle status. Kingston's best was on the mediocre side. He said, "They'd probably tell you they were filled up."

Max was indignant. "Because I'm a Lower? It's *election* day."

Joe said mildly, "Because they probably are filled up. But for that matter, they might brush you off. It's not as though an Upper went to a Middle or Lower hotel and asked for accommodations. But what do you want, justice?"

Max dropped it. He looked down into his glass. "Hey," he complained, "what'd they give me? This stuff tastes like weak hard cider."

Joe laughed. "What did you think it was going to taste like?"

Max took another unhappy sip. "I thought it was supposed to be the best drink you could buy. You know, really strong. It's just bubbly wine."

A voice said, dryly, "Your companion doesn't seem to be a connoisseur of the French vintages, captain."

Joe turned. Balt Haer and two others occupied the table next to them.

Joe chuckled amiably and said, "Truthfully, it was my own reaction, the first time I drank sparkling wine, sir."

"Indeed," Haer said. "I can imagine." He fluttered a hand. "Lieutenant Colonel Paul Warren of Marshal Cogswell's staff, and Colonel Lajos Arpad, of Budapest—Captain Joseph Mauser."

Joe Mauser came to his feet and clicked his heels, bowing from the waist in approved military protocol. The other two didn't bother to come to their feet, but did condescend to shake hands.

The Sov officer said, disinterestedly, "Ah yes, this is one of your fabulous customs, isn't it? On an election day, everyone is quite entitled to go anywhere. Anywhere at all. And, ah"—he made a sound somewhat like a giggle—"associate with anyone at all."

Joe Mauser resumed his seat then looked at him. "That is correct. A custom going back to the early history of the country when all men were considered equal in such matters as law and civil rights. Gentlemen, may I present Rank Private Max Mainz, my orderly."

Balt Haer, who had obviously already had a few, looked at him dourly. "You can carry these things to the point of the ludicrous, captain. For a man with your ambitions, I'm surprised."

The infantry officer the younger Haer had introduced as Lieutenant Colonel Warren, of Stonewall Cogswell's staff, said idly, "Ambitions? Does the captain have ambitions? How in Zen can a Middle have ambitions, Balt?" He stared at Joe Mauser superciliously, but then scowled. "Haven't I seen you somewhere before?"

Joes said evenly, "Yes, sir. Five years ago we were both with the marshal in a fracas on the Little Big Horn reservation. Your company was pinned down on a knoll by a battery of field artillery. The Marshal sent me to your relief. We sneaked in, up an arroyo, and were able to get most of you out."

"I was wounded," the colonel said, the superciliousness gone and a strange element in his voice above the alcohol there earlier.

Joe Mauser said nothing to that. Max Mainz was stirring unhappily now. These officers were talking above his head, even as they ignored him. He had a vague feeling that he was being defended by Captain Mauser, but he didn't know how, or why.

Balt Haer had been occupied in shouting fresh drinks. Now he turned back to the table. "Well, colonel, it's all very secret, these ambitions of Captain Mauser. I understand he's been an aide de camp to Marshal Cogswell in the past, but the marshal will be distressed to learn that on this occasion Captain Mauser has a secret by which he expects to rout your forces. Indeed, yes, the captain is quite the strategist." Balt Haer laughed abruptly. "And what good will this do the captain? Why on my father's word, if he succeeds all efforts will be made to make the captain a caste equal of ours. Not just on election day, mind you, but all three hundred sixty-five days of the year."

Joe Mauser was on his feet, his face expressionless. He said, "Shall we go, Max? Gentlemen, it's been a pleasure. Colonel Arpad, a privilege to meet you. Colonel Warren, a pleasure to renew acquaintance." Joe Mauser turned and, trailed by his orderly, left.

Lieutenant Colonel Warren, pale, was on his feet too.

Balt Haer was chuckling. "Sit down, Paul. Sit down. Not important enough to be angry about. The man's a clod."

Warren looked at him bleakly. "I wasn't angry, Balt. The last time I saw Captain Mauser I was slung over his shoulder. He carried, tugged and dragged me some two miles through enemy fire."

Balt Haer carried it off with a shrug. "Well, that's his profession. Category Military. A mercenary for hire. I assume he received his pay."

"He could have left me. Common sense dictated that he leave me."

Balt Haer was annoyed. "Well, then we see what I've contended all along. The ambitious captain doesn't have common sense."

Colonel Paul Warren shook his head. "You're wrong there. Common sense Joseph Mauser has. Considerable ability, he has. He's one of the best combat men in the field. But I'd hate to serve under him."

The Hungarian was interested. "But why?"

"Because he doesn't have luck, and in the dill you need luck." Warren grunted in sour memory. "Had the Telly cameras been focused on Joe Mauser, there at the Little Big Horn, he would have been a month long sensation to the Telly buffs, with all that means." He grunted again. "There wasn't a Telly team within a mile."

"The captain probably didn't realize that," Balt Haer snorted. "Otherwise his heroics would have been modified."

Warren flushed his displeasure and sat down. He said, "Possibly we should discuss the business before us. If your father is in agreement, the fracas can begin in three days." He turned to the representative of the Sov-world. "You have satisfied yourselves that neither force is violating the Disarmament Pact?"

Lajos Arpad nodded. "We will wish to have observers on the field, itself, of course. But preliminary observation has been satisfactory." He had been interested in the play between these two and the lower caste officer. He said now, "Pardon me. As you know, this is my first visit to the, uh *West*. I am fascinated. If I understand what just transpired, our Captain Mauser is a capable junior officer ambitious to rise in rank and status in your society." He looked at Balt Haer. "Why are you opposed to his so rising?"

Young Haer was testy about the whole matter. "Of what purpose is an Upper caste if every Tom, Dick and Harry enters it at will?"

Warren looked at the door through which Joe and Max had exited from the cocktail lounge. He opened his mouth to say something, closed it again, and held his peace.

The Hungarian said, looking from one of them to the other, "In the Sov-world we seek out such ambitious persons and utilize their abilities."

Lieutenant Colonel Warren laughed abruptly. "So do we here *theorteically*. We are *free*, whatever that means. However," he added sarcastically, "it does help to have good schooling, good connections, relatives in positions of prominence, abundant shares of good stocks, that sort of thing. And these one is born with, in this free world of ours, Colonel Arpad."

The Sov military observer clucked his tongue. "An indication of a declining society."

Balt Haer turned on him. "And is it any different in your world?" he said sneeringly. "Is it merely coincidence that the best positions in the Sov-world are held by Party members, and that it is all but impossible for anyone not born of Party member parents to become one? Are not the best schools filled with the children of Party members? Are not only Party members allowed to keep servants? And isn't it so that—"

VIII

Baron Malcolm Haer's field headquarters were in the ruins of a farm house in a town once known as Bearsville. His forces, and those of Marshal Stonewall Cogswell, were on the march but as yet their main bodies had not come in contact. Save for skirmishes between cavalry units, there had been no action. The ruined farm house had been a victim of an earlier fracas in this reservation which had seen in its comparatively brief time more combat than Belgium, that cockpit of Europe.

There was a sheen of oily moisture on the Baron's bulletlike head and his officers weren't particularly happy about it. Malcolm Haer characteristically went into a fracas with confidence, an aggressive confidence so strong that it often carried the day. In battles past, it had become a tradition that Haer's morale was worth a thousand men; the energy he expended was the despair of his doctors who had been warning him for a decade. But now, something was missing.

A forefinger traced over the military chart before them. "So far as we know, Marshal Cogswell has established his command here in Saugerties. Anybody have any suggestions as to why?"

A major grumbled, "It doesn't make much sense, sir. You know the marshal. It's probably a fake. If we have any superiority at all, it's our artillery."

"And the old fox wouldn't want to join the issue on the plains, down near the river," a colonel added. "It's his game to keep up into the mountains with his cavalry and light infantry. He's got Jack Alshuler's cavalry. Most experienced veterans in the field."

"I know who he's got," Haer growled in irritation. "Stop reminding me. Where in the devil is Balt?"

"Coming up, sir," Balt Haer said. He had entered only moments ago, a sheaf of signals in his hand. "Why didn't they make that date 1910, instead of 1900? With radio, we could speed up communications—"

His father interrupted testily. "Better still, why not make it 1945? Then we could speed up to the point where we could polish ourselves off. What have you got?"

Balt Haer said, his face in sulk, "Some of my lads based in West Hurley report concentrations of Cogswell's infantry and artillery near Ashokan reservoir."

"Nonsense," somebody snapped. "We'd have him."

The younger Haer slapped his swagger stick against his bare leg and kilt. "Possibly it's a feint," he admitted.

"How much were they able to observe?" his father demanded.

"Not much. They were driven off by a superior squadron. The Hovercraft forces are screening everything they do with heavy cavalry units. I told you we needed more—"

"I don't need your advice at this point," his father snapped. The older Haer went back to the map, scowling still. "I don't see what he expects to do, working out of Saugerties."

A voice behind them said, "Sir may I have your permission—"

Half of the assembled officers turned to look at the newcomer.

Balt Haer snapped, "Captain Mauser. Why aren't you with your lads?"

"Turned them over to my second in command, sir," Joe Mauser said. He was standing to attention, looking at Baron Haer.

The Baron glowered at him. "What is the meaning of this cavalier intrusion, captain? Certainly, you must have your orders. Are you under the illusion that you are part of my staff?"

"No, sir," Joe Mauser clipped. "I came to report that I am ready to put into execution—"

"The great plan!" Balt Haer ejaculated. He laughed brittlely. "The second day of the fracas, and nobody really knows where old Cogswell is, or what he plans to do. And here comes the captain with his secret plan."

Joe looked at him. He said, evenly, "Yes, sir."

The Baron's face had gone dark, as much in anger at his son, as with the upstart cavalry captain. He began to growl ominously, "Captain Mauser, rejoin your command and obey your orders."

Joe Mauser's facial expression indicated that he had expected this. He kept his voice level however, even under the chuckling scorn of his immediate superior, Balt Haer.

He said, "Sir, I will be able to tell you where Marshal Cogswell is, and every troop at his command."

For a moment there was silence, all but a stunned silence. Then the major who had suggested the Saugerties field command headquarters were a fake, blurted a curt laugh.

"This is no time for levity, captain," Balt Haer clipped. "Get to your command."

A colonel said, "Just a moment, sir. I've fought with Joe Mauser before. He's a good man."

"Not that good," someone else huffed. "Does he claim to be clairvoyant?"

Joe Mauser said flatly. "Have a semaphore man posted here this afternoon. I'll be back at that time." He spun on his heel and left them.

Balt Haer rushed to the door after him, shouting, "Captain! That's an order! Return—"

But the other was obviously gone. Enraged, the younger Haer began to shrill commands to a noncom in the way of organizing a pursuit.

His father called wearily, "That's enough, Balt. Mauser has evidently taken leave of his senses. We made the initial mistake of encouraging this idea he had, or thought he had."

"*We?*" his son snapped in return. "I had nothing to do with it."

"All right, all right. Let's tighten up, here. Now, what other information have your scouts come up with?"

IX

At the Kingston airport, Joe Mauser rejoined Max Mainz, his face drawn now.

"Everything go all right?" the little man said anxiously.

"I don't know," Joe said. "I still couldn't tell them the story. Old Cogswell is as quick as a coyote. We pull this little caper today, and he'll be ready to meet it tomorrow."

He looked at the two-place sailplane which sat on the tarmac. "Everything all set?"

"Far as I know," Max said. He looked at the motorless aircraft. "You sure you been checked out on these things, captain?"

"Yes," Joe said. "I bought this particular soaring glider more than a year ago, and I've put almost a thousand hours in it. Now, where's the pilot of that light plane?"

A single-engined sports plane was attached to the glider by a fifty-foot nylon rope. Even as Joe spoke, a youngster poked his head from the plane's window and grinned back at them. "Ready?" he yelled.

"Come on, Max," Joe said. "Let's pull the canopy off this thing. We don't want it in the way while you're semaphoring."

A figure was approaching them from the Administration Building. A uniformed man, and somehow familiar.

"A moment, Captain Mauser!"

Joe placed him now. The Sov-world representative he'd met at Balt Haer's table in the Upper bar a couple of days ago. What was his name? Colonel Arpad. Lajos Arpad.

The Hungarian approached and looked at the sailplane in interest. "As a representative of my government, a military attache checking upon possibile violations of the Universal Disarmament Pact, may I request what you are about to do, captain?"

Joe Mauser looked at him emptily. "How did you know I was here and what I was doing?"

The Sov colonel smiled gently. "It was by suggestion of Marshal Cogswell. He is a great man for detail. It disturbed him that an . . . what did he call it? . . . an *old pro* like yourself should join with Vacuum Tube Transport, rather than Continental Hovercraft. He didn't think it made sense and suggested that possibly you had in mind some scheme that would utilize weapons of a post 1900 period in your efforts to bring success to Baron Haer's forces. So I have investigated, Captain Mauser."

"And the marshal knows about this sail plane?" Joe Mauser's face was blank.

"I didn't say that. So far as I know, he doesn't."

"Then, Colonel Arpad, with your permission, I'll be taking off."

The Hungarian said, "With what end in mind, captain?"

"Using this glider as a reconnaissance aircraft."

"Captain, I warn you! Aircraft were not in use in warfare until—"

But Joe Mauser cut him off, equally briskly. "Aircraft were first used in combat by Pancho Villa's forces a few years previous to World War I. They were also used in the Balkan Wars of about the same period. But those were powered craft. This is a glider, invented and in use before the year 1900 and hence open to utilization."

The Hungarian clipped, "But the Wright Brothers didn't fly even gliders until—"

Joe looked him full in the face. "But you of the Sov world do not admit that the Wrights were the first to fly, do you?"

The Hungarian closed his mouth, abruptly.

Joe said evenly, "But even if Ivan Ivanovitch, or whatever you claim his name was, didn't invent flight of heavier than air craft, the glider was flown variously before 1900, including Otto Lilienthal in the 1890s, and was designed as far back as Leonardo da Vinci."

The Sov world colonel stared at him for a long moment, then gave an inane giggle. He stepped back and flicked Joe Mauser a salute. "Very well, captain. As a matter of routine, I shall report this use of an aircraft for reconnaissance purposes, and undoubtedly a commission will meet to investigate the propriety of the departure. Meanwhile, good luck!"

Joe returned the salute and swung a leg over the cockpit's side. Max was already in the front seat, his semaphore flags, maps and binoculars on his lap. He had been staring in dismay at the Sov officer, now was relieved that Joe had evidently pulled it off.

Joe waved to the plane ahead. Two mechanics had come up to steady the wings for the initial ten or fifteen feet of the motorless craft's passage over the ground behind the towing craft.

Joe said to Max, "did you explain to the pilot that under no circumstances was he to pass over the line of the military reservation, that we'd cut before we reached that point?"

"Yes, sir," Max said nervously. He'd flown before, on the commercial lines, but he'd never been in a glider.

They began lurching across the field, slowly, then gathering speed.

And as the sailplane took speed, it took grace. After it had been pulled a hundred feet or so, Joe eased back the stick and it slipped gently into the air, four or five feet off the ground. The towing airplane was still taxiing, but with its tow airborne it picked up speed quickly. Another two hundred feet and it, too, was in the air and beginning to climb. The glider behind held it to a speed of sixty miles or so.

At ten thousand feet, the plane leveled off and the pilot's head swiveled to look back at them. Joe Mauser waved to him and dropped the release lever which ejected the nylon rope from the glider's nose. The plane dove away, trailing the rope behind it. Joe knew that the plane pilot would later drop it over the airport where it could easily be retrieved.

In the direction of Mount Overlook he could see cumulus clouds and the dark turbulence which meant strong updraft. He headed in that direction.

Except for the whistling of wind, there is complete silence in a soaring glider. Max Mainz began to call back to his superior, was taken back by the volume, and dropped his voice. He said, "Look, captain. What keeps it up?"

Joe grinned. He liked the buoyance of glider flying, the nearest approach of man to the bird, and thus far everything was going well. He told Max, "An airplane plows through the air currents, a glider rides on top of them."

"Yeah, but suppose the current is going down?"

"Then we avoid it. This sailplane only has a gliding angle ratio of one to twenty-five, but it's a workhorse with a payload of some four hundred pounds. A really high performance glider can have a ratio of as much as one to forty."

Joe had found a strong updraft where a wind ran up the side of a mountain. He banked, went into a circling turn. The gauge indicated they were climbing at the rate of eight meters per second, nearly fifteen hundred feet a minute.

Max hadn't got the rundown on the theory of the glider. That was obvious in his expression.

Joe Mauser, even while searching the ground below keenly, went into it further. "A wind up against a mountain will give an updraft, storm clouds will, even a newly plowed field in a bright sun. So you go from one of these to the next."

"Yeah, great, but when you're between," Max protested.

"Then, when you have a one to twenty-five ratio, you go twenty-five feet forward for each one you drop. If you started a mile high, you could go twenty-five miles before you touched ground." He cut himself off quickly. "Look, what's that, down there? Get your glasses on it."

Max caught his excitement. His binoculars were tight to his eyes. "Sojers. Cavalry. They sure ain't ours. They must be Hovercraft lads. And look, field artillery."

Joe Mauser was piloting with his left hand, his right smoothing out a chart on his lap. He growled. "What are they doing there? That's at least a full brigade of cavalry. Here, let me have those glasses."

With his knees gripping the stick, he went into a slow circle, as he stared down at the column of men. "Jack Alshuler," he whistled in surprise. "The marshal's crack heavy cavalry. And several batteries of artillery." He swung the glasses in a wider scope and the whistle turned into a hiss of comprehension. "They're doing a complete circle of the reservation. They're going to hit the Baron from the direction of Phoenecia."

X

Marshal Stonewall Cogswell directed his old fashioned telescope in the direction his chief of staff indicated.

"What is it?" he grunted.

"It's an airplane, sir."

"Over a military reservation with a fracas in progress?"

"Yes, sir." The other put his glasses back on the circling object. "Then what is it, sir. Certainly not a free balloon."

"Balloons," the marshal snorted, as though to himself. "Legal to use. The Union forces had them toward the end of the Civil War. But practically useless in a fracas of movement."

They were standing before the former resort hotel which housed the marshal's headquarters. Other staff members were streaming from the building, and one of the ever-present Telly reporting crews were hurriedly setting up cameras.

The marshal turned and barked, "Does anybody know what in Zen that confounded thing, circling up there, is?"

Baron Zwerdling, the aging Category Transport magnate, head of Continental Hovercraft, hobbled onto the wooden veranda and stared with the others. "An airplane," he croaked. "Haer's gone too far this time. Too far, too far. This will strip him. Strip him, understand." Then he added, "Why doesn't it make any noise?"

Lieutenant Colonel Paul Warren stood next to his commanding officer. "It looks like a glider, sir."

Cogswell glowered at him. "A what?"

"A glider, sir. It's a sport not particularly popular these days."

"What keeps it up, confound it?"

Paul Warren looked at him. "The same thing that keeps a hawk up, an albatross, a gull—"

"A vulture, you mean," Cogswell snarled. He watched it for another long moment, his face working. He whirled on his chief of artillery. "Jed, can you bring that thing down?"

The other had been viewing the craft through field binoculars, his face as shocked as the rest of them. Now he faced his chief, and lowered the glasses, shaking his head. "Not with the artillery of pre-1900, No, sir."

"What can you do?" Cogswell barked.

The artillery man was shaking his head. "We could mount some Maxim guns on wagon wheels, or something. Keep him from coming low."

"He doesn't have to come low," Cogswell growled unhappily. He spun on Lieutenant Colonel Warren again. "When were they invented?" He jerked his thumb upward. "Those things."

Warren was twisting his face in memory. "Some time about the turn of the century."

"How long can the things stay up?"

Warren took in the surrounding mountainous countryside. "Indefinitely, sir. A single pilot, as long as he is physically able to operate. If there are two pilots up there to relieve each other, they could stay until food and water ran out."

"How much weight do they carry?"

"I'm not sure. One that size, certainly enough for two men and any equipment they'd need. Say, five hundred pounds."

Cogswell had his telescope glued to his eyes again, he muttered under his breath, "Five hundred pounds! They could even unload dynamite over our horses. Stampede them all over the reservation."

"What's going on?" Baron Zwerdling shrilled. "What's going on Marshal Cogswell?"

Cogswell ignored him. He watched the circling, circling craft for a full five minutes, breathing deeply. Then he lowered his glass and swept the assembled officers of his staff with an indignant glare. "Ten Eyck!" he grunted.

An infantry colonel came to attention. "Yes, sir."

Cogswell said heavily, deliberately. "Under a white flag. A dispatch to Baron Haer. My compliments and request for his terms.

While you're at it, my compliments also to Captain Joseph Mauser."

Zwerdling was bug-eyeing him. "Terms!" he rasped.

The marshal turned to him. "Yes, sir. Face reality. We're in the dill. I suggest you sue for terms as short of complete capitulation as you can make them."

"You call yourself a soldier—!" the transport tycoon began to shrill.

"Yes, sir," Cogswell snapped. "A soldier, not a butcher of the lads under me." He called to the Telly reporter who was getting as much of this as he could. "Mr. Soligen, isn't it?"

The reporter scurried forward, flicking signals to his cameramen for proper coverage. "Yes, sir. Freddy Soligen, marshal. Could you tell the Telly fans what this is all about, Marshal Cogswell? Folks, you all know the famous marshal. Marshal Stonewall Cogswell, who hasn't lost a fracas in nearly ten years, now commanding the forces of Continental Hovercraft."

"I'm losing one now," Cogswell said grimly. "Vacuum Tube Transport has pulled a gimmick out of the hat and things have pickled for us. It will be debated before the Military Category Department, of course, and undoubtedly the Sov-world military attaches will have things to say. But as it appears now, the fracas as we have known it, has been revolutionized."

"Revolutionized?" Even the Telly reporter was flabbergasted. "You mean by that thing?" He pointed upward, and the lenses of the cameras followed his finger.

"Yes," Cogswell growled unhappily. "Do all of you need a blueprint? Do you think I can fight a fracas with that thing dangling above me, throughout the day hours? Do you understand the importance of reconnaissance in warfare?" His eyes glowered. "Do you think Napoleon would have lost Waterloo if he'd had the advantage of perfect reconnaissance such as that thing can deliver? Do you think Lee would have lost Gettysburg? Don't be ridiculous." He spun on Baron Zwerdling, who was stuttering his complete confusion.

"As it stands, Baron Haer knows every troop dispensation I make. All I know of his movements are from my cavalry scouts. I repeat, I am no butcher, sir. I will gladly cross swords with Baron Haer another day, when I, too, have . . . what did you call the confounded things, Paul?"

"Glider," Lieutenant Colonel Warren said.

XI

Major Joseph Mauser, now attired in his best off-duty Category Military uniform, spoke his credentials to the receptionist. "I have no definite appointment, but I am sure the Baron will see me," he said.

"Yes, sir." The receptionist did the things that receptionists do, then looked up at him again. "Right through that door, major."

Joe Mauser gave the door a quick double rap and then entered before waiting an answer.

Balt Haer, in mufti, was standing at a far window, a drink in his hand, rather than his customary swagger stick. Nadine Haer sat in an easy-chair. The girl Joe Mauser loved had been crying.

Joe Mauser, suppressing his frown, made with the usual amenities.

Balt Haer without answering them, finished his drink in a gulp and stared at the newcomer. The old stare, the aloof stare, an aristocrat looking at an underling as though wondering what made the fellow tick. He said, finally, "I see you have been raised to Rank Major."

"Yes, sir," Joe said.

"We are obviously occupied, major. What can either my sister or I possibly do for you?"

Joe kept his voice even. He said, "I wanted to see the Baron."

Nadine Haer looked up, a twinge of pain crossing her face.

"Indeed," Balt Haer said flatly. "You are talking to the Baron, Major Mauser."

Joe Mauser looked at him, then at his sister, who had taken to her handkerchief again. Consternation ebbed up and over him in a flood. He wanted to say something such as, "Oh *no*," but not even that could he utter.

Haer was bitter. "I assume I know why you are here, major. You have come for your pound of flesh, undoubtedly. Even in these hours of our grief—"

"I . . . I didn't know. Please believe. . ."

". . . You are so constituted that your ambition has no decency. Well, Major Mauser, I can only say that your arrangement was with my father. Even if I thought it a reasonable one, I doubt if I would sponsor your ambitions myself."

Nadine Haer looked up wearily. "Oh, Balt, come off it," she said. "The fact is, the Haer fortunes contracted a debt to you, major. Unfortunately, it is a debt we cannot pay." She looked into his face. "First, my father's governmental connections do not apply to us. Second, six months ago, my father, worried about his health and attempting to avoid certain death taxes, transferred the family stocks into Balt's name. And Balt saw fit, immediately before the fracas, to sell all Vacuum Tube Transport stocks, and invest in Hovercraft."

"That's enough, Nadine," her brother snapped nastily.

"I see," Joe said. He came to attention. "Dr. Haer, my apologies for intruding upon you in your time of bereavement." He turned to the new Baron. "Baron Haer, my apologies for *your* bereavement."

Balt Haer glowered at him.

Joe Mauser turned and marched for the door which he opened then closed behind him.

On the street, before the New York offices of Vacuum Tube Transport, he turned and for a moment looked up at the splendor of the building.

Well, at least the common shares of the concern had skyrocketed following the victory. His rank had been upped to Major, and old Stonewall Cogswell had offered him a permanent position on his staff in command of aerial operations, no small matter of prestige. The difficulty was, he wasn't interested in the added money that would accrue to him, nor the higher rank—nor the prestige, for that matter.

He turned to go to his hotel.

An unbelievably beautiful girl came down the steps of the building. She said, "Joe."

He looked at her. "Yes?"

She put a hand on his sleeve. "Let's go somewhere and talk, Joe."

"About what?" He was infinitely weary now.

"About goals," she said. "As long as they exist, whether for individuals, or nations, or a whole species, life is still worth the living. Things are a bit bogged down right now, but at the risk of sounding very trite, there's tomorrow."

Damon Knight is too young to be a patriarch—"a person regarded as the father or founder of an order, class, etc."—but he has been described as one, and he certainly looks the part: huge grey beard, serious mein under long flowing locks. But no patriarch ever had such a hypertrophied sense of humor, or ever had such unerring aim with a peanut.

The order or class that Damon Knight is said to have fathered or foundered has a short (vaguely aquatic) name that Damon doesn't like, that isn't accurate anyhow, that critics have turned into an easy pejorative. All Damon asked was that science fiction be considered literature, not somehow immune to normal critical standards because of its free-wheeling subject matter or its commercial past; that science fiction writers bring to the way they write the same qualities of caring and imagination as the best ones apply to the things they write about.

Most of the stories in this book suggest an alternative to war by way of a surrogate institution, designed to satisfy whatever it is in human nature that needs war. A more permanent solution, of course, would be to change human nature.

RULE GOLDEN

by Damon Knight

I

A man in Des Moines kicked his wife when her back was turned. She was taken to the hospital, suffering from a broken coccyx.

So was he.

In Kansas City, Kansas, a youth armed with a .22 killed a school-mate with one shot through the chest, and instantly dropped dead of heart-failure.

In Decatur two middleweights named Packy Morris and Leo Oshinsky simultaneously knocked each other out.

In St. Louis, a policeman shot down a fleeing bank robber and collapsed. The bank robber died; the policemen's condition was described as critical.

I read those items in the afternoon editions of the Washington papers, and although I noted the pattern, I wasn't much impressed. Every newspaperman knows that runs of coincidence are a dime a dozen; *everything* happens that way—plane crashes, hotel fires, suicide pacts, people running amok with rifles, people giving away all their money; name it and I can show you an epidemic of it in the files.

What I was actually looking for were stories originating in two places: my home town and Chillicothe, Missouri. Stories with those datelines had been carefully cut out of the papers before I got them, so, for lack of anything better, I read everything datelined near either place. And that was how I happened to catch the Des Moines, Kansas City, Decatur and St. Louis items—all of those places will fit into a two-hundred-mile circle drawn with Chillicothe as its center.

I had asked for, but hadn't got, a copy of my own paper. That made it a little tough, because I had to sit there, in a Washington hotel room at night—and if you know a lonelier place and time, tell me—and wonder if they had really shut us down.

I knew it was unlikely. I knew things hadn't got that bad in America yet, by a long way. I knew they *wanted* me to sit there and worry about it, but I couldn't help it.

Ever since *La Prensa*, every newspaper publisher on this continent has felt a cold wind blowing down his back.

That's foolishness, I told myself. Not to wave the flag too much or anything, but the free speech tradition in this country is too strong; we haven't forgotten Peter Zenger.

And then it occurred to me that a lot of editors must have felt the same way, just before their papers were suppressed on the orders of an American President named Abraham Lincoln.

So I took one more turn around the room and got back into bed, and although I had already read all the papers from bannerlines to box scores, I started leafing through them again, just to make a little noise. Nothing to do.

I had asked for a book, and hadn't got it. That made sense, too; there was nothing to do in that room, nothing to distract me, nothing to read except newspapers—and how could I look at a newspaper without thinking of the *Herald-Star*?

My father founded the *Herald-Star*—the *Herald* part, that is, the *Star* came later—ten years before I was born. I inherited it from him, but I want to add that I'm not one of those publishers by right of primogeniture whose only function consists in supplying sophomoric by-lined copy for the front page; I started on the paper as a copy boy and I can still handle any job in a city room.

It was a good newspaper. It wasn't the biggest paper in the Middle West, or the fastest growing, or the loudest; but we'd had two Pulitzer prizes in the last fifteen years, we kept out practical bias on the editorial page, and up to now we had never knuckled under to anybody.

But this was the first time we had picked a fight with the U. S. Department of Defense.

Ten miles outside Chillicothe, Missouri, the Department had a little thousand-acre installation with three laboratory buildings, a small airfield, living quarters for a staff of two hundred and a one-story barracks. It was closed down in 1978 when the Phoenix-bomb program was officially abandoned.

Two years and ten months later, it was opened up again. A new and much bigger barracks went up in place of the old one; a two-company garrison moved in. Who else or what else went into the area, nobody knew for certain; but rumors came out.

We checked the rumors. We found confirmation. We published it, and we followed it up. Within a week we had a full-sized crusade started; we were asking for a congressional investigation, and it looked as if we might get it.

Then the President invited me and the publishers of twenty-odd other anti-administration dailies to Washington. Each of us got a personal interview with The Man; the Secretary of Defense was also present, to evade questions.

They asked me, as a personal favor and in the interests of national security, to kill the Chillicothe series.

After asking a few questions, to which I got the answers I expected, I politely declined.

And here I was.

The door opened. The guard outside looked in, saw me on the bed, and stepped back out of sight. Another man walked in: stocky build, straight black hair turning gray; about fifty. Confident eyes behind rimless bifocals.

"Mr. Dahl. My name is Carlton Frisbee."

"I've seen your picture," I told him. Frisbee was the Under Secretary of Defense, a career man, very able; he was said to be the brains of the Department.

He sat down facing me. He didn't ask permission, and he didn't offer to shake hands, which was intelligent of him.

"How do you feel about it now?" he asked.

"Just the same."

He nodded. After a moment he said, "I'm going to try to explain our position to you, Mr. Dahl."

I grinned at him. "The word you're groping for is 'awkward.' "

"No. It's true that we can't let you go in your present state of mind, but we can keep you. If necessary, you will be killed, Mr. Dahl. That's how important Chillicothe is."

"Nothing," I said, "is that important."

He cocked his head at me. "If you and your family lived in a community surrounded by hostile savages, who were kept at bay only because you had rifles—and if someone proposed to give them rifles—well?"

"Look," I said, "let's get down to cases. You claim that a new weapon is being developed at Chillicothe, is that right? It's something revolutionary, and if the Russians got it first we would be sunk, and so on. In other words, the Manhattan Project all over again."

"Right."

"Okay. Then why has Chillicothe got twice the military guard it had when it was an atomic research center, and a third of the civilian staff?"

He started to speak.

"Wait a minute, let me finish. Why, of the fifty-one scientists we have been able to trace to Chillicothe, are there seventeen linguists and philologists, three organic chemists, five physiologists, *twenty-six psychologists, and not one single physicist?*"

"In the first place—were you about to say something?"

"All right, go ahead."

"You know I can't answer those questions factually, Mr. Dahl, but speaking conjecturally, can't you conceive of a psychological weapon?"

"You can't answer them at all. My third question is, why have you got a wall around that place—not just a stockade, a wall, with guard towers on it? Never mind speaking conjecturally. Now I'll answer your question. Yes, I can conceive of psychological experimentation that you might call weapons research, I can think of several possibilities, and there isn't a damn one of them that wouldn't have to be used on American citizens before you could get anywhere near the Russians with it."

His eyes were steady behind the bright lenses. He didn't say, "We seem to have reached a deadlock," or "Evidently it would be useless to discuss this any further"; he simply changed the subject.

"There are two things we can do with you, Mr. Dahl; the choice will be up to you. First, we can indict you for treason and transfer you to a Federal prison to await trial. Under the revised Alien and Sedition Act, we can hold you incommunicado for at least twelve months, and, of course, no bail will be set. I feel bound to point out to you that in this case, it would be impossible to let you come to trial until after the danger of breaching security at Chillicothe is past. If necessary, as I told you, you would die in prison.

"Second, we can admit you to Chillicothe itself as a press representative. We would, in this case, allow you full access to all non-technical information about the Chillicothe project as it develops, with permission to publish as soon as security is lifted. You would be confined to the project until that time, and I can't offer you any estimate of how long it might be. In return, you would be asked to write letters plausibly explaining your absence to your staff and to close friends and relatives, and—providing that you find Chillicothe to be what we say it is and not what you suspect—to work out a series of stories for your newspaper which will divert attention from the project."

He seemed to be finished. I said, "Frisbee, I hate to tell you this, but you're overlooking a point. Let's just suppose for a minute that Chillicothe is what I think it is. How do I know that once I got inside I might not somehow or other find myself writing that kind of copy whether I felt like it or not?"

He nodded. "What guarantees would you consider sufficient?"

I thought about that. It was a nice point. I was angry enough, and scared enough, to feel like pasting Frisbee a good one and then seeing how far I could get; but one thing I couldn't figure out, and that was why, if Frisbee wasn't at least partly on the level, he should be here at all.

If they wanted me in Chillicothe, they could drag me there.

After a while I said, "Let me call my managing editor and tell him where I'm going. Let me tell him that I'll call him again—*on a video circuit*—within three days after I get there, when I've had time to inspect the whole area. And that if I don't call, or if I look funny or sound funny, he can start worrying."

He nodded again. "Fair enough." He stood up. "I won't ask you to shake hands with me now, Mr. Dahl; later on I hope you will." He turned and walked to the door, unhurried, calm, imperturbable, the way he had come in.

Six hours later I was on a westbound plane.

That was the first day.

The second day, an inexplicable epidemic broke out in the slaughterhouses of Chicago and surrounding areas. The symptoms were a sudden collapse followed by nausea, incontinence, anemia, shock, and in some cases, severe pain in the occipital and cervical regions. Or: as one victim, an A. F. of L. knacker with twenty-five years' experience in the nation's abbatoirs, succinctly put it: "It felt just like I was hit in the head."

Local and Federal health authorities immediately closed down the affected slaughterhouses, impounded or banned the sale of all supplies of fresh meat in the area, and launched a sweeping investigation. Retail food stores sold out their stocks of canned, frozen and processed meats early in the day; seafood markets reported their largest volume of sales in two decades. Eggs and cheese were in short supply.

Fifty-seven guards, assistant wardens and other minor officials of the Federal penitentiary at Leavenworth, Kansas, submitted a group resignation to Warden Hermann R. Longo. Their explanation of the move was that all had experienced a religious conversion, and that assisting in the forcible confinement of other human beings was incosonant with their beliefs.

Near Louisville, Kentucky, neighbors attracted by cries for help found a forty-year-old woman and her twelve-year-old daughter both severely burned. The woman, whose clothing was not even scorched although her upper body was covered with first and second degree burns, admitted pushing the child into a bonfire, but in her hysterical condition was unable to give a rational account of her own injuries.

There was also a follow-up on the Des Moines story about the man who kicked his wife. Remember that I didn't say he had a broken coccyx; I said he was suffering from one. A few hours after he was admitted to the hospital he stopped doing so, and he was released into police custody when X-rays showed no fracture.

Straws in the wind.

At five-thirty that morning, I was waking up my managing editor, Eli Freeman, with a monitored long-distance call—one of Frisbee's bright young men waiting to cut me off if I said anything I shouldn't. The temptation was strong, just the same, but I didn't.

From six to eight-thirty I was on a plane with three taciturn guards. I spent most of the time going over the last thirty years of my life, and wondering how many people would remember me two days after they wrapped my obituary around their garbage.

We landed at the airfield about a mile from the Project proper, and after one of my hitherto silent friends had finished a twenty-minute phone call, a limousine took us over to a long, temporary-looking frame building just outside the wall. It took me only until noon to get out again; I had been fingerprinted, photographed, stripped, examined, X-rayed, urinanalyzed, blood-tested, showered, disinfected, and given a set of pinks to wear until my own clothes had been cleaned and fumigated. I also got a numbered badge which I was instructed to wear on the left chest at all times, and an identity card to keep in my wallet when I got my wallet back.

Then they let me through the gate, and I saw Chillicothe.

I was in a short cul-de-sac formed by the gate and two walls of masonry, blank except for firing slits. Facing away from the gate I could see one of the three laboratory buildings a good half-mile away. Between me and it was a geometrical forest of poles with down-pointing reflectors on their crossbars. Floodlights.

I didn't like that. What I saw a few minutes later I liked even less. I was bouncing across the flat in a jeep driven by a stocky, moon-faced corporal; we passed the first building, and I saw the second.

There was a ring of low pillboxes around it. And their guns pointed *inward*, toward the building.

Major General Parst was a big, bald man in his fifties, whose figure would have been more military if the Prussian corset had not gone out of fashion. I took him for a Pentagon soldier; he had the Pentagon smoothness of manner, but there seemed to be a good deal more under it than the usual well-oiled vacancy. He was also, I judged, a very worried man.

"There's just one thing I'd like to make clear to you at the beginning, Mr. Dahl. I'm not a grudge-holding man, and I hope you're not either, because there's a good chance that you and I will be seeing a lot of each other during the next three or four years. But I thought it might make it a little easier for you to know that you're not the only one with a grievance. You see this isn't an easy job, it never has been. I'm just stating the fact: it's been considerably harder since your newspaper took an interest in us." He spread his hands and smiled wryly.

"Just what is your job, General?"

"You mean, what is Chillicothe." He snorted. "I'm not going to waste my breath telling you."

My expression must have changed.

"Don't misunderstand me—I mean that if I told you, you wouldn't believe me. I didn't myself. I'm going to have to show you." He stood up, looking at his wristwatch. "I have a little more than an hour. That's more than enough for the demonstration, but you're going to have a lot of questions afterward. We'd better start."

He thumbed his intercom. "I'll be in Section One for the next fifteen minutes."

When we were in the corridor outside he said, "Tell me something, Mr. Dahl: I suppose it occurred to you that if you were right in your suspicions of Chillicothe, you might be running a certain personal risk in coming here, in spite of any precautions you might take?"

"I considered the possibility. I haven't seen anything to rule it out yet."

"And still, I gather that you chose this alternative almost without hesitation. Why was that, if you don't mind telling me?"

It was a fair question. There's nothing very attractive about a Federal prison, but at least they don't saw your skull open there, or turn your mind inside out with drugs. I said, "Call it curiosity."

He nodded. "Yes. A very potent force, Mr. Dahl. More mountains have been moved by it than by faith."

We passed a guard with a T44, then a second, and a third. Finally Parst stopped at the first of three metal doors. There was a small pane of thick glass set into it at eye-level, and what looked like a microphone grill under that. Parst spoke into the grill: "Open up Three, Sergeant."

"Yes, sir."

I followed Parst to the second door. It slid open as we reached it and we walked into a large, empty room. The door closed behind us with a thud and a solid *click.* Both sounds rattled back startlingly; the room was solid metal, I realized—floor, walls and ceiling.

In the opposite wall was another heavy door. To my left was a huge metal hemisphere, painted the same gray as the walls, with a machine-gun's snout projecting through a horizontal slit in a deadly and impressive manner.

Echoes blurred the General's voice: "This is Section One. We're rather proud of it. The only entrance to the central room is here, but each of the three others that adjoin it is covered from a gun-turret like that one. The gun rooms are accessible only from the corridors outside."

He motioned me over to the other door. "This door is double," he said. "It's going to be an airlock eventually, we hope. All right, Sergeant."

The door slid back, exposing another one a yard farther in; like the others, it had a thick inset panel of glass.

Parst stepped in and waited for me. "Get ready for a shock," he said.

I loosened the muscles in my back and shoulders; my wind isn't what it used to be, but I can still hit. *Get ready for one yourself,* I thought, *if this is what I think it is.*

I walked into the tiny room, and heard the door thump behind me. Parst motioned to the glass pane.

I saw a room the size of the one behind me. There was a washbasin in it, and a toilet, and what looked like a hammock slung across one corner, and a wooden table with papers and a couple of pencils or crayons on it.

And against the far wall, propped upright on an ordinary lunch-counter stool, was something I couldn't recognize at all; I saw it and I didn't see it. If I had looked away then, I couldn't possibly have told anyone what it looked like.

Then it stirred slightly, and I realized that it was alive.

I saw that it had eyes.

I saw that it had arms.

I saw that it had legs.

Very gradually the rest of it came into focus. The top was about four feet off the floor, a small truncated cone about the size and shape of one of those cones of string that some merchants keep to tie packages. Under that came the eyes, three of them. They were round and oyster-gray, with round black pupils, and they faced in different directions. They were set into a flattened bulb of flesh that just fitted under the base of the cone; there was no nose, no ears, no mouth, and no room for any.

The cone was black; the rest of the thing was a very dark, shiny blue-gray.

The head, if that is the word, was supported by a thin neck from which a sparse growth of fuzzy spines curved down and outward, like a botched attempt at feathers. The neck thickened gradually until it became the torso. The torso was shaped something like a bottle gourd, except that the upper lobe was almost as large as the lower. The upper lobe expanded and contracted evenly, all around, as the thing breathed.

Between each arm and the next, the torso curved inward to form a deep vertical gash.

There were three arms and three legs, spaced evenly around the body so that you couldn't tell front from back. The arms sprouted just below the top of the torso, the legs from its base. The legs were bent only slightly to reach the floor; each hand, with five slender, shapeless fingers, rested on the opposite-number thigh. The feet were a little like a chicken's. . .

I turned away and saw Parst; I had forgotten he was there, and where I was, and who I was. I don't recall planning to say anything, but I heard my own voice, faint and hoarse:

"Did you *make* that?"

II

"Stop it!" he said sharply.

I was trembling. I had fallen into a crouch without realizing it, weight on my toes, fists clenched.

I straightened up slowly and put my hands into my pockets. "Sorry."

The speaker rasped.

"Is everything all right, sir?"

"Yes, Sergeant," said Parst. "We're coming out." He turned as the door opened, and I followed him, feeling all churned up inside.

Halfway down the corridor I stopped. Parst turned and looked at me.

"Ithaca," I said.

Three months back there had been a Monster-from-Mars scare in and around Ithaca, New York; several hundred people had seen, or claimed to have seen, a white wingless aircraft hovering over various out-of-the-way places; and over thirty, including one very respectable Cornell professor, had caught sight of something that wasn't a man in the woods around Cayuga Lake. None of these people had got close enough for a good look, but nearly all of them agreed on one point— the thing walked erect, but had too many arms and legs. . . .

"Yes," said Parst. "That's right. But let's talk about it in my office, Mr. Dahl."

I followed him back there. As soon as the door was shut I said, "Where did it come from? Are there any more of them? What about the ship?"

He offered me a cigarette. I took it and sat down, hitting the chair by luck.

"Those are just three of the questions we can't answer," he said. "He claims that his home world revolves around a sun in our constellation of Aquarius; he says that it isn't visible from Earth. He also—"

I said, "He talks—? You've taught him to speak English?" For some reason that was hard to accept; then I remembered the linguists.

"Yes. Quite well, considering that he doesn't have vocal cords like ours. He uses a tympanum under each of those vertical openings in his body—those are his mouths. His name is Aza-Kra, by the way. I was going to say that he also claims to have come here alone. As for the ship, he says it's hidden, but he won't tell us where. We've been searching that area, particularly the hills near Cayuga and the lake itself, but we haven't turned it up yet. It's been suggested that he may have launched it under remote control and put it into an orbit somewhere outside the atmosphere. The Lunar Observatory is watching for it, and so are the orbital stations, but I'm inclined to think that's a dead end. In any case, that's not my responsibility. He had some gadgets in his possession when he was captured, but even those are being studied elsewhere. Chillicothe is what you saw a few minutes ago, and that's all it is. God knows it's enough."

His intercom buzzed. "Yes."

"Dr. Meshevski would like to talk to you about the technical vocabularies, sir."

"Ask him to hold it until the conference if he possibly can."

"Yes, sir."

"Two more questions we can't answer," Parst said, "are what his civilization is like and what he came here to do. I'll tell you what he says. The planet he comes from belongs to a galactic union of highly advanced, peace-loving races. He came here to help us prepare ourselves for membership in that union."

I was trying hard to keep up, but it wasn't easy. After a moment I said, "Suppose it's true?"

He gave me the cold eye.

"All right, suppose it's true." For the first time, his voice was impatient. "Then suppose the opposite. Think about it for a minute."

I saw where he was leading me, but I tried to circle around to it from another direction; I wanted to reason it out for myself. I couldn't make the grade; I had to fall back on analogies, which are a kind of thinking I distrust.

You were a cannibal islander, and a missionary came along. He meant well, but you thought he wanted to steal your yamfields and your wives, so you chopped him up and ate him for dinner.

Or:

You were a West Indian, and Columbus came along. You treated him as a guest, but he made a slave of you, worked you till you dropped, and finally wiped out your whole nation, to the last woman and child.

I said, "A while ago you mentioned three or four years as the possible term of the Project. Did you—?"

"That wasn't meant to be taken literally," he said. "It may take a lifetime." He was staring at his desk-top.

"In other words, if nothing stops you, you're going to go right on just this way, sitting on this thing. Until What's-his-name dies, or his friends show up with an army, or something else blows it wide open."

"*That's* right."

"Well, damn it, don't you see that's the one thing you can't do? Either way you guess it, that won't work. If he's friendly—"

Parst lifted a pencil in his hand and slapped it palm-down against the desk-top. His mouth was tight. "It's *necessary*," he said.

After a silent moment he straightened in his chair and spread the fingers of his right hand at me. "One," he said, touching the thumb: "weapons. Leaving everything else aside, if we can get one strategically superior weapon out of him, or the theory that will enable us to build one, then we've *got* to do it and we've *got* to do it in secret."

The index finger. "Two: the spaceship." Middle finger. "Three: the civilization he comes from. If they're planning to attack us we've got to find that out, and when, and how, and what we can do about it." Ring finger. "Four: Aza-Kra himself. If we don't hold him in secret we can't hold him at all, and how do we know what he might do if we let him go? There isn't a single possibility we can rule out. Not one."

He put the hand flat on the desk. "Five, six, seven, eight, nine, ten, infinity. Biology, psychology, sociology, ecology, chemistry, physics, right down the line. Every science. In any one of them we might find something that would mean the difference between life and death for this country or this whole planet."

He stared at me for a moment, his face set. "You don't have to remind me of the other possibilities, Dahl. I know what they are; I've been on this project for thirteen weeks. I've also heard of the Golden Rule, and the Ten Commandments, and the Constitution of the United States. But this is *the survival of the human race* we're talking about."

I opened my mouth to say "That's just the point," or something equally stale, but I shut it again; I saw it was no good. I had one argument—that if this alien ambassador was what he claimed to be, then the whole world had to know about it; any nation that tried to suppress that knowledge, or dictate the whole planet's future, was committing a crime against humanity. That, on the other hand, if he was an advance agent for an invasion fleet, the same thing was true only a great deal more so.

Beyond that I had nothing but instinctive moral conviction; and Parst had that on his side too; so did Frisbee and the President and all the rest. Being who and what they were, they had to believe as they did. Maybe they were right.

Half an hour later, the last thought I had before my head hit the pillow was, *Suppose there isn't any Aza-Kra? Suppose that thing was a fake, a mechanical dummy?*

But I knew better, and I slept soundly.

That was the second day. On the third day, the front pages of the more excitable newspapers were top-heavy with forty-eight-point headlines. There were two Chicago stories. The first, in the early afternoon editions, announced that every epidemic victim had made a complete recovery, that health department experts had been unable to isolate any disease-causing agent in the stock awaiting slaughter, and that although several cases not involving stockyard employees had been reported, not one had been traced to consumption of infected meat. A Chicago epidemiologist was quoted as saying, "It could have been just a gigantic coincidence."

The later story was a lulu. Although the slaughterhouses had not been officially reopened or the ban on fresh-meat sales rescinded, health officials allowed seventy of the previous day's victims to return to work as an experiment. Within half an hour every one of them was back in the hospital, suffering from a second, identical attack.

Oddly enough—at first glance—sales of fresh meat in areas outside the ban dropped slightly in the early part of the day ("They *say* it's all right, but you won't catch me taking a chance"), rose sharply in the evening ("I'd better stock up before there's a run on the butcher shops").

Warden Longo, in an unprecedented move, added his resignation to those of the fifty-seven "conscience" employees of Leavenworth. Well-known as an advocate of prison reform, Longo explained that his subordinates' example had convinced him that only so dramatic a gesture could focus the American public's attention upon the injustice and inhumanity of the present system.

He was joined by two hundred and three of the Federal institution's remaining employees, bringing the total to more than eighty per cent of Leavenworth's permanent staff.

The movement was spreading. In Terre Haute, Indiana, eighty employees of the Federal penitentiary were reported to have resigned. Similar reports came from the State prisons of Iowa, Missouri, Illinois and Indiana, and from city and county correctional institutions from Kansas City to Cincinnati.

The war in Indo-China was crowded back among the stockmarket reports. Even the official announcements that the first Mars rocket was nearing completion in its sublunar orbit—frontpage news at any normal time—got an inconspicuous paragraph in some papers and was dropped entirely by others.

But I found an item in a St. Louis paper about the policeman who had collapsed after shooting a criminal. He was dead.

I woke up a little before dawn that morning, having had a solid fifteen hours' sleep. I found the cafeteria and hung around until it opened. That was where Captain Ritchy-loo tracked me down.

He came in as I was finishing my second order of ham and eggs, a big, blond, swimming-star type, full of confidence and good cheer. "You must be Mr. Dahl. My name is Ritchy-loo."

I let him pump my hand and watched him sit down. "How do you spell it?" I asked him.

He grinned happily. "It is a tough one, isn't it? French. R, i, c, h, e, l, i, e, u."

Richelieu. Ritchy-loo.

I said, "What can I do for you, Captain?"

"Ah, it's what I can do for *you*, Mr. Dahl. You're a VIP around here, you know. You're getting the triple-A guided tour, and I'm your guide."

I *hate* people who are cheerful in the morning.

We went out into the pale glitter of early-morning sunshine on the flat; the floodlight poles and the pillboxes trailed long, mournful shadows. There was a jeep waiting, and Ritchy-loo took the wheel himself.

We made a right turn around the corner of the building and then headed down one of the diagonal avenues between the poles. I glanced into the firing slit of one of the pillboxes as we passed it, and saw the gleam of somebody's spectacles.

"That was B building that we just came out of," said the captain. "Most of the interesting stuff is there, but you want to see everything, naturally, so we'll go over to C first and then back to A."

The huge barracks, far off to the right, looked deserted; I saw a few men in fatigues here and there, spearing stray bit of paper. Beyond the building we were heading for, almost against the wall, tiny figures were leaping rhythmically, opening and closing like so many animated scissors.

It was a well-policed area, at any rate; I watched for a while, out of curiosity, and didn't see a single cigarette paper or gum wrapper.

To the left of the barracks and behind it was a miniature town—

neat one-story cottages, all alike, all the same distance apart. The thing that struck me about it was that there were none of the signs of a permanent camp—no borders of whitewashed stones, no trees, no shrubs, no flowers. No *wives*, I thought.

"How's morale here, Captain?" I asked.

"Now, it's funny you should ask me that. That happens to be my job, I'm the Company B morale officer. Well, I should say that all things considered, we aren't doing too badly. Of course, we have a few difficulties. These men are here on eighteen-month assignments, and that's a kind of a long time without passes or furloughs. We'd like to make the hitches shorter, naturally, but of course you understand that there aren't too many fresh but seasoned troops available just now."

"No."

"*But*, we do our best. Now here's C building."

Most of C building turned out to be occupied by chemical laboratories: long rows of benches covered by rank growths of glassware, only about a fifth of it working, and nobody watching more than a quarter of that.

"What are they doing here?"

"Over my head," said Ritchy-loo cheerfully. "Here's Dr. Vitale, let's ask him."

Vitale was a little sharp-featured man with a nervous blink. "This is the atmosphere section," he said. "We're trying to analyze the atmosphere which the alien breathes. Eventually we hope to manufacture it."

That was a point that hadn't occurred to me. "He can't breathe our air?"

"No, no. Altogether different."

"Well, where does he get the stuff he does breathe, then?"

The little man's lips worked. "From that cone-shaped mechanism on the top of his head. An atmosphere plant that you could put in your pocket. Completely incredible. We can't get an adequate sample without taking it off him, and we can't take it off him without killing him. We have to deduce what he breathes in from what he breathes *out*. *Very* difficult." He went away.

All the same, I couldn't see much point in it. Presumably if Aza-Kra couldn't breathe our air, we couldn't breathe his—so anybody who wanted to examine him would have to wear an oxygen tank and a breathing mask.

But it was obvious enough, and I got it in another minute. If the prisoner didn't have his own air-supply, it would be that much harder for him to break out past the gun rooms and the guards in the corridors and the pillboxes and the floodlights and the wall. . . .

We went on, stopping at every door. There were storerooms, sleeping quarters, a few offices. The rest of the rooms were empty.

Ritchy-loo wanted to go on to A building, but I was being perversely thorough, and I said we would go through the barracks and the company towns first. We did; it took us three hours and thinned down Ritchy-loo's stream of cheerful conversation to a trickle. We looked everywhere, and of course we did not find anything that shouldn't have been there.

A building was the recreation hall. Canteen, library, gymnasium, movie theater, PX, swimming pool. It was also the project hospital and dispensary. Both sections were well filled.

So we went back to B. And it was almost noon, so we had lunch in the big air-conditioned cafeteria. I didn't look forward to it; I expected that rest and food would turn on Ritchy-loo's conversational spigot again, and if he didn't get any response to the first three or four general topics he tried, I was perfectly sure he would begin telling me jokes. Nothing of the kind happened. After a few minutes I saw why, or thought I did. Looking around the room, I saw face after face with the same blank look on it; there wasn't a smile or an animated expression in the place. And now that I was paying attention I noticed that the sounds were odd, too. There were more than a hundred people in the room, enough to set up a beehive roar; but there was so little talking going on that you could pick out individual sentences with ease, and they were all trochaic—*Want* some *su*gar? *No*, thanks. Like that.

It was infectious; I was beginning to feel it now myself—an execution-chamber kind of mood, a feeling that we were all shut up in a place that we couldn't get out of, and where something horrible was going to happen. Unless you've ever been in a group made up of people who had that feeling and were reinforcing it in each other, it's indescribable; but it was very real and very hard to take.

Ritchy-loo left half a chop on his plate; I finished mine, but it choked me.

In the corridor outside I asked him, "Is it always as bad as that?"

"You noticed it too? That place gives me the creeps, I don't know why. It's the same way in the movies, too, lately—wherever you get a lot of these people together. I just don't understand it." For a second longer he looked worried and thoughtful, and then he grinned suddenly. "I don't want to say anything against civilians, Mr. Dahl, but I think that bunch is pretty far gone."

I could have hugged him. Civilians! If Ritchy-loo was more than six months away from a summer-camp counselor's job, I was a five-star general.

We started at that end of the corridor and worked our way down. We looked into a room with an X-ray machine and a fluoroscope in it, and a darkroom, and a room full of racks and filing cabinets, and a long row of offices.

Then Ritchy-loo opened a door that revealed two men standing on opposite sides of a desk, spouting angry German at each other. The tall one noticed us after a second, said, "'St, 'st," to the other, and then to us coldly, "You might, at least, knock."

"Sorry, gentlemen," said Ritchy-loo brightly. He closed the door and went on to the next on the same side. This opened onto a small, bare room with nobody in it but a stocky man with corporal's stripes on his sleeve. He was sitting hunched over, elbows on knees, hands over his face. He didn't move or look up.

I have a good ear, and I had managed to catch one sentence of what the fat man next door had been saying to the tall one. It went like this: *"Nein, nein, das ist bestimmt nicht die Klaustrophobie; Ich sage dir, es ist das dreifüssige Tier, das sie störrt."*

My college German came back to me when I prodded it, but it creaked a little. While I was still working at it, I asked Ritchy-loo, "What was that?"

"Psychiatric section," he said.

"You get many psycho cases here?"

"Oh, no," he said. "Just the normal percentage, Mr. Dahl. Less, in fact."

The captain was a poor liar.

"Klaustrophobie" was easy, of course. *"Dreifüssige Tier"* stopped me until I remembered that the German for *"zoo"* is *"Tiergarten."* *Dreifüssige Tier:* the three-footed beast. The triped.

The fat one had been saying to the tall one, "No, no, it is absolutely not claustrophobia; I tell you, it's the triped that's disturbing them."

Three-quarters of an hour later we had peered into the last room in B building: a long office full of IBM machines. We had now been over every square yard of Chillicothe, and I had seen for myself that no skulduggery was going forward anywhere in it. That was the idea behind the guided tour, as Ritchy-loo was evidently aware.

He said, "Well, that just about wraps it up, Mr. Dahl. By the way, the General's office asked me to tell you that if it's all right with you, they'll set up that phone call for you for four o'clock this afternoon."

I looked down at the rough map of the building I'd been drawing as we went along. "There's one place we haven't been, Captain," I said. "Section One."

"Oh, well that's right, that's right. You saw that yesterday, though, didn't you, Mr. Dahl?"

"For about two minutes. I wasn't able to take much of it in. I'd like to see it again, if it isn't too much trouble. Or even if it is."

Ritchy-loo laughed heartily. "Good enough. Just wait a second, I'll see if I can get you a clearance on it." He walked down the corridor to the nearest wall phone.

After a few moments he beckoned me over, palming the receiver. "The General says there are two research groups in there now and it would be a little crowded. He says he'd like you to postpone it if you think you can."

"Tell him that's perfectly all right, but in that case I think we'd better put off the phone call, too."

He repeated the message, and waited. Finally, "Yes. Yes, uh-huh. Yes, I've got that. All right."

He turned to me. "The General says it's all right for you to go in for half an hour and watch, but he'd appreciate it if you'll be careful not to distract the people who're working in there."

I had been hoping the General would say no. I wanted to see the alien again, all right, but what I wanted the most was time.

This was the second day I had been at Chillicothe. By tomorrow at the latest I would have to talk to Eli Freeman; and I still hadn't figured out any sure, safe way to tell him that Chillicothe was a legitimate research project, not to be snipped at by the *Herald-Star*—and make him understand that I didn't mean a word of it.

I could simply refuse to make the call, or I could tell him as much of the truth as I could before I was cut off—two words, probably—but it was a cinch that call would be monitored at the other end, too; that was part of what Ritchy-loo meant by "setting up the call." Somebody from the FBI would be sitting at Freeman's elbow . . . and I wasn't telling myself fairy tales about Peter Zenger any more.

They would shut the paper down, which was not only the thing I wanted least in the world but a thing that would do nobody any good.

I wanted Eli to spread the story by underground channels—spread it so far, and time the release so well, that no amount of censorship could kill it.

Treason is a word every man has to define for himself.

Ritchy-loo did the honors for me at the gun-room door, and then left me, looking a little envious. I don't think he had ever been inside Section One.

There was somebody ahead of me in the tiny antechamber, I found: a short, wide-shouldered man with a sheepdog tangle of black hair.

He turned as the door closed behind me. "Hi. Oh—you're Dahl, aren't you?" He had a young, pleasant, meaningless face behind dark-rimmed glasses. I said yes.

He put a half-inch of cigarette between his lips and shook hands with me. "Somebody pointed you out. Glad to know you; my name's Connelly. Physical psych section—very junior." He pointed through the spy-window. "What do you think of him?"

Aza-Kra was sitting directly in front of the window; his lunch-counter stool had been moved into the center of the room. Around him were four men: two on the left, sitting on folding chairs, talking to him and occasionally making notes; two on the right, standing beside a waist-high enclosed mechanism from which wires led to the upper lobe of the alien's body. The ends of the wires were taped against his skin.

"That isn't an easy question," I said.

Donnelly nodded without interest. "That's my boss there," he said, "the skinny, gray-haired guy on the right. We get on each other's nerves. If he gets that setup operating this session, I'm supposed to go in and take notes. He won't, though."

"What is it?"

"Electroencephalograph. See, his brain isn't in his head, it's in his upper thorax there. Too much insulation in the way. We can't get close enough for a good reading without surgery. I say we ought to drop it till we get permission, but Hendricks thinks he can lick it. Those two on the other side are interviewers. Like to hear what they're saying?"

He punched one of two buttons set into the door beside the speaker grill, under the spy-window. "If you're ever in here alone, remember you can't get out while this is on. You turn on the speaker here, it turns off the one in the gun room. They wouldn't be able to hear you ask to get out."

Inside, a monotonous voice was saying, ". . . have that here, but what exactly do you mean by. . ."

"I ought to be in physiology," Donnelly said, lowering his voice. "They have all the fun. You see his eyes?"

I looked. The center one was staring directly toward us; the other two were tilted, almost out of sight around the curve of that bulb of blue-gray flesh.

". . . in other words, just what is the nature of this energy, is it— uh—transmitted by waves, or. . ."

"He can look three ways at once," I said.

"Three, with binocular," Donnelly agreed. "Each eye can function independently or couple with the one on either side. So he can have a series of overlapping monocular images, all the way around, or he can have up to three binocular images. They focus independently, too. He could read a newspaper and watch for his wife to come out of the movie across the street."

"Wait a minute," I said. "He has *six* eyes, not three?"

"Sure. Has to, to keep the symmetry and still get binocular vision."

"Then he hasn't got any front or back," I said slowly.

"No, that's right. He's trilaterally symmetrical. Drive you crazy to watch him walk. His legs work the same way as his eyes—any one can pair up with either of the others. He wants to change direction, he doesn't have to turn around. I'd hate to try to catch him in an open field."

"How did they catch him?" I asked.

"Luckiest thing in the world. Found him in the woods with two broken ankles. Now look at his hands. What do you see?"

The voice inside was still droning; evidently it was a long question. "Five fingers;" I said.

"Nope." Donnelly grinned. "One finger, four thumbs. See how they oppose, those two on either side of the middle finger? He's got a better hand than ours. One *hell* of an efficient design. Brain in his thorax where it's safe, six eyes on a stalk—trachea up there too, no connection with the esophagus, so he doesn't need an epiglottis. Three of everything else. He can lose a leg and still walk, lose an arm and still type, lose two eyes and still see better than we do. He can lose—"

I didn't hear him. The interviewer's voice had stopped, and Aza-Kra's had begun. It was frightening, because it was a buzzing and it was a voice.

I couldn't take in a word of it; I had enough to do absorbing the fact that there were words.

Then it stopped, and the interviewer's ordinary, flat Middle Western voice began again.

"—And just try to sneak up behind him," said Donnelly. "I dare you."

Again Aza-Kra spoke briefly, and this time I saw the flesh at the side of his body, where the two lobes flowed together, bulge slightly and then relax.

"He's talking with one of his mouths," I said. "I mean, one of those—" I took a deep breath. "If he breathes through the top of his head, and there's no connection between his lungs and his vocal organs, then where the hell does he get the air?"

"He belches. Not as inconvenient as it sounds. You could learn to do it if you had to." Donnelly laughed. "Not very fragrant, though. Watch their faces when he talks."

I watched Aza-Kra's instead—what there was of it: one round, expressionless, oyster-colored eye staring back at me. With a human opponent, I was thinking, there were a thousand little things that you relied on to help you: facial expressions, mannerisms, signs of emotion. But Parst had been right when he said, *There isn't a single possibility we can rule out. Not one.* And so had the fat man: *It's the triped that's disturbing them.* And Ritchy-loo: *It's the same way . . . wherever you get a lot of these people together.*

And I still hadn't figured out any way to tell Freeman what he had to know.

I thought I could arouse Eli's suspicion easily enough; we knew each other well enough for a word or a gesture to mean a good deal. I could make him look for hidden meanings. But how could I hide a message so that Eli would be more likely to dig it out than a trained FBI cryptologist?

I stared at Aza-Kra's glassy eye as if the answer were there. It was going to be a video circuit, I told myself. Donnelly was still yattering in my ear, and now the alien was buzzing again, but I ignored them both. Suppose I broke the message up into one-word units, scattered them through my conversation with Eli, and marked them off somehow—by twitching a finger, or blinking my eyelids?

A dark membrane flicked across the alien's oyster-colored eye.

A moment later, it happened again.

Donnelly was saying, ". . . intercostal membranes, apparently. But there's no trace of. . ."

"Shut up a minute, will you?" I said. "I want to hear this."

The inhuman voice, the voice that sounded like the articulate buzzing of a giant insect, was saying, "Comparison not possible, excuse me. If (*blink*) you try to understand in words you know, you (*blink*) tell yourself you wish (*blink*) to understand, but knowledge escape (*blink*) you. Can only show (*blink*) you from beginning, one (*blink*) little, another little. Not possible to carry all knowledge in one hand (*blink*)."

If you wish escape, show one hand.

I looked at Donnelly. He had moved back from the spy-window; he was lighting a cigarette, frowning at the match-flame. His mouth was sullen.

I put my left hand flat against the window. I thought, *I'm dreaming.*

The interviewer said querulously, ". . . getting us nowhere. Can't you—"

"Wait," said the buzzing voice. "Let me say, please. Ignorant man hold (*blink*) burning stick, say, this is breath (*blink*) of the wood. Then you show him flashlight—"

I took a deep breath, and held it.

Around the alien, four men went down together, folding over quietly at waist and knee, sprawling on the floor. I heard a thump behind me.

Donnelly was lying stretched out along the wall, his head tilted against the corner. The cigarette had fallen from his hand.

I looked back at Aza-Kra. His head turned slightly, the dark flesh crinkling. Two eyes stared back at me through the window.

"Now you can breathe," said the monster.

III

I let out the breath that was choking me and took another. My knees were shaking.

"What did you do to them?"

"Put them to sleep only. In a few minutes I will put the others to sleep. After you are outside the doors. First we will talk."

I glanced at Donnelly again. His mouth was ajar; I could see his lips fluttering as he breathed.

"All right," I said, "talk."

"When you leave," buzzed the voice, "you must take me with you."

Now it was clear. He could put people to sleep, but he couldn't open locked doors. He had to have help.

"No deal," I said. "You might as well knock me out, too."

"Yes," he answered, "you will do it. When you understand."

"I'm listening."

"You do not have to agree now. I ask only this much. When we are finished talking, you leave. When you are past the second door, hold your breath again. Then go to the office of General Parst. You will find there papers about me. Read them. You will find also keys to open gun room. Also, handcuffs. Special handcuffs, made to fit me. Then you will think, if Aza-Kra is not what he says, would he agree to this? Then you will come back to gun room, use controls there to open middle door. You will lay handcuffs down, where you stand now, then go back to gun room, open inside door. I will put on the handcuffs. You will see that I do it. And then you will take me with you."

. . . I said, "Let me think."

The obvious thing to do was to push the little button that turned on the audio circuit to the gun room, and yell for help; the alien could then put everybody to sleep from here to the wall, maybe, but it wouldn't do any good. Sooner or later he would have to let up, or starve to death along with the rest of us. On the other hand if I did what he asked—*anything* he asked—and it turned out to be the wrong thing, I would be guilty of the worst crime since Pilate's.

But I thought about it, I went over it again and again, and I couldn't see any loophole in it for Aza-Kra. He was leaving it up to me—if I felt like letting him out after I'd seen the papers in Parst's office, I could do so. If I didn't, I could still yell for help. In fact, I could get on the phone and yell to Washington, which would be a hell of a lot more to the point.

So where was the payoff for Aza-Kra? What was in those papers?

I pushed the button. I said, "This is Dahl. Let me out, will you please?"

The outer door began to slide back. Just in time, I saw Donnelly's head bobbing against it; I grabbed him by the shirt-front and hoisted his limp body out of the way.

I walked across the echoing outer chamber; the outermost door opened for me. I stepped through it and held my breath. Down the corridor, three guards leaned over their rifles and toppled all in a row, like precision divers. Beyond them a hurrying civilian in the cross-corridor fell heavily and skidded out of sight.

The clacking of typewriters from a nearby office had stopped abruptly. I let out my breath when I couldn't hold it any longer, and listened to the silence.

The General was slumped over his desk, head on his crossed forearms, looking pretty old and tired with his polished bald skull shining under the light. There was a faint silvery scar running across the top of his head, and I wondered whether he had got it in combat as a young man, or whether he had tripped over a rug at an embassy reception.

Across the desk from him a thin man in a gray pin-check suit was jackknifed on the carpet, half-supported by a chair-leg, rump higher than his head.

There were two six-foot filing cabinets in the right-hand corner behind the desk. Both were locked; the drawers of the first one were labeled alphabetically, the other was unmarked.

I unhooked Parst's key-chain from his belt. He had as many keys as a janitor or a high-school principal, but not many of them were small enough to fit the filing cabinets. I got the second one unlocked and began going through the drawers. I found what I wanted in the top one—seven fat manila folders labeled "Aza-Kra—Armor," "Aza-Kra—General information," "Aza-Kra—Power sources," "Aza-Kra—Space-flight" and so on; and one more labeled "Directives and related correspondence."

I hauled them all out, piled them on Parst's desk and pulled up a chair.

I took "Armor" first because it was on top and because the title puzzled me. The folder was full of transcripts of interviews whose subject I had to work out as I went along. It appeared that when captured, Aza-Kra had been wearing a lightweight bulletproof body armor, made of something that was longitudinally flexible and perpendicularly rigid—in other words, you could pull it on like a suit of winter underwear, but you couldn't dent it with a sledge hammer.

They had been trying to find out what the stuff was and how it was made for almost two months and as far as I could see they had not made a nickel's worth of progress.

I looked through "Power sources" and "Spaceflight" to see if they were the same, and they were. The odd part was that Aza-Kra's answers didn't sound reluctant or evasive; but he kept running into ideas for which there weren't any words in English and then they would have to start all over again, like Twenty Questions. . . . Is it animal? vegetable? mineral? It was a mess.

I put them all aside except "General information" and "Directives." The first, as I had guessed, was a catch-all for nontechnical subjects—where Aza-Kra had come from, what his people were like, his reasons for coming to this planet: all the unimportant questions; or the only questions that had any importance, depending on how you looked at it.

Parst had already given me an accurate summary of it, but it was surprisingly effective in Aza-Kra's words. *You say we want your planet. There are many planets, so many you would not believe. But if we wanted your planet, and if we could kill as you do, please understand, we are very many. We would fall on your planet like snowflakes. We would not send one man alone.*

And later: *Most young peoples kill. It is a law of nature, yes, but try to understand, it is not the only law. You have been a young people, but now you are growing older. Now you must learn the other law, not to kill. That is what I have come to teach. Until you learn this, we cannot have you among us.*

There was nothing in the folder dated later than a month and a half ago. They had dropped that line of questioning early.

The first thing I saw in the other folder began like this:

You are hereby directed to hold yourself in readiness to destroy the subject under any of the following circumstances, without further specific notification:

1, a: If the subject attempts to escape.

1, b: If the subject kills or injures a human being.

1, c: If the landing, anywhere in the world, of other members of the subject's race is reported and their similarity to the subject established beyond a reasonable doubt. . . .

Seeing it written down like that, in the cold dead-aliveness of black words on white paper, it was easy to forget that the alien was a stomach-turning monstrosity, and to see only that what he had to say was lucid and noble.

But I still hadn't found anything that would persuade me to help him escape. The problem was still there, as insoluble as ever. There was no way of evaluating a word the alien said about himself. He had come alone—perhaps—instead of bringing an invading army with him; but how did we know that one member of his race wasn't as dangerous to us as Perry's battleship to the Japanese? He might be; there was some evidence that he was.

My quarrel with the Defense Department was not that they were mistreating an innocent three-legged missionary, but simply that the problem of Aza-Kra belonged to the world, not to a fragment of the executive branch of the Government of the United States—and certainly not to me.

. . . There was one other way out, I realized. Instead of calling Frisbee in Washington, I could call an arm-long list of senators and representativves. I could call the UN secretariat in New York; I could call the editor of every major newspaper in this hemisphere and the head of every wire service and broadcasting chain. I could stir up a hornet's nest, even, as the saying goes, if I swung for it.

Wrong again: I couldn't. I opened the "Directives" folder again, looking for what I thought I had seen there in the list of hypothetical circumstances. There it was:

1, f: If any concerted attempt on the part of any person or group to remove the subject from Defense Department custody, or to aid him in any way, is made; or if the subject's existence and presence in Defense Department custody becomes public knowledge.

That sewed it up tight, and it also answered my question about Aza-Kra. Knocking out the personnel of B building would be construed as an attempt to escape or as a concerted attempt by a person or group to remove the subject from Defense Department custody, it didn't matter which. If I broke the story, it would have the same result. They would kill him.

In effect, he had put his life in my hands: and that was why he was so sure that I'd help him.

It might have been that, or what I found just before I left the office, that decided me. I don't know; I wish I did.

Coming around the desk the other way, I glanced at the thin man on the floor and noticed that there was something under him, half-hidden by his body. It turned out to be two things: a gray fedora and a pint-sized gray-leather briefcase, chained to his wrist.

So I looked under Parst's folded arms, saw the edge of a thick white sheet of paper, and pulled it out.

Under Frisbee's letterhead, it said:

By courier.

Dear General Parst:

Some possibility appears to exist that A. K. is responsible for recent disturbances in your area; please give me your thought on this as soon as possible—the decision can't be long postponed.

In the meantime you will of course consider your command under emergency status, and we count on you to use your initiative to safeguard security at all costs. In a crisis, you will consider Lieut. D. as expendable.

Sincerely yours,
CARLTON FRISBEE

cf/cf/enc.

"Enc." meant "enclosure"; I pried up Parst's arms again and found another sheet of stiff paper, folded three times, with a paperclip on it.

It was a First Lieutenant's commission, made out to Robert James Dahl, dated three days before, and with a perfect forgery of my signature at the bottom of it.

If commissions can be forged, so can court-martial records.

I put the commission and the letter in my pocket. I didn't seem to feel any particular emotion, but I noticed that my hands were shaking as I sorted through the "General information" file, picked out a few sheets and stuffed them into my pocket with the other papers. I wasn't confused or in doubt about what to do next. I looked around the room, spotted a metal locker diagonally across from the filing cabinets, and opened it with one of the General's keys.

Inside were two .45 automatics, boxes of ammunition, several loaded clips, and three odd-looking sets of handcuffs, very wide and heavy, each with its key.

I took the handcuffs, the keys, both automatics and all the clips.

In a storeroom at the end of the corridor I found a two-wheeled dolly. I wheeled it all the way around to Section One and left it outside they had given me when I arrived, and where the hell were my own clothes? I took a chance and went up to my room on the second floor, remembering that I hadn't been back there since morning.

There they were, neatly laid out on the bed. My keys, lighter, change, wallet and so on were on the bedside table. I changed and went back down to Section One.

In the gun room were two sprawled shapes, one beside the machine-gun that poked its snout through the hemispherical blister, the other under a panel set with three switches and a microphone.

The switches were clearly marked. I opened the first two, walked out and around and laid the three sets of handcuffs on the floor in the middle room. Then I went back to the gun room, closed the first two doors and opened the third.

Soft thumping sounds came from the loudspeaker over the switch panel; then the rattling of metal, more thumps, and finally a series of rattling clicks.

I opened the first door and went back inside. Through the panel in the middle door I could see Aza-Kra; he had retreated into the inner room so that all of him was plainly visible. He was squatting on the floor, his legs drawn up. His arms were at full stretch, each wrist manacled to an ankle. He strained his arms outward to show me that the cuffs were tight.

I made one more trip to open the middle door. Then I got the dolly and wheeled it in.

"Thank you," said Aza-Kra. I got a whiff of his "breath"; as Donnelly had intimated, it wasn't pleasant.

Halfway to the airport, at Aza-Kra's request, I held my breath again. Aside from that we didn't speak except when I asked him, as I was loading him from the jeep into a limousine, "How long will they stay unconscious?"

"Not more than twenty hours, I think. I could have given them more, but I did not dare, I do not know your chemistry well enough."

We could go a long way in twenty hours. We would certainly have to.

I hated to go home, it was too obvious and there was a good chance that the hunt would start before any twenty hours were up, but there wasn't any help for it. I had a passport and a visa for England, where I had been planning to go for a publishers' conference in January, but it hadn't occurred to me to take it along on a quick trip to Washington. And now I had to have the passport.

My first idea had been to head for New York and hand Aza-Kra over to the UN there, but I saw it was no good. Extraterritoriality was just a word, like a lot of other words; we wouldn't be safe until we were out of the country, and on second thought, maybe not then.

It was a little after eight-thirty when I pulled in to the curb down the street from my house. I hadn't eaten since noon, but I wasn't hungry; and it didn't occur to me until later to think about Aza-Kra.

I got the passport and some money without waking my housekeeper. A few blocks away I parked again on a side street. I called the airport, got a reservation on the next eastbound flight, and spent half an hour buying a trunk big enough for Aza-Kra and wrestling him into it.

It struck me at the last minute that perhaps I had been counting too much on that atmosphere-plant of his. His air supply was taken care of, but what about his respiratory waste products—would he poison himself in that tiny closed space? I asked him and he said, "No, it is all right. I will be warm, but I can bear it."

I put the lid down, then opened it again. "I forgot about food," I said. "What do you eat, anyway?"

"At Chillicothe I ate soya bean extract. With added minerals. But I am able to go without food for long periods. Please, do not worry."

All right. I put the lid down again and locked the trunk, but I didn't stop worrying.

He was being too accommodating.

I had expected him to ask me to turn him loose, or take him to wherever his spaceship was. He hadn't brought the subject up; he hadn't even asked me where we were going, or what my plans were.

I thought I knew the answer to that, but it didn't make me any happier. He didn't ask because he already knew—just as he'd known the contents of Parst's office, down to the last document; just as he'd known what I was thinking when I was in the anteroom with Donnelly.

He read minds. And he gassed people through solid metal walls.

What else did he do?

There wasn't time to dispose of the limousine; I simply left it at the airport. If the alarm went out before we got to the coast, we were sunk anyhow; if not, it wouldn't matter.

Nobody stopped us. I caught the stratojet in New York at 12:20, and five hours later we were in London.

Customs was messy, but there wasn't any other way to handle it. When we were fifth in line, I thought: *Knock them out for about an hour*—and held my breath. Nothing happened. I rapped on the side of the trunk to attract his attention, and did it again. This time it worked: everybody in sight went down like a rag doll.

I stamped my own passport, filled out a declaration form and buried it in a stack of others, put a tag on the trunk, loaded it aboard a handtruck, wheeled it outside and took a cab.

I had learned something in the process, although it certainly wasn't much: either Aza-Kra couldn't, or didn't, eavesdrop on my mind all the time—or else he was simply one step ahead of me.

Later, on the way to the harbor, I saw a newsstand and realized that it was going on three days since I had seen a paper. I had tried to get the New York dailies at the airport, but they'd been sold out—nothing on the stands but a lone copy of the Staten Island *Advance*. That hadn't struck me as odd at the time—an index of my state of mind—but it did now.

I got out and bought a copy of everything on the stand except the tipsheets—four newspapers, all of them together about equaling the bulk of one *Herald-Star*. I felt frustrated enough to ask the newsvendor if he had any papers left over from yesterday or the day before. He gave me a glassy look, made me repeat it, then pulled his face into an indescribable expression, laid a finger beside his nose, and said, "'Arf a mo'." He scuttled into a bar a few yards down the street, was gone five minutes, and came back clutching a mare's-next of soiled and bedraggled papers.

"'Ere you are, guvnor. Three bob for the lot."

I paid him. "Thanks," I said, "very much."

He waved his hand expansively. "Okay, bud," he said. "T'ink nuttin' of it!"

A comedian.

The only Channel boat leaving before late afternoon turned out to be an excursion steamer—round trip, two guineas. The boat wasn't crowded; it was the tag-end of the season, and a rough, windy day. I found a seat without any trouble and finished sorting out my stack of papers by date and folio.

British newspapers don't customarily report any more of our news than we do of theirs, but this week our supply of catastrophes had been ample enough to make good reading across the Atlantic. I found all three of the Chicago stories—trimmed to less than two inches apiece, but there. I read the first with professional interest, the second skeptically, and the third with alarm.

I remembered the run of odd items I'd read in that Washington hotel room, a long time ago. I remembered Frisbee's letter to Parst: *"Some possibility appears to exist that A.K. is responsible for recent disturbances in your area. . . ."*

I found two of the penitentiary stories, half smothered by stop press, and I added them to the total. I drew an imaginary map of the United States in my head and stuck imaginary pins in it. Red one, a little cluster: Des Moines, Kansas City, Decatur, St. Louis. Blue ones, a scattering around them: Chicago, Leavenworth, Terre Haute.

Down toward the end of the cabin someone's portable radio was muttering.

A fat youth in a checkered jacket had it. He moved over reluctantly and made room for me to sit down. The crisp, controlled BBC voice was saying, ". . . in Commons today, declared that Britain's trade balance is more favorable than at any time during the past fifteen years. In London, ceremonies marking the sixth anniversary of the death. . ." I let the words slide past me until I heard:

"In the United States, the mysterious epidemic affecting stockyard workers in the central states has spread to New York and New Jersey on the eastern seaboard. The President has requested Congress to provide immediate emergency meat-rationing legislation."

A blurred little woman on the bench opposite leaned forward and said, "Serve 'em right, too! Them with their beefsteak a day."

There were murmurs of approval.

I got up and went back to my own seat. . . . It all fell into one pattern, everything: The man who kicked his wife, the prizefighters, the policeman, the wardens, the slaughterhouse "epidemic."

It was the *lex talionis*—or the Golden Rule in reverse: Be done by as you do to others.

When you injured another living thing, both of you felt the same pain. When you killed, you felt the shock of your victim's death. You might be only stunned by it, like the slaughterhouse workers, or you might die, like the policeman and the schoolboy murderer.

So-called mental anguish counted too, apparently. That explained the wave of humanitarianism in prisons, at least partially; the rest was religious hysteria and the kind of herd instinct that makes any startling new movement mushroom.

And, of course, it also explained Chillicothe: the horrible blanketing depression that settled anywhere the civilian staff congregated—the feeling of being penned up in a place where something frightful was going to happen—and the thing the two psychiatrists had been arguing about, the pseudo-claustrophobia . . . all that was nothing but the reflection of Aza-Kra's feelings, locked in that cell on an alien planet.

Be done by as you do.

And I was carrying that with me. Des Moines, Kansas City, Decatur, St. Louis, Chicago, Leavenworth, Terre Haute—*New York.* After that, England. We'd been in London less than an hour—but England is only four hundred-odd miles long, from John o'Groat's to Lands End.

I remembered what Aza-Kra had said: *Now you must learn the other law, not to kill.*

Not to kill tripeds.

My body was shaking uncontrollably; my head felt like a balloon stuffed with cotton. I stood up and looked around at the blank faces, the inward-looking eyes, every man, woman and child living in a little world of his own. I had a hysterical impulse to shout at them, Look at you, you idiots! You've been invaded and half conquered without a shot fired, and you don't know it!

In the next instant I realized that I was about to burst into laughter. I put my hand over my mouth and half-ran out on deck, giggles leaking through my fingers; I got to the rail and bent myself over it, roaring, apoplectic. I was utterly ashamed of myself, but I couldn't stop it; it was like a fit of vomiting.

The cold spray on my face sobered me. I leaned over the rail, looking down at the white water boiling along the hull. It occurred to me that there was one practical test still to be made: a matter of confirmation.

A middle-aged man with rheumy eyes was standing in the cabin doorway, partly blocking it. As I shouldered past him, I deliberately put my foot down on his.

An absolutely blinding pain shot through the toes of my right foot. When my eyes cleared I saw that the two of us were standing in identical attitudes—weight on one foot, the other knee bent, hand reaching instinctively for the injury.

I had taken him for a "typical Englishman," but he cursed me in a rattling stream of gutter French. I apologized, awkwardly but sincerely—very sincerely.

When we docked at Dunkirk I still hadn't decided what to do.

What I had had in mind up till now was simply to get across France into Switzerland and hold a press conference there, inviting everybody from Tass to the UP. It had to be Switzerland for fairly obvious reasons; the English or the French would clamp a security lid on me before you could say NATO, but the Swiss wouldn't dare—they paid for their neutrality by having to look *both* ways before they cleared their throats.

I could still do that, and let the UN set up a committee to worry about Aza-Kra—but at a conservative estimate it would be ten months before the committee got its foot out of its mouth, and that would be pretty nearly ten months too late.

Or I could simply go to the American consulate in Dunkirk and turn myself in. Within ten hours we would be back in Chillicothe, probably, and I'd be free of the responsibility. I would also be dead.

We got through customs the same way we'd done in London.

And then I had to decide.

The cab driver put his engine in gear and looked at me over his shoulder. "*Un hôtel?*"

". . . Yes," I said. "A cheap hotel. *Un hôtel à bon marché.*"

"*Entendu.*" He jammed down the accelerator an instant before he let out the clutch; we were doing thirty before he shifted into second.

The place he took me to was a villainous third-rate commercial-travelers' hotel, smelling of urine and dirty linen. When the porters were gone I unlocked the trunk and opened it.

We stared at each other.

Moisture was beaded on his blue-gray skin, and there was a smell in the room stronger and ranker than anything that belonged there. His eyes looked duller than they had before; I could barely see the pupils.

"Well?" I said.

"You are half right," he buzzed. "I am doing it, but not for the reason you think."

"All right; you're doing it. *Stop it.* That comes first. We'll stay here, and I'll watch the papers to make sure you do."

"At the customs, those people will sleep only an hour."

"I don't give a damn. If the gendarmes come up here, you can put them to sleep. If I have to I'll move you out to the country and we'll live under a haystack. But no matter what happens we're not going a mile farther into Europe until I know you've quit. If you don't like that, you've got two choices. Either you knock me out, and see how much good it does you, or I'll take that air-machine off your head."

He buzzed inarticulately for a moment. Then, "I have to say no. It is impossible. I could stop for a time, or pretend to you that I stop, but that would solve nothing. It will be—it will do the greatest harm if I stop; you don't understand. It is necessary to continue."

I said, "That's your answer?"

"Yes. If you will let me explain—"

I stepped toward him. I didn't hold my breath, but I think half-consciously I expected him to gas me. He didn't. He didn't move; he just waited.

Seen at close range, the flesh of his head seemed to be continuous with the black substance of the cone; instead of any sharp dividing line, there was a thin area that was neither one nor the other.

I put one hand over the fleshy bulb, and felt his eyes retract and close against my palm. The sensation was indescribably unpleasant, but I kept my hand there, put the other one against the far side of the cone—pulled and pushed simultaneously, as hard as I could.

The top of my head came off.

I was leaning against the top of the open trunk, dizzy and nauseated. The pain was like a white-hot wire drawn tight around my skull just above the eyes. I couldn't see; I couldn't think.

And it didn't stop; it went on and on. . . . I pushed myself away from the trunk and let my legs fold under me. I sat on the floor with my head in my hands, pushing my fingers against the pain.

Gradually it ebbed. I heard Aza-Kra's voice buzzing very quietly, not in English but in a rhythm of tone and phrasing that seemed almost directly comprehensible; if there were a language designed to be spoken by bass viols, it might sound like that.

I got up and looked at him. Shining beads of blue liquid stood out all along the case of the cone, but the seam had not broken.

I hadn't realized that it would be so difficult, that it would be so painful. I felt the weight of the two automatics in my pockets, and I pulled one out, the metal cold and heavy in my palm . . . but I knew suddenly that I couldn't do that either.

I didn't know where his brain was, or his heart. I didn't know whether I could kill him with one shot.

I sat down on the bed, staring at him. "You knew that would happen, didn't you," I said. "You must think I'm a prize sucker."

He said nothing. His eyes were half-closed, and a thin whey-colored fluid was drooling out of the two mouths I could see. Aza-Kra was being sick.

I felt an answering surge of nausea. Then the flow stopped, and a second later, the nausea stopped too. I felt angry, and frustrated, and frightened.

After a moment I got up off the bed and started for the door.

"Please," said Aza-Kra. "Will you be gone long?"

"I don't know," I said. "Does it matter?"

"If you will be gone long," he said, "I would ask that you loosen the handcuffs for a short period before you go."

I stared at him, suddenly hating him with a violence that shook me.

"No," I said, and reached for the door-handle.

My body knotted itself together like a fist. My legs gave way under me, and I missed the door-handle going down; I hit the floor hard.

There was no sensation in my hands or feet. The muscles of my shoulders, arms, thighs, and calves were one huge, heavy pain. And I couldn't move.

I looked at Aza-Kra's wrists, shackled to his drawn-up ankles. He had been like that for something like fourteen hours. He had cramps.

"I am sorry," said Aza-Kra. "I did not want to do that to you, but there was no other way."

I thought dazedly, *No other way to do what?*

"To make you wait. To listen. To let me explain."

I said, "I don't get it." Anger flared again, then faded under something more intense and painful. The closest English word for it is "humility"; some other language may come nearer, but I doubt it; it isn't an emotion that we like to talk about. I felt bewildered, and ashamed, and very small, all at once, and there was another component, harder to name. A . . . threshold feeling.

I tried again. "I felt the other pain, before, but not this. Is that because—"

"Yes. There must be the intention to injure or cause pain. I will tell you why. I have to go back very far. When an animal becomes more developed—many cells, instead of one—always the same things happen. I am the first man of my kind who ever saw a man of your kind. But we both have eyes. We both have ears." The feathery spines on his neck stiffened and relaxed. "Also there is another sense that always comes. But always it goes only a little way and then stops.

"When you are a young animal, fighting with the others to live, it is useful to have a sense which feels the thoughts of the enemy. Just as it is useful to have a sense which sees the shape of his body. But this sense cannot come all at once, it must grow by a little and a little, as when a surface that can tell the light from the dark becomes a true eye.

"But the easiest thoughts to feel are pain thoughts, they are much stronger than any others. And when the sense is still weak—it is a part of the brain, not an organ by itself—when it is weak, only the strongest stimulus can make it work. This stimulus is hatred, or anger, or the wish to kill.

"So that just when the sense is enough developed that it could begin to be useful, it always disappears. It is not gone, it is pushed under. A very long time ago, one race discovered this sense and learned how it could be brought back. It is done by a class of organic chemicals. You have not the word. For each race a different member of the class, but always it can be done. The chemical is a catalyst, it is not used up. The change it makes is in the cells of all the body—it is permanent, it passes also to the children.

"You understand, when a race is older, to kill is not useful. With the change, true civilization begins. The first race to find this knowledge gave it to others, and those to others, and now all have it. All who are able to leave their planets. We give it to you, now, because you are ready. When you are older there will be others who are ready. You will give it to them."

While I have been listening, the pain in my arms and legs had slowly been getting harder and harder to take. I reminded myself that Aza-Kra had borne it, probably, at least ten hours longer than I had;

but that didn't make it much easier. I tried to keep my mind off it but that wasn't possible; the band of pain around my head was still there, too, a faint throbbing. And both were consequences of things I had done to Aza-Kra. I was suffering with him, measure for measure.

Justice. Surely that was a good thing? Automatic instant retribution, mathematically accurate: an eye for an eye.

I said, "That was what you were doing when they caught you, then—finding out which chemical we reacted to?"

"Yes. I did not finish until after they had brought me to Chillicothe. Then it was much more difficult. If not for my accident, all would have gone much more quickly."

"The walls?"

"Yes. As you have guessed, my air machine will also make other substances and expel them with great force. Also, when necessary, it will place these substances in a—state of matter, you have not the word—so that they pass through solid objects. But this takes much power. While in Chillicothe my range was very small. Later when I can be in the open, it will be much greater."

He caught what I was thinking before I had time to speak. He said, "Yes. You will agree. When you understand."

It was the same thing he had told me at Chillicothe, almost to the word.

I said, "You keep talking about this thing as a gift but I notice you didn't ask us if we wanted it. What kind of a gift is that?"

"You are not serious. You know what happened when I was captured."

After a moment he added, "I think if it had been possible, if we could have asked each man and woman on the planet to say yes or no, explaining everything, showing that there was no trick, that most would have said yes. For people the change is good. But for governments it is not good."

I said, "I'd like to believe you. It would be very pleasant to believe you. But nothing you can say changes the fact that this thing, this gift of yours could be a weapon. To soften us up before you move in. If you were an advance agent for an invasion fleet, this is what you'd be doing."

"You are thinking with habits," he said. "Try to think with logic. Imagine that your race is very old, with much knowledge. You have ships that cross between the stars. Now you discover this young race, these Earthmen, who only begin to learn to leave their own planet. You decide to conquer them. Why? What is your reason?"

"How do I know? It could be anything. It might be something I couldn't even imagine. For all I know you want to eat us."

His throat-spines quivered. He said slowly, "You are partly serious. You really think . . . I am sorry that you did not read the studies of the physiologists. If you had, you would know. My digestion is only for vegetable food. You cannot understand, but—with us, to eat meat is like with you, to eat excretions."

I said, "All right, maybe we have something else you want. Natural resources that you've used up. Some substance, maybe some rare element."

"That is still habit thinking. Have you forgotten my air machine?"

"—Or maybe you just want the planet itself. With us cleared off it, to make room for you."

"Have you never looked at the sky at night?"

I said, "All *right*. But this quiz was your idea, not mine. I *admit* that I don't know enough even to make a sensible guess at your motives. And that's the reason why I can't trust you."

He was silent a moment. Then: "Remember that the substance which makes the change is a catalyst. Also it is a very fine powder. The particles are of only a few molecules each. The winds carry it. It is swallowed and breathed in and absorbed by the skin. It is breathed out and excreted. The wind takes it again. Water carries it. It is carried by insects and by birds and animals, and by men, in their bodies and in their clothing.

"This you can understand and know that it is true. If I die another could come and finish what I have begun, but even this is not necessary. The amount of the catalyst I have already released is more than enough. It will travel slowly, but nothing can stop it. If I die now, this instant, still in a year the catalyst will reach every part of the planet."

After a long time I said, "Then what did you mean by saying that a great harm would be done, if you stopped now?"

"I meant this. Until now, only your Western nations have the catalyst. In a few days their time of crisis will come, beginning with the United States. And the nations of the East will attack."

IV

I found that I could move, inchmeal, if I sweated hard enough at it. It took me what seemed like half an hour to get my hand into my pocket, paw all the stuff out onto the floor, and get the key-ring hooked over one finger. Then I had to crawl about ten feel to Aza-Kra, and when I got there my fingers simply wouldn't hold the keys firmly enough.

I picked them up in my teeth and got two of the wristcuffs unlocked. That was the best I could do; the other one was behind him, inside the trunk, and neither of us had strength enough to pull him out where I could get at it.

Then the pins-and-needles started, as Aza-Kra began to flex his arms and legs to get the stiffness out of them. Between us, after a while, we got him out of the trunk and unlocked the third cuff. In a few minutes I had enough freedom of movement to begin massaging his cramped muscles; but it was three-quarters of an hour before either of us could stand.

We caught the mid-afternoon plane to Paris, with Aza-Kra in the trunk again. I checked into a hotel, left him there, and went shopping: I bought a hideous black dress with imitation-onyx trimming, a black coat with a cape, a feather muff, a tall black hat and the heaviest mourning veil I could find. At a theatrical costumer's near the Place de l'Opera I got a reasonably lifelike old-woman mask and a heavy wig.

When he was dressed up, the effect was startling. The tall hat covered the cone, the muff covered two of his hands. There was nothing to be done about the feet, but the skirt hung almost to the ground, and I thought he would pass with luck.

We got a cab and headed for the American consulate, but halfway there I remembered about the photographs. We stopped off at an amusement arcade and I got my picture taken in a coin-operated machine. Aza-Kra was another problem—that mask wouldn't fool anybody without the veil—but I spotted a poorly-dressed old woman and with some difficulty managed to make her understand that I was a crazy American who would pay her fifty francs to pose for her picture. We struck a bargain at a hundred.

As soon as we got into the consulate waiting-room, Aza-Kra gassed everybody in the building. I locked the street door and searched the offices until I found a man with a little pile of blank passport books on the desk in front of him. He had been filling one in on a machine like a typewriter except that it had a movable plane-surface platen instead of a cylinder.

I moved him out of the way and made out two passports; one for myself, as Arthur James LeRoux; one for Aza-Kra, as Mrs. Adrienne LeRoux. I pasted on the photographs and fed them into the machine that pressed the words "*Photograph attached U. S. Consulate Paris,*

France" into the paper, and then into the one that impressed the consular seal.

I signed them, and filled in the blanks on the inside covers, in the taxi on the way to the Israeli consulate. The afternoon was running out, and we had a lot to do.

We went to six foreign consulates, gassed the occupants, and got a visa stamp in each one. I had the devil's own time filling them out; I had to copy the scribbles I found in legitimate passports at each place and hope for the best. The Israeli one was surprisingly simple, but the Japanese was a horror.

We had dined in our hotel room—steak for me, water and soy-bean paste, bought at a health-food store, for Aza-Kra. Just before we left for Le Bourget, I sent a cable to Eli Freeman:

BIG STORY WILL HAVE TO WAIT SPREAD THIS NOW ALL STOCKYARD SO-CALLED EPIDEMIC AND SIMILAR PHENOMENA DUE ONE CAUSE STEP ON SOMEBODY'S TOE TO SEE WHAT I MEAN.

Shortly after seven o'clock we were aboard a flight bound for the Middle East.

And that was the fourth day, during which a number of things happened that I didn't have time to add to my list until later.

Commercial and amateur fishermen along the Atlantic seaboard, from Delaware Bay as far north as Portland, suffered violent attacks whose symptoms resembled those of asthma. Some—who had been using rods or poles rather than nets—complained also of sharp pains in the jaws and hard palate. Three deaths were reported.

The "epidemic" now covered roughly half the continental United States. All livestock shipments from the West had been canceled, stockyards in the affected area were full to bursting. The President had declared a national emergency.

Lobster had disappeared completely from east-coast menus.

One Robert James Dahl, described as the owner and publisher of a Middle Western newspaper, was being sought by the Defense Department and the FBI in connection with the disappearance of certain classified documents.

The next day, the fifth, was Saturday. At two in the morning on a Sabbath, Tel Aviv seemed as dead as Angkor. We had four hours there, between planes; we could have spent them in the airport waiting room, but I was wakeful and I wanted to talk to Aza-Kra. There was one

ancient taxi at the airport; I had the driver take us into the town and
leave us there, down in the harbor section, until plane time.

We sat on a bench behind the sea wall and watched the moonlight
on the Mediterranean. Parallel banks of faintly-silvered clouds arched
over us to northward; the air was fresh and cool.

After a while I said, "You know that I'm only playing this your way
for one reason. As far as the rest of it goes, the more I think about it
the less I like it."

"Why?"

"A dozen reasons. The biological angle, for one. I don't like violence, I don't like war, but it doesn't matter what I like. They're
biologically necessary, they eliminate the unfit."

"Do you say that only the unfit are killed in wars?"

"That isn't what I mean. In modern war the contest isn't between
individuals, it's between whole populations. Nations, and groups of
nations. It's a cruel, senseless, wasteful business, and when you're in
the middle of it it's hard to see any good at all in it, but it works—the
survivors *survive*, and that's the only test there is."

"Our biologists do not take this view." He added, "Neither do
yours."

I said, "How's that?"

"Your biologists agree with ours that war is not biological. It is
social. When so many are killed, no stock improves. All suffer. It is as
you yourself say, the contest is between nations. But their wars kill
men."

I said, "All right, I concede that one. But we're not the only kind
of animal on this planet, and we didn't get to be the dominant species
without fighting. What are we supposed to do if we run into a hungry
lion—argue with him?"

"In a few weeks there will be no more lions."

I stared at him. "This affects lions, too? Tigers, elephants, everything?"

"Everything of sufficient brain. Roughly, everything above the
level of your insects."

"But I understood you to say that the catalyst—that it took a different catalyst for each species."

"No. All those with spines and warm blood have the same ancestors. Your snakes may perhaps need a different catalyst, and I believe
you have some primitive sea creatures which kill, but they are not
important."

I said, "My God." I thought of lions, wolves, coyotes, housecats, lying dead beside their prey. Eagles, hawks and owls tumbling out of the sky. Ferrets, stoats, weasels. . .

The world a big garden, for protected children.

My fists clenched. "But this is a million times worse than I had any idea. It's insane. You're upsetting the whole natural balance, you're knocking it crossways. Just for a start, what the hell are we going to do about rats and mice? That's—" I choked on my tongue. There were too many images in my mind to put any of them into words. Rats like a tidal wave, filling a street from wall to wall. Deer swarming out of the forests. The sky blackening with crows, sparrows, jays.

"It will be difficult for some years," Aza-Kra said. "Perhaps even as difficult as you now think. But you say that to fight for survival is good. Is it not better to fight against other species than among yourselves?"

"Fight!" I said. "What have you left us to fight with? How many rats can a man kill before he drops dead from shock?"

"It is possible to kill without causing pain or shock. . . . You would have thought of this, although it is a new idea for you. Even your killing of animals for food can continue. We do not ask you to become as old as we are in a day. Only to put behind you your cruelty which has no purpose."

He had answered me, as always; and as always, the answer was two-edged. It was possible to kill painlessly, yes. And the only weapon Aza-Kra had brought to Earth, apparently, was an anesthetic gas. . . .

We landed at Srinagar, in the Vale of Kashmir, at high noon: a sea of white light under a molten-metal sky.

Crossing the field, I saw a group of white-turbaned figures standing at the gate. I squinted at them through the glare; heatwaves made them jump and waver, but in a moment I was sure. They were bush-bearded Sikh policemen, and there were eight of them.

I pressed Aza-Kra's arm sharply and held my breath.

A moment later we picked our way through the sprawled line of passengers to the huddle of bodies at the gate. The passport examiner, a slender Hindu, lay a yard from the Sikhs. I plucked a sheet of paper out of his hand.

Sure enough, it was a list of the serial numbers of the passports we had stolen from the Paris consulate.

Bad luck. It was only six-thirty in Paris now, and on a Saturday morning at that; we should have had at least six hours more. But something could have gone wrong at any one of the seven consulates—an after-hours appointment, or a worried wife, say. After that the whole thing would have unraveled.

"How much did you give them this time?" I asked.

"As before. Twenty hours."

"All right, good. Let's go."

He had overshot his range a little: all four of the hack-drivers waiting outside the airport building were snoring over their wheels. I dumped the skinniest one in the back seat with Aza-Kra and took over.

Not for the first time, it occurred to me that without me or somebody just like me Aza-Kra would be helpless. It wasn't just a matter of getting out of Chillicothe; he couldn't drive a car or fly a plane, he couldn't pass for human by himself; he couldn't speak without giving himself away. Free, with no broken bones, he could probably escape recapture indefinitely; but if he wanted to go anywhere he would have to walk.

And not for the first time, I tried to see into a history book that hadn't been written yet. My name was there, that much was certain, providing there was going to be any history to write. But was it a name like Blondel . . . or did it sound more like Vidkun Quisling?

We had to go south; there was nothing in any other direction but the highest mountains in the world. We didn't have Pakistan visas, so Lahore and Amritsar, the obvious first choices, were out. The best we could do was Chamba, about two hundred rail miles southeast on the Srinagar-New Delhi line. It wasn't on the principal air routes, but we could get a plane there to Saharanpur, which was.

There was an express leaving in half an hour, and we took it. I bought an English-language newspaper at the station and read it backward and forward for four hours; Aza-Kra spent the time apparently asleep, with his cone, hidden by the black hat, tilted out the window.

The "epidemic" had spread to five Western states, plus Quebec, Ontario and Manitoba, and parts of Mexico and Cuba . . . plus England and France, I knew, but there was nothing about that in my Indian paper; too early.

In Chamba I bought the most powerful battery-operated portable radio I could find; I wished I had thought of it sooner. I checked with the airport: there was a flight leaving Saharanpur for Port Blair at eight o'clock.

Port Blair, in the Andamans, is Indian territory; we wouldn't need to show our passports. What we were going to do after that was another question.

I could have raided another set of consulates, but I knew it would be asking for trouble. Once was bad enough; twice, and when we tried it a third time—as we would have to, unless I found some other answer—I was willing to bet we would find them laying for us, with gas masks and riot guns.

Somehow, in the few hours we were to spend at Port Blair, I had to get those serial numbers altered by an expert.

We had been walking the black, narrow dockside streets for two hours when Aza-Kra suddenly stopped.

"Something?"

"Wait," he said. ". . . Yes. This is the man you are looking for. He is a professional forger. His name is George Wheelwright. He can do it, but I do not know whether he will. He is a very timid and suspicious man."

"All right. In here?"

"Yes."

We went up a narrow unlighted stairway, chocked with a kitchen-midden of smells, curry predominating. At the second-floor landing Aza-Kra pointed to a door. I knocked.

Scufflings behind the door. A low voice: "Who's that?"

"A friend. Let us in, Wheelwright."

The door cracked open and yellow light spilled out; I saw the outline of a head and the faint gleam of a bulbous eye. "What d'yer want?"

"Want you to do a job for me, Wheelwright. Don't keep us talking here in the hall."

The door opened wider and I squeezed through into a cramped, untidy box of a kitchen. A faded cloth covered the doorway to the next room.

Wheelwright glanced at Aza-Kra and then stared hard at me; he was a little chicken-breasted wisp of a man, dressed in dungarees and a striped polo shirt. "Who sent yer?"

"You wouldn't know the name. A friend of mine in Calcutta." I took out the passports. "Can you fix these?"

He looked at them carefully, taking his time. "What's wrong with 'em?"

"Nothing but the serial numbers."

"What's wrong with *them*?"

"They're on a list."

He laughed, a short, meaningless bark.

I said, "Well?"

"Who'd yer say yer friend in Calcutter was?"

"I haven't any friend in Calcutta. Never mind how I knew about you. Will you do the job or won't you?"

He handed the passports back and moved toward the door. "Mister, I haven't got the time to fool with yer. Perhaps yer having me on, or perhaps yer've made an honest mistake. There's another Wheelwright over on the north side of town. You try him." He opened the door. "Good night, both."

I pushed it shut again and reached for him, but he was a yard away in one jump, like a rabbit. He stood beside the table, arms hanging, and stared at me with a vague smile.

I said, "I haven't got time to play games, either. I'll pay you five hundred American dollars to alter these passports—" I tossed them onto the table—"or else I'll beat the living tar out of you." I took a step toward him.

I never saw a man move faster: he had the drawer open and the gun out and aimed before I finished that step. But the muzzle trembled slightly. "No nearer," he said hoarsely.

I thought, *Five minutes,* and held my breath.

When he slumped, I picked up the revolver. Then I lifted him—he weighed about ninety pounds—propped him in a chair behind the table, and waited.

In a few minutes he raised his head and goggled at me dazedly. "How'd yer do that?" he whispered.

I put the money on the table beside the passports. "Start," I said.

He stared at it, then at me. His thin lips tightened. "Go ter blazes," he said.

I stepped around the table and cuffed him backhand. I felt the blow on my own face, hard and stinging, but I did it again. I kept it up. It wasn't pleasant; I was feeling not only the blows themselves, but Wheelwright's emotional responses, the shame and wretchedness and anger, and the queasy writhing fear: Wheelwright couldn't bear pain.

At that, he beat me. When I stopped, sickened and dizzy, and said as roughly as I could, "Had enough, Wheelwright?" he answered, "Not if yer was ter kill me, yer bloody barstid."

His voice trembled, and his face was streaked with tears, but he meant it. He thought I was a government agent, trying to bully him into signing his own prison sentence, and rather than let me do it he would take any amount of punishment; prison was the one thing he feared more than physical pain.

I looked at Aza-Kra. His neck-sines were erect and quivering; I could see the tips of them at the edges of the veil. Then inspiration hit me.

I pulled him forward where the little man could see him, and lifted the veil. The feathery spines stood out clearly on either side of the corpse-white mask.

I won't touch you again," I said. "But look at this. Can you see?"

His eyes widened; he scrubbed them with the palms of his hands and looked again.

"And this," I said. I pulled at Aza-Kra's forearm and the clawed blue-gray hand came out of the muff.

Wheelwright's eyes bulged. He flattened himself against the back of the chair.

"Now," I said, "six hundred dollars—or I'll take this mask off and show you what's behind it."

He clenched his eyes shut. His face had gone yellowish-pale; his nostrils were white.

"Get it out of here," he said faintly.

He didn't move until Aza-Kra had disappeared behind the curtain into the other room. Then, without a word, he poured and drank half a tumblerful of whisky, switched on a gooseneck lamp, produced bottles, pens and brushes from the table drawer, and went to work. He bleached away the first and last digits of both serial numbers, then painted over the areas with a thin wash of color that matched the blue tint of the paper. With a jeweler's loupe in his eye, he restored the obliterated tiny letters of the background design; finally, still using the loupe, he drew the new digits in black. From first to last, it took him thirty minutes; and his hands didn't begin to tremble until he was done.

V

The sixth day was two days—because we left Otaru at 3:30 p.m. Sunday and arrived at Honolulu at 4:00 a.m. Saturday. We had lost five hours in traversing sixty-one degrees of longitude—but we'd also gained a day by crossing the International Date Line from west to east.

On the sixth day, then, which was two days, the following things happened and were duly reported:

Be Done By As Ye Do was the title of some thousands of sermons and, by count, more than seven hundred front-page newspaper editorials from Newfoundland to Oaxaca. My cable to Freeman had come a little late; the *Herald-Star's* announcement was lost in the ruck.

Following this, a wave of millennial enthusiasm swept the continent; Christians and Jews everywhere feasted, fasted, prayed and in other ways celebrated the imminent Second (or First) Coming of Christ. Evangelistic and fundamentalist sects garnered souls by the million.

Members of the Apostolic Overcoming Holy Church of God, the Pentecostal Fire Baptized Holiness Church and numerous other groups gave away most or all of their worldly possessions. Others were more practical. The Seventh Day Adventists, who are vegetarians, pooled capital and began an enormous expansion of their meatless-food factories, dairies and other enterprises.

Delegates to a World Synod of Christian Churches began arriving at a tent city near Smith Center, Kansas, late Saturday night. Trouble developed almost immediately between the Brethren Church of God (Reformed Dunkers) and the Two-Seed-in-the-Spirit Predestinarian Baptists—later spreading to a schism which led to the establishment of two rump synods, one at Lebanon and the other at Athol.

Five hundred Doukhobors stripped themselves mother-naked, burned their homes, and marched on Vancouver.

Roman Catholics in most places celebrated the Feast of the Transfiguration as usual, awaiting advice from Rome.

Riots broke out in Chicago, Detroit, New Orleans, Philadelphia and New York. In each case the original disturbances were brief, but were followed by protracted vandalism and looting which local police, state police, and even National Guard units were unable to check. By midnight Sunday property damage was estimated at more than twenty million dollars. The casualty list was fantastically high. So was the proportion of police-and-National-Guard casualties—exactly fifty per cent of the total. . . .

In the British Isles, Western Europe and Scandinavia, the early symptoms of the Western hemisphere's disaster were beginning to appear: the stricken slaughterers and fishermen, the unease in prisons, the freaks of violence.

An unprecedented number of political refugees turned up on the West-German side of the Burnt Corridor early Saturday morning.

Late the same day, a clash between Sikh and Moslem guards on the India-Pakistan border near Sialkot resulted in the annihilation of both parties.

And on Sunday it hit the fighting in Indo-China.

Allied and Communist units, engaging at sixty points along the eight-hundred-mile front, fell back with the heaviest casualties of the war.

Red bombers launched a successful daylight attack on Luangprabang: successful, that is, except that nineteen out of twenty planes crashed outside the city or fell into the Nam Ou.

Forty Allied bombers took off on sorties to Yen-bay, Hanoi and Nam-dinh. None returned.

Nobody knew it yet, but the war was over.

Still other things happened but were not recorded by the press:

A man in Arizona, a horse gelder by profession, gave up his business and moved out of the county, alleging ill health.

So did a dentist in Tacoma, and another in Galveston.

In Breslau an official of the People's Police resigned his position with the same excuse; and one in Buda; and one in Pest.

A conservative Tajik tribesman of Indarab, discovering that his new wife had been unfaithful, attempted to deal with her in the traditional manner, but desisted when a critical observer would have said he had hardly begun; nor did this act of compassion bring him any relief.

And outside the town of Otaru, just two hundred and fifty miles across the Sea of Japan from the eastern shore of the Russian Socialist Federated Soviet Republic, Aza-Kra used his anesthetic gas again—on me.

I had been bone-tired when we left Port Elair shortly before midnight, but I hadn't slept all the long dark droning way to Manila; or from there to Tokyo, with the sun rising half an hour after we cleared the Philippines and slowly turning the globe underneath us to a white disk of fire; or from Tokyo north again to Otaru, bleak and windy and smelling of brine.

In all that time, I hadn't been able to forget Wheelwright except for half an hour toward the end, when I picked up an English-language broadcast from Tokyo and heard the news from the States.

The first time you burn yourself playing with matches, the chances are that if the blisters aren't too bad, you get over it fast enough; you forget about it. But the second time, it's likely to sink in.

Wheelwright was my second time; Wheelwright finished me.

It's more than painful, it's more than frightening, to cause another living creature pain and feel what he feels. It tears you apart. It makes you the victor and the victim, and neither half of that is bearable.

It makes you love what you destroy—as you love yourself—and it makes you hate yourself as your victim hates you.

That isn't all. I had felt Wheelwright's self-loathing as his body cringed and the tears spilled out of his eyes, the helpless gut-twisting shame that was as bad as the fear; and that burden was on me too.

Wheelwright was talented. That was his own achievement; he had found it in himself and developed it and trained himself to use it. Wheelwright had courage. That was his own. But who had made Wheelwright afraid? And who had taught him that the world was his enemy?

You, and I, and every other human being on the planet, and all our two-legged ancestors before us. Because we had settled for too little. Because not more than a handful of us, out of all the crawling billions, had ever had the will to break the chain of blows, from father to daughter to son, generation after generation.

So there was Wheelwright; that was what we had made out of man: the artistry and the courage compressed to a needlethin, needle-hard core inside him, and that only because we hadn't been able to destroy it altogether; the rest of him self-hatred, and suspicion, and resentment, and fear.

But after breakfast in Tokyo, it began to seem a little more likely that some kind of a case could be made for the continued existence of the human race. And after that it was natural to think about lions, and about the rioting that was going on in America.

For all his moral nicety, Aza-Kra had no trouble in justifying the painful extinction of carnivores. From his point of view, they were better off dead. It was regrettable, of course, but. . .

But, *sub specie deternitatis*, was a man much different from a lion?

It was a commonplace that no other animal killed on so grand a scale as man. The problem had never come up before: could we live without killing?

I was standing with Aza-Kra at the top of a little hill that overlooked the coast road and the bay. The bus that had brought us there was dwindling, a white speck in a cloud of dust, down the highway toward Cape Kamui.

Aza-Kra sat on a stone, his third leg grotesquely bulging the skirt of his coat. His head bent forward, as if the old woman he was pretending to be had fallen asleep, chin on massive chest; the conical hat pointed out to sea.

I said, "This is the time of crisis you were talking about, for America."

"Yes. It begins now."

"When does it end? Let's talk about this a little more. This justice. Crimes of violence—all right. They punish themselves, and before long they'll prevent themselves automatically. What about crimes of property? A man steals my wallet and runs. Or he smashes a window and takes what he wants. Who's going to stop him?"

He didn't answer for a moment; when he did the words came slowly and the pronunciation was bad, as if he were too weary to attend to it. "The wallet can be chained to your clothing. The window can be made of glass that does not break."

I said impatiently, "You know that's not what I mean. I'm talking about the problem as it affects everybody. We solve it by policemen and courts and prisons. What do we do instead?"

"I am sorry that I did not understand you. Give me a moment. . . ."

I waited.

"In your Middle Ages, when a man was insane, what did you do?"

I thought of Bedlam, and of creatures with matted hair chained to rooftops.

He didn't wait for me to speak. "Yes. And now, you are more wise?"

"A little."

"Yes. And in the beginning of your Industrial Revolution, when a factory stopped and men had no work, what was done?"

"They starved."

"And now?"

"There are relief organizations. We try to keep them alive until they can get work."

"If a man steals what he does not need," Aza-Kra said, "is he not sick? If a man steals what he must have to live, can you blame him?"

Socrates, in an onyx-trimmed dress, three-legged on a stone.

Finally I said, "It's easy enough to make us look foolish, but we have made some progress in the last two thousand years. Now you want us to go the rest of the way overnight. It's impossible; we haven't got time enough."

"You will have more time now." His voice was very faint. "Killing wastes much time. . . . Forgive me, now I must sleep."

His head dropped even farther forward. I watched for a while to see if he would topple over, but of course he was too solidly based. A tripod. I sat down beside him, feeling my own fatigue drag at my body, envying him his rest; but I couldn't sleep.

There was really no point in arguing with him, I told myself; he was too good for me. I was a savage splitting logic with a missionary. He knew more than I did; probably he was more intelligent. And the central question, the only one that mattered, couldn't be answered the way I was going at it.

Aza-Kra himself was the key, not the doctrine of non-violence, not the psychology of crime.

If he was telling the truth about himself and the civilization he came from, I had nothing to worry about.

If he wasn't, then I should have left him in Chillicothe or killed him in Paris; and if I could kill him now, that was what I should do.

And I didn't know. After all this time, I still didn't know.

I saw the bus come back down the road and disappear towards Otaru. After a long time, I saw it heading out again. When it came back from the cape the second time, I woke Aza-Kra and we slogged down the steep path to the roadside. I waved as the bus came nearer; it slowed and rattled to a halt a few yards beyond us.

Passengers' heads popped out of the windows to watch us as we walked toward the door. Most of them were Japanese, but I saw one Caucasian, leaning with both arms out of the window. I saw his features clearly, narrow pale nose and lips, blue eyes behind rimless glasses; sunlight glinting on sparse yellow hair. And then I saw the flat dusty road coming up to meet me.

I was lying face-up on a hard sandy slope; when I opened my eyes I saw the sky and a few blades of tough, dry grass. The first thought that came into my head was, *Now I know. Now I've had it.*

I sat up. And a buzzing voice said, "Hold your breath!"

Turning, I saw a body sprawled on the slope just below me. It was the yellow-haired man. Beyond him squatted the gray form of Aza-Kra.

"All right," he said.

I let my breath out. "What—?"

He showed me a brown metal ovoid, cross-hatched with fragmentation grooves. A grenade.

"He was about to arm it. There was no time to warn you. I knew you would wish to see for yourself."

I looked around dazedly. Thirty feet above, the slope ended in a clean-cut line against the sky; beyond it was a short, narrow white stripe that I recognized as the top of the bus, still parked at the side of the road.

"We have ten minutes more before the others awaken."

I went through the man's pockets. I found a handful of change, a wallet with nothing in it but a few yen notes, and a folded slip of glossy white paper. That was all.

I unfolded the paper, but I knew what it was even before I saw the small teleprinted photograph on its inner side. It was a copy of my passport picture—the one on the genuine document, not the bogus one I had made in Paris.

On the way back, my hands began shaking. It got so bad that I had to put them between my thighs and squeeze hard; and then the shaking spread to my legs and arms and jaw. My forehead was cold and there was a football-sized ache in my belly, expanding to a white pain every time we hit a bump. The whole bus seemed to be tilting ponderously over to the right, farther and farther but never falling down.

Later, when I had had a cup of coffee and two cigarettes in the terminal lunchroom, I got one of the most powerful irrational impulses I've ever known: I wanted to take the next bus back to that spot on the coast road, walk down the slope to where the yellow-haired man was, and kick his skull to flinders.

If we were lucky, the yellow-haired man might have been the only one in Otaru who knew we were here. The only way to find out was to go on to the airport and take a chance; either way, we had to get out of Japan. But it didn't end there. Even if they didn't know where we were now, they knew all the stops on our itinerary; they knew which visas we had. Maybe Aza-Kra would be able to gas the next one before he killed us, and then again maybe not.

I thought about Frisbee and Parst and the President—damning them all impartially—and my anger grew. By now, I realized suddenly, they must have understood that we were responsible for what was happening. They would have been energetically apportioning the blame for the last few days; probably Parst had already been court-martialed.

Once that was settled, there would be two things they could do next. The could publish the truth, admit their own responsibility, and warn the world. Or they could destroy all the evidence and keep silent. If the world went to hell in a bucket, at least they wouldn't be blamed for it. . . . Providing I was dead. Not much choice.

After another minute I got up and Aza-Kra followed me out to a taxi. We stopped at the nearest telegraph office and I sent a cable to Frisbee in Washington:

HAVE SENT FULL ACCOUNT CHILLICOTHE TO TRUSTWOR-
THY PERSON WITH INSTRUCTIONS PUBLISH EVENT MY
DEATH OR DISAPPEARANCE. CALL OFF YOUR DOGS.

It was childish, but apparently it worked. Not only did we have
no trouble at Otaru airport—the yellow-haired man, as I'd hoped, must
have been working alone—but nobody bothered us at Honolulu or
Asuncion.

Just the same, the mood of depression and nervousness that settled on me that day didn't lift; it grew steadily worse. Fourteen hours'
sleep in Asuncion didn't mend it; Monday's reports of panics and bank
failures in North America intensified it, but that was incidental.

And when I slept, I had nightmares: dreams of stifling-dark jungles, full of things with teeth.

We spent twenty-four hours in Asuncion, while Aza-Kra pumped
out enough catalyst to blanket South America's seven million square
miles—a territory almost as big as the sprawling monster of Soviet
Eurasia.

After that we flew to Capetown—and that was it. We were
finished.

We had spiraled around the globe, from the United States to
England, to France, to Israel, to India, to Japan, to Paraguay, to the
Union of South Africa, trailing an expanding invisible cloud behind us.
Now the winds were carrying it westward from the Atlantic, south from
the Mediterranean, north from the Indian Ocean, west from the
Pacific.

Frigate birds and locusts, men in tramp steamers and men in jet
planes would carry it farther. In a week it would have reached all the
places we had missed: Australia, Micronesia, the islands of the South
Pacific, the Poles.

That left the lunar bases and the orbital stations. Ours and Theirs.
But they had to be supplied from Earth; the infection would come to
them in rockets.

For better or worse, we had what we had always said we wanted.
Ahimsa. The Age of Reason. The Kingdom of God.

And I still didn't know whether I was Judas, or the little Dutch
boy with his finger in the dike.

I didn't find out until three weeks later.

We stayed on in Capetown, resting and waiting. Listening to the
radio and reading newspapers kept me occupied a good part of the

time. When restlessness drove me out of doors, I wandered aimlessly in the business section, or went down to the harbor and spent hours staring out past the castle and the breakwater.

But my chief occupation, the thing that obssessed me now, was the study of Aza-Kra.

He seemed very tired. His skin was turning dry and rough, more gray than blue; his eyes were blue-threaded and more opaque-looking than ever. He slept a great deal and moved little. The soy-bean paste I was able to get for him gave him insufficient nourishment; vitamins and minerals were lacking.

I asked him why he didn't make what he needed in his air machine. He said that some few of the compounds could be inhaled, and he was making those; that he had had another transmuter, for food-manufacture, but that it had been taken from him; and that he would be all right; he would last until his friends came.

He didn't know when that would be; or he wouldn't tell me.

His speech was slower and his diction more slurred every day. It was obviously difficult for him to talk; but I goaded him, I nagged him, I would not let him alone. I spent days on one topic, left it, came back to it and asked the same questions over. I made copious notes of what he said and the way he said it.

I wanted to learn to read the signs of his emotions; or failing that, to catch him in a lie.

A dozen times I thought I had trapped him into a contradiction, and each time, wearily, patiently, he explained what I had misunderstood. As for his emotions, they had only one visible sign that I was able to discover: the stiffening and trembling of his neck-spines.

Gestures of emotion are arbitrary. There are human tribes whose members never smile. There are others who smile when they are angry. Cf. Dodgson's Cheshire Cat.

He was doing it more and more often as the time went by; but what did it mean? Anger? Resentment? Annoyance? *Amusement?*

The riots in the United States ended on the 9th and 10th when interfaith committees toured each city in loudspeaker trucks. Others began elsewhere.

Business was at a standstill in most larger cities. Galveston, Nashville and Birmingham joined in celebrating Hallelujah Week: dancing in the streets, bonfires day and night, every church and every bar roaring wide open.

Russia's delegate to the United Nations, who had been larding his speeches with mock-sympathetic references to the Western nations' difficulties, arose on the 9th and delivered a furious three-hour tirade accusing the entire non-Communist world of cowardly cryptofascistic biological warfare against the Soviet Union and the People's Republics of Europe and Asia.

The new staffs of the Federal penitentiaries in America, in office less than a week, followed their predecessors in mass resignations. The last official act of the wardens of Leavenworth, Terre Haute and Alcatraz was to report the "escape" of their entire prison populations.

Police officers in every major city were being frantically urged to remain on duty.

Queen Elizabeth, in a memorable speech, exhorted all citizens of the Empire. to remain calm and meet whatever might come with dignity, fortitude and honor.

The Scots stole the Stone of Scone again.

Rioting and looting began in Paris, Marseilles, Barcelona, Milan, Amsterdam, Munich, Berlin.

The Pope was silent.

Turkey declared war on Syria and Iraq; peace was concluded a record three hours later.

On the 10th, Warsaw Radio announced the formation of a new Polish Provisional Government whose first and second acts had been, respectively, to abrogate all existing treaties with the Soviet Union and border states, and to petition the UN for restoration of the 1938 boundaries.

On the 11th East Germany, Austria, Czechoslovakia, Hungary, Rumania, Bulgaria, Latvia and Lithuania followed suit, with variations on the boundary question.

On the 12th, after a brief but by no means bloodless putsch, the Spanish Republic was re-established; the British government fell once and the French government twice; and the Vatican issued a sharp protest against the ill-treatment of priests and nuns by Spanish insurgents.

Not a shot had been fired in Indo-China since the morning of the 8th.

On the 13th the Karelo-Finnish S. S. R., the Estonian S. S. R., the Byelorussian S. S. R., the Ukrainian S. S. R., the Azerbaijan S. S. R., the Turkmen S. S. R. and the Uzbek S. S. R. declared their independence of the Soviet Union. A horde of men and women escaped or released from forced-labor camps, the so-called Slave Army, poured westward out of Siberia.

VI

On the 14th, Zebulon, Georgia (pop. 312), Murfreesboro, Tennessee (pop. 11,190) and Orange, Texas (pop. 8,470) seceded from the Union.

That might have been funny, but on the 15th petitions for a secession referendum were circulating in Tennessee, Arkansas, Louisiana and South Carolina. Early returns averaged 61% in favor.

On the 16th Texas, Oklahoma, Mississippi, Alabama, Kentucky, Virginia, Georgia and—incongruously—Rhode Island and Minnesota added themselves to the list. Separatist fever was rising in Quebec, New Brunswick, Newfoundland and Labrador. Across the Atlantic, Catalonia, Bavaria, Moldavia, Sicily and Cyprus declared themselves independent states.

And that might have been hysteria. But that wasn't all.

Liquor stores and bars were sprouting like mushrooms in dry states. Ditto gambling halls, horse rooms, houses of prostitution, cockpits, burlesque theaters.

Moonshine whisky threatened for a few days to become the South's major industry, until standard-brand distillers cut their prices to meet the competition. Not a bottle of the new stocks of liquor carried a Federal tax stamp.

Mexican citizens were walking across the border into Arizona and New Mexico, swimming into Texas. The first shipload of Chinese arrived in San Francisco on the 16th.

Meat prices had increased by an average of 60% for every day since the new control and rationing law took effect. By the 16th, round steak was selling for $10.80 a pound.

Resignations of public officials were no longer news; a headline in the Portland *Oregonian* for August 15th read:

WILL STAY AT DESK, SAYS GOVERNOR.

It hit me hard.

But when I thought about it, it was obvious enough; it was such an elementary thing that ordinarily you never noticed it—that all governments, not just tyrannies, but *all* governments were based on violence, as currency was based on metal. You might go for months or years without seeing a silver dollar or a policeman; but the dollar and the policeman had to be there.

The whole elaborate structure, the work of a thousand years, was coming down. The value of a dollar is established by a promise to pay; the effectiveness of a law, by a threat to punish.

Even if there were enough jailers left, how could you put a man in jail if he had ten or twenty friends who didn't want him to go?

How many people were going to pay their income taxes next year, even if there was a government left to pay them to?

And who was going to stop the landless people from spilling over into the nations that had land to spare?

Aza-Kra said, "These things are not necessary to do."

I turned around and looked at him. He had been lying motionless for more than an hour in the hammock I had rigged for him at the end of the room; I had thought he was asleep.

It was raining outside. Dim, colorless light came through the slotted window blinds and striped his body like a melted barber pole. Caught in one of the bars of light, the tips of two quivering neck-spines glowed in faint filigree against the shadow.

"All right," I said. "Explain this one away. I'd like to hear you. Tell me why we don't need governments any more."

"The governments you have now—the governments of nations—they are not made for use. They exist to fight other nations."

"That's not true."

"It is true. Think. Of the money your government spends, in a year, how much is for war and how much for use?"

"About sixty per cent for war. But that doesn't—"

"Please. This is sixty per cent now, when you have only a small war. When you have a large war, how much then?"

"Ninety per cent. Maybe more, but that hasn't got anything to do with it. In peace *or* wartime there are things a national government does that can't be done by anybody else. Now ask me for instance, what."

"Yes. I ask this."

"For instance, keeping an industrial country from being dragged down to coolie level by unrestricted immigration."

"You think it is better for those who have much to keep apart from those who have little and give no help?"

"In principle, no, but it isn't just that easy. What good does it do the starving Asiatics if we turn America into another piece of Asia and starve along with them?"

He looked at me unwinkingly.

"What good has it done to keep apart?"

I opened my mouth, and shut it again. Last time it had been Japan, an island chain a little smaller than California. In the next one, half the world would have been against us.

"The problem is not easy, it is very difficult. But to solve it by helping is possible. To solve it by doing nothing is not possible."

"Harbors," I said. "Shipping. Soil conservation. Communications. Flood control."

"You do not believe these things can be done if there are no nations?"

"No. We haven't got time enough to pick up all the pieces. It's a hell of a lot easier to knock things apart than to put them together again."

"Your people have done things more difficult than this. You do not believe now, but you will see it done."

After a moment I said, "We're supposed to become a member of your galactic union now. Now that you've pulled our teeth. Who's going to build the ships?"

"Those who build them now."

I said, "Governments build them now."

"No. Men build ships. Men invent ships and design ships. Government builds nothing but more government."

I put my fists in my pockets and walked over to the window. Outside, a man went hurrying by in the rain, one hand at his hat-brim, the other at his chest. He didn't look around as he passed; his coffee-brown face was intent and impersonal. I watched him until he turned the corner, out of sight.

He had never heard of me, but his life would be changed by what I had done. His descendants would know my name; they would be bored by it in school, or their mothers would frighten them with it after dark. . . .

Aza-Kra said, "To talk of these things is useless. If I would lie, I would not tell you that I lie. And if I would lie about these things, I would lie well; you would not find the truth by questions. You must wait. Soon you will know."

I looked at him. "When your friends come."

"Yes," he said.

And the feathery tips of his neck-spines delicately trembled.

They came on the last day of August—fifty great rotiform ships drifting down out of space. No radar spotted them; no planes or interceptor rockets went up to meet them. They followed the terminator around, landing at dawn: thirteen in the Americas, twenty-five in Europe and Asia, five in Africa, one each in England, Scandinavia, Australia, New Zealand, New Guinea, the Phillipines, Japan.

Each one was six hundred feet across, but they rested lightly on the ground. Where they landed on sloping ground, slender curved supporting members came out of the doughnut-shaped rim, as dainty as insect's legs, and the fat lozenge of the hub lowered itself on the five fat spokes until it touched the earth.

Their doors opened.

In twenty-four days I had watched the nations of the Earth melt into shapelessness like sculptures molded of silicone putty. Armies, navies, air forces, police forces lost their cohesion first. In the beginning there were individual desertions, atoms escaping one at a time from the mass; later, when the pay failed to arrive, when there were no orders or else orders that could not be executed, men and women simply went home, orderly, without haste, in thousands.

Every useful item of equipment that could be carried or driven or flown went with them. Tractors, trucks, jeeps, bulldozers gladdened the hearts of farmers from Keokuk to Kweiyang. Bombers, small boats, even destroyers and battleships were in service as commercial transports. Quartermasters' stores were carried away piecemeal or in ton lots. Guns and ammunition rusted undisturbed.

Stock markets crashed. Banks failed. Treasuries failed. National governments broke down into states, provinces, cantons. In the United States, the President resigned his office on the 18th and left the White House, whose every window had been broken and whose lawn was newly landscaped with eggshells and orange rind. The Vice-President resigned the next day, leaving the Presidency, in theory, to the Speaker of the House; but the Speaker was at home in his Arkansas farm; Congress had adjourned on the 17th.

Everywhere it was the same. The new governments of Asia and Eastern Europe, of Spain and Portugal and Argentina and Iran, died stillborn.

The Moon colonies had been evacuated; work had stopped on the Mars rocket. The men on duty in the orbital stations, after an anxious week, had reached an agreement for mutual disarmament and had come down to Earth.

Seven industries out of ten had closed down. The dollar was worth half a penny, the pound sterling a little more; the ruble, the Reichsmark, the franc, the sen, the yen, the rupee were waste paper.

The great cities were nine-tenths deserted, gutted by fires, the homes of looters, rats and roaches.

Even the local governments, the states, the cantons, the counties, the very townships, were too fragile to stand. All the arbitrary lines on the map had lost their meaning.

You could not say any more, "Japan will—" or "India is moving toward—" It was startling to realize that; to have to think of a sprawling, amorphous, unfathomable mass of infinitely varied human beings instead of a single inclusive symbol. It made you wonder if the symbol had ever had any connection with reality at all: whether there had ever been such a thing as a nation.

Toward the end of the month, I thought I saw a flicker of hope. The problem of famine was being attacked vigorously and efficiently by the Red Cross, the Salvation Army, and thousands of local volunteer groups: they commandeered fleets of trucks, emptied warehouses with a calm disregard of legality, and distributed the food where it was most needed. It was not enough—too much food had been destroyed and wasted by looters, too much had spoiled through neglect, and too much had been destroyed in the field by wandering, half-starved bands of the homeless—but it was a beginning; it was something.

Other groups were fighting the problem of these wolf-packs, with equally encouraging results. Farmers were forming themselves into mutual-defense groups, "communities of force." Two men could take any property from one man of equal strength without violence, without the penalty of pain; but not from two men, or three men.

One district warned the next when a wolf-pack was on the way, and how many to expect. When the pack converged on a field or a storehouse, men in equal or greater numbers were there to stand in the way. If the district could absorb, say, ten workers, that many of the pack were offered the option of staying; the rest had to move on. Gradually, the packs thinned.

In the same way, factories were able to protect themselves from theft. By an extension of the idea, even the money problem began to seem soluble. The old currency was all but worthless, and an individual's promise to pay in kind was no better as a medium of exchange; but promissory notes obligating those communities could and did begin to circulate. They made an unwieldy currency, their range was limited, and they depreciated rapidly. But it was something; it was a beginning.

Then the wheel-ships came.

In every case but one, they were cautious. They landed in conspicuous positions, near a city or a village, and in the dawn light, before any man had come near them, oddly-shaped things came out and hurriedly unloaded boxes and bales, hundreds, thousands, a staggering array. They set up sun-reflecting beacons; then the ships rose again and disappeared, and when the first men came hesitantly out to investigate, they found nothing but the beacon, the acre of carefully-stacked boxes, and the signs, in the language of the country, that said:

THIS FOOD IS SENT BY THE PEOPLES OF OTHER WORLDS TO HELP YOU IN YOUR NEED. ALL MEN ARE BROTHERS.

And a brave man would lift the top of a box; inside he would see other boxes, and in them oblong pale shapes wrapped in something transparent that was not cellophane. He would unwrap one, feel it, smell it, show it around, and finally taste it; and then his eyebrows would go up.

The color and the texture were unfamiliar, but the taste was unmistakable! Tortillas and beans! (Or taro; or rice with beansprouts; or stuffed grape leaves; or herb omelette!)

The exception was the ship that landed outside Capetown, in an open field at the foot of Table Mountain.

Aza-Kra woke me at dawn. "They are here."

I mumbled at him and tried to turn over. He shook my shoulder again, buzzing excitedly to himself. "Please, they are here. We must hurry."

I lurched out of bed and stood swaying. "Your friends?" I said.

"Yes, yes." He was struggling into the black dress, pushing the peaked hat backward onto his head. "*Hurry.*"

I splashed cold water on my face, and got into my clothes. I pulled out the top dresser drawer and looked at the two loaded automatics. I couldn't decide. I couldn't figure out any way they would do me any good, but I didn't want to leave them behind. I stood there until my legs went numb before I could make up my mind to take them anyhow, and the hell with it.

There were no taxis, of course. We walked three blocks along the deserted streets until we saw a battered sedan nose into view in the intersection ahead, moving cautiously around the heaps of litter.

"Hold your breath!"

The car moved on out of sight. We found it around the corner, up on the sidewalk with the front fender jammed against a railing. There were two men and a woman in it, Europeans.

"Which way?"

"Left. To the mountains."

When we got to the outskirts and the buildings began to thin out, I saw it up ahead, a huge silvery-metal shelf jutting out impossibly from the slope. I began to tremble. *They'll cut me up and put me in a jar*, I thought. *Now is the time to stop, if I'm going to.*

But I kept going. Where the road veered away from the field and went curving on up the mountain the other way, I stopped and we got out. I saw dark shapes and movements under that huge gleaming bulk. We stepped over a broken fence and started across the dry, uneven clods in the half-light.

Light sprang out: a soft, pearl-gray shimmer that didn't dazzle the eye although it was aimed straight toward us, marking the way. I heard a shrill worldless buzzing, and above that an explosion of chirping, and under them both a confusion of other sounds, humming, droning, clattering. I saw a half-dozen nightmare shapes bounding forward.

Two of them were like Aza-Kra; two more were squat things with huge humped shells on top, like tortoise-shells the size of a card table, with six long stump-ended legs underneath, and a tangle of eyes, tentacles, and small wriggly things peeping out in front; one, the tallest, had a long sharp-spined column of a body rising from a thick base and four startlingly human legs, and surmounted by four long whiplike tentacles and a smooth oval head; the sixth looked at first glance like an unholy cross between a grasshopper and a newt. He came in twenty-foot bounds.

They crowded around Aza-Kra, humming, chirping, droning, buzzing, clattering. Their hands and tentacles went over him, caressingly; the Newt-grasshopper thing hoisted him onto its back.

They paid no attention to me, and I stayed where I was, with my hands tight and sweating on the grips of my guns. Then I heard Aza-Kra speak, and the tallest one turned back to me.

It reeked: something like brine, something like wet fur, something rank and indescribable. It had two narrow red eyes in that smooth knob of a head. It put one of its tentacles on my shoulder, and I didn't see a mouth open anywhere, but a droning voice said, "Thank you for caring for him. Come now. We go to ship."

I pulled away instinctively, quivering, and my hands came out of my pockets. I heard a flat- echoing *crack* and a yell, and I saw a red wetness spring out across the smooth skull; I saw the thing topple and lie in the dirt, twitching.

I thought for an instant that I had done it, the shot, the yell and all. Then I heard another yell, behind me: I whirled around and heard a car grind into gear and saw it bouncing away down the road into town, lights off, a black moving shape on the dimness. I saw it veer wildly and slew into the fence at the first turn; I heard its tired popping as it went through and the muffled crash as it turned over.

Dead, I thought. But the next time I looked I saw two figures come erect beyond the overturned car and stagger toward the road. They disappeared around the turn, running.

I looked back at the others, bewildered. They weren't even looking that way; they were gathered around the body, lifting it, carrying it toward the ship.

The feeling—the black depression that had been getting stronger every day for three weeks—tightened down on me as if somebody had turned a screw. I gritted my teeth against it, and stood there wishing I were dead.

They were almost to that open hatch in the oval hub that hung under the rim when Aza-Kra detached himself from the group and walked slowly back to me. After a moment one of the others—a hump-shelled one—trundled along after him and waited a yard or two away.

"It is not your fault," said Aza-Kra. "We could have prevented it, but we were careless. We were so glad to meet that we did not take precautions. It is not your fault. Come to the ship."

The hump-shelled thing came up and squeaked something, and Aza-Kra sat on its back. The tentacles waved at me. It wheeled and started toward the hatchway. "Come," said Aza-Kra.

I followed them, too miserable to care what happened. We went down a corridor full of the sourceless pearl-gray light until a doorway suddenly appeared, somehow, and we went through that into a room where two tripeds were waiting.

Aza-Kra climbed onto a stool, and one of the tripeds began pressing two small instruments against various parts of his body; the other squirted something from a flexible canister into his mouth.

And as I stood there watching, between one breath and the next, the depression went away.

I felt like a man whose toothache has just stopped; I probed at my mind, gingerly, expecting to find that the feeling was still there, only hiding. But it wasn't. It was gone so completely that I couldn't even remember exactly what it had been like. I felt calm and relaxed—and safe.

I looked at Aza-Kra. He was breathing easily; his eyes looked clearer than they had a moment before, and it seemed to me that his skin was glossier. The feathery neck-spines hung in relaxed, graceful curves.

. . . It was all true, then. It had to be. If they had been conquerors, the automatic death of the man who had killed one of their number, just now, wouldn't have been enough. An occupying army can never be satisfied with an eye for an eye. There must be retaliation.

But they hadn't done anything; they hadn't even used the gas. They'd seen that the others in the car were running away, that the danger was over, and that ended it. The only emotions they had shown, as far as I could tell, were concern and regret—

Except that, I remembered now, I had seen two of the tripeds clearly when I turned back to look at them gathering around the body: Aza-Kra and another one. And their neck-spines had been stiff. . . .

Suddenly I knew the answer.

Aza-Kra came from a world where violence and cruelty didn't exist. To him, the Earth was a jungle—and I was one of its carnivores.

I knew, now, why I had felt the way I had for the last three weeks, and why the feeling had stopped a few minutes ago. My hostility toward him had been partly responsible for his fear, and so I had picked up an echo of it. Undirected fear is, by definition, anxiety, depression, uneasiness—the psychologists' *Angst*. It had stopped because Aza-Kra no longer had to depend on me; he was with his own people again; he was safe.

I knew the reason for my nightmares.

I knew why, time and again when I had expected Aza-Kra to be reading my mind, I had found that he wasn't. He did it only when he had to; it was too painful.

And one thing more:

I knew that when the true history of this time came to be written, I needn't worry about my place in it. My name would be there, all right, but nobody would remember it once he had shut the book.

Nobody would use my name as an insulting epithet, and nobody would carve it on the bases of any statues, either.

I wasn't the hero of the story.

It was Aza-Kra who had come down alone to a planet so deadly that no one else would risk his life on it until he had softened it up. It was Aza-Kra who had lived for nearly a month with a suspicious, irrational, combative, uncivilized flesh-eater. It was Aza-Kra who had used me, every step of the way—used my provincial loyalties and my self-interest and my prejudices.

He had done all that, weary, tortured, half-starved . . . and he'd been scared to death the whole time.

We made two stops up the coast and then moved into Algeria and the Sudan: landing, unloading, taking off again, following the dawn line. The other ships, Aza-Kra explained, would keep on circling the planet until enough food had been distributed to prevent any starvation until the next harvest. This one was going only as far as the middle of the North American continent—to drop me off. Then it was going to take Aza-Kra home.

I watched what happened after we left each place in a vision device they had. In some places there was more hesitation than in others, but in the end they always took the food: in jeep-loads, by pack train, in baskets balanced on their heads.

Some of the repeaters worried me. I said, "How do you know it'll get distributed to everybody who need it?"

I might have known the answer: "They will distribute it. No man can let his neighbor starve while he has plenty."

The famine relief was all they had come for, this time. Later, when we had got through the crisis, they would come back; and by that time, remembering the food, people would be more inclined to take them on their merits instead of shuddering because they had too many eyes or fingers. They would help us when we needed it, they would show us the way up the ladder, but we would have to do the work ourselves.

He asked me not to publish the story of Chillicothe and the month we had spent together. "Later, when it will hurt no one, you can explain. Now there is no need to make anyone ashamed; not even the officials of your government. It was not their fault; they did not make the planet as it was."

So there went even that two-bit chance at immortality.

It was still dawn when we landed on the bluff across the river from my home; sky and land and water were all the same depthless cool gray, except for the hairline of scarlet in the east. Dew was heavy on the grass, and the air had a smell that made me think of wood smoke and dry leaves.

He came out of the ship with me to say good-by.

"Will you be back?" I asked him.

He buzzed wordlessly in a way I had begun to recognize; I think it was his version of a laugh. "I think not for a very long time. I have already neglected my work too much."

"This isn't your work—opening up new planets?"

"No. It is not so common a thing, that a race becomes ready for space travel. It has not happened anywhere in the galaxy for twenty thousand of your years. I believe, and I hope, that it will not happen again for twenty thousand more. No, I am ordinarily a maker of—you have not the word, it is like porcelain, but a different material. Perhaps some day you will see a piece that I have made. It is stamped with my name."

He held out his hand and I took it. It was an awkward grip; his hand felt unpleasantly dry and smooth to me, and I suppose mine was clammy to him. We both let go as soon as we decently could.

Without turning, he walked away from me up the ramp. I said, "Aza-Kra!"

"Yes?"

"Just one more question. The galaxy's a big place. What happens if you miss just one bloodthirsty race that's ready to boil out across the stars—or if nobody has the guts to go and do to them what you did to us?"

"Now you begin to understand," he said. "That is the question the people of Mars asked us about you . . . twenty thousand years ago."

The story ends there, properly, but there's one more thing I want to say.

When Aza-Kra's ship lifted and disappeared, and I walked down to the bottom of the bluff and across the bridge into the city, I knew I was going back to a life that would be a lot different from the one I had known.

For one thing, the *Herald-Star* was all but done for when I came home: wrecked presses, half the staff gone, supplies running out. I worked hard for a little over a year trying to revive it, out of sentiment, but I knew there were more important things to be done than publishing a newspaper.

Like everybody else, I got used to the changes in the world and in the people around me: to the peaceful, unworried feel of places that had been electric with tension; to the kids—the wonderful, incredible kids; to the new kind of excitement, the excitement that isn't like the night before execution, but like the night before Christmas.

But I hadn't realized how much I had changed, myself, until something that happened a week ago.

I'd lost touch with Eli Freeman after the paper folded; I knew he had gone into pest control, but I didn't know where he was or what he was doing until he turned up one day on the wheat-and-dairy farm I help run, south of the Platte in what used to be Nebraska. He's the advance man for a fleet of spray planes working out of Omaha, aborting rabbits.

He stayed on for three days, lining up a few of the stiff-necked farmers in this area that don't believe in hormones or airplanes either; in his free time he helped with the harvest, and I saw a lot of him.

On his last night we talked late, working up from the old times to the new times and back again until there was nothing more to say. Finally, when we had both been quiet for a long time, he said something to me that is the only accolade I am likely to get, and oddly enough, the only one I want.

"You know, Bob, if it wasn't for that unique face of yours, it would be hard to believe you're the same guy I used to work for."

I said, "Hell, was I that bad?"

"Don't get shirty. You were okay. You didn't bleed the help or kick old ladies, but there just wasn't as much *to* you as there is now. I don't know," he said. "You're—more human."

More human.

Yes. We all are.

*Bill Nabors has every right to see all things military
through a dense filter of irony. When his draft notice arrived,
during the Vietnam war, Bill was flat on his back in a
hospital. He dutifully snuck out of the hospital and made it
to the induction center for his physical. The doctors said
"Egad, son, you've got a bleeding ulcer—you ought to be in
hospital!", and the military hasn't bothered him since.*

*He hasn't stopped bothering the military, though.
Witness this short chronicle of Field Marshal Sea Boy D.
Brown's fall to grace.*

THE STATE OF ULTIMATE PEACE

by William Nabors

I.

succubus

At the very best moment of his conference with Lord Byron, E.
E. Cummings and T. S. Eliot, an explosion of raucous laughter awoke
Field Marshal Sea Boy D. Brown. Angry, confused and quite disap-
pointed, he sat up in bed and screamed for his orderly, *goodpal*, the
way he had learned from old movies and volumes of apocryphal war
memoirs. Then, aware that the walls were soundproof; his orderly out
for re-programming and his need indeterminate, the field marshal
quieted down. What he really wanted, he decided, was to think. The
possibility that he had war psychosis must be considered. After all, it
flashed hundreds of times every day—PEACE, BROTHERHOOD,
PUT AN END TO WAR—all that goddamn nonsense, and always the
letters were bigger, brighter and overlay a more ominous scene. Once,
he'd been moved to tears and just the past few days, he was almost
certain he had heard his name stage whispered in the backgrounds.
Was he losing his grip? Not likely—but? "It couldn't be," he mumbled.
He was a patriot. He still ordered the bombardments. Shit—gracious
glory, sometimes he even accelerated them! He couldn't have it; not
war psychosis, peace madness, as the secret reports called it. It was
unthinkable! He wasn't some snotty-nosed little conscript. He was a
field marshal; such things did not happen to field marshals. A man of
his rank, Chief of the General Staff, couldn't possibly contract such a

disease; especially that particular strain. Why, there hadn't been any V. D. in the officer corp since the formation of Econoland, when the world's richest nations merged under the Governing Directors to hold back the fanatic millions of Third World's strike force. The old condom shop was as much a military tradition as the salute. If his fears proved correct, he could be the only officer to contract anything like this since. . .

Field Marshal Brown halted the terrible train of thought. This craving for poetry would stop. It was probably nothing more than the late blossoming of his mother's sensitivity. He couldn't actually have caught peace madness. He'd simply read the secret reports about the cases in London, Washington and Moscow, and like some ignorant hypochondriac, assumed that he'd caught it. "You, Brown, are a fool," he said and gazed at the tattered copy of *Guernica* he'd purchased on the negative culture market. Chances were, his behavior could be attributed to an inordinate fear of approaching old age! There's been only the one incident with that crass young sculptress, Gloria Tenable. Other than that he hadn't touched a female in ten years. He was certain of his health! The only thing wrong with him was a little nostalgia for less complicated times.

"Stop worrying," he ordered himself, "and get rid of that goddamn Picasso and the books. Do you want to wind up in one of those convalescent centers for the senile and treacherous?"

But he could not stop worrying. Each day the field marshal seemed to spend more time pursuing poetry, music and other joys and much less time at his destructive duties. He devoted long brooding hours to contemplation of Dylan Thomas's poems, "The Hand That Signed A Paper Felled A City" and "Among Those Killed In The Dawn Raid Was A Man Aged One Hundred." The planning of attacks became almost unbearable. Military History, the chief passion of his life, bored and depressed him. For the first time, rank seemed a burden; glory, folly. It was as if a stranger had entered his body. He could not explain his behavior. Just yesterday, he'd ordered the Military Police to overlook the soldier's use of *Consolation* and *Fly,* volatile pschedelics, which severely curbed agressive tendencies. Recent pictures from the front upset him so much, that he sent hordes of prostitutes and entertainers to soothe the troops. When the Chairman Director consulted him about new war plans, the field marshal became evasive. He talked of fanciful new weapons systems. He promised his chairman bigger bombardments and world domination for Econoland's forces. In his heart, however, even as he raved on about Econoland's military might, there lurked the seeds of a mysterious and inhuman pacifism. He could no longer tolerate the thought of ordering operatives, even smart-assed conscripts and cultural laggards, to their demise.

Abruptly, the field marshal threw back the covering and crawled out of bed. He opened a virgin bottle of mescal and poured it in the fetal chair's umbilical supplier. "Innocence," he mused, "should aid the search for truth." He eased into the chair's suspension seat, adjusted the temperature and cast aside his sleeping garments. He put on the breather helmet and fastened the umbilical cord to his abdominal connection. He waited for the plastic bubble to cover the chair; then secured his body and signaled for suspension. The room went black. His limbs eased into position as the chair elevated him. The apprehension he sometimes felt when using the device passed as the warm fluid filled the bubble. He smiled; his breather helmet immersed and he eagerly awaited the first shot of mescal. "Nothing like liquor through the cord," he said and closed his eyes as the mescal burned his throat. It never ceased to amaze him, that whatever you put in the umbilical supplier profoundly affected the senses of taste and smell, even though it wasn't ingested through the mouth. There was no better way to dine, especially for lonely old bachelors. A great step forward, the fetal chair. Why, he hadn't had to see a physician or a psycho-priest in all the years since he was awarded his first unsophisticated model. It gave him an unrivaled sense of security. Too bad the directors didn't see fit to mass produce them for the goddamn conscripts and civilians. If the people could relax in their fetal chairs now and again, there might not be such an epidemic of social unrest. It was barely safe to go out. Look what had happened to him—trapped nearly three days in that cellar with Gloria Tenable—he'd never be able to explain it. It looked like the last bombardment had arrived. And they dared to call that a peace demonstration. That wicked little strumpet! He'd been caught off his guard. To resist all that time and then be abused in your sleep; it was unjust. He'd awakened to find her taking full advantage of his morning erection, humping like the devil and brandishing a big chisel to insure his continued cooperation. He hadn't even seen the reports then. A condom might have been useless anyhow, at least against that particular strain. Look what had happened to that Moscow propaganda expert. He was fortified with a permanent condom and still had picked it up from a member of the Bolshoi Ballet Company. Now the best ad man in Econoland was sitting in a convalescent center in Siberia, dabbing paint and writing a book already titled, *Conversations With Michelangelo*.

When at last he pushed the birth button, a panic gripped Field Marshal Brown as he felt himself being ejected. The room seemed momentarily vacant; full of petty terrors he had never before noticed. The flashing commenced—STOP THE WAR—DON'T KILL HUNGRY PEOPLES. An enormous mosaic of a crowd of emaciated Asians stood in the background. Somehow, he knew they were to be neutralized—gassed. He heard the dead poet, Jed Kristian, speak softly, "Brown, Brown—*children of these anonymous slain shall bring to justice. . ."*

"Damn you; damn you," screamed the field marshal. "What do I have to do with this? It's nothing to do with me! I never did anything to these people . . . I."

Field Marshal Brown vomited his mescal. He sat naked on the cold floor and wept. Vaguely, he regretted his part in the slaughter. He had not wanted to be blamed for the carnage. He had not forseen such an event. His career was ruined. Thoughts of violence made his stomach retch; he had it all right—peace madness. Of that he was certain.

II.

"I think that we are in rats' alley
Where the dead men lost their bones."[1]

There was something wrong about the way *goodpal,* his "magic nigger," put him back to bed and it disturbed the field marshal. It wasn't just that his dark little orderly had found him sitting there naked, half asleep; mumbling the lines from Sandburg's "Buttons." It was the indifferent way *goodpal* had handled him, tossing him on the bed like a bundle of soiled garments and then just leaving him there alone in the darkened room, without inquiring what the field marshal's preference might be. It seemed as if the natural distance between robot and man had suddenly expanded. Brown realized he could no longer consider *goodpal* a harmless and neutral machine. It must be deemed a threat; perhaps even a keeper. Certainly the "magic nigger" was now more an observer than an orderly. A metamorphosis had occurred. For the first time, the field marshal understood the true relationship of servant and master. An orderly knew everything about you; much more than a wife, mother, father, sibling, cat, psycho-priest, mistress—and in terms of objectivity—an orderly knew you much better than you could ever know yourself. It knew what troubled you, even if it did not know the origin of your difficulty and was not programed to term it peace madness. Brown realized that a robot like *goodpal* might prove extremely dangerous to someone who had fallen under official scrutiny and he was almost certain that he had made himself suspect. If he were brought before the Directors—a lower bureaucracy wouldn't dare proceed against a field marshal—this little electronic "darky" could do him boundless injury. His *goodpal* could make the difference between a life sentence to a convalescent center for peace maniacs and an indefinite term on the limbo-mechanism for the most serious offense in Econoland—peace mongering. *Goodpal* could make the field marshal's toilet habits the brunt of common jokes. The little robot could list its master's most innocent liaisons like taxes with numerous computers, boards, investigators and other petty bureaucrats. Every "magic nigger" in Econoland would receive data on him. *Goodpal* knew the stains; dirt, general frailties, whims, fears, lust, and unconscious habits of the honorable field marshal. The little robot was a nemesis such as he had not seen on the field of conflict. His *goodpal* was no longer his humble orderly, but his policeman; his jailer. Brown trembled. It seemed obvious. He was trapped! He could not do it violence. He could not smash it or follow the example of his ancestors and lynch it. Even the thought of assaulting it made him nauseous. He wrote a poetic note to compensate and put it where the robot would be sure to scan it—*on goodpal i rely, my robot friend; my true ally*—he went on for pages, each word a tribute, endearing him more to the machine that would, he feared, add so bountifully to his misery. He looked over the note—"By holy shit, reminds me of 'Gunga Din,'" if I do say so myself."

No, the field marshal could not hate his *goodpal*! He could not even dislike it. When he got even a little angry at it, he became ill and had to lie down until his aggression passed. Regardless of how he approached the matter, he could not justify eliminating the robot. Neither could he convert it to pacifism. A *goodpal* made the worst kind of enemy—an enemy without volition. You could not reason with it; its performance was pre-ordained. There was nothing to do, Brown determined, but try to escape. After all, a poet of his stature was practically obligated to spread his joy among the masses. Besides, he wanted to see his Gloria, sweet little chiseler, and thank her for what she'd done.

The field marshal was perched on the antique commode pondering his dilemma, when Sandburg appeared. The old poet carried a battered guitar, a walking staff and a rucksack. He was accompanied by seven goats, two dogs and a large mist-grey cat. He was clothed in heavy work garments, suited to the early decades of the twentieth century. His skin was dark and weatherbeaten from working and wandering the forgotten landscapes of his country. He appeared as gaunt as historic pictures of the man, Lincoln, about whom he'd written the scandalous and forbidden volumes of biography. His message for the field marshal was not subtle. It was plain like his clothes and his lost land. The poet spoke: *"In the old wars drum of hoofs and the beat of shod feet./ In the new wars hum of motors and the tread of rubber tires./ In the wars to come silent wheels and the whir of rods not yet dreamed out in the heads of man."*[2]

The field marshal arose; pulled up his pants, nodded and offered his hand. "I've always admir. . ."

The old poet smiled and faded away with his goats and dogs. Only the cat remained. A silver trinket dangled from its collar. The field marshal knelt and removed it. It was shaped like soldier's tags he'd seen in museums. A small key was taped to one side of the tag and on the reverse side was stamped: *"Yes, tell your sins/ And know how careless a pearl fog is/Of the laws you have broken."*[3]

Brown patted the cat. He thought he understood the lines from "Pearl Fog." He slipped the tape loose from the tag and held the key up to the light—*"goodpal*—md OX991." The field marshal smiled. He didn't quite know what to pack. His *goodpal* usually took care of that sort of thing.

Sandburg's visit had put Brown in a very good frame of mind. In honor of his new tranquillity, he named his cat "Happy"; called for the *goodpal*, slipped the key in the proper slot and erased the accumulated data. The machine stopped—dead silent. The cat purred. Brown picked it up and headed for the negative culture market. He would try EMILIANO'S first. Just from scuttlebutt, it seemed the sort of place where Gloria would eventually appear and a not at all bad place to satiate his sudden passion for the works of Thoreau. In addition, he knew he would be quite safe there, since no police were allowed in the market, a street prison, differing from the normal convalescent center in that the state did not sentence you there, or prevent you from haphazardly wandering in. Once you were interred, it was a different matter, a special dispensation was required in order to be released. Otherwise, the *goodpals* on duty at the gates would not let you out. The institution seemed to work well and it was self-supporting. Disgruntled conscripts; artists, general misfits, criminals and cultural laggards flocked willingly to the market, while normal operatives were aware that it was a prison and a place to be avoided. On the other hand, operatives who wished to purchase the forbidden commodities which supported the prison were channeled to a large warehouse on the market's edge, where drug dealers, pimps, book salesmen, and artists carried on the business of vice. The state attached no stigma to functioning operatives who made purchases at the warehouse. It expected them to do so, though it was a serious offense to do it openly. Operatives were permitted to visit brothels, buy drugs, books, paintings; satisfy any deviate taste so long as they attempted, no matter how feebly, to hide their vice. In reality, of course, no vice could be concealed; all *goodpals* were programed to detect crime. Still, it was a necessary act of patriotism to attempt to hide deviations. Sincere secretiveness was the true measure of respect for authority. Should an operative lapse into open vice, he was guilty of treason and thus fodder for the limbo-mechanism.

III.

incubus

Field Marshal Brown entered EMILIANO'S. He looked in the small establishment and decided to sit by the window. When the waiter appeared, the field marshal ordered rum for himself and a saucer of milk for "Happy," who had already stretched out on the table for a nap. "Do you expect Miss Tenable today?"

"Gloria," the waiter said. "Oh sure, she comes in 'bout every day. Say ain't that there outfit. . ."

"It's a uniform," said Brown. "That will be all."

"O.K.," said the waiter. "I wasn't bein' nosey."

Brown peered out at the cobblestone street. Perhaps he would see Gloria as she neared EMILIANO'S. He hoped he would recognize her without too much difficulty. It had been so dark in that cellar and with her waving the chisel, he had been completely confused! He was certain he could pick her silhoutte out of a large crowd, but about the color of her hair, eyes and complexion; the intricacies of her features, he could only guess. When they dug him out of the rubble, the *goodpals* in charge had rushed him away in an emergency vehicle to keep him safe from the raving horde of pacifists. He hadn't even been able to tell her goodbye; though, truthfully, at the time he probably would have had her sentenced to the limbo-mechanism.

"Your order, sir," said the waiter "and the *Market Times*. You mentioned Gloria and I . . . well let the news speak for itself!"

A page of headlines blared out at the field marshal: GIRLS INFECT THIRD DIVISION, SCULPTRESS TENABLE ELECTED NEW LEADER WOMEN'S FUCK FOR PEACE—FIELD MARSHAL DESERTS, GOODPAL DISARMED—FRONT LINE TROOPS THROW DOWN WEAPONS—BROWN TO BE LIMBOED WHEN CAPTURED—ZACHARIAH THE PIMP RECEIVES ANOTHER FUCKER MEDAL OF HONOR—DIRECTORS REMAIN UNINFECTED, RESIST PEACE PLEAS, THREATEN TO MOBILIZE GOODPALS—THIRD WORLD OFFENSIVE EXPECTED SOON— PEACE VIRUS BAFFLES RESEARCHERS, NO KNOWN ANTIDOTE!

The field marshal was overcome—excited. He could not even read his Thoreau. He waited for Gloria. He wanted to get into this fight. A military man couldn't sit out a war, not so long as there was a place for him. He had just assumed when he came down with peace madness, that his career was over, but now he could get right back into the fight and fuck his heart out for peace! Why there was no end to the glory he might bring to humanity. He wasn't much of a poet—he realized that—but as a war hero, perhaps the new state would allow him a pension. He could start a little magazine—call it *Brown's Journal of Verse*. Why there was no limit to where he could go! He got an erection, just thinking about it. He might have to change uniforms but he was still in an army.

[1]T. S. Eliot, "The Waste Land" (from *The Waste Land And Other Poems:* Harcourt, Brace & World Inc., third edition, 1962) p. 33. Lines 15-16.
[2]Carl Sandburg. "Wars" (*Complete Poems:* Harcourt, Brace & Company, 1950) p. 42. Lines 1-4.
[3]Carl Sandburg, "Pearl Fog" (from *Complete Poems:* Harcourt, Brace & Company, 1950) p. 54. Lines 8-10.

Isaac Asimov is not the only science fiction writer to have produced more than a hundred books. But most of the others rose to the century mark on a mountain of throwaway adventure novels, pornographic quickies and other such hurried buckmakers. Dr. Asimov has done few of these (forgiving one almost-pseudonymous bit of harmless ribaldry) and anyone scanning a list of his titles can only be awe-struck by the breadth of this man's scholarship and by the sheer size of the projects he has successfully tackled.

In this essay, the Good Doctor offers us a cybernetic prescription for peace and plenty in the modern world.

BY THE NUMBERS
by Isaac Asimov

Hypocrisy is a universal phenomenon. It ends with death, but not before. When the hypocrisy is conscious, it is, of course, disgusting, but few of us are conscious hypocrites. It is so easy to argue ourselves into views that pander to our own self-interests and prejudices and *sincerely* find nobility in them.

I do it myself, I'm certain; but by the very nature of things, it is difficult for me to see self-examples clearly. Let me give you, instead, an example involving a good friend of mine.

He was talking about professors. He could have been one, he said, if he had followed the proper path after college graduation. Now, he said, he was glad he hadn't for he wouldn't want to be associated with so uniformly cowardly a profession. He wouldn't want to bear a title borne by those who so weakly and supinely gave in to the vicious demands of rascally students.

His eyes glinted feverishly at this point, and he lifted his arms so that they cradled an imaginary machine-gun. He said, from between gritted teeth, "What I would have given those bastards would have been a rat-tat-tat-tat." And he sprayed the entire room with imaginary bullets, killing (in imagination) every person in it.

I was rather taken aback. My friend was, under ordinary conditions, one of the most kindly and reasonable persons I know and I made excuses (hypocritically doing for a friend what I would not have done for an enemy). He had had a few drinks, and I knew that he had had a lonely, miserable and scapegoated youth. No doubt at the other end of that machine-gun were the shades of those young men who had hounded him for sport so many years ago.

So I made no comment and changed the subject, bringing up a political campaign then in progress. It quickly turned out, again to my discomfiture, that my friend, who usually saw eye to eye with me, had deserted our standard and was voting for the other fellow. I could not help expressing dismay and my friend at once began to explain at great length his reasons for deserting.

I shook my head, eager to cut him short. "It's no use," I said. "You won't convince me. I hate your man too much ever to vote for him."

Whereupon my friend threw himself back in his chair with a simper of self-conscious virtue* and said, "I'm afraid I'm not a very good hater."

And the vision of the imaginary machine-gun with which he had imaginarily killed hundreds of students not three minutes before rose in front of my eyes. I sighed and changed the subject again. What was the use of protesting? It was clear he honestly thought he was not a good hater.

Heaven only knows how many people are now occupied in denouncing our technological society and all the evils it has brought upon us. They do so with a self-conscious virtue that tends to mask the fact that they are all as eager a group of beneficiaries of that society as anyone else. They may denounce the other guy's electric razor, so to speak, but do so while strumming on an electric guitar.

There must be some idealists who "return to the soil" and remain there for longer than the month or two required to develop callouses. I may conceive of them using sticks and rocks as tools, scorning the fancy metal devices manufactured by modern blast furnaces and factories. And *even so*, they are free to do this only because they take advantage of the fact that our technological society can feed (however imperfectly) billions of human beings and still leave land for simple-lifers to grub in.

Our technological society was not forced on mankind. It grew out of the demand of human beings for plenty of food, for warmth in winter, coolness in summer, less work and more play. Unfortunately, people want all of this plus all the children they feel like having, and

---

1*If self-conscious virtue could be sold at a dollar a pound we'd all be rich. Me, too, for I am loaded down with as many tons of self-conscious virtue as anyone.

the result is that technology* in its command-performance has brought us to a situation of considerable danger.

Very well, we must pull through safely—but how? To me, the only possible answer is through the continued and wiser use of technology. I don't say that this will surely work. I *do* say, though, that nothing else will.

For one thing, it seems to me that we must continue, extend and intensify the computerization of society.

Is that thought offensive? Why?

Is it that computers are soul-less? Is it that they don't treat human beings as human beings, but merely as punch-cards (or as the electronic equivalent).

Well, then, let's get it straight. Computers don't treat anyone as anything. They are mathematical tools designed to store and manipulate data. It is the human beings who program and control computers who are responsible, and if they sometimes hide behind the computer to mask their own incapacity, that is really a human fault rather than a computer fault, isn't it?

Of course, one might argue that if the computer weren't there to hide behind, the human beings in charge would be flushed out and be forced to treat us all more decently.

Don't you believe it! The history of administrative ineptitude, of bureaucratic savagery, of all the injustices and tyranny of petty officialdom, long antedates the computer. And that's what you'd be dealing with if you abolished the computer.

Of course, if you dealt with a human being, you could reason and persuade which means that a person with intelligence and articulacy would have an advantage over others with just as good a case, who are unsophisticated, inarticulate and scared. Or you might be able to bend an official decision by slipping someone a few dollars, by doing a favor, or by calling upon an influential friend. In which case, those with money or importance have the advantage over those without.

---

*Mind you, I say "technology" and not "science." Science is a systematic method of studying and working out those generalizations that seem to describe the behavior of the universe. It could exist as a purely intellectual game that would never affect the practical life of human beings either for good or evil, and that was very nearly the case in ancient Greece, for instance. Technology is the application of scientific findings to the tools of everyday life, and that application can be wise or unwise, useful or harmful. Very often, those who govern technological decisions are not scientists and know little about science but are perfectly willing to pander to human greed for the immediate short-term benefit and the immediate dollar.

But that's wrong, isn't it. It is to soul-less impartiality that we all give lip-service. The laws, we proclaim, must be enforced without favor. The law, we maintain, is no respecter of persons. If we really believe that, then we should welcome computerization, which would apply the rules of society without the capacity for being blarneyed or bribed out of it. To be sure, cases may be different from person to person, but the more elaborately a computer is programmed, the more the difference in cases can be taken into account.

Or is it that we don't really want to be treated impartially? Very likely, and that's why I suspect hyporcisy has a lot to do with the outcry against computerization.

Do we lose our individuality in a computerized society? Do we become numbers instead of people?

Alas, we can't be people without having handles. We are all coded and *must* be. If you must deal with someone who resolutely refuses to give you a name you will refer to him by some description, such as "The guy with the red hair and bad breath." Eventually, you will reduce that to "Old bad-breath."

With time and generations that could become "Obreth" or something and may even come to be considered an aristocratic name.

In other words, we *are* coded. We can't be a "person" to more than the bare handful of people who deal with us every day. To everyone else, we are known only as a code. The problem, then, is not whether we are to be coded; the problem is whether we are to be coded *efficiently*.

It amounts to a difference between a number and a name. Most people seem to think that a number is much more villainous than a name. A name is somehow personal and endearing while a number is impersonal and wicked.

I recognize the feeling. I happen to love my own name, and I invariably make a big fuss if it is misspelled or mispronounced (both of which are easy to do). But I find excuses for myself. In the first place, my name is intensely personal. I am the only Isaac Asimov in the world, as far as I know; certainly the only one in the United States. Furthermore, if anyone knows my name without knowing me, it is entirely because of what I myself, personally, have done with my life.

And yet it has its drawbacks. My name is difficult to spell and difficult to pronounce, and I spend what seems several hours a year negotiating with telephone operators and attempting to persuade them, in vain, to pronounce my name just approximately correctly.

Ought I to have some simpler and more pronounceable name? But then I would be lost in a nominal ocean. There must be many people who prefer names to numbers and have names like Fred Smith, Bob Jones and Pat McCarthy. Each of these is shared by myriads, and of what real value is a sound combination endlessly duplicated? Imagine the history of mistakes such duplication has led to, from the billing of someone for an article he didn't buy to the execution of someone for a crime he didn't commit.

Numbers are names also but are *efficient* names. If they are properly distributed, there need be no duplications *ever*. Every single number-name can be unique through all of Earthly space and time. And they would all be equally amenable to spelling and pronunciation.

Naturally, we should distinguish between a man's official code-designation and his personal one. Even today, a man may have the name of Montmorency Quintus Blodgett, and no document involving him may be legal without every letter of that name carefully formed in his own handwriting yet his friends may call him Spike. To have an official number does not mean that you must be *called* by that number.

Just have that number on record. Have it unique. Have it convenient. And have it easily stored and manipulated by computer. You will be infinitely more a person because there is something that is uniquely and ineradicably you forever reachable, than by having a meaningless name dubiously known to a few dozen people.

The day of the number is upon us already, in fact, although in a very primitive fashion. It is here because we insist on it. We insist on overloading the post-office to a further extent each year, so we need zip-codes to expedite delivery. As true hypocrites, we complain bitterly about those zip-codes and would complain just as bitterly if we abandoned them and delayed our mail, as we would then necessarily have to do.

In the same way, the upward-spiralling number of long distance calls we all make and the reluctance of people to be telephone-operators rather than telephone-users (or to pay telephone bills that will enable the phone companies to lure operators to the switch-boards) makes area-codes necessary.

And as for social security numbers, try running the tax-system without them.

Of course, you are about to say, who needs the tax-system, and oh boy, do those words fall upon sympathetic ears. My tax-payments each year are higher by an order of magnitude than I ever dreamed (when I got my doctorate) I would ever make as total income and I pay none of it joyously.

Nevertheless those taxes are there, despite the objections of everyone of us, because of the absolute demand—of every one of us. We insist that the government maintain various expensive services, and that means enormous and complicated taxes. To demand the service and complain of the payment is hypocrisy if the contradiction is understood and idiocy if it is not.

The greatest and most expensive of our demands is that the government maintain an enormous military establishment of the most advanced and expensive type in order to protect us in our position as richest and most powerful nation against the envious hordes without.

What, you don't demand it? You don't either? I guess that is because you and I are anti-militaristic and believe in peace and love. The fact is, however, that the American people, by a large majority, would rather pay for arms than for anything else. If you doubt it, study the record of Congressional votes and remember that there are few Senators and Representatives who would dream of offending their constituents and risking the loss of their precious jobs.

Yes, you're for cutting government spending. And I'm for cutting government spending. The only catch is that you and I and all the rest of us are for cutting it only in those areas which don't hurt us either emotionally or economically. Which is natural for hypocrites.

And if we all yell for reduction but all keep our heads firmly in the trough, there will be no reduction as long as our technological civilization remains stable.

Now, then, if we insist on huge and expensive government activities, and if we therefore expect the government to collect about a quarter of a trillion dollars a year from generally reluctant taxpayers who, by and large, find nothing unpatriotic in cheating, you place the government in a difficult spot.

It is because of that difficult spot that the Internal Revenue Service has the most unpopular job in the country (and I tell you frankly that I myself hate them from top to bottom being, unlike my friend, a fairly good hater). Yet that hateful job is essential, and it couldn't be done at all without social security numbers and computers.

Since the job must be done, let's make it less hateful. To me, it seems, the way out is to develop a national computer-bank, government-run (inevitably) which will record in its vitals every bit of ascertainable information about every individual in the United States (or in the world, if we are ever intelligent enough to work out a world government).

I don't look forward to this with sad resignation, or with fearful apprehension, but with longing.

I want to see every man receive a long and complicated code of identification, with symbols representing age, income, education, housing, occupation, family size, hobbies, political views, sexual tastes, *everything* that can be conceivably coded. I would like to have all these symbols periodically brought up to date so that every birth, every death, every change of address, every new job, every new degree earned, every arrest, every sickness, be constantly recorded. Naturally, any attempt to evade or falsify such symbols would clearly be an anti-social act and would be treated and punished as such.

Wouldn't such coding be an invasion of privacy? Yes, of course, but why bring that up? We lost *that* fight long ago. Once we agreed to an income tax at all, we gave the government the right to know what our income was. Once we insisted on having the income tax made equitable by permitting deductions for business expenses and losses, for contributions, depreciation, and who knows what else, we made it necessary for the government to deal with it all, to pry into every check we make out, to poke into every meal in every restaurant, to leaf through our every record.

I don't like it. I hate and resent being treated as though I were guilty until I prove myself innocent. I hate dealing in an unequal fight with an agency that is at once prosecutor and judge.

And yet it is necessary. I myself have never been caught, so far, in anything but overpayments, and have therefore received only refunds, but I understand this is not typical. The I.R.S. by turning everyone upside down and shaking hard, collects millions of dollars which rightfully belongs to them by law.

Well, what if we were all thoroughly encoded and that all this encoding were manipulated and handled by computers? Our privacy would be no more destroyed than it is now, but the effects of that destruction might be less noticeable and irritating. The I.R.S. would not need to fumble over our records. They would *have* our records.

I, for one, would love to be in a situation where I couldn't possibly cheat, as long as no one else could possibly cheat, either. For most of us, it would mean a saving in taxes.

In fact, I would like to see a cashless society. I would like to see everyone work through a computerized credit-card arrangement. I would like to see every transaction of whatever nature and size, from the purchase of General Motors to the purchase of a newspaper, involve that credit-card, so that money is always transferred electronically from one account to another.

Everyone would know what his assets are at any time. Furthermore, the government could take its cut out of every transaction, and adjust matters, plus or minus, at the end of each year. You cannot cheat, you will not be concerned.

Will all this personal snooping enable the government to control and repress us more ruthlessly? Is it compatible with democracy?

The truth is that no government is ever at a loss for methods of controlling its population. No computer is needed, no codes, no dossiers. The history of mankind is a history of tyranny and of government by repression, and some of the most repressive and efficiently despotic governments have had very little in the way of technology at their service.

Did the Spanish Inquisition use computers to track down heretics? Did the Puritans of New England? The Calvinists of Geneva?

The difficulty, in fact, is finding a government that is not repressive. Even the most liberal and gentle government, in which civil liberties are ordinarily scrupulously respected, quickly turns repressive when an emergency arises and it feels threatened. It does this without any difficulty at all, breaking through any legal barriers as though they weren't there.

In World War II, for instance, the United States government, which I love and respect, placed thousands of Americans of Japanese descent into concentration camps without any trace of legal right. It could not even be considered a necessary war measure, since the same was not done (or even dreamed of) with respect to Americans of German or Italian descent, although we were at war with Germany and Italy as well as with Japan. Yet the action met with little resistance from the population generally and was actually popular, entirely because of our suspicion of people with funny-looking eyes and because of our fear of Japan in the immediate aftermath of Pearl Harbor.

That's the key word: "fear." Every repression is aroused by fear. If not by general fear, then by the fear of a tyrant for his own safety.

In the absence of detailed knowledge about its population, a government can only feel safe if it represses *everybody*. In the absence of knowledge, a government *must* play if safe, *must* react to rumors and suppositions, and *must* strike hard at everybody, lest it be struck. The worst tyrannies are the tyrannies of fearful men.

If a government knows its population thoroughly, it need not fear uselessly; it will know *whom* to fear. There will be repression, certainly, since the government never existed that did not repress those it considered dangerous, but the repression will not need to be as general, as enduring, or as forceful. In other words, there will be less fear at the top and *therefore* more freedom below.

Might not a government repress just for the hell of it, if it has the kind of opportunity computerization gives it? Not unless it is psychotic. Repression makes enemies and conspirators, and however efficiently a computer may help you fight them, why have them if you don't need to create them?

Then, too, a thorough knowledge of the characteristics of its population can make more efficient those government services we now demand. We cannot expect the government to act intelligently if it does not, at any time, know what it is doing; or what, in detail, is being demanded of it. We must buy service with money in the first place, as all taxpayers know; but we must then buy useful and efficient service by paying out, in return, information about ourselves.

Nor is this something new. The decennial census has grown steadily more complex with the years, to the benefit of the businessman and the administrator, who find in it the information that can help guide their responses. Well, I only suggest this be carried to its ultimate conclusion.

With such an ultimate computerization, such a total conversion into a society following a by-the-number organization, wipe out initiative and creativity and individualism?

Such as in what society that we have ever had?

Show me the society at any time in the world's history in which there was no war, no famine, no pestilence, no injustice. We have had societies in which there was initiative and creativity and individualism, yes, but in only a small upper layer of aristocrats and sophisticates.

The philosophers of Athens had time to think and speculate because Athenian society was rich in slaves that had no free time at all. The Roman Senators lived lives of luxury by plundering all the Mediterranean world. The royal courts of every nation, our own southern gentry, our own nothern industrialists, lived easy on the back of peasants, and slaves, and laborers.

Do you want those societies? If so, where will you yourself fit in, given such a society? Do you see yourself as an Athenian slave, or as an Athenian philosopher; as an Italian peasant or as a Roman senator; a southern share-cropper or a southern plantation-owner. Would you like to be transported into such a society and run your fair share of risk as to the position you will occupy in it, remembering that for every one in comfort there were a hundred or a thousand scrabbling in the dark.

Hypocrite! You don't want the simple societies anyway. The only thing we can legitimately aspire to, is exactly the complex society we now have but *one that works*. And that means complete computerization, because the society has grown too complex to be made to work in any other way. The only alternative, the *only* alternative, is utter destruction.

If we program our computers properly, we will be able to apply minimum taxes; we will be able to hold corruption to a minimum; we will be able to minimize social injustice. After all, any society in which the people are plundered, in which the few enrich themselves, in which large segments of the population are poor, hungry, alienated and angry, contributes to its own instability.

Individuals may be short-sighted enough to prefer their own immediate benefit and the hell with all others, including their children, but computers are not that soulless. They would be geared to the working of a society and not to the comfort of individuals and, unlike the uncontrolled human being, would not sell out society's birthright for an individual's mess of pottage.

Again, individuals may be emotional enough to want war to enforce their views, even though a war almost invariably ends with both sides generally losing (though particular individuals may profit), and no war can conceivably be as useful as a sensible compromise. But a computer, properly programmed, can't possibly be so soulless as to recommend war as an optimum solution.

And if the various nations all computerized themselves in a properly-programmed fashion, I suspect that all the national computers would, so to speak, agree on solutions. They would all recommend compatible programs since it is clear that in this day, and even more so in future days, no one portion of the Earth can profit from evil to another. The world is small. We rise together, all of us; or we sink together.

So that's what I want, a world without war and without injustice, made possible by the computer.

And, because I try *not* to be a hypocrite, I will admit frankly that I want such a world for purely selfish reasons. It will make me feel good.

*Howard Hughes was still alive when I wrote this story, and
James McPhee's excellent book,* The Curve of Binding
Energy *(Ballantine, 1975) hadn't yet been published.*

*If this story, being merely fiction, doesn't scare you, try
McPhee's book: it isn't, and should.*

*Joe Haldeman (b. Oklahoma City 1943, B.S. physics and
astronomy, M.F.A. English) has been writing full-time for
seven years. Among his books are three science fiction novels
published by St. Martin's Press:* All My Sins Remembered
(1977), Mindbridge *(1976), and* The Forever War *(1974),
which won both Hugo and Nebula Awards for best science
fiction novel of the year.*

TO HOWARD HUGHES: A MODEST PROPOSAL
by JOE HALDEMAN

11. 13 October 1975

Shark Key is a few hundred feet of sand and scrub between two
slightly larger islands in the Florida Keys: population, one.

Not even one person actually lives there—perhaps the name has
not been attractive to real estate developers—but there is a locked gar-
age, a dock and a mailbox fronting on US 1. The man who owns this bit
of sand—dock, box, and carport—lives about a mile out in the Gulf of
Mexico and has an assistant who picks up the mail every morning and
gets groceries and other things.

Howard Knopf Ramo is this sole "resident" of Shark Key, and he
has many assistants besides the delivery boy. Two of them have docto-
rates in an interesting specialty, of which more later. One is a helicopter pilot; one ran a lathe under odd conditions; one is a youngish ex-
colonel (West Point, 1960); one was a contract killer for the Mafia; five
are doing legitimate research into the nature of gravity; several dozen
are dullish clerks and technicians; and one, not living with the rest off
Shark Key, is a U.S. Senator who does not represent Florida but
nevertheless does look out for the interests of Howard Knopf Ramo.
The researchers and the delivery boy are the only ones in Ramo's
employ whose income he reports to the IRS, and he only reports one
tenth at that. All the other gentlemen and ladies also receive ten-

times-generous salaries, but they are all legally dead, and so the IRS has no right to their money, and it goes straight to anonymously numbered Swiss accounts without attrition by governmental gabelle.

Ramo paid out little more than one million dollars in salaries and bribes last year; he considered it a sound investment of less than one fourth of one per cent of his total worth.

2.   7 May 1955

Our story began, well, many places with many people. But one pivotal person and place was 17-year-old Ronald Day, then going to high school in sleepy Winter Park, Florida.

Ronald wanted to join the Army, but he didn't want to just *join* the Army. He had to be an officer, and he wanted to be an Academy man.

His father had served gallantly in World War II and in Korea until an AP mine in Ch'unch'on (Operation "Ripper") forced him to retire. At that time he had had for two days a battlefield commission, and he was to find that the difference between NCO's retirement and officer's retirement would be the difference between a marginal life and a comfortable one, subsequent to the shattering of his leg. Neither father nor son blamed the Army for having sent the senior Day marching through a muddy mine field, 1953 being what it was, and neither thought the military life was anything but the berries. More berries for the officers, of course, and the most for Westpointers.

The only problem was that Ronald was, in the jargon of another trade, a "chronic underachiever." He had many fascinating hobbies and skills and an IQ of 180, but he was barely passing in high school, and so had little hope for an appointment. Until Howard Knopf Ramo came into his life.

That spring afternoon, Ramo demonstrated to father and son that he had the best interests of the United States at heart, and that he had a great deal of money (nearly a hundred million dollars, even then), and that he knew something rather embarrassing about senior Day, and that in exchange for certain reasonable considerations he would get Ronald a place in West Point, class of 1960.

Not too unpredictably, Ronald's intelligence blossomed in the straitjacket discipline at the Point. He majored in physics, that having been part of the deal, and took his commission and degree—with high honors—in 1960. His commission was in the Engineers, and he was assigned to the Atomic Power Plant School at Fort Belvoir, Virginia. He took courses at the School and at Georgetown University nearby.

He was Captain Ronald Day and bucking for major, one step from being in charge of Personnel & Recruitment, when he returned to his billet one evening and found Ramo waiting for him in a stiff-backed chair. Ramo was wearing the uniform of a brigadier general, and he asked a few favors. Captain Day agreed gladly to co-operate, not really believing the stars on Ramo's shoulders; partly because the favors seemed harmless if rather odd, but reasonable in view of past favors; mainly because Ramo told him something about what he planned to do over the next decade. It was not exactly patriotic but involved a great deal of money. And Captain Day, O times and mores, had come to think more highly of money than of patriotism.

Ramo's representatives met with Day several times in the following years, but the two men themselves did not meet again until early 1972. Day eventually volunteered for Vietnam, commanding a battalion of combat engineers. His helicopter went down behind enemy lines, such lines as there were in that war, in January, 1972, and for one year he was listed as MIA. The North Vietnamese eventually released their list, and he became KIA, body never recovered.

By that time his body, quite alive and comfortable, was resting a mile off Shark Key.

3.   5 December 1959

1   Andre Charvat met Ronald Day only once, at Fort Belvoir, five years before they would live together under Ramo's roof. Andre had dropped out of Iowa State as a sophomore, was drafted, was sent to the Atomic Power Plant School, learned the special skills necessary to turn radio-active metals into pleasing or practical shapes, left the Army and got a job running a small lathe by remote control, from behind several inches of lead, working with plutonium at an atomic power applications research laboratory in Los Alamos—being very careful not to waste any plutonium, always ending up with the weight of the finished piece and the shavings exactly equal to the weight of the rough piece he had started with.

But a few milligrams at a time, he was substituting simple uranium for the precious plutonium shavings.

He worked at Los Alamos for nearly four years and brought 14.836 grams of plutonium with him when he arrived via midnight barge off Shark Key, 12 November 1974.

Many other people in similar situations had brought their grams of plutonium to Shark Key. Many more would, before the New Year.

4.   1 January 1975

"Ladies. Gentlemen." Howard Knopf Ramo brushes long white hair back in a familiar, delicate gesture and with the other hand raises a tumbler to eye level. It bubbles with good domestic champagne. "Would anyone care to propose a toast?"

An awkward silence, over fifty people crowded into the television room. On the screen, muted cheering as the Allied Chemical ball begins to move. "The honor should be yours, Ramo," says Colonel Day.

Ramo nods, gazing at the television. "Thirty years," he whispers and says aloud: "To *our* year. To our world."

Drink, silence, sudden chatter.

5.   2 January 1975

Curriculum Vitae

My name is Philip Vale and I have been working with Howard Knopf Ramo for nearly five years. In 1967 I earned a doctorate in nuclear engineering at the University of New Mexico and worked for two years on nuclear propulsion systems for spacecraft. When my project was shelved for lack of funding in 1969, it was nearly impossible for a nuclear engineer to get a job, literally impossible in my specialty.

We lived off savings for a while. Eventually I had to take a job teaching high school physics and felt lucky to have any kind of a job, even at $7000 per year.

But in 1970 my wife suffered an attack of acute glomerulonephritis and lost both kidneys. The artificial dialysis therapy was not covered by our health insurance, and to keep her alive would have cost some $25,000 yearly. Ramo materialized and made me a generous offer.

Three weeks later, Dorothy and I were whisked incognito to Shark Key, our disappearance covered by a disastrous automobile accident. His artificial island was mostly unoccupied in 1970, but half of one floor was given over to medical facilities. There was a dialysis machine, and two of the personnel were trained in its use. Ramo called it "benevolent blackmail" and outlined my duties for the next several years.

6.   4 April 1970

When Philip Vale came to Ramo's island, all that showed above water was a golden geodesic dome supported by massive concrete pillars and arm-thick steel cables that sang basso in the wind. Inside the dome were living quarters for six people and a more-or-less legitimate research establishment called Gravitics, Inc. Ramo lived there with two technicians, a delivery boy and two specialists in gravity research. The establishment was very expensive, but Ramo claimed to love pure science, hoped for eventual profit, and admitted that it made his tax situation easier. It also gave him the isolation that semibillionaires traditionally prefer; because of the delicacy of the measurements necessary to his research, no airplanes were allowed to buzz overhead, and the Coast Guard kept unauthorized ships from coming within a one-mile radius. All five employees did do research work in gravity; they published with expected frequency, took out occasional patents, and knew they were only a cover for the actual work about to begin downstairs.

There were seven underwater floors beneath the golden dome, and Dr. Philip Vale's assignment was to turn those seven floors into a factory for the construction of small atom bombs. Twenty-nine Nagasaki-sized fission bombs.

7.   August 1945

Howard Knopf Ramo worked as a dollar-a-year man for several years, the government consulting him on organizational matters for various secret projects. He gave as good advice as he could, without being told classified details.

In August, 1945, Ramo learned what that Manhattan Project had been all about.

8.   5 April 1970—3 February 1972

Dr. Philip Vale was absorbed for several weeks in initial planning: flow charts, lists of necessary equipment and personnel, timetables, floor plans. The hardest part of his job was figuring out a way to steal a lot of plutonium without being too obvious about it. Ramo had some ideas, on this and other things, that Vale expanded.

By the middle of 1971 there were thirty people living under Gravities, Inc., and plutonium had begun to trickle in, a few grams at a time, to be shielded with lead and cadmium and concrete and dropped into the Gulf of Mexico at carefully recorded spots within the one-mile limit. In July they quietly celebrated Ramo's 75th birthday.

On 3 February 1972, Colonel Ronald Day joined Vale and the rest. The two shared the directorship amicably, Day suggesting that they go ahead and make several mock-up bombs, both for time-and-motion studies within the plant and in order to check the efficiency of their basic delivery system: an Econoline-type van, specially modified.

9.   Technological Aside

One need not gather a "critical mass" of plutonium in order to make an atom bomb of it. It is sufficient to take a considerably smaller piece and subject it to a neutron density equivalent to that which prevails at standard temperature and pressure inside plutonium at critical mass. This can be done with judiciously shaped charges of high explosive.

The whole apparatus can fit comfortably inside a Ford Econoline van.

10.   9 September 1974

Progress Report
Delivery Implementation Section.

TO: Ramo, Vale, Day, Sections 2, 5, 8.

As of this date we can safely terminate R & D on the following vehicles: Ford, Fiat, Austin, VW. Each has performed flawlessly on trial runs to Atlanta.

On-the-spot vehicle checks assure us that we can use Econolines for Ghana, Bombay, Montevideo, and Madrid, without attracting undue attention.

The Renault and Soyuz vans have not been road-tested because they are not distributed in the United States. One mock-up Renault is being smuggled to Mexico, where they are fairly common, to be tested. We may be able to modify the Ford setup to fit inside a Soyuz shell. However, we have only two of the Russian vans to work with, and will proceed with caution.

The Toyota's suspension gave out in one out of three Atlanta runs; it was simply not designed for so heavy a load. We may substitute Econolines or VW's for Tokyo and Kyoto.

Ninety per cent of the vehicles were barged to New Orleans before the Atlanta run, to avoid suspicions at the Key Largo weigh station.

We are sure all systems will be in shape well before the target date.

(signed) Maxwell Bergman,
Supervisor

11.   14 October 1974

Today they solved the China Problem: automobiles and trucks are still fairly rare in China, and its border is probably the most difficult to breach. Ramo wants a minimum of three targets in China, but the odds against being able to smuggle out three vans, load them with bombs, smuggle them back in again and drive them to the target areas without being stopped—the odds are formidable.

Section 2 (Weapons Research & Development) managed to compress a good-sized bomb into a package the size of a large suitcase, weighing about 800 pounds. It is less powerful than the others and not as subtly safeguarded—read "booby-trapped"—but should be adequate to the task. It will go in through Hong Kong in a consignment of Swiss heavy machinery, bound for Peking; duplicates will go to Kunming and Shanghai, integrated with farm machinery and boat hulls, respectively, from Japan. Section 1 (Recruiting) has found delivery agents for Peking and Shanghai, is looking for a native speaker of the dialect spoken around Kunming.

12.   Naming

Ramo doesn't like people to call it "Project Blackmail," and so they just call it "the project" when he's around."13.   1 July 1975

Everything is in order: delivery began one week ago. Today is Ramo's 79th birthday.

His horoscope for today says "born today, you are a natural humanitarian. You aid those in difficulty and would make a fine attorney. You are attracted to the arts, including writing. You are due for domestic adjustment, with September indicated as a key month."

None of the above is true. It will be in October.

14.   13 October 1975

7:45 on a grey Monday morning in Washington, D.C., a three-year-old Econoline van rolls up to a park-yourself lot on 14th Street. About a quarter mile from the White House.

The attendant gives the driver his ticket. "How long ya gonna be?"

"Don't know," he said. "All day, probably."

"Put it back there then, by the Camaro."

The driver parks the van and turns on a switch under the dash. With a tiny voltmeter he checks the dead-man switch on his arm: a constant-readout sphygmomanometer wired to a simple signal generator. If his blood pressure drops too low too quickly, downtown Washington will be a radioactive hole.

Everything in order, he gets out and locks the van. This activates the safeguards. A minor collision won't set off the bomb, and neither would a Richter-6 earthquake. It will go off if anyone tries to X-ray the van or enter it.

He walks two blocks to his hotel. He is very careful crossing streets.

He has breakfast sent up and turns on the *Today* show. There is no news of special interest. At 9:07 he calls a number in Miami. Ramo's fortune is down to fifty million, but he can still afford a suite at the Beachcomber.

At 9:32, all American targets having reported, Ramo calls Raykjavik.

"Let me speak to Colonel Day, This is Ramo."

"Just a moment, sir." One moment. "Day here."

"Things are all in order over here, Colonel. Have your salesmen reported yet?"

"All save two, as expected," he says: everyone but Peking and Kunming.

"Good. Everything is pretty much in your hands, then. I'm going to go down and do that commercial."

"Good luck, sir."

"We're past the need for luck. Be careful, Colonel." He rings off.

Ramo shaves and dresses, white Palm Beach suit. The reflection in the mirror looks like somebody's grandfather; not long for this world, kindly but a little crotchety, a little senile. Perhaps a little senile. That's why Colonel Day is co-ordinating things in Iceland, rather than Ramo. If Ramo dies, Day can decide what to do. If Day dies, the bombs all go off automatically.

"Let's go," Ramo shouts into the adjoining room. His voice is still clear and strong.

Two men go down the elevator with him. One is the ex-hit man, with a laundered identiy (complete to plastic surgery) and two hidden pistols. The other is Philip Vale, who carries with him all of the details of Project Blackmail and, at Ramo's suggestion, a .44 Magnum single-shot derringer. He watches the hit man, and the hit man watches everybody else.

The Cadillac that waits for them outside the Beachcomber is discreetly bulletproof and has under the front and rear seats, respectively, a Thompson submachine gun and a truncated 12-gauge shotgun. The ex-hit man insisted on the additional armament, and Ramo provided them for the poor man's peace of mind. For his own peace of mind

Ramo, having no taste for violence on so small a scale, had the firing
pins removed last night.

They drive to a network-affiliated television station, having spent a
good deal of money for ten minutes of network time. For a paid political announcement.

It only cost a trifle more to substitute their own men for union
employees behind the camera and in the control room.

15. Transcript

FADE IN LONG SHOT: RAMO, PODIUM, GLOBE
RAMO

My name is Howard Knopf Ramo.

SLOW DOLLY TO MCU RAMO
RAMO

Please don't leave your set; what I have to say is extremely important to you and your loved ones. And I won't take too much of your
time.

You've probably never heard of me, though some years ago my
accountants told me I was the richest man in the world. I spent a good
deal of those riches staying out of the public eye. The rest of my fortune I spent on a project that has taken me thirty years to complete.

I was born just twenty-one years after the Civil War. In my
lifetime, my country has been in five major wars and dozens of small
confrontations. I didn't consider the reasons for most of them wor-
thwhile. I didn't think that any of them were worth the price we paid.

And at that, we fared well compared to many other countries,
whether they won their wars or lost them. Still, we continue to have
wars. Rather. . .

TIGHT ON RAMO

. . . our *leaders* continue to declare wars, advancing their own
political aims by sending sons and brothers and fathers out to bleed and
die.

CUT TO:

MEDIUM SHOT, RAMO SLOWLY TURNING GLOBE
RAMO

We have tolerated this situation through all of recorded history. No
longer. China, the Soviet Union, and the United States have stockpiled
nuclear weapons sufficient to destroy all human life, twice over. It has

gone beyond politics and become a matter of racial survival.

I propose a plan to take these weapons away from them—every one, simultaneously. To this end I have spent my fortune constructing 29 atomic bombs. 28 of them are hidden in various cities around the world. One of them is in an airplane high over Florida. It is the smallest one, a demonstration model, so to speak.

CUT TO:

REMOTE UNIT; PAN SHORELINE

RAMO

VOICE OVER SURF SOUND
This is the Atlantic Ocean, off one of Florida's Keys. The bomb will explode seven miles out, at exactly 10:30. All shipping has been cleared from the area and prevailing winds will disperse the small amount of fallout harmlessly.

Florida residents within fifty miles of Shark Key are warned not to look directly at the blast.

FILTER DOWN ON REMOTE UNIT

Watch. There!

AFTER BLAST COMES AND FADES

CUT TO:

TIGHT ON RAMO
RAMO
Whether or not you agree with me, that all nations must give up their arms, is immaterial. Whether I am a saint or a power-drunk madman is immaterial. I give the governments of the world three days' notice—not just the atomic powers, but their allies as well, Perhaps less than three days, if they do not follow my instructions to the letter.

Atomic bombs at least equivalent to the ones that devastated Hiroshima and Nagasaki have been placed in the following cities:

MCU RAMO AND GLOBE

RAMO

TOUCHES GLOBE AS HE NAMES EACH CITY

Accra, Cairo, Khartoum, Johannesburg, London, Dublin, Madrid, Paris, Berlin, Rome, Warsaw, Budapest, Moscow, Leningrad, Novosibirsk, Ankara, Bombay, Sydney, Peking, Shanghai, Kunming, Tokyo, Kyoto, Honolulu, Akron, San Francisco, New York, Washington.

The smaller towns of Novosibirsk, Kunming and Akron—one for each major atomic power—are set to go off eight hours before the others, as a final warning.

These bombs will also go off if tampered with, or if my representatives are harmed in any way. The way this will be done, and the manner in which atomic weapons will be collected, is explained in a letter now being sent through diplomatic channels to the leader of each threatened country. Copies will also be released to the world press.

A colleague of mine has dubbed this effort "Project Blackmail." Unflattering, but perhaps accurate.

CUT TO:

LONG SHOT RAMO, PODIUM, GLOBE

RAMO

Three days. Good-by.

FADE TO BLACK

16. Briefing

"They didn't *catch* him?" The President was livid.

"No, sir. They had to find out what studio the broadcast originated from and then get—"

"Never mind. Do they know where the bomb is?"

"Yes, sir, it's on page six." The aide tentatively offered the letter, which a courier from the Polish embassy had brought a few minutes after the broadcast.

"Where? Has anything been done?"

"It's in a public parking lot on 14th Street. The police—"

"Northwest?"

"Yes, sir."

"Good God. That's only a few blocks from here."

"Yes, sir."

"No respect for . . . nobody's fiddled with it, have they?"

"No, sir. It's booby-trapped six ways from Sunday. We have a bomb squad coming out from Belvoir, but it looks pretty foolproof."

"What about the 'representative' he talked about? Let me see that thing." The aide handed him the report.

"Actually, he's the closest thing we've got to a negotiator. But he's also part of the booby-trap. If he's hurt in any way. . ."

"What if the son of a bitch has a heart attack?" The President sat back in his chair and lowered his voice for the first time. "The end of the world."

17.   Statistical Interlude

One bomb will go off if any of 28 people dies in the next three days. They will all go off if Ronald Day dies.

All of these men and women are fairly young and in good physical condition. But they are under considerable strain and also perhaps unusually susceptible to "accidental" death. Say each of them has one chance in a thousand of dying within the next three days. Then the probability of accidental catastrophe is one minus .999 to the 29th power.

This is .024 or about one chance out of 42.

A number of cautionary cables were exchanged in the first few hours, related to this computation.

18.   Evening

The Secretary of Defense grips the edge of his chair and growls: "That old fool could've started World War III. Atom . . . bombing . . . Florida."

"He gave us ample warning," the Chairman of the AEC reminds him.

"Principle of the goddamn thing."

The President isn't really listening; what's past is over and there is plenty to worry about for the next few days. He is chain-smoking, something he never does in public and rarely in conference.

"How can we keep from handing over all of our atomics?" The President stubs out his cigarette, blows through the holder, lights another.

"All right," the chairman says. "He has a list of our holdings, which he admits is incomplete." Ticks off on his fingers. "He will get a similar list from China: locations, method of delivery, yield, Chinese espionage has been pretty efficient. Another list from Russia. Between the three, that is among the three, I guess—" Secretary of Defense makes a noise. "—he will probably be able to disarm us completely."

He makes a tent of his fingers. "You've thought of making a deal, I suppose. Partial lists from—"

"Yes. China's willing, Russia isn't. And Ramo is also getting lists from England, France and Germany. Fairly complete, if I know our allies."

"Wait," says the secretary, "France has bombs too—"

"Halfway to Reykjavik already."

"What the hell are we going to do?"

Similar queries about the same thing, in Moscow and Peking.

19. Morning

Telegrams and cables have been arriving by the truckload. The President's staff abstracted them into a 9-page report. Most of them say "Don't do anything rash." About one in ten says "call his bluff," most of them mentioning a Communist plot. One of these even came from Akron.

It didn't take them long to find Ramo. Luckily, he had dismissed the bodyguard after returning safely to the Beachcomber, and so there was no bloodshed. Right now he is in a condition something between house arrest and protective custody, half of Miami's police force and large contingents from the FBI and CIA surrounding him and his very important phone.

He talks to Reykjavik, and Day tells him that all of the experts have arrived: 239 atomic scientists and specialists in nuclear warfare, a staff of technical translators and a planeload of observers from the UN's International Atomic Energy Agency.

Except for the few from France, no weapons have arrived. Day is not surprised and neither is Ramo.

Ramo is saddened to hear that several hundred people were killed in panicky evacuations, in Tokyo, Bombay and Khartoum. Evacuation of London is proceeding in an orderly manner. Washington is under martial law. In New York and Paris a few rushed out and most people are just sitting tight. A lot of people in Akron have decided to see what's happening in Cleveland.

20. Noon

President's intercom buzzes. "We found Ramo's man, sir."

"I suppose you searched him. Send him in."

A man in shirt sleeves walks in between two uniformed MP's. He is a hawk-faced dark man with a sardonic expression.

"This is rather premature, Mr. President. I was supposed to—"

"Sit down."

He flops into an easy chair. "—supposed to call on you at 3:30 this afternoon."

"You no doubt have some sort of a deal to offer."

The man looks at his watch. "You must be hungry, Mr. President. Take a long lunch hour, maybe a nap. I'll have plenty to say at—"

"You—"

"Don't worry about me, I've already eaten. I'll wait here."

"We can be very hard on you."

He rolls up his left sleeve. Two small boxes and some wiring are taped securely to his forearm. "No, you can't. Not for three days—you can't kill me or even cause me a lot of pain. You can't drug me or hypnotize me." (This last, a lie.) "Even if you could, it wouldn't bring any good to you."

"I believe it would."

"We can discuss that at 3:30." He leans back and closes his eyes.

"What *are* you?"

He opens one eye. "A professional gambler." That is also a lie. Back when he had to work for a living, he ran a curious kind of a lathe.

21.   3:30 P.M.

The President comes through a side door and sits at his desk. "All right, you have your say."

The man nods and straightens up slowly. "First off, let me explain my function."

"Reasonable."

"I am a gadfly, a source of tension."

"That is obvious."

"I can also answer certain questions about that bomb in your backyard."

"Here's one: how can we disarm it?"

"That I can't tell you."

"I believe we can convince—"

"No, you don't understand. I don't know *how* to turn it off. That's somebody else's job." Third lie. "I do know how to blow it up—hurt me or kill me or move me more than ten miles from ground zero. Or I can just pull this little wire." He touches a wire and the President flinches.

"All right. What else are you here for?"